John Harding was born in a small Fenland village in the Isle of Ely in 1951. After local village and grammar schools, he read English at St Catherine's College, Oxford, where he once sat next to Martin Amis during a lecture. He worked first as a newspaper reporter, then as a writer and editor in magazines, before becoming a freelance writer. He lives in Richmond upon Thames with his wife and two sons.

WHAT WE DID ON OUR HOLIDAY

John Harding

BLACK SWAN

WHAT WE DID ON OUR HOLIDAY
A BLACK SWAN BOOK : 0 552 99847 8

First publication in Great Britain

PRINTING HISTORY
Black Swan edition published 2000

1 3 5 7 9 10 8 6 4 2

Set in 10.5/13pt Melior by
County Typesetters, Margate, Kent.

Black Swan Books are published by Transworld Publishers,
61–63 Uxbridge Road, London W5 5SA,
a division of The Random House Group Ltd,
in Australia by Random House Australia (Pty) Ltd,
20 Alfred Street, Milsons Point, Sydney, NSW 2061, Australia,
in New Zealand by Random House New Zealand Ltd,
18 Poland Road, Glenfield, Auckland 10, New Zealand
and in South Africa by Random House (Pty) Ltd,
Endulini, 5a Jubilee Road, Parktown 2193, South Africa.

Reproduced, printed and bound in Great Britain by
Clays Ltd, St Ives plc.

For Norah

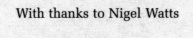

With thanks to Nigel Watts

First Week

One
Friday

'*Toilet.*'

I pretend not to hear. Or if I have heard, not to understand. Either is possible. When Dad's voice manages to rise above a whisper, which is rare, it is slurred, as though thick with alcohol, the words staggering out of his mouth and falling over one another, delirious and incoherent, like drunks ejected from a pub at closing time. And here he's up against the whine of the jet engines, too. I turn my face away from him and look out of the window, where, thousands of feet below, I can see mountains still capped by snow even though it's August. The Alps. Still the whole of Italy, and then some, to go.

'*Toilet!*'

This time it's too loud and too precise to ignore. When he wants something, *really* wants something, Dad can summon up near normal volume and clarity. And, of course, *toilet* is what he most often wants, apart from, perhaps, Cadbury's chocolate eclairs. So it's a word he's had plenty of practice on. In fact, if you just heard him say *toilet,* you wouldn't know there was anything wrong with him, so long as you closed your eyes, of course.

In the seat in front of Dad, Mum's head, a grey

cauliflower from the back because it has been tightly permed and sprayed to the texture of a Brillo pad in preparation for the holiday, jerks to one side. I hear her gasp, 'Oh no!' and give a nervous laugh.

I turn to look at Dad. His eyes, watery and grey as a February sky, stare back at me in blank, mute appeal. We none of us know how much or how little Dad can see. Certainly glaucoma and cataracts have done for the left eye, so it looks as lifeless as glass, and sees as well as glass too. And the peripheral sight of the right eye, the one we call, without irony, his 'good eye', has been eaten away, leaving only what the opticians call pinhole vision. But just how big the hole is and how much he can actually see through it we don't know. The last time he managed to read anything was the headline GOTCHA! in the *Sun* because the letters were so big, and that was six years ago during the Falklands War. Sometimes we try to test him, by pointing at things and asking him to name them, but his responses are so indistinct we don't know if he's right or wrong anyway. The only sure test would be to stand him in front of the lavatory bowl and ask him what it was. Except, if he said *toilet* with sufficient distinction to be understood, it would probably be because he wanted to go anyway (always a possibility) and was saying the word independently of our test.

All I hope now is he can't see the fear in my eyes. *He* wants to go to the lavatory and I'm shitting myself.

'*Toilet!*' It's starting to sound desperate.

'You don't want to go now, Jim,' says Mum. The cauliflower is twisting and weaving about, but she can't turn round because her eighteen stone bulk is wedged tightly into the narrow aircraft seat by the armrest on one side and my wife, Laura, on the other, the armrest between them having been raised to 'give us more room' as Mum put it, convinced as she is that my skinny little wife and she are separated by only a dress size or two.

12

Mum has a vision problem too. When she looks at herself in the mirror it's as though through the wrong end of a telescope, her vast poundage shrunk to normal size. We have learned, over the years, not to challenge this perspective.

'You'll have to wait, Jim,' she says. 'I can't do nothing now. Not with this thing pinning me down,' and she indicates the fold-down table bearing her plastic lunch tray, which is resting on the top layer of her stomach.

'It's OK,' I say, shaking off my lethargy and assuming the role of caring son taking his parents on holiday, for whom nothing is too much trouble. 'There's no problem. I'll see to you, Dad.'

Dad smiles. It's hard to tell, since the mask-like expression which is a feature of his illness permits only a baring of the upper dentures rather than a gallery of different smiling nuances, but I could swear it's not just with relief but triumph too. And why not? After all, he's just played his trump card. No matter how bad things get, no matter how much he is pushed and pulled around, *toilet* will always give him a little bit of power.

For a moment I can't think what to do. Dad is sitting to my left in the aisle seat. When we boarded the plane I put him there because his mobility problems made it impossible to get him into the one next to the window. He can't move sideways on his own. And while you can pull him sideways, you can't push him since his feet remain rooted to the spot and he just falls over. So I slid into the window seat and pulled Dad into the aisle seat next to me. Now I have to get over him and into the aisle to pull him out. The first thing I need to do is get rid of the meal trays so I can fold up the little tables on the seat backs in front of us. I look around and see both the stewardesses are up the other end of the plane, still doling out lunch. I gather up all the plastic cutlery and cups from my table and stuff them back on to the tray, cramming the perspex lid down over them. It won't close. I open it again, take out cup, knife, fork, paper towel and moist wipe, and try to arrange them as I think they were when the meal was delivered to me. I glance at Dad, who is making a big show of going red in the face and gritting his teeth, the latter the more worrying in someone with such loose dentures. Finally the jigsaw is almost in place and I repeat the exercise with Dad's tray. Again the lid won't close. I try to force it and a piece of lemon meringue pie shoots out of the side and bounces off Dad's best check sports jacket and on to the floor. Dad immediately starts fussing with the jacket, pulling the bottom of it out from under the fold-down table, and making brushing motions over it with his hands.

All at once I want to hit him.

'It's OK, Dad, no harm done.'

He ignores this.

'It's OK, Dad. It didn't go on your jacket.'

The cauliflower throws itself back against its headrest. 'Oh no, he hasn't gone and spilt something on his best jacket already!'

'No, no, it's perfectly all right,' I say. 'His jacket is all right. DAD, IT'S ALL RIGHT. YOU CAN STOP THAT NOW.'

People are beginning to turn and look at us. I dispense smiles. Some of them stare at Dad for a moment, then politely look away. I realise he has crumbs in his moustache and tomato sauce on his chin. I wrench his plastic tray open, retrieve the moist wipe, rub his face, perhaps a little more harshly than is strictly necessary, drop the wipe back on the tray and wrestle it closed again. I put both trays on Dad's table and begin to fold my table up. Dad immediately opens the lid of the top tray and starts taking out the sugar, salt and pepper packets. I let go of my table so it drops down with a thump and reach across to take the packets from Dad, quite forcefully, and ram them back into the tray and jam the lid down. As my table thumps down, Mum's voice from in front says, 'Oh dear, what is the man up to now?'

'Leave the trays alone, Dad,' I say, but he's still trying to fiddle with them. I put my left hand over them, holding them together and closed, and with my right, fold up my table and do up the clip that holds it in place. At last I can stand up. I lift the two trays over the seat in front to Laura, who says, 'What am I supposed to do with them?' but takes them anyway. I reach down and fold Dad's table up. At once Dad starts fiddling with the clasp and trying to get the table down again. I grab both his hands and say, 'Leave that, Dad, I thought you wanted to go to the loo.'

'Toilet?' he translates, knowing full well what loo means.

'Yes, toilet.'

He says something which might be 'About bloody time too', but equally well might not be, and puts his hands on the armrests of his chair. He strains for a moment or two, during which he fails to rise even an inch from the seat. I stand up and lift my left leg over Dad's legs. Somehow I manage to stretch it over and get it down on to the floor of the aisle. I lift my right leg and pull it after me, holding on to the top of Mum's seat to keep my balance, while trying to keep my leg out of Dad's way as it comes over. To get it right out, I have to lean so far into the aisle that I no longer have control over it. My heel grazes Dad's jacket. His jaw drops open and he yells out, 'Arrgh!' My leg clears him and I put my foot on the ground. Dad sits holding his chest as though he has been stabbed.

Mum's head jerks round again. 'What are you doing to the poor man?' she says.

'It's all right, he's just making a fuss about nothing,' I say, leaning round and giving her a smile. 'I scarcely touched him. He's not hurt.'

'You don't know that,' she says. 'Nobody knows the

15

pain that man puts up with day after day, and never a word of complaint. If only he could talk we'd know just what suffering he goes through.'

I can't be bothered to point out the contradiction here. I put my hand under Dad's left elbow and say, 'Push down hard with your hands, Dad, so we can get you up out of your seat.'

He clenches his dentures and begins straining, pushing with all his might. His face begins to turn red, not just the usual bright red of the eczema that is a side-effect of one of his tablets, but much darker, until it is almost purple. I try not to think about his blocked arteries and high blood pressure, but fail, and immediately a picture of a body bag being taken from a plane, probably from some Vietnam War movie, jumps into my brain. I'm just deciding I will stop this now, when I notice his body begin to lift out of the seat. He is stiff and heavy to lift, a dead weight, and I can feel sweat breaking out on my forehead. But it's all right. He's made it. He's up.

'Well done,' I say. 'Not the best designed seats in the world, are they?'

Dad looks at me, dentures bared in a smile tinged with the slight hysteria of relief and speaks fast for at least a minute, making himself laugh as he does so. I can't make out a single word.

'You're right there,' I say.

He suddenly looks worried and confused and I realise that once again I've opted for the wrong response. He acknowledges my mistake with a weak smile. It makes me think of what I will have to tell him before this holiday is over and I suddenly feel like someone taking an old and trusting dog for a final walk before having him put down. Quickly, before it has chance to stick, I wipe the image from my mind. 'Anyway,' I say with a bonhomie so fake I can taste it, 'you're up now. Let's get you to the loo.'

I start to pull him, to move him sideways, out of the

gap between his seat and the one in front, and into the aisle. He lurches towards me and almost falls over.

In my anxiety to get him to the loo, which I can see is empty and, for the moment, queue-free, I've forgotten one potent effect of his illness. The fall in blood pressure everyone suffers when they stand up is sluggish in returning to normal in people like him. The problem is exacerbated by his medication. So for a minute or so after rising from a chair he is always dizzy and even more immobile than usual.

I catch him before he can fall and steady him so he's standing upright again. I take a deep breath and remember the technique for moving him sideways. I begin to rock him from side to side, taking it very slowly at first and then gently allowing the rhythm to speed up. I'm aware that people are staring at us and find I enjoy showing off my obvious expertise in the secrets of caring for someone like Dad. After a minute or so he's in a strong steady rhythm and his feet are almost lifting off the ground. I pull him towards me slightly and gradually rock him into the aisle. Once he's there I let him stand for a moment to stabilise himself.

Now he's got his breath back, I stand facing him and begin lifting my feet and swinging my arms in a marching manner. 'Come on, Dad, imagine it's forty years ago and you're on your way here in the army. March.'

Slowly he begins to swing his arms and lift his feet in a pathetic parody of a military step. With his bent back, shrunken physique and bared teeth he looks like a chimpanzee. All at once I want to hug him, but of course I don't. He's marching really well now, enjoying the rhythm and activity after being cramped up for so long. I give him a little tug to slip him into first gear and he begins to move forward. Once he starts there's no stopping him and he makes it to the loo almost at a run.

I call out, 'Left wheel!' and with the merest tug on his

elbow, swivel him into the lavatory, pushing open the door so he can march right up to the bowl. I try to go in with him, but the cubicle is too small to accommodate me as well. I begin to retreat, but notice Dad is turning his head towards me and looking helpless. I realise he is struggling with his zip. I reach around him and pull it down for him. I stand in the doorway for a few moments and it's obvious nothing is happening. I notice his arms are moving almost frantically and know he is having trouble finding his penis. I try to reach around him again, but it's too difficult in the confined space.

'OK, Dad, march on the spot,' I say. 'Come on, hup two, three, four, hup two, three, four.' He is soon marching away again and by strategic pushing and pulling, I manage to make him turn 180 degrees so that he's facing me. I put my hand inside his fly, find the opening in the front of his old-fashioned underpants, slip a couple of fingers in and grope around until they feel the soft warm flesh of his penis. Not wanting to grab hold of it, I put my fingers underneath and lift them, so that it flops out of his underpants and trousers.

Suddenly I see us thirty odd years ago, when I was four or five, with our roles reversed and Dad helping me extricate my little willy from the leg of my short grey trousers, the two of us standing either side of the lavvy in the outhouse, aiming our spray into the bowl together, and I remember how immense the thing in his hands seemed then.

'Excuse me, but is there a problem?'

I look up and see the purple gingham uniform of a stewardess. I follow her alarmed gaze and realise I still have my hand on Dad's penis.

'No, no problem. Just helping my father go to the loo. He's disabled.'

'Need any help?' she says calmly, as if she sees this sort of thing every day of her life.

18

'No thanks, I can manage. Thanks anyway.' I say.

Dad blurts something out, but at such speed neither of us can understand any of it, which is just as well as it is almost certainly something lewd. The stewardess bows out and I get Dad marching again, his penis bobbing up and down with the movement. I manage to get him turned around and pull the door closed behind him just as another passenger, a woman of twenty or so in a lime-green T-shirt and stone-washed denims, arrives and stands behind me, in what she assumes to be the queue for the lavatory.

Suddenly, it goes dark inside the loo and I realise Dad has done something to the light switch. I open the door and see his shoulder is leaning against the wall. I tug him upright, a bit sharply, and he cries out 'Whoa!' I grope along the wall, find the light switch and flick it on. I pull the door to once more and turn to look at the woman, who, fortunately, is facing the other way. I turn back to the loo. The light's gone out again. I think about trying to switch it back on, but decide there's no point. So I just stand outside and hold the door closed, since there's no way Dad can lock it behind himself, to give him some privacy. I reflect that it's just as well Dad is almost blind anyway, since he is, in all truth, pissing in the dark.

Whole minutes tick by. The woman beside me is moving from one white high heel to the other, and I realise she is probably quite desperate to go.

'Some people!' she says finally, a pinched expression on her face. 'What on earth do they do in there?'

'It's my father,' I say. 'I'm sorry about the delay, but he's disabled.'

'Oh, I'm sorry, I didn't know,' she says. 'How awful for you.'

I enjoy the look of dismay and embarrassment on her face for a few moments, but then the long wait takes over. The worst thing is I know Dad hasn't even started yet. He has prostate trouble, an affliction completely independent of his illness, which means he is always wanting to go to the lavatory and then has trouble starting once he gets there. The woman beside me is beginning to sweat now and looks desperately towards the rear of the aircraft where there are more lavatories.

'I think I'll try the other end,' she says and dashes off with a funny, pained walk, which can't just be down to the tightness of her jeans and the impracticality of her footwear. Just then I hear the sound of a fitful stream hitting the metal bowl of the lavatory. After another age Dad starts trying to move. I get him marching again and wheel him round. His penis has been put away and only the tail of his shirt exposes itself from his fly. I tuck it in, ignore the damp stain on his trouser front, zip him up and march him back to his seat.

'Oh God, what a performance,' says Mum as we pass. I slip into my seat and pull Dad into his. When he sits down I notice his shoes are all wet.

'Well, we made it,' I say.

'Yes,' he says, and begins laughing uncontrollably, his top teeth flapping up and down. And then he leans across and says, slowly and clearly so I can hear every single word, 'Mind you, I don't know how much hit the target.'

During the remaining half-hour or so of the flight a number of people approach the loo, look inside and then stalk off towards the rear of the plane. Dad is still laughing to himself. It is an as yet scientifically unexplained feature of his condition that a man who was fastidious about cleanliness all his life, and who eschewed dirty jokes and vulgarity, now finds the merest mention of anything lavatorial or remotely sexual totally hilarious.

'What are you two laughing about?' asks Mum, her tray gone so she is now able to look round at us.

'I'll tell you later,' I say, and turn to look out of the

20

window. Below me I can see the Mediterranean, blue as a travel brochure promise. And then I see land, a lump of honey-coloured rock unrelieved by any hint of greenery or the rise and fall of mountains or striations suggesting rivers. I assume it's some uninhabited place we're flying over until I hear the man behind me say to his companion, 'Look, we're here. Malta.'

As the aircraft approaches the runway, people around me are craning their necks to catch a glimpse of the island. I'm glad they are too busy to notice what now seems to me to be a small river gushing out from the loo. A few minutes later, after we've landed and I' m shuffling Dad towards the exit, I see Laura ahead of me staring at two stewardesses kneeling by the lavatory, one of them passing a huge wad of paper towels to the other who is mopping frantically at the floor. Laura turns and catches my eye with a look that says, 'I told you this was a bloody crazy idea.'

She did, too. The moment I suggested it as our Christmas present to Mum and Dad last year, she flicked angrily through the travel brochure I'd brought home, screwed up her mouth in a way I knew meant trouble, and started listing the drawbacks:

'Your dad has advanced Parkinson's disease. He has so many things wrong with him. He can't walk – '

'He's OK once you get him going.'

' – not properly. He can't talk, he's practically blind, he can't eat because his dentures don't fit and he can't swallow properly. For God's sake, what's he going to do there? What are we going to do with him?'

'He'll like it because he was there during the war. It was the place he liked best, better even than Italy. He always says he left a bit of himself there.'

'I know, his appendix, ha bloody ha. It's enough reason not to do it just to avoid hearing him make that

21

joke again. Not that I would hear it, of course, but I'd know he was doing it.'

'But, anyway, it's not just for him,' I argued. 'It's for Mum too. She'd like a holiday. It would show her there are still possibilities, that even though he is getting gradually worse – '

'Gradually!'

' – gradually worse, there are still things to look forward to, surprises.'

'Well, I don't think they'll enjoy it and I think it's mad to sacrifice our holiday for them.'

'If you don't mind me saying so, I know they're my parents, but I think that's a bit of a selfish attitude.'

'It's all right for you to pontificate about being selfish.' She tossed the brochure on to the sofa beside her. 'You're not the one who has to do things for him, like wash him and put cream on the bloody pressure sore on his bottom. Why can't we give them something else for a present?'

'OK, you tell me – what?' That stopped her dead. It was a hard one to answer because over the years we've bought them everything we could think of and now there's nothing else they need. Their sheltered council flat is so small that there's no room for luxuries. Even the things we have given them, though inspiring awe at the time, have disappointed. There are the clothes they never wear because they never go out; the video recorder, whose controls Mum still cannot work no matter how often I show her: the microwave which she uses to keep her bread in.

I retrieved the brochure and began flicking through it, trying to imagine the look of wonder on Mum and Dad's faces when they saw it.

'Look, we have to give them something nice. We can't not give them something as good as the video last year.'

'Why do we have to top last year's present?' she said.

Lately, I've noticed a hard edge to her voice which used not to be there before and it's beginning to make me nervous.

'So what if you disappoint them? Why must you spend your whole life trying to please your father, instead of yourself, or me?'

'That's stupid,' I said. 'I'm not bothered about pleasing them. If that was all that mattered I'd just have given you the bloody baby you're obsessed with, wouldn't I? That would have pleased them more than anything, wouldn't it? Well, you have to agree, wouldn't it?'

'I hear what you're saying,' Laura said and switched on the TV.

Of course, Laura was probably right. Whatever we bought them never matched up in later use to their initial reaction to it. When we gave them the video recorder, Mum said, 'I never thought we'd own one of them.' Dad sat and stroked it as if it was a new kitten, babbling away in wonder even though he can hardly see anything on TV.

But the holiday tickets would be different, I was certain. This time we weren't giving them an object, but an experience. This time the enjoyment of the present would far surpass the impact of its presentation. Even so, that presentation promised to be dramatic. Laura had come up with a brainwave for wrapping the tickets. That's the thing about Laura, she can be side-tracked by details. Her opposition to everything to do with this holiday was overwhelmed by her love of gift wrapping. She did up the cardboard wallet containing the tickets, luggage labels and so on, in bright blue and yellow gift paper. 'I know it's unseasonal,' she said, 'but it suggests sun and sea and holidays.' Then she put it into a cracker she'd made out of yellow crêpe paper. Then she put that into a shoebox and wrapped that in blue paper. That went into a bigger box, with Pampers Disposable Nappies written all over it.

She wrapped that. And then put it in another box and wrapped that too.

Christmas Day finds me so excited I can hardly wait for Mum and Dad to open the present. It's like being a kid all over again. 'You made a brilliant job of the wrapping,' I tell Laura as we drive up the A10 towards Cambridge-shire, with the bright blue package sitting on the back seat like a bomb, waiting to explode. 'You've turned it into a proper present, because tickets aren't really like having a present. They're all about the future. There's nothing you can do with them on the day. I can't wait to see them unwrap it.'

Laura turns her head and stares at me for a moment, and I realise it isn't working any more. After ten years, something is going badly wrong here.

When we open the door of the flat we hear Mum shout-ing, 'Get in there, bugger you, get in!' I wonder what aspect of Dad's illness is frustrating her now, but we walk in to find him sitting alone in the living room, half asleep. His head leans over to the right, something to do with the way the Parkinson's affects his neck muscles, especially when he's tired, so that now it dangles precariously over the side of his chair. On the TV someone is giving presents to children in a hospital.

I peep into the open door of the kitchen. Mum is push-ing a roasting tin containing a huge turkey back into the oven. 'There, that's got you, you bugger,' she says.

I give her a kiss and ask how she is.

She wipes the sweat from her face with the bottom of her apron. The kitchen is hot and steamy. 'Fed up. There's no room in this place. I don't know why they have to make them so small. You couldn't hang a cat in this kitchen.'

I don't bother to correct her. It would only start an

argument, with her so hot and flustered, the way she always is cooking Christmas dinner.

'Well, you won't come to us.'

'Not at Christmas,' she says, adjusting saucepans and gas and pausing to lift a wooden spoon from a pan of gravy to taste it. 'This is our home, me and Dad's, even though it's not our real home because we had to give that up because of him being a bit disabled, but it's still our home, and while we can we'll have our family for Christmas dinner if it's the last thing I do.'

'It probably will be,' I say. Mum wipes her hands on her apron and takes the single step across the kitchen which is all that's needed to bring her into the living room. She greets Laura with a hug and a kiss.

'Happy Christmas,' says Laura.

'Oh no, look at that man!' Mum rushes across the room and begins tugging at Dad's head to lift it up. 'Get that neck up, Jim,' she shouts. 'I do wish he wouldn't do that.'

'Sorry, dear,' she turns to Laura. 'I could put up with all the rest of it if it wasn't for that neck. It drives me round the wall.'

'I know,' says Laura, 'but Dad can't help it, you know that.'

'Bloody Parkinson's,' says Mum and begins to cry. Laura hugs her. Dad looks suitably chagrined. Mum breaks abruptly from Laura's grasp. 'The Yorkshire's burning!' she yells and runs back into the kitchen. For some reason, Mum always insists that a Christmas dinner without Yorkshire pudding isn't a proper Christmas dinner.

We sit and talk to Dad, who begins a long rambling story about Christmas 1944, when he would have been in Burma, or possibly 1934, when he was a fourteen-year-old schoolboy. It's impossible to know which, especially with the noise of the telly and all the banging and stage sighing coming from the kitchen. But finally the din subsides, save for the hissing of steam from a saucepan of Brussels sprouts and the sound of Mum basting the turkey. There's a bit more banging and another, 'Get in there! Get in, will you!' and finally Mum emerges. She leans against the door jamb of the kitchen and wipes her forehead with the back of her hand, silent-screen style.

'Oh dear, I feel faint,' she says.

'Sit down. You should have let me help,' says Laura.

'Let you help! I can see you fitting into that poky little hole as well!' Mum says, gesturing at the kitchenette.

'Shall I get you a glass of water?'

'No, I'm all right now.' She brightens immediately. 'Let's get the presents over, before *they* get here.'

They are my sister, Pauline, and her husband Derek. They always come for Christmas dinner too.

I produce a bottle of whisky and pour a glass for Dad. I overpour slightly and the glass, which is a sherry glass Mum has given me because she and Dad, not being real drinkers, don't know the difference, is full to the brim. Dad begins to lift it to his mouth, his lips already slurping with an anticipation his hand cannot keep up with.

'Careful you don't spill it,' I say.

'He won't,' says Mum. 'His hands don't shake.' She turns to Laura and says, 'He hasn't got the shaking kind', as though this is something she's never mentioned to her before. In fact she says it to almost everybody the first time she meets them. 'That's one thing I am thankful for, that it's not the shaking kind.'

Dad has heard this so often he immediately begins to laugh, his hand shakes and a splash of whisky goes on to his trousers.

'Trust you to make a liar out of me,' says Mum. 'Honestly,' and again she turns to Laura, 'I think he just does it to defy me.'

Warmed by the whisky, which he is sipping eagerly,

26

since he is not often allowed alcohol because it might interfere with his many tablets, Dad smiles subversively.

Now we've all got a drink, Laura begins dishing out presents from the two carrier bags she has brought in from the car. There isn't much time to linger over them because Mum, whose whole life is conducted at a rush, has one eye on the clock. 'Get a move on, Jim,' she says. '*They'll* be here soon.'

Dad scratches frantically at wrapping paper but can't find the joins, so Laura unwraps his presents for him. A bottle of single malt whisky. A sweet-shop size jar of Cadbury's chocolate eclairs, from which he immediately takes one and sucks it while he sips a glass of malt, which I can't help thinking is almost certainly a capital offence in Scotland.

Mum has soap and a new apron. I get a book token and a Manchester United diary. Mum gives Laura her favourite perfume, having asked me on the telephone what she wanted. As usual, I asked Laura, but pretended to Mum that I hadn't.

When everything else has been opened, Laura produces the big blue box and places it on Dad's lap. 'Happy Christmas, Mum and Dad,' she says. 'Happy Christmas,' I say.

'Whatever is it?' says Mum. 'Not a telly for the bedroom?'

'Nothing so grand,' I reply.

'Not a slow cooker?' she says.

I begin to wonder if she would have preferred something electrical.

'Why don't you open it?' says Laura. Dad makes a few feeble passes at the paper without any success, so Laura offers the package to Mum.

'Not with my arthritic fingers,' says Mum. 'You do it, dear.'

I'm secretly pleased as Laura unveils one layer after

another, opening each and taking out the new package inside with a little Ta-ra! to try to inject some excitement into having your present opened by proxy. I enjoy all of Laura's careful preparation being so pointless.

Dad giggles uncontrollably as each new layer is peeled away, eyes bright as a child's. Mum is ducking and weaving, moving with amazing speed and agility for someone so huge, trying to catch pieces of wrapping paper as Laura tosses them aside and muttering about 'waste'. She's breathing heavily and looks relieved when at last Laura makes a brave show of pulling the pretend cracker with herself and produces the final small packet.

Dad points at it, teeth going like castanets and dribble cascading down his chin. Mum sticks the wrapping paper on the sideboard and wipes his face with the tea towel he always has safety-pinned round his neck at home.

Laura hands the packet to Mum, saying, 'It must be a small telly. You'd better unwrap this, Mum.'

Mum looks up at the clock, then begins to unpick the Sellotape, careful not to tear the paper. 'It's such pretty paper it will come in again another year,' she says. 'Though you don't often see blue for Christmas.'

She peels back the paper and the brightly coloured wallet with the words 'Your holiday documents' emblazoned on it rests in her hands. She lets out a gasp. 'Oh Jim, it's a holiday! I never thought you'd take us on another one, not after Yorkshire last year. Not with Dad getting so much worse.'

'Well, aren't you going to read it?' I say. 'Don't you want to know where you're going?'

'I haven't got my glasses,' she says. She hands the wallet to me. 'You read it, Nick love. Go on.'

'Well,' I say, drawing out the papers. 'This is a voucher for two weeks at the Villa Francesca.'

'Two weeks!'

'Well, it's not worth going all that way for one.'

'All what way?' says Mum.

'All the way to Malta,' says Laura.

It's as though a sudden gust of cold wind has caught Mum pulling a funny expression and frozen her face for ever, the way she always warned would happen to us when we were little. Her lips are so pinched it's as if her mouth has eaten itself.

'What's wrong?' I ask and turn to look at Dad. 'You do want to go, don't you?'

'Just try and stop us,' he says, loud and clear.

Mum begins picking up the discarded paper and boxes from the floor. There's a lot of angry rustling and wasteful screwing up of re-usable paper.

'What's the matter, Mum?' I say. 'Aren't you pleased?'

'Course I am. It's just a shock, that's all.'

'But – '

Just then, the door opens, and Pauline and Derek walk in.

After she has given Laura and me a perfunctory kiss each on the cheek, Pauline rushes over to Dad, flings her arms around him and says, 'Happy Christmas, Pops!'

I flinch. She never called him this when we were children. Pauline grabs his cheek between thumb and forefinger, the way you might a baby's, and says, 'Look at him, he's all excited about Christmas, aren't you, lovey? Are you drinking whisky? Are you? That's it, Pops, get tiddly, it only comes once a year.'

Laura has left the room and I can hardly bear to listen, but Dad is laughing with delight, his teeth flapping as he says something in reply.

'Yes I know, dear, you loves your little Pauline, don't you.' It's hard not to laugh at this as Pauline is nearly six feet tall and at least a stone overweight. 'Bless you, Pops!' She kisses him on top of the head, as if he were a dog. He's smiling all over his face, lapping it up and I don't know which of them is annoying me more. I can't believe he likes all this goo.

I'm relieved to be able to turn away to Derek, who shakes hands. I only ever see him at Christmas. I don't go out of my way to see Pauline, even though she only lives a few miles from Mum and Dad, and when I do drop in, Derek's nearly always away, driving his lorry.

We stand awkwardly for a moment, not knowing what to say to one another. 'Which way did you come?' he asks, finally. 'M25, M11?'

'No, North Circular and A10,' I say.

He thinks about this for a moment. 'Oh, you came that way, did you? Course you could have come North Circular, A10, M25, M11, that might have been quicker.'

We start discussing routes and Derek embarks upon a long monologue about the various ways of getting to different parts of London from East Anglia, as though, if we could only find the right route, it would somehow bring us closer together.

'Malta!' Pauline's voice suddenly booms out. 'Well, who's a lucky Pops then? I wouldn't mind going there myself.'

'What's this then?' asks Derek.

'Nick and Laura are taking Mum and Pops to Malta for a holiday,' Pauline tells him. 'All right for some, isn't it. How the other half live. Still, we're happy with a couple of weeks at Cromer, aren't we, Derek? That's good enough for us.'

There's an embarrassed silence. Pauline disappears into the kitchen to help Mum. There's renewed banging of pans and plates.

'Where are you flying from?' asks Derek.

'Gatwick,' I say.

'Do you go A316, M3, M25, M23, or go through Kingston and Reigate on the 240 and 217 till you link up with the A23?' he asks.

'That's just what I wanted to ask you,' I say.

There's a bit more handing out of presents and then dinner is ready. Derek brings the fold-down gateleg table out of the bedroom and sets it up in the living room. The room's too small for a permanent table, so normally Mum eats off a tray on her lap and Dad from a little table on a stand that can be pushed over his armchair. Derek positions the table so Dad can eat without having to leave his chair. Mum goes to sit on Dad's right, the side he has to be fed from because of the way his head leans.

'Oh no you don't, Mother,' says Pauline, jumping into the seat first. 'You have a rest today. I'll feed Pops. You like your little Pauline feeding you, don't you, Pops? She looks after you well, doesn't she?'

'Yis,' says Dad, a corruption of 'yes' he employs whenever he wants to sound especially childish and vulnerable.

'Have another whisky Dad,' I say.

'Not too much,' says Mum.

'It's Christmas.' I begin to pour and receive a smile from Dad in return.

The meal is, as always, sumptuous. The turkey is huge. I'm given a leg because that was always a special treat when I was a child. Dad and I always got the legs and it's no use now trying to tell Mum I'd prefer breast meat. Dad can't eat leg any more, so the other one goes to Derek.

'What do you want, Jim?' says Mum.

'Give him a nice bit of breast, Mum,' says Pauline. 'He likes a bit of breast, don't you, Pops. I say, you like a bit of breast, don't you?'

Of course this is enough to send Dad into hysterics, the teeth flapping up and down, and Pauline joins in, cackling loudly.

'You want to watch that laugh, girl,' says Derek. 'You could end up on the table with this turkey.'

31

We all laugh, Pauline more than anyone, and I wonder to myself why I don't see her more often as I'm always so pleased when I do.

There is too much food to fit on the little table, and the wide windowsills of the flat are co-opted as serveries. There are Brussels sprouts cooked, like all the vegetables, without mercy to be soft enough to require no chewing so that even Dad can eat them. There are carrots; mashed swede; frozen peas; runner beans; leeks; roasted parsnips; huge crispy roast potatoes; great wedges of Yorkshire pudding, which cause Pauline to say, 'Christmas dinner wouldn't be Christmas dinner without Yorkshire pudding,' and Mum to reply, 'That's just what I always say,' as though they've never discussed the subject before; turkey, of course, and chipolatas, wrapped in rings of bacon and baked alongside the bird until they're brown and crispy. Everyone's plate is swimming to the brim in thick gravy. There is bread sauce and lashings of cranberry jelly.

Derek produces a bottle of Lambrusco and pours everyone a glass, including Laura who, even after ten years, still cannot bring herself to tell them she doesn't like sweet wine.

Silence descends on the table, other than the clicking of knife and fork on china. Food is much too important in our family to be talked over.

Occasionally someone says something, but it's always an isolated remark, pertaining strictly to the meal ('Lovely parsnips', 'Where did you get these chipolatas, Mum?') and never meant to be an opener for conversation.

After eating enough to end a small famine, Mum looks at her nearly empty plate and says, 'You never enjoy it when you cook it yourself, do you?'

'That's just what I always say,' says Pauline, who will no doubt say this tomorrow when she cooks dinner for her three hulking teenage sons (who have pleaded the lack of space in Mum and Dad's flat as an excuse to stay at home today) and Derek's widowed mum.

There is more clicking of cutlery and an occasional, 'Someone finish these Brussels up, *please*,' from Mum, or 'Pass the gravy, *lovely* gravy,' from Pauline. Once Mum leaps up suddenly, saying, 'Jim! Jim! Don't dribble your gravy like that. I ask you, what does the man look like!'

'It's all right, Mother,' says Pauline, 'I'll clean him up. It's no big deal. What's a little dribble when we're only family.'

'I don't mind,' says Mum, subsiding into her chair again. 'But it's not very nice for Laura.'

'Well Laura will just have to put up with it,' says Pauline. 'Dad can't help it, can you, Pops?'

'I have to say I'm quite a dribbler myself,' says Laura to lighten the atmosphere and dabs theatrically at her chin with her paper napkin. We all laugh. So Laura dabs even more ferociously.

'Isn't she a scream?' says Pauline. 'Laura, you do make me laugh. It's a gift that, you know, making people laugh. It's so much more important than good looks.'

After the turkey, Mum switches on the telly for the Queen. 'I never miss her,' she says, although in fact no one, least of all Mum, pays any attention to what the monarch is saying. We're too busy filling up our drinks and pulling crackers and reading silly mottoes. Then Pauline takes the bread out of the microwave and microwaves the Christmas pudding and we eat huge chunks of it with Marks & Spencer brandy butter, all except Laura, for whom Mum has to search the cupboards for a can of Bird's custard powder.

The meal over at last, Laura and Pauline wash up, while Derek and I have more to drink and feed Dad chocolate eclairs because he's by now well over his whisky quota for the day, if not for the whole of next year. Then the table is put away and we sink into our chairs. Dad is fast asleep. The rest of us look at but don't really watch the telly until it's time for Pauline and Derek to go because they have to call in on Derek's mum. There's a lot more chucking Dad under the chin and calling him Pops before they eventually leave. As soon as the door is closed Mum sinks back into her chair, points the remote control at the telly to switch it off and says, 'Thank God for a bit of peace and quiet!'

There's a long silence. I sense a tension in the air. Laura suddenly says, 'I know,' and goes to one of her carrier bags. She pulls out the travel brochure and goes over and plonks herself down next to Mum. 'We can have a look at our holiday now,' she says.

She begins leafing through the brochure. 'Here's Valletta, that's the capital,' she says.

'Very nice,' says Mum, not really looking.

It's obvious Laura doesn't know what to say. 'Did you go to Valletta, Dad?' she says, but it's no use. Dad's head hangs over the arm of his chair and he's snoring audibly.

'Jim!' Mum shouts. 'Put that head up! PUT IT UP!'

Dad wakes with a start and in panic thrusts a still-wrapped chocolate eclair into his mouth.

Mum is up and across the room at a speed that belies her size. She grabs Dad's head in what looks like a wrestling hold, as though she's about to wrench it off, and forces it upright. Dad looks like a startled animal, eyes wide in fear.

'We're just talking about Malta, Dad,' says Laura. 'We're relying on you to remember the best bits.'

Dad looks completely lost. He's obviously forgotten all about the holiday and thinks this is some kind of game. He begins speaking, very quietly and at such a lick that all the words elide, so that what comes out is a drone broken by only the occasional pause, presumably where one sentence, known only to him, ends and another begins.

We all listen politely. But suddenly Laura says, 'Mum, what's up?' I turn and see Mum biting her upper lip. Her eyes brim with moisture.

'Whatever is it, Mum?' I say. 'Is it something to do with the holiday?'

'Its no good, you'll have to know,' she says. 'Dad's said he wants you to know and that's all there is to it.'

I look at Dad, who stares back with an expression that says he doesn't understand what she's talking about any more than I do.

Mum drags herself up out of her chair and waddles over to the sideboard, the same ancient sideboard that was in the old house when I was a child. It's a plain utility model from just after the war, when Mum and Dad were first married. As long as I can remember it's always been stuffed with old papers and bills, although a highlight of my childhood was finding a copy of *Treasure Island* that Dad had received as a prize at grammar school in there. It was the only book in the house.

Mum sinks to her knees in front of the sideboard, opens a door and begins pulling at papers. A whole pile of them slides out and cascades on to the floor. It's funny how someone as neat and tidy as Mum is so haphazard about any kind of document. There must be all sorts in there. She prods her podgy fingers under a pile of family photos and probes around. Finally she seems to have made contact with what she's looking for. She stretches her hand further in and pulls. More papers and photos pour on to the floor, but Mum ignores them as she takes out an old biscuit tin with a picture of a Scots piper on it. Clutching it under one arm, she lifts one leg so the foot is on the ground and uses her free arm to grasp the edge of the sideboard and pull herself up. She walks back to her chair and sits down with the tin on her lap. She lifts one hand to wipe the sweat from her brow. Tears dribble down her cheeks. I look at Dad and realise he is staring at her and that, no matter how little he can see, he knows exactly what is going on here.

'You've got to remember', Mum says, taking the lid off the tin and laying it on the sofa beside her, 'that boys like Dad were away years on end in the war. It was a funny old time. It wasn't like now.'

She begins rifling through piles of yellowed newspaper clippings, old postcards, sepia photos and ancient letters, their envelopes brittle with age, the writing on them faded to a washed-out green.

'Besides, Dad and I weren't courting at this time. He'd been giving me the run-around and I just decided there was no point sitting around waiting for him to ask me to marry him, so I wrote and told him it was all over between us. I got engaged to Harry Finch instead. But he was on an aircraft carrier that was torpedoed by the Japanese and lost with all hands.'

Here she starts to lift her hand to stifle a tear when she realises she's already crying anyway, so doesn't bother and instead reaches into the pile of letters and pulls one out.

'So that's how come I ended up marrying your Dad.' The story finished now, she opens the envelope with great care, an archaeologist disturbing a tomb, fearful of curses. I see the envelope has a foreign stamp on it. Using her thumb and forefinger like tweezers, Mum extracts some sheets of yellowed writing paper and a photograph flutters to the floor.

I bend and pick it up and stare at it. It's no more than an inch by two inches, black and white. A young woman with jet hair, black flashing eyes and dark skin smiles out with a mixture of hope and pride. In her arms she holds a small baby, done up in a big white bonnet much too large for its tiny head and great swathes of lace, which fall almost to the ground as though the baby is wearing an adult's dress. The woman is wearing a white peasant shirt. It's impossible to tell anything from the background, which looks dry and dusty, except that it must be foreign.

Laura comes to sit by me, and peers at the photo too. 'Who is she?' she asks.

'Here, take it. I can't read it,' says Mum, thrusting the letter at us. 'Only promise me you won't think any the worse of your Dad.'

I glance at Dad and see he is now bright red and chewing ferociously on a chocolate eclair.

I take the letter from Mum and open it out. The address at the top of the page ends with the word 'Malta'. I begin to read:

Dear Jimmy,

I am sorry not to write before but is terrible hard and I do get a Scottish sailor to help put my words into English for me. Here is a picture of me with our fine wee son whose name is Anthony. I think this is a very British name, which is only right. Do you no think the bairn is awful bonny? He is now eight weeks old and a frisky puppy. In the picture he is two weeks and not so very frisky. Please to come soon or write or send money. Here we have food but not anything else for a baby without money and life is awful hard.

Your bonny lassie,
Maria

'And there's this too,' says Mum, handing me another letter, written in the same hand. I see it is dated a month later, September 1945.

Dear Jimmy

I am sure a good man like yourself will ken how awful hard it is for a wee lassie to have a bairn and no man in a place as strong on religion as Malta. It would do a body the world of good to hear from you, even a wee line or two. Just to ken you will stand by your lassie will be enough to keep her spirits high. Besides, it is your bairn and you have a duty, man.

Your ever-loving bonny wee lassie,
Maria

'Is that all?' I ask.

Mum nods.

'And this Maria was some Maltese girl who Dad . . . '

Dad is suddenly talking. He's very agitated, his hands twitching and, as always happens when he's upset, he speaks so fast it's even harder than usual to understand anything. It goes on for three or four minutes, during which time Laura and I stare at him, eyes screwed up in concentration, trying to catch a single word. Finally the gabble slows and then dries up, like water running down a plughole when the tap is suddenly turned off. He stares at us, a question in his tired old eyes.

There's silence. We don't know what reply is required. He's obviously got something dreadfully important off his chest, but we don't know whether 'Yes' or 'No' is appropriate, if indeed either is.

In the end it's Mum who breaks the silence. 'It's easy to be hard now,' she says, lumbering out of her chair at a speed which for her counts as springing. She pads across the room to Dad and stands beside him, putting her arm, like a soft, fleshy pillow, around him in an understanding embrace, while at the same time taking the opportunity to lift his head up. 'He was young, just off the farm. He'd had no experience of life. These foreign girls were mad for our boys. They'd do anything for a pair of stockings or a packet of cigarettes.'

Dad's head jerks up and he says something which I'd swear is, 'Not even a packet!' but I decide it's better to let it go.

'Don't sit there and judge him too hard,' says Mum. 'It wasn't his fault. I've forgiven him long ago, not that there's anything to forgive because he wasn't my fella when it happened.'

'We're not judging him,' I say. 'I'm thirty-five years old Mum. I know about things. It's just, well, such a shock . . . '

'So Dad got this girl Maria pregnant, then?' says Laura, never one to beat about the bush.

Mum nods.

'But what happened? Did he go back to see her? Has he seen his son?'

'That's just it,' says Mum, 'he wasn't able to. These letters only reached us in 1952. That was after you were born, Nick, and Pauline was already a toddler. It was a real shock to your Dad all them years later, I can tell you. And to me too. I never knew he had a past when I married him. I thought *I* was his past. I'd known him since we was fifteen.'

'What do you mean, wasn't able to?' I ask.

'Well, we wrote back straight away, soon as we got the letters, but our letters just came back marked "No such address". Dad wrote to the War Office and the Maltese government, but we couldn't find nothing out, except that nobody knew where this Maria had gone. We did our best, but that was that.'

I look at Dad. He stares back at me, eyes conveniently blank for once.

'Does this mean you don't want to go to Malta now?' I ask. 'The holiday's off, then?'

Dad begins talking again, getting very animated and

waving his arms. It's impossible to catch anything.

When he stops Mum says, 'Course we want to go, but not just for an ordinary holiday. We could never afford to go before. But Dad wants to go. He wants to find his lost son.'

'And you, Mum, you don't mind that?'

'I understand his wishes. We don't know how long we've got left, neither of us. I wouldn't want Dad going with any unfinished business on his conscience. Besides, Nick, it's not just for him. I think we should find Anthony for you too. After all, he's not just Dad's son, he's your half-brother.'

Two

Saturday

I awake to the hissing of water and think it is raining, which will be a relief after the baking temperature yesterday. It might help to cool all our tempers. Then the rain stops, as though someone has suddenly turned it off, and I hear a door open and close. I open my eyes and see Laura, one towel wrapped round her body, another her head. She has just had a shower.

'Morning,' I say breezily.

She begins pulling on clothes and avoids looking at me.

'What's good about it?' she says. 'The fact that we've got two whole weeks here? What an almighty fuck up!'

I don't try to argue, there's not much point after yesterday. I shut my eyes and rewind it all. The flight was OK in the end. We all had a good laugh about Dad and the lavatory. And afterwards Mum was quite jolly on the coach from the airport to the villa.

'I did like those little trays,' she kept saying, referring to the meal on the plane. 'I thought that was a very good idea. Handy giving you that plastic knife and fork. And that moist wipe. Very useful.'

So useful in fact that Mum didn't use hers, but put it

41

away because you never knew when it would come in handy.

The trouble started when the coach dropped us at the Villa Francesca.

'Dumped,' was the word Laura used.

'Dumped without ceremony,' said Mum.

As soon as we were off the coach the driver handed us our luggage, gave me a door key, pointed to the villa and said, 'Villa Francesca. Good holiday.' And drove off.

The villa turned out to be one of half a dozen on a small estate surrounded by wasteland. There's an old saying we have in the house-selling business: 'There are three things that sell a house: location, location and location.' Well, in that case, offloading the Villa Francesca would be hard. It was in the middle of nowhere. All around was scrubland, sparse and treeless. The only vertical objects in view were a huge radio mast half a mile away, a concrete water tower and an electricity pylon. I was glad to be on holiday, and that it wasn't my job to shift this one, or any of the other houses here. I was so relieved at the thought I could even spare a bit of sympathy for the poor, unknown Maltese sod who would have to do it one day. But thankfully it wasn't all bad. The property did have some attractive features. The building itself was clean and pleasant, a well-presented modern villa with a little patio at the front and stucco walls fringed with purple bougainvillaea. I unlocked the ornately carved wooden front door and we entered a large hallway, which opened up to the second floor. On our right was a sweeping staircase of polished black marble with a natural wood banister.

We explored the ground floor first, and found just two rooms, identical to one another, each a bedroom containing twin beds and a wardrobe.

'Where's everything else?' said Mum. 'Where's all the other rooms?'

'Toilet?' said Dad.

'Stay here,' I said, 'Laura and I will look upstairs.'

The staircase consisted of twenty-five steps, each one so glossily marbled as to be a potential death trap to Mum, let alone Dad. At the top we found a kitchen with all the latest appliances, even a washing machine, a bathroom with a bath, shower and loo, a sitting room with two sofas, some wicker armchairs, a huge oak table and dining chairs, and a balcony from which you could look out over several miles of undulating wasteland followed by what looked like a huge town and finally the sea, winking at us in the late afternoon light.

'This is fucking crazy,' I said. 'If this is what you get when you specify disabled, imagine what it must be like if you don't.'

'Your Dad will never get up here,' said Laura. 'We can't stay here.'

'Don't worry, I'll speak to the rep. We'll sort it out. Just try to make the best of it for now. Keep Mum and Dad happy.'

We went downstairs.

'What's up there?' asked Mum.

'Living room, kitchen, bathroom – '

'Toilet?'

'Yes, Dad, toilet. It's very nice, really lovely furniture. Very high standard. Fabulous view.'

'Not much good if we can't see it,' said Mum. 'I wouldn't call this suitable for the disabled. How's Dad supposed to wee?'

'Well, I think the stairs might be a bit tricky for him. They're very slippy. But . . . '

'Oh no, not with my feet! I can't go up slippy steps with my feet.'

One of the many medical problems Mum suffers from, which are overshadowed by Dad's, are her feet. They have developed an increasing aversion to surfaces which are in any way glossy. Because of it she cannot go into Woolworths on her own without 'coming over all funny'. She has graded all the shops at home according to the polish of their floors. It's like film certificates. There are some she won't venture into at all, some only with another adult to hang on to, and some where she can cruise freely, supported only by her trusty shopping trolley.

'Yes, but don't worry, I'll phone the rep up. We'll sort it out. They must have something more suitable.'

'*Toilet!*'

Laura and I looked at one another in consternation.

'What do you want to go for?' I asked.

'*Toilet!*'

'Yes, Dad, I know, but what for?'

'Jimmy riddle,' he mumbled.

I sighed with relief. One often fortunate side-effect of Dad's tablets is they render him chronically constipated, so that at difficult moments – and this was shaping up to be one – at least you didn't have to worry about dealing with, as Mum put it, *that.*

'OK, hold on a minute.'

Dad immediately winced with pain, and Laura began stroking his shoulder in sympathy while I raced up the stairs, slipping on the second or third step and nearly falling flat on my face. On the landing I found a large cupboard and inside it a broom, Hoover, mop and plastic bucket. I grabbed the bucket and dashed back downstairs. I helped Dad get his penis out while Laura held the bucket just below it, the penis draped over the rim. We stood like that for ten minutes, waiting for him to start.

'Come on, man, for goodness' sake!' said Mum. 'This is the way he always is, hounding you to take him to the toilet all the time and then can't do anything when he gets there.'

'All right, Mum,' said Laura, 'there's no problem. I'm the one holding the bucket.'

'Yes,' said Mum, 'and I'm the one desperate to use it next.'

There was no point in all three of us standing there making him more anxious, so I decided to go and take a look at the car. I'd noticed a white Seat parked in the driveway next to the villa. I went out and tried the driver's door, which I was surprised to find was unlocked, but then this was Malta, not London, and crime here, according to the guidebook, was virtually unknown. I sat in the driver's seat and began searching for the keys. They weren't under the dashboard or the floor mat, in the glove compartment or on top of the sun visor, all the places where people generally leave keys.

'Can I help you?' It was a Liverpool accent

I looked up to see a man of about fifty, immediately identifiable as British by his polo shirt, too-short khaki shorts, sandals and blue cotton socks, looking down at me. He was obviously amused.

'Just looking for my car keys,' I said.

'Well, I shouldn't think you'll find them in my car,' he replied.

'Your car?'

'Yes. If you look you'll see it's actually nearer to my villa than yours. Your parking place is round the other side of your villa.'

'But there's no car there. My holiday includes a hire car.'

'They'll deliver it tomorrow morning. That's what happened with us.'

'But what are we supposed to do for food? There don't seem to be any shops around here.'

'About two miles to the nearest decent one. I'll run you down if you like.'

'That's very kind of you. I wouldn't trouble you, only I

have my parents with me and my father's disabled.'

'It's no trouble. Someone did the same for me when we arrived last week. See you in ten minutes.'

'Is there a phone there where I can phone the rep?'

'No point. Nobody there at the moment. Don't worry, though, she'll be round tomorrow when they bring the car.'

We spent a miserable evening camped in Mum and Dad's bedroom, sitting on the beds, the solid wood dining chairs upstairs being much too heavy and the wicker armchairs too cumbersome, to be lugged down the treacherous steps. We ate cheese sandwiches and funny Maltese crisps, washed down with Marsovin, a local wine made from imported Sicilian grapes.

'Still, a bit better than the last time you were here,' I said to Dad, trying to lift things a bit. 'A bit more comfortable than in the war.'

Dad struggled to remove a piece of crisp from his moustache by stretching his tongue up to it, like an iguana. It took all his concentration for a moment or two.

'Well, answer the boy,' said Mum. 'It's not his fault everything's such a mess. He done his best.'

Dad retrieved the crisp and chewed it for a moment or two. At first I thought he had forgotten my question, but then I realised he was chewing over his words, getting the feel of them in his mouth so they'd come out right.

'I'm not so sure about that,' he said, spraying fragments of crisps as he spoke. 'At least we had a bloody latrine.'

Now I reach out a hand and pat Laura's buttocks by way of conciliation. She twists her bottom, shaking off my hand like a troublesome fly.

'I'm not in the mood,' she says, dropping the towel and pulling on a pair of knickers. She turns to face me. 'It's all just such a mess, this place,' she says, gesturing with her arms to indicate the villa, so that her breasts move up and

46

down. With the movement I find myself beginning to get aroused and have to turn instead to look out of the window.

'Looks like it's going to be fine,' I say.

'Fine!' she replies. 'It must be seventy out there already. We'll be lucky if your father doesn't have a bloody stroke and end up being re-united with his bloody appendix.'

I'm about to reply when I hear a loud *thud*! Then another, and another. I could swear the whole house is shaking and immediately think it must be an earthquake. I jump out of bed, grab the towel Laura has just discarded and run out into the hallway. There's another thud, followed by another and another as though someone is manhandling a heavy trunk, step by step, down the stairs. I look up and see Mum, clad only in her enormous bra and knickers, sitting down halfway up the staircase. As I watch, she lowers herself on to the next step and then the next. Suddenly she realises I'm here.

'Oh sorry, love, hope I didn't wake you up,' she says. 'Had to get upstairs. Number twos.'

'Are you all right?' I say.

'Yes, but I don't think much of this marble stuff. My bottom's freezing.'

I think about helping her up, but decide she's safer shuffling down on her backside. When she moves from one step to the next her breasts and the many layers of her stomach flop up in the air and then back down again in a series of little slapping sounds, like waves against a river bank when a boat has just passed by.

I think of the half-hour or so in bed last night when Laura and I were happy for once, giggling as we tried to imagine how Mum would manage to squat over a plastic bucket to pee. Now she looks like a grotesque oversized child and I suddenly feel bad about laughing at her.

Before I can say anything, there's a loud banging at the

front door. I call Laura to look after Mum and go to open it. On the doorstep is a plump Maltese girl, very tanned, with teeth so white they seem to dazzle in the already strong sunlight. She's wearing the navy and red uniform of our travel company and a name badge which says 'Martina'.

'Good morning, I am your holiday representative. Sorry, you are not up,' she says, nodding at the towel. 'I have brought you the car. It's parked outside. Here are the keys. I hope everything is all OK? Yes?'

She has the guttural, throaty voice that I'm already beginning to recognise as Maltese.

'Well, no, it bloody well isn't, actually,' I say. 'I'm not happy with this villa.'

'You don't like it?' she says, eyes wide in surprise. 'It is a very nice villa, nice furniture, microwave, panoramic view. You must surely agree?'

'Oh, it's a lovely villa,' I say, 'but not if you're disabled. My father is nearly seventy years old. He can hardly walk and he's almost blind.'

'And he's in the Villa Francesca?' Through the open doorway Martina indicates the stairs with a sweep of one hand. I look round and see Mum, at the foot of them, scuttle away, anxious not to be seen in her underwear.

'But you have to be crazy to stay here with him. This accommodation is totally unsuitable for disabled persons. What are you thinking about? Just look at all these stairs. And so slippery too.' She looks at me as though I must be mad or patricidal, or both.

'I know that, for Christ's sake.' I say. 'I specified somewhere suitable for a disabled person and this is where you've put us.'

'It's not good enough,' calls Mum's voice from her bedroom. 'After all he did for you people in the war.'

Martina looks mystified. 'War?' she says. 'What is this about war?'

'Forget the bloody war,' I say. 'Just get us out of here.'

Martina comes in and sits down on the bottom step of the staircase – 'Ooh, cold!' she says – and consults various papers which she has on a clipboard. I recognise her as one of those pleasant people who do not understand the ill-temper of others and find myself feeling sorry for her. I know how she feels. One of the many ways in which I am not good at my job is my inability to deal with clients who become angry and upset, which is most of them at some time or another. Selling a house affects people like that.

Suddenly Martina's face brightens into a smile.

'Ah, I see now. There has been what we call in Malta a bit of a cock up. You have been given the wrong villa.' She goes to the front door, opens it and points across the little square. 'There is your house, you see, single-floor for disabled persons. This one is for Mr Ferguson, who is over there also by mistake. He's probably plenty mad too. He requested a panoramic view.'

'God,' I say, 'I hope he made it through the night OK without it.'

My sarcasm is lost on Martina, who merely looks puzzled, and all at once I realise she is a simple soul and feel guilty for having abused her.

'So what do we do?' I say. 'I suppose it's going to involve a mass of paperwork and bureaucracy to sort this mess out.'

'No, of course not,' she replies, the teeth flashing. 'We just make a swap. No problem.'

As she leaves she turns to look up at the staircase again and then at me with a face full of pity. 'Disabled!' she says, and departs, shaking her head in disbelief.

Ten minutes later two retirement-age couples, the Fergusons and their friends, arrive, carrying suitcases and piles of clothes as well as bedding. They stand impatiently in the hallway. 'Come on, get a move on,' says one of the men, laughing. 'We don't want to waste any more of our holidays over this do we?'

'I'm sorry, but there may be quite a delay,' I say. 'We have a bit of a problem.'

The problem is getting Dad up, which on a bad day at home can take Mum until lunchtime. Although Dad has been spared the most well-known symptom of his illness, the one that identifies Parkinson's disease for most people – the tremor – he has all the other problems, both major disabilities and minor irritations and annoyances, in abundance. Specifically akinesia, slowness in beginning a movement. He knows what to do, but his brain no longer produces the neural transmitters to tell his body to do it. So even simple actions, like sitting up or walking, are hard for him to begin unless you jog him physically by pulling his arms or touching his elbow. Then there's the rigidity caused by over-contraction of the muscles, so that Parkinson's patients have increased muscle tone and there's more resistance if you try to move their bodies. In practical terms this means that Dad is a dead weight, his limbs as stiff and unwieldy as those of a corpse, something he often resembles because of the slightly wet, marbled look of his pale skin – another effect of his drugs. He has great difficulty in rising, especially from a low chair, and this is heightened first thing in the morning. When he does get up, he is often dizzy for a few minutes and liable to fall over if he is not supported. There has been a loss of dexterity too, so that he has problems carrying out even the simplest of tasks: the doing up of buttons, the tying of shoelaces (although, after seventeen years of the disease, he can no longer reach these anyway), combing his hair.

On holiday Laura always assists Mum. In the past I've tried helping, but somehow I'm not very good at it and

Mum and Laura have eased me out of it, so I've become convinced that all nursing is, like childbirth, women's work. They have about them a practicality, a roughness, so that they pull and push Dad about to get him to do what they want, whereas I want to treat him with great delicacy, like something that's about to break.

And how will strangers handle him I ask myself? How will he fare in the brusque, professional hands of those who are unfamiliar with his many little foibles and his illness with all its annoying idiosyncrasies? I don't want to think about that now. There are two whole weeks before I have to think about that.

The first thing Mum and Laura do is sit him up. This is not too difficult, since he is sleeping with five pillows under his head, the last of these a large 'V' pillow we have brought from home which is designed to stop his wayward neck from tilting during the night. So it is only a short pull and then he is sitting. Next, by degrees, they shuffle him closer to the edge of the bed. Then Laura supports his body so he can't slip back again, while Mum grabs his feet and swivels his pale, emaciated legs so they hang over the side of the bed. Laura lets go of his body, then goes round in front of him, pulls off his pyjama bottoms and puts his socks on. At the same time Mum jerks his chin up, usually saying 'Get that head up. GET IT UP!' at least once, and inserts drops in his eyes for his glaucoma. This is when, if one of them remembers, they put his false teeth in, a difficult operation in itself since he will never open his mouth wide enough and Mum often becomes frustrated, grabs his jaws with both hands and yanks them open while Laura rams the teeth in. Once his dentures are in place there's an outside chance they may be able to understand something he says. Without them, there is none at all.

Now Laura takes his hands from Mum and holds him in balance while Mum produces a wide-necked plastic bottle. She inserts his penis into it and holds it there while Dad attempts his first pee of the day.

Once he's finally emptied his bladder, on a count of one-two-three Laura pulls his arms sharply. At the same time Mum pushes him and, with luck, he comes to his feet. It's at this point his balance goes and he's liable to fall over. If that happens, and he goes sideways, Laura, who is holding his hands, will not be able to stop him so Mum must support his body for a while. Gradually Dad, who is standing with knees and pelvis bent, begins to straighten up. The blood returns to his brain and he is able to stand unaided.

In normal circumstances they would march him to the bathroom and wash him down, but of course that's impossible today with the Ferguson party waiting out in the hall. Laura sits on the bed behind Dad and Mum hands her a jar of Sudocrem, which Laura applies to the pressure sore on Dad's bottom, a souvenir of a long stay in hospital when he fell and broke his pelvis three years ago. The pelvis recovered, but his backside never has and requires daily treatment if it is not to break out into a raw, weeping mess again. It's like treating a baby for nappy rash, except that it takes much more cream to cover Dad's behind. The pressure sore is one of Mum's principal obsessions and the greatest compliment she can pay Laura at the end of a holiday is, 'You've kept his bottom lovely,' which always gets a laugh from Dad.

He's ready now to be dressed. Mum stands next to him and puts his arm around her shoulder, holding him up, while Laura crouches on the floor on the same side and tries to lift his foot. Not only can Dad not lift the foot, something is also holding it to the ground. It's as though somehow, in the brief moment he has been standing, it has grown roots. With a bit of a push from Mum and a sharp tap on the foot from Laura, the message eventually gets through and the foot lifts. Laura takes advantage of this brief opportunity to slip the leg of his underpants and trousers, already prepared, with the one inside the other, over it. Only when all the trouser leg is safely over the foot do they allow it to sink back to the ground. Then they repeat the whole thing with the other leg, until eventually pants and trousers are on and can be pulled up.

Next they pull off the pyjama jacket and put on a clean vest. They do this even today, although the temperature is likely to be in the nineties again, as it was yesterday. Mum says, as she does every morning, 'Jim, put that head up, PUT IT UP!', before rolling the vest up and slipping the neck over Dad's head quite roughly, making him call out. For a moment or two his head is trapped inside the vest and pulled against it. Eventually it springs free, his still-full head of hair standing up on end, as though in shock at the rough treatment meted out to him. Sometimes he will reach up and rub weakly at his nose or eyes by way of protest. At this moment he has as much dignity as a two-year-old child. His arms are inserted into the armholes, with Laura and Mum operating each side of him in tandem, still without ceremony, so that he again calls out if a finger is caught on the way through. The shirt follows, with Mum beginning to button it up because she is always in such a fierce hurry to get the job over with and finds Laura slow, until she abandons the task, saying, 'It's no use, this arthritis in my fingers, you'll have to do it, dear,' and leaves it to Laura after all. Next they slip on his jumper, which today is a sleeveless one in deference to the foreign climate, Mum not being one to take risks with colds, or anything else, where Dad is concerned. Now Mum takes out a comb and combs his hair, which as well as having hardly thinned over the years, is only just beginning to turn grey. But even this part of his body is not untouched. Overactive sebaceous glands mean his scalp flakes like a cake of dried-out soap, so that

53

when she's finished, Mum has to scrape bits of dead skin from the comb.

Lastly, she applies steroid cream to the eczema on his face, yet another bonus from his medication. Now Mum steps back to admire him. He stands there, back stooped, head hanging slightly to the right, face red and raw, hair flaking, eyes dim, his right hand useless, its muscles seized up so it is held in a permanent clench and resembles a bird's claw, knees bent, and whole body wavering. It's the best she can do. Mum pecks him on the cheek and says, 'There, you'll do.'

Dad mumbles something which is totally indecipherable, but is almost certainly 'I'll have to' and smiles. He's ready to begin his day. The whole thing, on a good day, will have taken at least an hour.

While all this is going on, I pack Mum and Dad's things, then pull on some clothes and start to clear our possessions from the rest of the villa, assembling them all in the hall, where the Fergusons are standing around, shuffling from foot to foot and giving one another meaningful glances. They wear nylon leisure suits with elasticated waistbands and little zip-up jackets, the men's grey and blue, the women's pink and purple. They look like they're in uniform, as if they are members of some holiday police force and have been sent to chuck us out.

I begin with our bedroom, mine and Laura's, wondering why someone as dedicated to untidiness as Laura is at home, where her clothes are strewn about our bedroom as if we've just been burgled, should have a fetish about unpacking her things and putting them neatly away in drawers and wardrobes the moment she reaches her holiday accommodation. And why do it yesterday when she had every reason to expect we'd be moving elsewhere today?

I open one of our suitcases and chuck in stuff from the

wardrobe, adding the things Laura has already managed to leave on the floor, and then move to the chest of drawers on her side of the bed. I open the top drawer and begin taking out her neatly stacked underwear, delighting in throwing it into the case any old how in reprisal for her bothering to be so arbitrarily tidy, and have just taken out the last little pile when something slips out from between the knickers and on to the floor. I bend to pick it up and realise it's her packet of contraceptive pills. For some reason, perhaps some primitive intuition, I glance at it and notice that the little holes below the words Monday, Tuesday and Wednesday have been punched open, the pills gone, but that Thursday and Friday, yesterday and the day before, remain perfectly intact, the pills securely in place and not safely inside Laura. I know she has not forgotten to take them. It's one of the things Laura is always efficient about, taking her pill. She might forget it one night, but she'd always take it next morning. She'd never miss two days running. It's obvious something is going on here. I need to think about it, but there isn't time now with the four nylon bailiffs waiting outside. I stuff the packet inside a pair of knickers, so Laura won't be able to tell I've seen it, and cram them in the case with everything else. I strip the sheets from the bed and put them in the case too. I rush upstairs and collect the few grocery items from the kitchen and our towels from the bathroom. I fetch Mum and Dad's cases and carry the whole lot out to our bright red Seat, put them in the boot and on the back seat, and drive the hundred yards or so across the little square to our new home.

I open the front door, noting that it has no carving, dump all our stuff inside and return to the Villa Francesca for my family. Dad's ready now and we all troop across the square.

'Did you get all our things?' Laura says.

'Yes,' I say, 'I even remembered to empty the drawers.'

I watch her reaction to this, but she doesn't even blink.

The bungalow is simple. The bedrooms are smaller and less airy. The kitchen is a galley and doesn't have a microwave or a washing machine. The floors are plain stone, and dull enough for even Mum's satisfaction. The living room is small and ordinary, with glass doors opening on to a patio which looks out over the dusty square and another window opening on to wasteland at the side, where I can see rusty tin cans and plastic bags flapping about, as though people throw their rubbish there.

We all look around.

'It's a bit poky,' says Laura. 'Pretty well equipped, though.' She's opening kitchen cupboards. 'There's a food processor. And a coffee filter.' She rifles through a drawer. 'Plenty of cutlery.' She lifts out what looks like a small hammer. 'Even a steak tenderiser.' She pulls more objects out of the drawer and holds them up for our inspection. 'A turkey baster, too. And a meat thermometer. Can't imagine we'll be using those.' She closes the drawer. 'Everything we could possibly need. Though there's a crack in the handbasin in the bathroom – and there are only three egg cups.'

Laura is expert at noticing such minor flaws in rented accommodation. It's her job. That's how I met her. There was this property in Kingston we'd been asked to sell. I went to put a valuation on it. I'd been told it was empty, so I was surprised when I let myself in to hear the washing machine going. When I got into the kitchen, the dishwasher and tumble-dryer were on too. It was spooky because the house was obviously not being lived in. Sure there was furniture, but nothing personal, no packets of food on the worktops, no coats in the hall. With all this noise from the appliances, I didn't hear her walk into the room and turned to find myself staring into her big brown eyes.

'Sorry,' I mumbled. 'I would have rung the bell, but I was led to believe the house was empty.'

'It is,' she said, and I felt her eyes running up and down me, appraising me, the way, I later learned, she appraised flats and houses, looking for stains and cracks and more than reasonable wear and tear. 'It was let out for the last six months. I'm just running the appliances to make sure they're all working OK. I'm the inventory clerk from the letting agent.'

'Inventory clerk?'

'Yes, before we let a property I go round and make a note of the condition. Any marks on the paintwork, damaged furniture and so on. I write it all down. Then, when the tenants move out, I go round again and see if there's any new damage and if there is we take it off their deposit before we give it back.'

'Sounds fascinating,' I say.

'Oh it is, it's like being a detective. I hardly ever meet the people, but I feel as if I know their most intimate secrets.'

'Such as?'

'Well, I don't know what the couple who had this place have been up to in the bath, but it's got a bloody great crack in it.'

It was the way she looked me straight in the eye when she said it that assured me I wouldn't be turned down if I asked her out. I'd passed the inspection.

Laura's professional interest is all in the condition of a place. So even now the aesthetics of the bungalow don't engage her. Not so Mum.

'Not such nice furniture,' she says.

'No microwave,' says Laura, her inventory finished. 'It's not the same standard as the villa.'

'For God's sake, you went on enough about how bad that was. Aren't you ever satisfied?' I feel hot and bothered after lugging everything around.

'Don't you worry Nick, you done your best. It's perfectly all right,' says Mum. 'As a matter of fact, I prefer it. It's more homely. Besides, you can't have everything, can you?'

It was something she said a lot when we were kids, when not having everything meant more or less the same as not having very much. I knew we weren't rich, and that there were things we couldn't have: a Scalextric for me, a Rosebud doll for Pauline. A dog. The difference is, when Mum said it then, it was me who was disappointed. Now the same words seem to express her disappointment in me.

Once we've unpacked again, Laura and I drive to the nearest town and stock up on food and drink. We buy bread at a bakery and a big round local cheese, olives, olive oil and plenty of Marsovin and beer at a general store. On the way home we stop at a van parked by the roadside and buy huge red tomatoes, orange peaches, shiny green peppers and a cos lettuce.

We have lunch on the patio, sitting in deckchairs. Dad, wearing a panama hat Laura and I bought him for the holiday, is perfectly happy to sit in the sun, perhaps having forgotten he's in Malta, but not caring. Mum cuts off half a pound of cheese and puts it on her plate, with a tiny piece of lettuce and a slice of tomato. She starts slicing bits off the cheese and putting them on a piece of bread.

'I don't mind just having a bit of salad, it doesn't bother me,' she says. 'I don't feel that hungry in this heat.'

And it is hot, probably in the mid-nineties in the shade. We decide that today will be a rest day, to let Dad recover from yesterday's journey so he'll be raring to go tomorrow. Laura and I drink bottles of beer and get quite tipsy.

'I think I'll go and have a bit of a lie down,' says Mum. 'That's what all these foreigners do, isn't it, have a fiesta in the afternoon.'

'Siesta,' I say.

'Trust Mum to get it wrong,' she says, and ambles off to her new bedroom.

Dad is already snoring away in his deckchair and Laura and I push it round so he's out of the sun. She looks up at me from the other side of the chair, her face flushed from the booze.

'Why don't we have a little fiesta?' she says.

I feel a stirring in my loins as she takes my hand and leads me towards our room. She hasn't been like this for ages. She hasn't been interested in sex at all.

Inside the bedroom she leans towards me and thrusts her tongue into my mouth, shoving it against mine, and pushes her pelvis forward, pressing herself against my blossoming hard-on.

'What's got into you?' I say, and then all at once I remember the packet slipping out of her underwear drawer and I know.

'It must be the heat,' she says. 'I'm feeling really horny. I'm glad your mum went to bed, I might have had to have you there and then.'

She starts pulling at my clothes, tugging at my belt and sliding her hand down inside my underpants. I like this and half my brain is saying, 'Go on, why not?' But I know why not.

'Hang on a minute,' I say. 'Let me get us another beer first.'

'OK then,' she says, stroking my penis, 'but hurry up.'

I walk out to the kitchen, open the fridge and take out two more bottles. My mind is racing, trying desperately to think of a way out of this, to find a plausible excuse not to fuck my wife. The harder I try to think, the more my mind stalls and seizes up. It's no good. Time's running out. I have to do something, create some kind of diversion. I let one of the bottles slide from my hand and hit the stone floor where it smashes with a bang like a bomb going off, sending foaming beer and fragments of glass in every direction. I rush back to the bedroom.

'What was that?' Laura is naked on the bed.

'I dropped a beer,' I say. 'There's glass everywhere.'

'Leave it, we'll clear up afterwards.'

'I can't. What if Mum wakes up? She might step on it and cut herself.'

I don't wait for her to argue, but rush out and begin banging cupboard doors open and shut, until I find a dustpan and brush. I bend down and start sweeping up glass. I hear the bed creak as though Laura's just got off it. If she comes out here she'll have the mess cleared up in no time at all. I hear the door of our wardrobe open. She must be putting on her dressing gown. She'll be here in seconds. I'm panicking. I'm ready to do something desperate. Anything. But what? And then I spot a small piece of glass glinting up at me from the floor just in front of me and suddenly I know what to do. I grit my teeth and kneel on it, grinding it into the ground with my bare knee.

Laura emerges from the bedroom in her dressing gown. 'Come on, hurry up,' she says.

'Damn!' I cry out. 'I've cut myself.'

I stand up and see a satisfying thread of blood trickling down my leg. I think how fortunate it is that the knee is one of the most insensitive parts of the body.

Laura's annoyance disappears and she bends to look at the knee.

'We'll have to clean it up,' she says. 'It's all dirty from the floor. We'll have to make sure there's no glass in it.'

I sit on a stool while Laura fetches the Dettol from our holiday first-aid kit and boils a kettle of water. She begins dabbing at the knee with a bit of cotton wool.

'Ooow!' I cry.

'Does it hurt that much? It doesn't seem to be very deep.'

'Probably a small piece of glass,' I say. 'It's really sore. Really, really sore. I feel a bit sick from it.'

Eventually she gets it clean. 'It's only a scratch,' she says. 'You'll live. Do you think you can limp back to the bedroom?'

'I think I'd rather sit here for a minute or two if you don't mind, I feel a bit faint. Must just be the shock.'

She rolls her eyes.

'Besides,' I add, 'we'd better get the glass cleared up off the floor.'

Glaring at me, she picks up the dustpan and brush and sweeps up the debris, taking great care, I notice, to squat and not put her knees to the ground. She brushes fast and roughly, as though it's the floor she's annoyed with for not fucking her.

'You do make a fuss about nothing,' she says.

'It may not look much, but it bloody hurts,' I say.

She's just finished wrapping the glass in newspaper and putting it in the kitchen bin when Mum walks in, rubbing her eyes, and says, 'Oh dear, I just had a horrible dream about a bomb going off. Scared the life out of me, it did.'

Behind Mum's back, Laura rolls her eyes again, but this time in conspiracy with me, not in anger. I give her a wan smile back, as though I too am seething with sexual frustration. Then I turn it on Mum and feel it expand with genuine warmth.

After all, she's just stopped herself becoming a grandmother.

By early evening I sense everyone is flagging. We've been here a whole day now and our holiday hasn't really begun, let alone our mission to find my lost brother. I feel everyone looking towards me to do something to rescue

61

things. As Laura's downcast look says, this was my big idea after all. So we all get dressed up, Dad in a long-sleeved shirt and his best sports jacket, just in case there's a sudden freeze, me out of my shorts and T-shirt into chinos and shirt, and Laura and Mum into fresh dresses. Mum's is a huge purple floral number that prompts her to say, 'Look, I match the boulanvigar,' and Laura to begin trying to teach her the word all over again.

The two of them take ages to get ready, enjoying the idea of getting poshed up for Saturday night out. It's a novelty for Mum, who only ever goes out in the evening when she's on holiday with us. When they've finished it takes even longer getting Dad ready, changing his clothes, putting cream on his bottom and making sure he's had all his tablets. Finally he's done, right down to having his eye drops in and his hair brushed. We're just about to go out of the front door, when he says, *'Toilet!'*

'Oh no,' says Mum. 'What for, not number twos I hope?'

'Yis,' says Dad, and I swear I can see a hint of a smile.

'You can't want to go now, Jim, not at this moment of all moments.'

Dad licks his lips and stares at her resolutely.

'Can't wait.'

Mum grabs him by the wrist and tugs him off towards the loo. It's the one thing Laura won't do for him, and we stand and make faces at one another. A moment later Mum returns, red with fury. She's left Dad on the loo since she knows there's no urgency. It's four days since he had a bowel movement so another hour or two won't make any difference.

'He does it on purpose,' she says. 'He waits till we're going out and then he wants to go.'

I nod, but Laura is more generous.

'I'm sure he can't help it,' she says. 'He's probably worried about getting stuck out somewhere and wanting to go. Besides, there's no rush, it's only seven, and the guidebook says the Maltese don't eat till late.'

This doesn't carry much weight with a woman who has always got tea over by six o'clock at the latest.

'The speed he eats at, we'll still be feeding him his dinner at breakfast time,' she says. She shakes her head with frustration and sinks on to the sofa, suddenly weary, dark rings around her eyes. I realise it is at a vulnerable moment like this that I have to catch her and say what I have to say, when she might be more willing to listen, to entertain the awfulness of the idea. But not now, not now. I cannot do it now.

I go to check on Dad. He's sitting on the loo, face red, perhaps from exposure to the sun, but more likely from straining to produce something, his head leaning perilously to the right, his hair just brushing the wall.

'How's it going?' I ask.

'It's not!' he replies, or at least I think he does.

We wait half an hour, and then Mum goes in to sort him out.

'Have you done anything?' she says.

Dad shakes his head. She pulls him roughly to his feet, anger giving her abnormal strength, tugs up his pants and trousers, and begins fastening them.

'Toilet . . . ?' Dad says.

'No, Jim, you don't want to do anything, you know you don't. Stop messing me around.' And she lugs him out of the room. As he lurches past me, he smiles out of . . . conspiracy? embarrassment? apology? I don't know. I take his arm and lead him outside to the car. Mum and Laura get in the back and I notice the wheelbase creak on Mum's side. I place a plastic carrier bag on the front passenger seat and back Dad towards it. When he's as close as he can get, I push him backwards at the same time holding his head and thrusting it downwards so he doesn't bang it on the top of the door frame. Once he's sitting on the carrier bag I grab his ankles and swivel him around, the shininess of the carrier bag making the movement smooth and effortless. He laughs like a child on a swing.

I jump in the car and we set off.

'Where's the seat belts?' says Mum from the back.

'There don't appear to be any,' I say. 'There's no law about them here, they're not compulsory.'

'Thank gawd for that,' says Mum. 'They're always too tight anyway, don't you find, Laura?'

I'm not sure what I expected Malta to look like, but it definitely wasn't what I see as we drive along, which confirms the impression I had on the coach from the airport. I suppose I thought it would be a kind of Anglicised version of a Greek island. Instead it appears to be one large town. Or rather a series of little towns which all sprawl into one another, so that we travel for mile after mile through dull streets of modern concrete houses, interspersed with hardware and television shops. Every so often there's the splendour of a baroque church, nestling in the ugliness around it, or sometimes a whole row of ornate eighteenth-century buildings with fabulously carved doors and balconies.

Not that I get much time to look. The guidebook has warned me about driving in Malta, but nothing has prepared me for this. The good thing about it is that they drive on the left, but it's little compensation for the way they drive. After a few minutes I realise that signals are rarely given and learn to assume that any car near me may do its best to collide with me without warning. Everyone drives too fast, so that when I slow down to try to get my bearings and because I'm fearful of the vehicles hurtling at me from all directions, I'm blasted by a rage of car horns. Every time I take a bend, because of the heat, the tyres squeal out like small animals being tortured and add to the tension. At a roundabout I'm shocked to see a car coming from my left at right angles to us and just carry on as though we weren't there, so that I have to hit the brakes hard. It takes only another roundabout to realise there are no rules at roundabouts and who goes first is a matter of nerve and bluff, like a mechanised form of poker. The faint-hearted can stoke themselves up with alcohol too, as there's no drink-drive limit here. I've already told myself there's no way I'm driving home sober. No one gives way if they can beat you to where you're going, even if it means you have to brake for all you're worth. We've only been driving for twenty minutes and we've already seen two collisions. It dawns on me that virtually every vehicle, including the one I'm driving, has one or more dents, or a cracked bumper, or a broken windscreen. It's war out here.

I start to become hysterical. I drive across a roundabout, narrowly missed by a car from both left and right, which pass us with horns screaming. Mum has her hands over her eyes.

'Oh dear, do be careful, Nick, this will give me another heart attack, I know it will.'

Laura strokes her soothingly. Dad is laughing hysterically, loving the craziness of it all. He starts talking, trying to shout above the roar of the traffic, as we all bounce up and down, hitting one pothole after another. I turn and grin at him as a car shoots out of a side road in front of us and I swerve just in time to miss it.

'They'll be shooting at us next!' I say and Dad starts laughing all over again.

Soon though I'm getting used to it and starting to enjoy myself. I realise it's true what they say about the Maltese, that they're smiling, happy-go-lucky people. When they hit their horns, it's never in anger but to tell you to get out of the way, and they often wave at you when you do.

Suddenly Mum speaks from the back. 'Have we got to

go through this much longer?' she asks. I look at the dash-board clock and realise it's half-past eight. We've been travelling for an hour – on an island that's so small you can drive right across it in that time. I have no idea where we are. There are hardly any road signs. It's like England during the war, when they took them all down to confuse German paratroopers. Nearly half a century later and they're doing the same thing here to German tourists.

I ask Laura for the map book and get Dad to hold it open on his lap. I keep glancing at it but it doesn't help. I can't get where I want to go because I don't know where I am. We drive around like this for another twenty min-utes. Suddenly we're on a big dual carriageway, and a sign says 'Valletta'.

'Thank God. We can eat here,' I say.

'No chance,' says Laura, who's studying the guidebook. 'There aren't any restaurants and nothing opens in the evenings.'

'But it's the capital,' I say.

'Well, it's not my fault, it's no use getting shirty with me.'

'I'm not getting shirty, it's very stressful driving under these conditions.'

'Specially when you're hungry,' says Mum. 'Starving even.'

Suddenly I see a sign. It says St Julian's Bay. I know that's a tourist area, so it must have restaurants. By the time I spot it we're past it, so I floor the brake and do a U-turn. Sound of large animal being tortured.

'Oh dear,' says Mum, 'I'm glad I'm not driving.'

After the sign to St Julian's, there aren't any more, so I just keep driving in the general direction. Eventually we see the sea and everyone cheers. I don't care where it is, I can see people walking up and down a sort of prom-enade. Lots of them are olive skinned locals but then I spot a flash of pink and purple and grey and blue.

66

'Look, it's the Fergusons!' says Laura. 'They must be eating here. This will do, Nick.'

It takes me another twenty minutes or so to find a place to park, but we're finally all out of the car and on the promenade in front of the sea. Dad's legs have seized up from sitting in the car so long and we have a little walk to loosen them up.

'I never thought we'd get here in one piece,' Mum confesses to Laura. 'I think it's taken away my appetite, all that rushing about.'

'Well,' says Laura, 'I'm hungry. Besides, you don't want to get back in the car and drive home straight away, do you?'

'Oh no,' Mum says. 'I wish you hadn't said that. I never thought about getting home again.'

The place is bustling. There are Maltese families walking up and down, everyone dressed up for Saturday night. There are gangs of British youths, loud and swigging from beer bottles, and British and Scandinavian girls walking along with their noses in the air, pretending to ignore them but stopping every now and then for a conspiratorial giggle. We cross the coast road to look for a restaurant, but all we find are bars, mostly empty still, and pumping out deafening music to attract customers. We walk for ages but don't see anywhere to eat.

'There's a sign up there for pizza,' says Laura, pointing ahead.

'Dad doesn't like pisa,' says Mum, pronouncing it like the city, even though Laura has just said it. 'Come to that, I don't much care for it myself, either. Not with my teeth.'

'Perhaps they'll do other things,' I say, but when we get there we find there's nothing but pizza on the menu.

'Oh, let's give up and go home,' says Mum. 'There's nowhere here Dad can eat.'

'I'm not getting straight back in that car and going

67

through all that again just because you and Dad won't eat pizza,' I say.

'It's not a question of "won't", your Dad doesn't like pisa. This is meant to be a holiday, not torture.'

A huge involuntary sigh escapes me, something I must have learned from Mum over the years.

'All right, we'll give it another five minutes, and if we don't find anything, we'll go home,' I say.

A hundred yards down the road we come to a restaurant. We're all so relieved we bundle in without really looking at it. It's only when we're inside and a waiter in a smart white jacket, black bow tie and trousers is welcoming us that I notice the crisp white tablecloths, the rolled napkins and the heavy, expensive-looking cutlery. It may not be the sort of place that will welcome Dad once they see him eating.

'Table for four?' asks the waiter.

'Yes,' I say.

'Can we go in a corner, please?' says Mum. 'Only my husband is a bit disabled and he doesn't like people looking at him when he's eating.'

Dad smiles at this, as though to say he doesn't give a toss, which Laura and I are sure is the case. It's Mum who's embarrassed by his table manners.

The waiter gives a sympathetic smile and almost manages not to be shocked by Dad's appearance. You hardly ever see anyone with Parkinson's disease out in public. They tend to shut themselves away from the world, locked inside their homes as well as themselves.

At the table, Mum and Laura sit with backs to the wall. I lift the table and push it as close to them as Mum's stomach will allow. Then I march Dad up to the edge of the table, so he's pressed right up against it. I put a chair behind him and push him down on to it, at the same time thrusting the chair forward before he makes contact with it so as to get it as far under the table as possible. Once he's sitting down there's still a bit of a gap between him and the table, but I lift it up and put it back where it started. I'm on form tonight, it's touching Dad's tummy.

Mum looks round the restaurant, which is empty apart from a Maltese family on the other side of it, near the window. Despite the bustle outside, it's still early to eat by Maltese standards.

'Nice and empty,' says Mum. 'If we get a move on we can get our food down us and be out of here before anyone else turns up.'

'Mum,' I put my hand on hers, 'stop worrying. You're on holiday. The idea is to relax and enjoy your food, not to give yourself indigestion because you're worried about Dad's eating.'

'*I'm* not worried,' she says. 'It's your dad. He hates people staring at him while he's eating.'

I'm about to say, 'How would he know?' when I catch Laura's warning glance.

'Well, we're OK here,' I say. 'No one can see him except us.'

Dad ignores all this and is studying the menu, holding it in one hand and the frame of his glasses in the other, as though straining to read it. The menu is upside down.

Laura reads the menu out to Dad. It's something I wish she wouldn't do, since she always reads out every item and doesn't omit the things that are difficult or impossible for him to eat. But it's too late now, she's started and nothing will stop her.

'What do you fancy for a starter?' I ask him, when she's finished.

'We don't want a starter,' says Mum. 'It will take all night to get done if we go having starters.'

'Mum, we're out for a meal. It doesn't matter how long we take. We're on holiday.'

'Well, Dad doesn't want to sit too long, not on his bottom. Not after all that time in the car.'

'Well I don't care about anyone else,' says Laura, bless her, 'I'm having one. I'm having garlic mushrooms.'

'Dad, what about you?'

'He'll have some soup,' says Mum. 'He can eat that all right.'

'Soup OK, Dad?'

'Prawn cocktail,' he says.

'Now Jim, you know you'll only make a mess with prawns. Why not have some nice tomato soup? You like that.'

'Prawn cocktail,' Dad says, appealing to me.

'All right, Dad,' I say. 'I'll help you with it. And to follow?'

Mum, Laura and I order local seafood specialities, giant prawns in garlic butter for them and calamari for me.

'Dad? What about your main course?'

'Prawn cocktail?' he says, hopefully.

'Yes, you're having that to start, but what about afterwards, for your main meal?'

'What do you want for your dinner, Jim?' says Mum. 'Hurry up, we haven't got all night.'

'Shall I read you the menu again?' says Laura.

'No thanks!' cries Mum.

Dad struggles for a moment, looking worried and confused, trying to remember anything at all from the menu.

'Rabbit stew.'

'Oh no! Not stew. Trust that man to want something messy. Have some scampi, Jim. You like scampi.'

'Rabbit stew.'

Mum starts to protest, but I wave her down.

'It's OK, I'll help him. After all, it is a Maltese speciality.'

'I've got nothing against rabbits,' says Mum. 'I used to eat them all the time when we were first married. Your dad does like rabbit.'

I call the waiter over and give him our order, and ask for a bottle of wine too. Mum puts in a request for a dessert spoon for Dad. 'He's a bit disabled with his hands,' she says. As the waiter's about to leave, Dad looks up at him and says, 'Ice cream?'

'Not yet, Dad,' I tell him.

Dad looks at me, and then at Mum.

'No ice cream?'

'Yes, Dad, but you don't order it yet.'

'You have your dinner first, then you order your afters, Jim,' says Mum. 'When you know if you've still got room for it.'

'Oh, I think Dad always has room for ice cream, don't you, Dad?' says Laura.

It's true: it's one of his big passions, like chocolate eclairs. He will eat whole litres of ice cream, regardless of flavour, and will keep at it until you take it away from him. At home he always has ice cream after lunch and tea, as much as Mum will give him.

He smiles back at Laura, and you'd almost swear his dead old eyes are twinkling, an ice-cream eater and all-round rogue.

When Mum had her heart attack, seven years ago, they were staying in a hotel in Eastbourne. Dad had had Parkinson's for ten years by then and the last three years had been ones of big decline, so that Mum was having to do more and more for him and getting more and more exhausted day by day. It was before Laura and I began taking them on holiday and they'd gone off on a trip organised by one of those associations for the elderly. On the first night we had a phone call from the tour operator to say Mum was in hospital with a suspected heart attack and Dad was in the hotel, helpless without her. We jumped into the car and rushed down to Sussex.

* * *

71

At the hospital we found Mum sitting up in bed, great black rings round her eyes, monitoring discs taped to her chest, heart-beat machine bleeping on a trolley beside her.

'How are you?' I asked.

'I'm all right, but the doctors here are no good,' she said. 'They've told me I need to lose some weight. I never heard nothing so daft. I've worn myself to a shadow looking after that man.'

'Well, I wouldn't worry about that now,' I said. 'Just try to rest and get better.'

'But what's going to happen to Dad?'

'Never mind about Dad, we'll go to the hotel and put him to bed and then tomorrow we'll take him home with us. Laura will look after him while I come back here to be with you.'

'Tell him I love him,' she said. 'Tell him I'm sorry to let him down.'

At the hotel we found Dad sitting in the residents' lounge with all the other people from the trip. They'd just finished dinner and the conversation when we walked in was all about coronary seizures, sparked off, of course, by Mum's attack but prolonged as a subject close to the statistically vulnerable hearts of everyone there.

Dad was subdued and visibly shocked by what had happened. In those days his speech was better and it was possible to understand whole sentences of what he said. I got him a large whisky and bought drinks for the other people around him.

'My brother used to eat four eggs a day for breakfast,' one man was saying. 'Every day of his life, plus he had eggs in cakes and Yorkshire pudding and so on. Then one day he had a massive heart attack. Just fell down in the street. He was lucky to survive, they said. But the doctor told him it was the eggs that done it. "They're bad for the heart," he said. "No more eggs."'

Dad's face was now suddenly more full of concern than it had shown so far for Mum. He leaned forward towards the man.

'This doctor,' he said, 'did he mention anything about ice cream?'

Now we're halfway through our starters and I'm leaning over Dad trying to rescue prawns from his lap.

'There, what did I tell you?' says Mum. 'I know this man so well. I told you he would have preferred soup.'

'It's all right, Mum, they're only going on his napkin.'

Dad has now abandoned the small knife and fork that accompany his food and is picking the prawns out one by one, using the index finger and thumb of his left hand, the claw being useless for feeding unless you put a dessert spoon into it. At this moment I hear the door open behind me. Mum looks up and says, 'Oh no!'

I turn around and see the Fergusons have just come in. One of the men, the one in blue, lifts a hand and gives us a cheery wave. There's a rustle of nylon and they're standing over us. Mum stops eating and gives them an annoyed look.

'Well, it's a small world, isn't it?' says Grey.

'Yes,' I reply, trying to alleviate the fallout from Mum's scowl. 'Don't tell me you've already booked this table?'

We all laugh, except Dad, who has a prawn stuck to the palm of his left hand and is lifting the hand, tongue outstretched, trying to lick the prawn off with all the intense concentration you see in apes at the zoo when they're picking fleas from one another's coats.

The Ferguson party stare at him for a moment.

'It's all right,' says Mum, 'there's no need to stare. He's not drunk, he's a bit disabled, that's all.'

Dad immediately begins mumbling something, causing a thin dribble of Marie Rose sauce to trickle from his

73

mouth and down his chin. I can't hear a word he's saying, but I imagine it's something to do with the remark about being drunk, so I lift the bottle and top his glass up. Dad reaches out, picks up the glass, salutes the Fergusons and says, 'Cheers.'

They all laugh and Pink Woman says, 'He's got the right idea. I think we'll sit down and get stuck into some of that ourselves.'

The waiter appears and sees us all talking.

'You are friends?' he says. 'You want to sit together? I can push the tables together.'

'No thank you very much,' says Mum. 'We do not.'

Grey points to a table over by the window and mutters something about the view, and they troop off over there. For the rest of the meal Mum leans her head on her left hand to shield her face from any stray Ferguson glances.

'Dad hates anyone looking at him when he's eating,' she says. 'Poor devil, it's the only pleasure he's got left to him and they have to spoil it by staring at him.'

Dad looks up from his rabbit stew and smiles at me.

'Are you enjoying that?' I ask.

'Tough,' he says.

'What, the rabbit?'

'Yis. Tough as old boots.'

'You don't have to eat it, Dad, if you don't want it. Have you had enough?'

'Yis. Ice cream?'

The rabbit stew has been so messy to get from Dad's plate to his mouth, and so difficult for him to chew once it gets there, that it's been a real struggle trying to feed him and eat my own meal. The stress of it all is making me drink faster than normal and I order a second bottle. Laura is obviously feeling some of the pressure too, probably because, since I'm so busy, she's stuck talking to Mum all the time, and she's drinking even faster than I am. As I shovel pistachio ice cream into Dad's mouth, adding bright green stains to the pink Marie Rose ones on his moustache, I suddenly feel Laura's naked foot slide on top of mine. The big toe slowly insinuates itself up the leg of my trousers and caresses my shin. I look up and find Laura's eyes beaming messages to me. I immediately decide I won't drink any more, it's too risky, and that I'll reverse normal romantic practice and ply Laura with drink in the hope that she'll fall asleep and I won't have to make love to her.

Eventually the meal is over. I suggest coffee, as this will provide an opportunity to get some Tamakari, the evil Maltese liqueur I've read about in the guidebook, down Laura and possibly knock her out immediately, but Mum declines.

'We don't want to bother about coffee,' she says. 'It will only hold us up. We can have a cup when we get home. Besides, Dad prefers his Horlicks last thing before bed.'

There's an argument about who's going to pay, but I force Mum to back down, mainly because I'm the only one with any local currency. Then we're off.

On the way home I'm so relaxed from all the drink that I'm able to ignore the bedlam of the traffic. My mind seems as clear as the night sky, in which you can see all the stars, and I know exactly how to get home. But I catch Laura's face in the rearview mirror and see she's wide awake. So I deliberately take a wrong turning and pretend I'm lost. I drive around for half an hour, cursing loudly, until suddenly I realise I really am lost. Trying to navigate is even worse in the dark and it takes us two hours to get home. Everyone is shattered. I have to get Dad out of the car and settle him in his room, and then go and lift the sleeping Laura from the back seat. As I put her into bed, she opens her eyes, says, 'I have never been one for deferred gratification,' and falls fast asleep again. I go back and help Mum put Dad to bed. I heat some milk up for his Horlicks and take it into him, but he's too tired to drink more than a few sips and then he's asleep and snoring loudly. As I'm about to leave the room, Mum hugs me.

'Thank you for a lovely day, Nicholas dear. We had a nice relaxing time. But we mustn't do that every day. It's not what we come for. Tomorrow we've got to look for Anthony.'

Three

Sunday

Even though it's only ten o'clock in the morning, the heat is already oppressive as we drive towards the south-west of the island, heading for the small town where Maria lived when she wrote to Dad. Tension sits in the car like a fifth passenger and manifests itself differently in each of us. Dad eats Cadbury's chocolate eclairs, chewing them in a frenzy, jaws working all the time, while Mum busies herself unwrapping them for him. I drive like a maniac, taking advantage of the empty roads because all the local maniacs are still in bed, probably recuperating after Saturday night, which seems to be something the Maltese go in for in a big way. Laura and I both nurse hangovers, hers undoubtedly worse than mine, neither helped by the potholes in the roads. Every so often I see her face in the rearview mirror and catch her staring at the back of my head, as though trying to penetrate my skull and discover the secrets it holds.

This morning, when she woke up, I kissed her on the forehead, with a warmth she won't have felt for years and said, 'That's for last night. It may have been the apex of our entire love life. We'll have to take a case of Marsovin home with us.'

She rubbed her eyes and looked around the room, as though what she needed to unlock her fogged memory might have been left lying around somewhere, like a bunch of car keys.

'I don't remember. Did we . . . ?'

'Come on, you're kidding me. I can't believe you've forgotten. Wait till you get up, you said you wouldn't be able to walk.'

I strode off to the shower, whistling with what I hoped sounded like sexual contentment, but was, in fact, pleasure at imagining the confused expression on her face behind me.

Laura's misgivings about our quest surface in annoyance at Mum who, it has to be said, is being very annoying. Mum can't stop talking, everything she says inconsequential and unconnected with anything else.

'Oh dear, talk about roads!' she says every time we hit another pothole. Or, 'This heat! I don't like the heat. I never have done.'

Laura, I know, wants silence, space for her thoughts about last night, about the day ahead. So she stares out of the window, turning her head away from Mum, making a point of not answering. Being ignored makes Mum feel even more nervous, so she talks even more.

'Look, Laura!' She punches Laura on the upper arm, perhaps not only to gain her attention but also as punishment for ignoring her, so Laura is forced to turn and follow Mum's pointing finger. 'Boo-gan-villa', says Mum.

'Mmm,' says Laura.

'Pretty, isn't it?' says Mum.

'Mmm,' says Laura.

Mum settles back in her seat and is silent for all of thirty seconds. Then:

'This heat!'

Silence.

'Well, answer someone,' says Mum. 'What are you all being so funny about?'

'No one's being funny, Mum,' I say.

'Yes you are.'

'I'm driving. I have to find the way. It's not easy without signposts.'

'Laura's not driving.'

'What's that supposed to mean?' asks Laura.

'It means you could answer when I'm making conversation.'

'Answer what?' asks Laura.

'Answer me about the heat.'

'What about the heat?'

'I said, "This heat!"'

'I'm sorry, I thought you were just commenting on the heat. I didn't think it required an answer.'

'You could have agreed with me. That might have been more polite.'

'Well I shouldn't think anyone's going to disagree with you. It's obviously bloody hot. The bloody tar's melting on the bloody road.'

'Language,' Mum mutters into her bosom. She withdraws into herself, hunching up her body, as much as you can hunch up eighteen stones. The car is completely silent now except for Dad's furious chomping of chocolate eclairs. When he eats them he sounds like a pig, all snuffles and snorts, because he's trying to breathe through his nose, which is always congested.

'Oh dear, listen to the man!' says Mum. 'Jim, stop eating them things, the rest of us can't hear ourselves think. Laura would like some peace and quiet back here, wouldn't you, dear?'

'If only . . . ' Laura says.

'Stop it!' says Mum, reaching forward, grabbing Dad's head and pushing it sideways. 'And get that neck up. GET

IT UP! No wonder you can't breathe properly! You're almost on top of Nicholas. How's the poor boy supposed to drive?'

'Don't worry, I can manage,' I say.

'Yes, and very nice it would be if we was all killed in an accident because his neck is all over your controls. Jim, get it up. GET IT UP!'

I know she is nervous at what she will find. She wants Dad to have his son, but she's jealous of any bit of his life that doesn't derive from her. And because this episode of his life has always been so firmly buried in the past, she expects to exhume it uncorrupted by time. I'm sure that in her mind this Maria remains the dark siren of the faded snapshot, ready to lure Dad away from the straight and narrow again. When I asked Mum what she felt about it this morning, she said, 'It's like water, it draws you. Like when I used to walk across the bridge in the village and I'd look down at the water and be frightened I'd fall in, so it was all I could do to stop myself jumping in anyway to get it over and done with.'

And Dad? We can't tell what he's thinking about this possibly momentous re-union any more than we could tell what he wanted for dinner last night. His anxiety may be because he's about to confront the mistake of half a lifetime ago, but could equally well be because he is worried about wanting to pee and sees no sign of a lavatory anywhere. He may be upset at recalling his lost youth, his healthy young body and that of the woman who loved him, or it may be simply the rawness of his wasted old bottom bouncing up and down on the hard plastic seat of the Seat that's bothering him. For all we know, he may not even remember he is in Malta. He's definitely feeling the heat. He never even suggested wearing his jacket today, but just shook his head when Mum proffered it, and then said, 'Wallet?'

I saw Mum slip his black leather wallet from the inside

breast pocket of the jacket and noticed it was thick and bulging.

'Hang on,' I said, 'What's he got in there?'

I snatched it from her before she could deposit it in her handbag. It was almost splitting at the seams with banknotes.

'How much is there here?' I demanded, knowing Mum would know down to the last penny. She looked sheepish.

'None of your business.' She fired me the look of a defiant three-year-old.

'It is if you get mugged and lose it all. Come on, Mum, don't make me count it.'

'Two thousand, four hundred and sixty-five pounds,' she said. 'And you said there wasn't any crime here.'

Laura and I exchanged the sort of glance shocked parents might on learning their unmarried teenage daughter was pregnant.

Laura, sharp as ever, noticed Mum pushing her handbag behind her mountainous bottom.

'What's in the bag?' she snapped. 'How much more have you got?'

'Well, I can't put it in the bank or the social will find out and I'll lose some of my rent rebate,' Mum said. 'And I wasn't going to leave it in that flat. There's all sorts got keys to that place, wardens, maintenance men . . . they're in and out like yo-yos.'

'How much, Mum?'

'Four thousand five hundred.'

'You're crazy, you know that. That's seven grand you've got on you. God, there are pickpockets anywhere, you know, even here. They could just have lifted Dad's wallet out of his pocket.'

'Well, they won't now. I'm putting it in my bag.' She produced her bag from its hiding place, opened it, dropped the wallet in and closed the clasp with a resounding snap. 'And I don't want to hear no more about it. It's got nothing to do with you.'

'It's got everything – ' I started to say, but then saw Laura shaking her head at me.

'It's no use going on at her,' she whispered to me as we got in the car. 'We'll just have to keep our eyes glued to her bag when we're out, that's all.'

If the money is a source of anxiety for Laura and me, it's even more so for Dad. For the first twenty minutes of the journey he turned round every couple of minutes and said, 'Lil, wallet?' to which Mum replied, 'Yes, stop whittling, man. I've got your wallet.'

But eventually he sank into the snuffling and snorting which are the nearest he gets to silence. Now when I ask him if he's OK, he just lets out a little moan, which could be of pleasure or of pain, it's impossible to tell, since his dentures are welded together by toffee.

When I see the honey stone houses of the town appearing before us, it's obvious it's only a small place and I realise a part of me is disappointed, the part secretly hoping for a metropolis so big Maria and my half-brother would be impossible to find. Although there is plenty of new building here, it still looks the sort of town where everyone might know everyone else. The road leads into a central square, one side of which is taken up by a huge church, almost a mini-cathedral, out of all proportion to the size of the population but perhaps not to the depth of their faith. I park opposite the church, get out of the car and go round to the other side to help Dad out. There's something different about this place, as though we've suddenly come to another country. A breeze, warm but dry and refreshing after the sticky humidity at the bungalow, tousles my hair. The feel of the town is North African, with a canopy of palm trees shading the square and the scent of aromatic plants and herbs wafting from little courtyards in front of some of the houses. I notice a couple of the houses have minaret-shaped windows and there are elaborate carvings on some of the front doors, as well as heavily mosaicked front porches and steps, relics of the island's Moorish past which here, at least, have not been expunged.

In contrast, the church is a massive baroque confection, the elaboration of its stonework jarring with the simplicity of the houses around it, like an overdressed whore who has gatecrashed a garden party. The bell is ringing, since it's time for Mass, and one or two late worshippers, a man in black trousers and a green anorak (the latter surely an item of formality rather than necessity) and an old woman in a black dress with a black lace shawl over her head, are hurrying towards the big wooden doors. Outside an old man sits smoking on a bench. I walk over to him and notice his black suit is shiny with age and as wrinkled at the elbows and knees as the face under the grey trilby. He doesn't look up, but applies all his concentration to his cigarette, as though he's afraid he'll miss some of it.

I say, 'Excuse me, but can you tell me where I can find Triq San Gwann Battista?'

He draws on his cigarette so hard that the end glows as if it is about to burst into flames. He doesn't reply, but I can tell he's thinking about it. I take off my panama and wipe the sweat off my forehead with the back of my hand. I move a couple of steps to claim the shelter of the palm the old man is sitting under, away from the ferocity of the sun.

He lifts his arm and points to one corner of the square. Then he says something in Malti and gestures with his hand, moving the fingers as if I'm a dog he is shooing away.

I realise he's trying to tell me that it's a bit of a way, that I have to go to the corner of the square and then keep walking. I mime steering a car and then walking. I point to my legs. 'Walk?' I say.

'*Iva*,' he replies.

I go and get the others, who are sitting on a bench on the other side of the square. 'It's this way,' I tell them.

'Oh dear,' says Mum, getting up with unusual speed, and smoothing down her dress, trying to look her best. 'I never thought we'd find it so quick.'

'We haven't yet,' says Laura.

We walk across the square and enter the street the old man indicated. It's deserted apart from a black-and-white cat, like an Egyptian statue, with saucer-shaped eyes and pointed ears, which is sitting licking itself in a doorway, and pauses, one paw still raised to its mouth, to watch us as we walk by. We probably seem a curious convoy. In front Laura supports Mum, who has no need of physical support but is fearful of overbalancing if she doesn't feel another arm beneath her own, ready to catch her should she fall or 'go all of a sudden' as she puts it. In the event, of course, the only thing Laura, at five feet three and seven and a half stones, could do if Mum fell is try to get out of the way to avoid being crushed. At the moment the likelihood of Mum's longtime fear of falling actually reaching fruition is increased by the fact that she's tearing along like a charging elephant. Dad and I follow, me holding his hand in case he trips, which is always possible since he can't see anything on the ground. But he doesn't need help in moving. Once you start him off, slip him into first gear with a little tug, he changes rapidly into overdrive so that he's all but running. It's the festinating walk that's a paradoxical feature of Parkinson's, always hurrying, getting nowhere fast.

The street is lined with shops whose names belie its architecture and the hot sun. It's as if my mind has slipped out of sync into the England of the 1950s: CYNTHIA Gift Shop; HI SPOT Snooker Hall; JAY'S

MOTORING SCHOOL. STICK NO BILLS, says a sign on a wall, translating it below, NON AFFIGERE, to remind us this is not the Britain of forty years ago, as does a small bas relief of Christ on the wall of the next house, the words beneath it proclaiming *Viva Gesu*.

After a hundred yards another street, narrow and dark, joins the one we're in and on the corner house is painted a sign saying 'Triq San Gwann Battista'. We turn into it, grateful for its gloomy shade. The houses here are more Italianate, with little wrought-iron balconies projecting from the upper storeys. There's a smell of cooking and I catch a whiff of oregano. Somewhere a woman's voice is shouting angrily in Malti and I know it is at some hapless man. Laura and I leave Mum and Dad leaning against one another, like two playing cards propping each other up, and look at the numbers on the doors.

'Number 48 must be at the other end,' I say, and we set off. I hear Mum say 'Come on, Jim,' and turn to see her seize Dad by the wrist and drag him along like a recalcitrant child, while he resists, holding his glasses in one hand and still trying to read the street sign, looking at it as though it has a hidden meaning that has escaped the rest of us. By the time they catch up with us, Mum is panting and sweat rolls down her cheeks, which burn red from the effort.

'Why have you stopped?' she asks, assuming it's to prevent her having another heart attack. 'We're all right. Dad and me can manage.'

'I stopped because we're there,' I say. 'This is number 48. Or what's left of it.'

We stand and stare at the pile of rubble which is all there is in the spot where Maria's old home should be. You can see it's old rubble because grass and moss have long grown over the stonework that remains, softening and blurring the lines so that soon it will be impossible to tell this was ever a place where someone lived.

'Where's it gone?' says Mum. 'Who's took it away?'

I feel someone's eyes on me and turn, but there's no one there. A curtain blows out from a first-floor balcony across the street, as though someone has been standing there watching. Almost immediately there's the sound of a bolt being drawn back and the front door of the house opens. A young woman, wearing tight jeans and a leopard print T-shirt, comes out, pausing to push a small girl in a long white dress, who attempts to follow her, back inside. Closing the door behind her, she walks across the street, suspicion in her dark eyes.

'Yes please,' she says. 'You want something?'

'Yes,' says Mum, her tone quarrelsome, as though this young mother is somehow responsible. 'What have they done with this house?'

'Done? Who?' says the woman. 'Nobody does anything to any house.'

'I'm sorry,' I say, smiling at her, realising she is very attractive, her eyes almond-shaped and almost black, her skin brown as Mum's fingers after peeling potatoes. 'We wondered what had happened to number 48.'

'Oh, it is destroyed,' she says. 'It blows up.'

'Blew up? What, in the war?'

'No, after war. 1957, 1958 or sometime like that. I dunno. Anyway, there is a bomb dropped by . . . ' she waves at the sky.

'A plane?'

'Germans. It bury itself in the garden and no one know it is there, and then one day it just blow up.'

'Was anybody killed?'

'No. I don't think so. I don't know. I am not born. Maybe.'

'We're looking for someone who used to live here. Maria Spiteri. You know her, or her son, Anthony? She lived here in 1945.'

'Ah, no, I was not born then.'

'Of course not. Well, do you have any family who might know? An elderly neighbour, perhaps?'

She shrugs. She's losing interest.

'No, I dunno anything. I have to go now. Sorry.'

We stand and look at the ruin for a moment or two. The young woman walks back to her house, opens the door and goes inside. The door slams shut with a bang, which sounds even more final in the Sunday morning silence.

Somewhere far off a rooster crows, as though it too has woken late with a hangover.

Dad shakes his head and I wonder if he understands everything after all, and is disappointed. Mum looks suddenly smaller, as though someone has let all the air out of her. They both seem tired and old.

'It looks like the trail has gone cold,' I say. 'We might as well go.'

We make our way back along the street, no longer hurrying, Dad's feet dragging on the pavement.

'I didn't think it would be like this,' says Mum, dabbing at her eyes with her hankie. 'I thought we'd find Dad's little boy.'

'I know,' says Laura, patting her arm. 'It's ever so disappointing after coming all this way.'

Suddenly there's the sound of footsteps, lighter than our own. Someone is running behind us and I turn to see the little girl who tried to follow the woman out of the house. She is chasing after us, her tiny arms pumping the air with effort, her white dress billowing in the breeze.

'Mister! Mister!' she calls.

I stop and wait for her. She runs up to me and stands in front of me, panting to get her breath. 'Mama says you must ask the priest. He is very old. He lives here a long time. Knows everybody.'

I reach inside my pocket and find a few coins, which I hand to the little girl. She backs off, wary of taking them.

I stretch out my hand. 'Go on, take it,' I say. 'It's for running so well and telling us about the priest.'

She snatches the money and runs off, shouting *'Grazzi!'* as she goes.

With Mass over, the main square is transformed. People are pouring out of the church, standing around in groups, gossiping, the men reaching into the pockets of their mostly worn and old-fashioned suits, taking out packets of cigarettes, which are offered around, and lighting up. Children run about laughing, a motorbike is kicked into life, cars are started up. We find a seat in the shade occupied by a couple of plump old women, who immediately shuffle up to the other end when they see Dad's condition, leaving an exaggerated amount of room, even for Mum, to get into. Mum and Dad sit down.

'Thank you very much,' says Mum to the women. 'My husband doesn't like this heat. He's a bit disabled, you see.'

One of the women says, 'Nobody likes the sun so hot. Especially not if you are on the heavy side.'

'No,' says Mum, looking the woman up and down, 'it must be difficult.'

I fetch a bottle of water from the car and pour Mum and Dad out a plastic cup each, but Dad waves his away.

'He's worried about the toilet,' says Mum.

'There's one here,' I say, pointing to a concrete building on one side of the square which couldn't be anything but a public lavatory. 'I'll take him in a minute. I want to catch the priest before he goes.

I enter the church as the last worshippers are leaving, slowed down by the burden of gossip they have to unload on one another. I'm amazed by the interior of the building. It's stuffed with statues of saints, oil paintings of biblical scenes which look as if they might be valuable, and wood panelling overlaid with gold leaf at almost every opportunity, like an over-iced cake. 'Excellent decorative order', as we say at work. There's no sign of the priest, but at the crux of the nave I feel a breeze coming from one side and follow it around the back of the altar, where there's an open door. I walk through it and find myself outside once more. The priest, still in his vestments, is sitting on a little wall in the shade, smoking a cigarette, his back to me. I walk over to him and cough.

'Excuse me . . .'

He turns, and I see at once he is not the man I'm looking for. He can't be more than thirty. He reads the disappointment in my face.

'Yes?' he says. 'There is something I can do for you?'

'I was expecting an older man. You are the priest of this church?'

'Yes, I am. You were hoping to find Father Joseph. May I ask why?'

'It's on some business of my father's,' I say. 'He was here during the war. He's disabled now and he's returned to look for a Maltese person he met here, someone who was very close to him.'

'I see. Forgive me for asking, but I have a reason. You see, Father Joseph is very ill. He is in the hospital at B'Giba. He has suffered a stroke and is unlikely to recover. I have to make sure he is not bothered for frivolous purposes.'

'My father loved a woman here. After he left, she had a son. My father has never seen him.'

The priest takes another drag from his cigarette, holding it now between thumb and index finger as it is almost burned down. He watches it as though he has never really looked at a cigarette burning before.

'You will find him in the Hospice of the Sisters of Mercy, just outside B'Giba. But I have to tell you he is a very sick man. His mind is not all it was. He may not be able to help you. Also, his old housekeeper may know something, she was with him for many years. But naturally I will have to ask her permission before I tell you her address. Please leave me yours and I will contact you.'

I pat my pockets and purse my lips in frustration. The priest reaches under his surplice and produces a biro. He holds it out to me and then hands me his cigarette pack to write on.

I scribble down the address and hand the pack back to him. 'Please, it's very kind of you to help at all, but we're only here for another twelve days.'

'Ah yes, after nearly half a century your father is now in a great hurry to see his Maltese son.' He smiles. 'Better late than never. That's a wise British saying.'

'Yes. Thank you, Father.'

I turn and walk away. I'm just about to round the end of the church when he calls out to me. I turn, not having heard.

'I hope you find what you are looking for,' he says and waves his hand, which I notice now holds a fresh cigarette.

On the way home the atmosphere inside the car is flat. We don't know what to do with ourselves now the search is in limbo. I've vetoed going straight to the hospital to see Father Joseph. Mum and Dad have had enough excitement for one day and it's obvious they are both exhausted. So we do what we always do in our family at such times. We eat. I notice a roadside restaurant, a lovely old building covered in crimson bougainvillaea and with a small garden to one side where the tables and chairs are shaded by pergolas hung with grapevines.

'How about some lunch?' I say. 'Anybody hungry?'

'I could manage a little something,' says Mum. 'Just a bite. And anyway Dad will have to have something so he can take his tablets.'

It's one of the features of our holiday lives, Dad having to have food at certain hours because he's not supposed to take his tablets on an empty stomach. Laura often suggests a biscuit or two would do, but Mum insists 'a couple of biscuits isn't going to stop your stomach being empty, the man needs a proper meal'. So we always end up eating out.

Seated in the garden we sip chilled white wine, except for Laura, who only has mineral water.

'I think I had enough wine last night,' she says, when Mum looks surprised at this. 'I don't think the wine here agrees with me.'

She looks at me and then quickly down at the table, where she drags a fork slowly across the white tablecloth, making a pattern. All at once I wonder if there's another reason she's not drinking. If she thinks something happened last night and believes she may be pregnant, she might not drink because it would be bad for the baby. Suddenly I get a sense of what it would be like to have a wife who is pregnant and I feel a funny kind of pride, but only for a moment.

We order omelettes, 'and some chips for Dad', says Mum. 'He could manage some chips.'

'Sounds like a good idea,' I say. 'What about you, Mum? Would you like chips?'

'Oh, go on then, just to be sociable. After all, I'm on my holidays, why shouldn't I?'

The omelettes are fluffy and buttery and deep yellow. The chips are crisp and golden from the olive oil they've been fried in. It all tastes clean and fresh out here in the open air. We eat in silence, finding a sudden hunger, the way you do after a period of stress. There is only the clatter of our knives and forks as one of us occasionally puts them down to take another sip of the wine.

When it's over Dad has ice cream, a massive concoction of three different flavours under a mound of whipped

91

cream, and Mum has a banana split, 'To keep him company'. Laura and I take it in turn to feed Dad and we're all happy because he's loving every spoonful, swallowing it down and opening his mouth ready for the next one, like a baby bird being fed by its mother.

Afterwards Mum and Laura go off to the lavatory. I'm sitting opposite Dad, and the wine bottle is on the table between us, the outside of it still sweating in the heat, even though it's a long time out of the fridge. I pour us each another glass. Dad lifts his and says, 'Bottoms up,' and takes a deep sip.

'Bottoms up,' I say and fake a smile to try to lift his spirits. And while I'm doing it, I'm suddenly aware of how the smile is made, the mechanics of the corners of the mouth moving outwards, stretching the lips until the teeth are revealed for maximum effect. Of course, they are tightly clenched to prevent what I ought to say from escaping.

I know I can't tell Dad until I tell Mum, but that means letting it explode under him all at once, without the merest hint of a warning.

I close my eyes, as though against the glare of the sun, and the clear blue sky is swapped for the stormy grey of a February day six months ago when Mum, Pauline and I went to look at The Willows.

Outside The Willows, Mum refused to get out of Pauline's car. 'I'm not going into that place,' she said, folding her arms resolutely like a sit-down protester preparing to resist attempts at removal by the police.

'They're expecting us,' I said. 'We've got to go in.'

'I haven't got to do anything. I'm my own person. It just don't seem right going behind Dad's back when the poor man's flat out in hospital.'

There was a paradox here. If Dad had not been in hospital, Mum would not have been there anyway, since his hospitalisations are the only times she leaves his company for a moment, which is part of the problem. Dad was laid up in a geriatric ward with one of his increasingly frequent bouts of bronchitis. The doctors were hinting he was reaching the stage when he would need permanent professional nursing care. His GP, Dr Large, had suggested we take a look at The Willows, which he said was good as private nursing homes go, especially as its weekly fees did not exceed the amount state benefit would pay.

'Come on, Mum,' said Pauline, switching off the engine, putting her arm around Mum and giving her a hug while at the same time undoing the clasp of her seat belt. 'We might as well look at it now we're here.'

Mum didn't reply, but sat staring out of the windscreen at the three large willow trees in front of the single-storey, 1950s red-brick building, their foliage a trio of disembodied skirts dancing a frenzied rumba in the fierce north-easterly wind which had howled its way from the Russian steppes to assault this exposed Fenland village.

Pauline got out of the car, walked around the other side and opened Mum's door.

'Come on,' she said. 'It doesn't do any harm to look. He doesn't have to come here if you don't want him to.'

'Don't worry, I won't. I know I won't,' said Mum, but nevertheless she began to move. 'I'll keep going as long as I can.'

Pauline rolled her eyes at me as I got out of the car. We each took one of Mum's arms and helped her lift herself out.

At the front door we were met by a short, round woman in her early fifties. With her sharp curved nose and large, black-rimmed spectacles, she reminded me of an owl.

'I'm Janet Cooper,' she said as she ushered us inside. 'My husband Len and I have been running The Willows for twenty-three years. No, I tell a lie, twenty-four, come March. Not a very nice day, is it?'

'It's bitter out there, bitter,' said Mum. 'Mind you, it's not exactly sheltered here, is it? Bleak, I'd call it. Very bleak.'

'It's lovely in the summer, dear,' said Mrs Cooper. 'Now, let me ask you, is it yourself you're considering The Willows for?'

'Me?' Mum turned purple. 'Me? I should think not! Let me tell you you won't get me in a place like this. I'd throw myself in the river first.'

'It's our father who's the patient,' Pauline said quickly.

'Resident, dear,' said Mrs Cooper. 'We say resident here. This isn't a hospital, it's their home and we like to make them feel it as such.'

'Well, that's something, I suppose,' said Mum. She looked with approval at the multicoloured carpet and the pink-painted walls as Mrs Cooper led us along a short corridor which opened out into a large room. It was full of big, upright vinyl armchairs ranged all round the walls and in two rows, back to back, along the centre. About half of them were occupied by elderly people.

'The lounge,' said Mrs Cooper with an all-embracing sweep of her arm. 'We don't say "day room" the way they might at some other establishments. We say "lounge". What I was saying about it being their home, you see?'

Mum, Pauline and I surveyed the twenty or so people in the room. We were looking at the various stages of decay the human form goes through before it returns to dust. In one corner a group were dozing in front of a large television, which was showing an old Randolph Scott western, the volume turned so low it was unlikely any of them who were awake could be following the plot.

'It's company for them,' said Mrs Cooper, reading my thoughts. 'If they really want to watch a programme, they can do so in their own rooms.'

On the other side of the room, a couple of brighter-eyed old women were reading books, the lips of one of them mouthing the words, while a man next to them slept with his head back, mouth wide open and a copy of the *Sun* on his lap. Beside him another man smiled at us and waved a hand. 'Nice to see you again!' he shouted. There was a bird cage with a couple of budgerigars. A tall old man, a hump on his bent back, tapped feebly on the side of the cage and said something to them. The birds ignored him, clinging to the metal bars of the cage with their claws, staring out across the room, apparently at Randolph Scott, perhaps attracted by the faint sound of gunfire. Two old men were playing cards and laughing. Three women sat side by side, knitting and chatting together. Beside them a wizened little woman had removed one of her slippers and was holding it to her mouth, nibbling at the toe. Mrs Cooper strode over to her.

'I don't think we want to do that, do we, Gwendoline dear?' she said, pulling the slipper from her reluctant fingers. 'Not hygienic.' She bent down and gently slid the slipper back on to the woman's foot.

'As you can see, a fair amount of activity. I like to keep my old people stimulated. Yes, they do get tired and some of them sleep. But we try to interest them in such activities as they can do. And we have various entertainments.'

'Entertainments?' I asked.

'We have a lady comes from Cambridge every other Friday. She plays the electric keyboard and sings songs from the shows. There are two ladies from the village who come on a voluntary basis and do craftwork with the residents. And another who reads to them on a Wednesday afternoon. Very nice for those who can't read themselves. And we have a magician from time to time. They love that, the old people do, especially the rabbits. Animals are very therapeutic.' As if rehearsed, she bent and picked up a large tabby cat which was walking past. 'This is Flopsy. We have three cats. There's Topsy and Mopsy as well. Silly names, I know, but it is a scientific

95

fact that petting an animal can relieve stress and depression. Now, I'll show you a room.'

She led us along another corridor. There was a smell of overcooked vegetables which reminded me of school dinners. Ahead, with her back to us, a frail old lady rested on her Zimmer frame. She was in the middle of the passage.

'Excuse us, Lily,' said Mrs Cooper and squeezed past the Zimmer. Mum tried to follow, but there was not enough space for her expansive figure. For a moment I thought she was going to elbow the old lady out of the way. Instead she bustled back and tried to get through on the other side. But the old lady was bang in the middle of the corridor and there was no way through. Mrs Cooper squeezed back to join us and there was an awkward silence as we slowly edged our way along the corridor, like mourners behind a coffin, at Lily's pace.

Eventually Lily passed an open doorway and Mrs Cooper ushered us through it. The room was obviously uninhabited. It contained a metal hospital bed, a white melamine dressing table with drawers, a white melamine wardrobe, a vinyl-covered armchair and a small wooden chair. The atmosphere was cold and forbidding.

'Not very homely, I know,' Mrs Cooper smiled. 'But it gives you an idea of size and so on. And residents can have whatever they like from home, television, video, pictures for the walls.'

There was silence as we tried to find something to look at in the room, but in all truth, it was so bare one glance had been enough. Mum let out a little whimper, as though she was trying to stifle a full-blown sob. 'I couldn't put my Jim in here,' she sniffed. 'It's like a prison cell.'

Mrs Cooper put her arm around her. 'I know, dear, I know,' she said. 'But it's as I was saying, this is just the bare bones. Let me take you to see what can be made of it.'

Outside in the corridor Lily was talking to another old lady with a walking frame, the two of them facing one another over their Zimmers like neighbours chatting over a garden fence. A bell started ringing, loud and insistent, like a fire alarm. 'That will be one of the residents,' smiled Mrs Cooper over her shoulder. 'Each room has a bell to summon the staff should a resident need assistance.' A young woman in a white nurse's tunic rushed past us in the direction of the bell, turning sideways on the run to pass Lily and her friend en route.

We were shown into another room. 'Here we are,' said Mrs Cooper. 'Hello, Bill,' she said to a small bald man in pyjamas lying in the bed. 'You don't mind me just showing Mrs Taylor and her family your room, do you? It's such a lovely room.'

Bill smiled a gummy smile and I noticed his teeth grinning at us from a glass on his bedside table. He muttered something incomprehensible and turned away to watch the television, which was on a bracket on the wall at the end of his bed. It was a quiz show.

'As you can see, Bill's family have made his room into a proper home for him.'

It was true. The walls were covered from waist height to ceiling in children's drawings and photographs of smiling kids. I found myself facing a picture of a cat done in green crayon. Underneath was written, 'I love you, Granddad.' Next to it was an old tinted photograph of a wedding couple, the bride in white, the man in a blue RAF uniform, his hair unnaturally red. Instead of the institutional furniture, Bill had a large pine wardrobe and a comfortable, cloth-upholstered armchair. His bed had blue sheets and a duvet instead of blankets. There were potted plants on the windowsill. On a wooden chest of drawers there were more photos, a couple of vases of artificial flowers, a pair of antelope carved in wood and a small metal model of Ely Cathedral. Above his head was a little bookshelf holding a few books, a Walkman and several neat stacks of tapes.

Suddenly the bell started ringing again. I wondered how often this happened, as the sound was deafening. But Bill seemed oblivious and had almost dozed off to sleep.

The nurse we saw earlier tapped on the open door and said, 'Mrs Cooper, could you come and look at Violet for a minute, please?'

'Yes, of course,' said Mrs Cooper. She turned to us. 'Excuse me for just a minute.' She disappeared. Bill's eyes closed. The duvet slipped from his bed. Mum tried to catch it, but it slid to the floor before she could manage it. Bill was wearing only a pyjama jacket, his lower body naked. Underneath him, on the bottom sheet, was a strip of pale blue material, which I suddenly realised was an incontinence pad. He was lying with his knees up, so his thigh concealed his pubic area. On the bed I saw a thick, transparent plastic bag, full of dark, amber liquid, the colour of strong beer. From the bag a plastic tube protruded and snaked its way along the bed and over his thigh. A deep sigh escaped him and his body relaxed into sleep. His legs slid flat, and I was able to follow the plastic tube up over his thigh to where it was swallowed by the gaping mouth in the tip of his penis, the small red lips of the opening gripping it tight, like the mouth of a fish devouring a worm.

'Catheter,' Mum explained. 'They're all on them in these places. They say it's because they can't do a wee on their own, but it's just for the convenience of the staff if you ask me. It saves them the trouble of messing with bottles. Same as that thing underneath. They let them do their business in the bed and just pull that thing out and chuck it away like a nappy. I seen it up the hospital. They'd have your Dad like this. His prostate is all the excuse they'd need. They'd have one of them tubes in his

98

willy before he'd been here five minutes.'

On the table beside Bill was a tray containing a few medical implements. There was a plastic bag containing another tube. I noticed it had what looked like a small rubber balloon on one end.

'That's a new catheter,' said Mum. 'They have to change them every so often.'

Beside the plastic bag was a small booklet. I picked it up. The front said, 'Using a Catheter'. And underneath, 'Your questions answered'.

I flicked through it. I started to read the section headed 'Inserting a catheter'. It explained how the tube was pushed into the penis and up into the bladder by a doctor, who then inflated air into the balloon in the bladder. It seemed to operate like a ballcock in a lavatory cistern, letting fluid out whenever the bladder was full without any need for recourse to the wearer.

Can a penis wince? I think mine did, as I recalled the sharp pain when a woman's fingernail had once accidentally caught in its opening during lovemaking, or the needle sting when a hair somehow entered it. I turned a few pages. 'Can I have sex while wearing a catheter?' it asked. 'Yes, you can,' came the reply. 'Simply double the catheter along the underside of your penis and slip a condom over both. You can then have sex in the normal way.'

I put the booklet back on the bedstand and glanced back at Bill as we left the room. The transparent plastic tube now appeared orange and the level of liquid in the bag on the bed was rising. Fluid was being effortlessly transferred from one container to another. Bill was pissing, blissfully asleep.

In the car there was silence until we hit the outskirts of Ely.

'Well, Mum, what did you think?' said Pauline, making an exaggerated display of consulting her rearview mirror, in an attempt to give the question a casual spin which fooled no one, least of all Mum.

'All right, I suppose, as them places go.'

'I thought it was quite nice, really,' said Pauline. 'Very homely.'

'Oh yes,' I said quickly. 'Not very flash perhaps, but definitely comfortable.'

'I know what you're up to,' said Mum, 'and you can stop it now. I'd never put your Dad in one of them places, not in a million years. The only way he'll end up somewhere like that is over my dead body.'

I want to tell Dad all about The Willows right now, and what a nice place it is and how he'll be well looked after and what fun it will be having other people to talk to and cats and budgies and entertainments, only I don't. Not because I know none of it is true, but because to do so would render me a child once again, confessing a misdemeanour to him, that I have gone behind his back and kept this a secret all these months, my deceit earning once again his stony disapproval.

I decide to start paving the way for the moment before the end of next week when, to satisfy Pauline's ultimatum, I will have to confront Mum.

'You know, Dad, Mum's not as fit as she used to be,' I say.

He mumbles something, which sounds like, 'None of us are,' and laughs.

'What I mean is, she's finding it hard to manage.'

He suddenly looks frightened and his eyes flicker back and forth, as though searching for an enemy in the foliage around us, although if there were anybody there he probably couldn't see them anyway.

'Dad, I'm talking about Mum.'

He licks his lips, and mumbles something.

'What?' I say. 'Speak slowly and louder.'

'Mum does a good job,' he says and stares off into the

distance, perhaps thinking about what I've said but, more probably, unaware of its import. I wait for a moment to see if there's anything else, but nothing comes. It's as if he's disappeared again, the way he often seemed to when I was a child. I look at his worn-out old body, the vacant eyes, and it's hard to imagine him ever having an affair with anyone, just as it's hard for me to remember who he was before he became like this.

I close my eyes and cut my mind loose, let it drift away from the heat and the whine of the cicadas. If I squeeze my eyelids tight I get flashbacks of myself as a small boy, only I'm outside myself, watching, never inside seeing it through my own eyes. It's always in black-and-white, like the photos we have from that time. And it's a silent movie. People open their mouths and speak and laugh, but the sound hasn't been recorded. I see Dad hauling me up on to his shoulders and running round and round the old garden at home with me. I see myself sitting looking out of the front-room window, dying for him to come home soon before I burst with wanting to tell him about something that happened that day. I press my eyelids tighter and he's teaching me to play chess and, even though he gives me a queen advantage, he still has to work hard to let me win. I look across the board, up into his face, I'm squeezing my eyes so tight now it's giving me a headache, trying to see how he looked before his eyes went dead and his smile froze to a mask, and the eczema burst all over his cheeks like the bougainvillaea over the walls of the Villa Francesca. Tighter and tighter I squeeze, I'm really concentrating now, willing his face to appear and . . . nothing. Only the way he is if I open my eyes and look at him now.

There's this theory about Parkinson's, although, of course, a theory — and one of many — is all that it is. Nobody knows for sure how or why it starts. It could be an accident, or exposure to some chemical, or maybe even a virus. But whatever the trigger, the result is the same. A part of the brain called the substantia nigra is damaged and stops producing dopamine, a chemical which helps transmit messages from the brain to the rest of the body, like telling you to lift your foot when you want to start walking. Even in normal people, the amount of dopamine you have decreases as you get older, and when it gets below a certain level, you begin to exhibit symptoms of Parkinson's disease. Normally this happens in very old age. The theory says, suppose something happens to you to kill off some of your dopamine production while you're still young. Suppose the damage is not enough to make a difference that anyone can notice. Then as you grow older your remaining dopamine supply declines at the normal rate. But because you've got less to start with, you reach the point at which you don't have enough much sooner. Bingo! You have Parkinson's disease. Dad was diagnosed at the age of fifty-one. But, if the theory's right, that was just the day when his dopamine dropped to a sufficiently low level to manifest symptoms a doctor could recognise. The day before it was not quite so bad, and the day before that a little less bad than that, making a sliding scale right back to the day the catastrophe, whatever it was, happened to him in the first place. In that case wouldn't you be able to look back and see the clues long before the doctors had? Things like not having the energy to play with me or forgetting to ask about my maths exam. Didn't I spot the first signs years before the medics, the day I decided he'd just lost interest in me? It's a theory I cling to, like a small child to a favourite teddy bear on a stormy night. It was nothing to do with Dad and me, after all. It was just a chemical that wasn't there.

*   *   *

'Get that neck up! GET IT UP!' I open my eyes. Dad has fallen asleep, his head hanging over the side of his chair. Mum is trying to tug it upright. It's time to leave.

It's not just Dad who is tired. Mum too is wilting from heat and disappointment. We spend the afternoon resting on the bungalow patio and at six o'clock Laura goes inside to make supper.

'I think we all need an early night,' she says, widening her eyes at me behind Mum's back. 'It will do us good.'

During the meal I try to get Laura drunk again, but she refuses to touch a drop of wine. 'No thanks,' she says, her voice dripping with innuendo which fortunately Mum is too busy eating to notice, 'I think I'll enjoy my evening better without it.'

Not that there's much of an evening anyway. No sooner are our plates empty than Laura whisks them away. Dad is tugged out of his seat and off to his bedroom before he's even had chance to lick the last drops of ice cream from his moustache. Laura has him undressed, Horlicked and tableted in such record time she even earns Mum's approval. 'You see what you can achieve by getting your meal over and done with quick,' says Mum.

I try to play for time by starting the washing up, but Laura takes the dishcloth from my hand and whispers, 'We can do this in the morning. Let's get to bed.'

In our bedroom, Laura has our clothes off before I know what's happening. She pushes me on to the bed and climbs on top of me, her tongue forcing its way between my clenched teeth. Her hand reaches down to my genitals where, like the traitor it is, my penis immediately stiffens.

I grab her shoulders and manage to roll her off me.

'Why are you stopping?' she says, even though I don't think I can properly be said to have started yet. 'What's the matter?'

'Haven't cleaned my teeth,' I improvise.

'I don't mind.'

'Well, I do. They're all furry with garlic. Besides, I need a pee.'

'OK,' she says, as I make for the door. 'But don't be long.' She indicates my erection which I'm just covering with my dressing gown. 'Timewise, that is.'

I wander around the kitchen, absent-mindedly brushing my teeth, while my penis attempts to push its way through the front of my dressing gown as though it is so impatient for sex it is on an independent search for a vagina to bury itself in. I'm aware of something right at the very back of my mind nagging at me, as if the few grey cells not under the tyranny of my penis are trying to tell me something.

Suddenly, an image from yesterday flashes into my brain: Laura pulling things out of the cutlery drawer and holding them up.

I walk over to the drawer and open it. I put down my toothbrush and take out the steak tenderiser. It's like a small mallet with a piece of bumpy metal covering the bit you hit the meat with. I lay my penis on the worktop and imagine giving it a short, sharp blow, and inducing instant, temporary (I hope) impotence. I raise the tenderiser. And then, just as I'm about to strike, I find myself thinking about the word and there doesn't seem to be anything very tender about what I'm contemplating. I move so that my penis, which is still erect and unperturbed by all this, is no longer resting on the worktop. Carefully and quietly I lay the steak tenderiser back in the drawer and then I notice something else beside it. A light goes on in my head and the bit of my brain that's working says, 'Idiot! *This* is what I meant all along.'

I lift out the turkey baster. I have never really seen one before. It consists of a plastic tube with a rubber bulb over one end. The idea seems to be that you stick the end of the tube in the fat around your roasting turkey and by depressing and releasing the bulb suck fat into it, which you then squirt over the bird. A sort of culinary water pistol.

'Nick!' Laura calls softly from the bedroom. 'What are you doing?'

'Just coming,' I say. 'Soon as I've flossed.'

Frantic, I look around the kitchen and my eyes light on the pan in which Laura heated the milk for Dad's Horlicks. The words 'milky white substance' leap into my mind. It was how they always described semen in school biology textbooks. Thank goodness we didn't wash up — there's some milk left in the bottom of the pan. I dip a finger in. It's still pretty warm. How hot is semen, I wonder? I remember something I read once about your balls being outside your body to keep the sperm cool. I notice the meat thermometer in the drawer and wonder if I can use it to check the temperature of the milk.

'Nick!'

I decide there's no point in worrying about temperature as I haven't time to cool it anyhow. Then I wonder if the texture's all wrong. It's too thin and runny, not thick and sticky like semen should be. I spot the Horlicks jar on the worktop by the hob. I grab a teaspoon and ladle a bit of Horlicks into the milk and give it a good stir to thicken it up. I take the turkey baster, depress the rubber bulb, stick the other end in the milk, and suck up a tube full. Then I stick it in my dressing gown pocket and dash back to the bedroom.

As I enter the door, Laura gives me a suspicious look and for a moment I almost expect her to say, 'Is that a turkey baster in your pocket or are you just pleased to see me?' But instead she just smiles and says, 'About time too,' and pats the bed beside her. I walk around to my side of the bed and switch off the bedside lamp. It's pitch black.

'Oh, don't you want it on?' Laura says.

'Not tonight. More romantic this way.'

I slip out of my dressing gown, taking the turkey baster out of the pocket at the same time. As I climb into bed, I place it carefully between Laura's pillow and the wall behind it, making sure the open end is up. I don't want a premature premature ejaculation.

After a bit of kissing and stroking, I push Laura on to her back and move my hand down between her legs. I begin to massage her clitoris.

'Aaah!' she gasps, 'That's nice.'

As I stroke her, I turn on to my side and press my penis against her thigh. I rub myself gently against her.

'Ooh, I like that great heavy thing on my leg,' she says and her pelvis begins to gyrate as she pushes herself hard against my fingers.

We do this for some time and then she begins to moan, long and slow at first, then in short little gasps.

'Oh! Oh! Oh!' she goes.

'Aaaah!' I groan 'Ah! Ah! Ah!' taking on the rhythm of her movement as I rub myself against her faster and faster.

'Oh! Oh! Oh!'

'Ah! Ah! Ah!'

She pulls my head to her. We kiss. She bites my lower lip so hard I can taste blood. I reach up behind the pillow, grab the turkey baster and drop it behind my back.

'Ooooooooo!' It's a long, drawn-out sigh. I'm still rubbing myself against her.

I lift my left hand from her now-sated clitoris, fumble behind myself and find the turkey baster. I place the end of the tube close to my still-moving penis and depress the bulb.

'Aaaaaaaaaaa!' I moan and fling the turkey baster over my shoulder.

'Oh my goodness!' says Laura.

'Sorry,' I say. 'Sorry, I just couldn't control myself.'

106

Laura puts her arms around me and holds me tight. The sheet beneath our thighs seems to be soaking wet.

'It's OK, baby, it's OK,' she says.

'I'm really sorry,' I say. 'It's never happened to me before. I guess I was just so excited.'

'I could tell. There was so much of it! And so hot too! I've never known it so hot.'

'I feel such a failure.'

'It's all right. Honestly. I find it really flattering you can still get that way after ten years together. All that moaning too. You've never done that before.'

'Are you sure you don't mind? Really really sure?'

'Of course not.'

'I don't think I'll be able to – '

'Don't even think about it. I'm perfectly happy. Let's just snuggle down and go to sleep in each other's arms.'

I lie there for ages, until her breathing takes on the slow, heavy rhythm of deep sleep. Then I carefully unwrap her arms from around me, slip from the bed, feel around on the floor until I find the turkey baster and take it into the kitchen, where I wash and dry it and return it to its drawer.

I have just faked an orgasm.

Four

Monday

There are four old men in the hospital ward, which is clean but cramped in spite of the sparse furnishings. Each patient lies on an old-fashioned metal hospital bed, his only other furniture a small bedside cabinet. In the middle of the room is a portable TV on a metal trolley. The walls are painted white and are bare except for a wooden crucifix on the wall facing the door, next to the single small window, which is wide open. A large ceiling fan oscillates with a *whump whump*. We stand awkwardly in the doorway, wondering which of the patients is Father Joseph.

'Father Joseph?' I say to the young nun who has been asked to show us to the ward. She almost laughs, she is so surprised. It's possible she has never before encountered people visiting a total stranger. But I've already explained our mission to the sister in charge of the ward and can't be bothered to go through it again, so I'm happy to leave her in confusion.

'You don't know?'

'No.'

She raises her eyebrows and indicates the man farthest from the door on the right-hand side. 'You must be quick.

Really no more than two visitors are allowed. It's all right now for a short time, because no one else has any visitors, but be as fast as you can. Oh, and please try not to let him upset himself, he is very ill.'

We walk past the man in the first bed. He is old but very powerfully built, as though he has done hard physical work all his life. He is lying flat on his back and evidently trying to lift himself up, pushing his arms against the white sheets so hard his face is contorted with the effort. On the opposite side of the room another man is asleep, mouth wide open, toothless gums exposed. Once again, I'm reminded how old age resembles baby-hood, but as if seen in a fairground mirror, what's appealing in the child now a grotesque distortion. The man facing Father Joseph is sitting up, watching the TV on the trolley, which is at the end of his bed. It's an old episode of *Cheers*.

He waves at us, and shouts something in Malti. I smile back and Mum says, 'He looks a nice clean old man.' The man looks puzzled, so Mum walks over and shouts at him, 'You look lovely and clean.' She reaches in her bag and hands him one of Dad's chocolate eclairs, which the man unwraps and pops into his mouth. He smiles, jaws working away on the sweet. Watching him, a sudden vision of Dad's future life in The Willows flashes before me: a solitary confinement version of this, reliant upon the sporadic and infrequent visits of the staff even for a sweet, his only entertainment a television he can neither see nor understand. The old man waves again and Mum turns to Laura and says, 'They love a bit of praise, these old people.'

Father Joseph is on his back, his head and shoulders supported by several pillows so he's almost sitting. His body is covered by a single sheet, which allows its out-line to be clearly seen, short and thin, like a child's. His head is totally bald, the eyes sunken into dark sockets, the cheekbones hollow. It's like a skull. His hands rest on top of the sheet, so neat and symmetrical it looks as if someone has placed them very carefully there. In his left arm is a tube connected to a drip feed by his side.

'He looks like a Belsen victim,' says Mum, without moderating the volume of her voice. Whispering is something she leaves entirely to Dad, since he is capable of little else. The old priest's eyes, which are almost as pale and dim as Dad's, wander towards her so slowly you can almost see them following the sound. Laura and I gather up chairs from around the other beds and place them next to Father Joseph's. It's a job to fit everyone in, especially Mum. We sit down, me on one side of the old priest's head, Dad on the other.

'Father Joseph,' I begin. 'You don't know us . . . '

'Don't I?' he says, his eyes flicking from one to the other of us, his head completely static. I notice when he speaks that the right half of his mouth doesn't move and remember about his stroke. His words are almost as blurred and indistinct as Dad's.

'We're looking for a woman.'

'Ah, yes, yes. Who isn't?' He starts laughing, a dirty chuckle, throaty with catarrh and sexual innuendo.

'No, you don't understand, this was a woman my father knew during the war. This is my father.'

The eyes slide slowly from right to left and fix on Dad for a long minute.

'He's a bit disabled. Parkinson's,' says Mum. 'But it's not the shaking kind, thank God.' She suddenly realises she's talking to a priest and mumbles, 'So to speak,' and is quiet.

'The war?' says the priest.

'Yes. Her name was Maria Spiteri.'

'The war? I remember the war. We ate rats you know. We ate all sorts, anything to keep us alive. I had a very fine cat called Gregory and we ate him. A beautiful ginger tom. Have you ever tasted cat? No? Well, let me tell you, it's not unlike squirrel. But I loved that cat. I almost choked on every mouthful. Poor Gregory!' Suddenly his body begins to shake until finally he lets out a great sob. 'Poor, poor Gregory. What a way to serve a friend.'

'I know it was hard here during the war. My father has told me about it many times.'

'The raids never stopped. Some days they were at it from dawn till dusk. We had no protection. Stukas bombed the town.'

'Stukas!' Dad says the word as plainly as anything. Then he's off on a long incoherent ramble, in which we may or may not be able to make out words like 'North Africa', 'Churchill', 'lazy Eyeties'.

He stops for breath and it's Father Joseph's turn, but his speech soon tires to a slur and he too becomes impossible to understand, except for occasional words or phrases he spits out on to the sheet with globules of saliva as if for greater emphasis: 'nettle soup', 'stewed lizards', 'boiled mice.'

Dad's really animated now. There's a mad glint in his good eye and words spill out of him, like water bubbling over from a boiling pan. As soon as he pauses, usually to wipe a line of dribble from his mouth, the priest starts up again, talking faster and faster. He's just as incoherent as Dad and I begin to wonder if somehow they are speaking the same language and are making perfect sense to one another while the rest of us can only catch the occasional word. I try to get Father Joseph back on the right track, but he's too busy staring back across the years to hear me.

'NAAFI . . . Lancasters . . . tail-end Charlies,' says Dad.

'Roast frogs . . . devilled beetles . . . mixed rodent grill,' replies the priest who must, I think, be in some crazed fantasy of the past now. Once again, I try to intervene.

'Father . . . I . . . '

'Bat pie . . . baked starlings . . . grasshopper stew.'

'I have a photograph . . . '

111

'Lee Enfield,' Dad throws out, leaning towards the priest as though making an important point. 'Pack drill. Shoulder arms!'

'Snails à la Grecque. Mouth-watering if you have enough garlic. Garlic covers a multitude of sins, but be sure they will find you out in the end. God sees all, God sees all. Dog sweetbreads.'

'Limpet mines. Mills bombs. Remove the pin, count three and throw.'

'Sparrow fricassée. Turnip soup.'

'Kill that cigarette! Don't you know there's a blackout!'

'Squirrel *hâché*. Made me gag. Never could abide raw meat!'

'Squad, squad shun!'

'Listen, I hate to interrupt, but . . . '

'Spaghetti bolognese with worms . . . owl curry.'

'MARIA SPITERI. DO YOU REMEMBER HER? THINK, PLEASE!'

'Jerries advancing . . . Panzer division . . . bazookas requested immediately.'

'DAD BE QUIET A MOMENT. DAD, SHUT UP, PLEASE!'

'Please, what is going on here? We cannot have all this shouting. You are disturbing the other patients.'

It's the nun again. I look around the ward. The sleeping man is still asleep. The man by the door has stopped trying to lift himself up and is dozing off. The man opposite is laughing loudly at something Ted Danson is saying, wiping tears from his eyes.

'I'm sorry, I was just trying to ask him about someone my father knew during the war.'

'Look at him,' she says. 'he doesn't remember his own name. The stroke damaged his brain. He couldn't tell you what happened half an hour ago, never mind all those years.'

I look at the old priest. He has gone quiet again and is

making a low humming sound to himself, like a child singing. He picks at the sheets, the ends of his fingers the yellow of old letters, from a lifetime's cigarettes, pulling off imaginary pieces of something and putting them in his mouth.

'Please,' I say to the nun, 'one last try.'

I hold the photograph right under the priest's eyes. 'This woman was called Maria Spiteri, do you remember her? Do you recognise the face?'

The old man continues his humming noise, his eyes looking straight through the photograph, not seeing it at all, focusing only on what he sees on the sheet, which is as white and blank as virgin snow.

It's white outside as well, with the midday sun bouncing off the concrete walls of the hospital. Dad lifts a hand to shield his eyes as if warding off a blow, his glaucoma making him extra sensitive to bright light. Another dead end and everyone's disappointment is exposed here. I rack my brains for a way to lift them out of it.

'Why don't we make a hospital day of it, while we're at it?' I say. 'Let's see if we can find the one Dad was in. See if it jogs any memories for him.'

'We might even find your appendix, Dad,' says Laura, taking his arm. 'That would be something, wouldn't it?'

'Four inches long,' he says, in a sudden spurt of clarity. 'Ready to burst any minute.'

We have the address of the hospital from a letter Dad wrote to Mum when he was there.

'What was he doing writing to you when you were engaged to someone else?' says Laura, as we drive towards M'dina.

'Well, it was the war then,' says Mum. 'It was all different. He knew he was the one I loved. He knew I only got engaged to the other fella to spite him.'

'Did it make you jealous, Dad?' Laura says.

113

He laughs.

'Well, if it did,' I say, 'it didn't stop him carrying on with this Maltese piece.'

The teeth flap like castanets played *presto*.

The hospital is on what passes for a hill on this uncontoured island. At first, I'm not sure if it is the hospital, and have to ask a white-suited man who's just got out of his car and is entering what looks like a newly built villa a hundred yards or so down the road.

'Yes, this was the military hospital,' he says. 'But it became a school some years ago. It's for boys who don't do so well in their exams. They learn practical things here.'

I thank him and he disappears into his house. A sign on the gate says Dr D. B. Bacciolotto, so we can trust his information about the hospital. The name of his house is Windsong and it's accurate, the wind is whistling around the former hospital as we enter the grounds, a pleasant relief after the suffocating stagnant air virtually everywhere else we've been on the island.

In the dusty driveway a sign says PATIENTS AND VISITORS CAR PARK, its still being there an indication, perhaps, of the status of the exam failures who now use the building. There's a general air of decay. The spacious grounds, as we say in the trade, are mostly laid out to scrubby grass and forlorn, abandoned shrubs, with just the odd defiant oleander bloom for colour. The drainpipes are rusting and rust marks stain the walls, like old dried blood on a bandage. A sign over the main entrance of the building says

DAVID BRUCE
ROYAL NAVAL HOSPITAL

and a foundation stone bears the date 1914. The military

architects did their best to render the soft yellow stone of the island unattractive and succeeded wonderfully. The building is square and dour and defiantly un-baroque with not the slightest hint of a frill to be seen. It has all the brooding massiveness of a prison. To enhance this effect, the frames of the ugly flat windows – row after row of them on all three floors – are painted institution green.

We amble around the building, which seems not only closed for the school holidays but also completely uninhabited. Somewhere a door bangs monotonously in the wind. Ripe for conversion.

I try to picture Dad being wheeled out of the French doors in his bed, or perhaps a wheelchair, to get the fresh air and the sun, while a couple of miles away the Luftwaffe was doing its best to pound Valletta into submission. But it's a task beyond my imagination.

I'm surprised to see no one about, apart from a man loading a rusty boiler on to a truck. He looks at us either suspiciously or furtively, I can't decide which.

Mum and Laura are walking around the garden. I notice Mum take a pair of nail scissors from her pocket and snip off a couple of oleander blooms. She pops the flowers in her handbag and smiles at me like a naughty infant. I stand with Dad on the terrace in front of the building. He lifts his glasses to stare up at it and then turns to gaze at the view.

'Is it coming back to you?' I ask.

'I think so, yes, Nick.'

'What can you remember about this place?' I say.

He looks around him for a minute or two and shakes his head. He gazes off towards the horizon for another minute. At last he turns to me and says, 'What country is this?'

Dad's confusion is partly the result of the Parkinson's and partly the side-effects of the various tablets he takes, especially the levodopa, which sometimes causes hallucinations. Getting the dosage of levodopa just right is a tricky business. If it's too low, then the lack of dopamine Dad's getting means all the symptoms of the illness become worse, especially rigidity. But increasing the dosage doesn't necessarily have the opposite effect, and even if it does it can increase his mental confusion too.

Once, ten years after he was first diagnosed, they decided to take him into hospital for a 'drug holiday' to assess his condition without all the drug side-effects to complicate and mask things. So they withdrew all his medication and sat back to watch what happened.

Pauline phoned me after the second day. 'Nick, I don't like what they're doing to him,' she said. 'They're torturing the poor man. He doesn't know where he is.'

'That's not unusual,' I say.

'It's not funny. You should see him. He keeps seeing things, animals and things that aren't there.'

They had him in a little side room on his own because his shouts were alarming the other patients. I stood and watched him from the doorway, seeing him as a stranger might. He was looking round and round the room, his eyes never still, and focusing especially on the floor around the bed. His hands gripped the bedclothes, pulling them to him like a protective cloak. His knees were bunched up in front of him, making him smaller, as though the bed were an island and he was fearful of something dreadful rising up out of the water around him and snapping at his ankles.

I stepped into the room. 'It's OK, Dad, I'm here.'

His eyes swivelled to me, full of milky relief, like a child who has lost sight of his mother in a crowd and suddenly finds her again. I took his hand from the blankets and tucked them back in. He gripped my fingers so tightly I thought they would snap.

'Nick, boy, you've got to get me out of here,' he said.

This was in the days when you could still understand most of what he said. 'There are things in here. They're after me. They climb up the walls.'

'What do? What things?'

'Animals. Little furry animals. They're trying to get on to the bed.'

'What sort of animals? Cats and dogs?'

'No-oo, no-oo, not nice animals. Vicious ones. Vermin. They would give you a nasty bite.'

'What – rats, mice, voles?'

'There have been, but not now. Now it's little furry things. I don't know what they are.'

I looked around the room, and made a sweeping gesture with my hand. 'But Dad, there's nothing here. The room's empty.'

He sat up and leaned forward, peering over the edge of the bed, his head turning, eyes patrolling the room.

'Aaaargh!' He pointed at a corner.

'What?'

'There's one! There!'

'What is it? What does it look like?'

'Small and furry with big teeth.'

'And where exactly is it?'

'Over there, in the corner.'

I walked over to the corner and made a big show of stamping my feet up and down.

'There's nothing here, see?'

'But I can see it.'

I walked back over to the bed and sat down on it, taking both his hands in mine. He continued to stare at the floor in the corner area.

'Dad. Dad, look at me. Come on, leave that and look at me for a moment.'

Reluctantly his head turned and he stared at me, eyes full of mad hope, like someone in a Bible illustration about to be cured by Christ.

'Dad, you're having hallucinations. It's because they've taken you off the levodopa. It's playing tricks with your mind, making you see things that aren't there.'

'But it's there now, in the corner. It's real, I know it is.'

'No, it's not, Dad. Listen to me. It's just an hallucination. Remember when I was a kid and you used to tell me about mirages in the desert, how people could see rivers and swimming pools and things?'

'Yis.'

'Well, it's like that. Your mind tells you it's there, but it's not. It's all just a figment of your imagination. You know that, don't you?'

'Yes, Nick, I understand. I know what you're saying is true.'

'Good, just remember that and you'll be all right. You can't see anything because there isn't anything there.'

'All right, Nick. Thank you.'

'Feel better now?'

'Yes thank you, Nick. Much better.'

'Good.'

'Nick?'

'Yes?'

'That thing in the corner . . . ?'

'The thing that isn't there?'

'Yis.'

'What about it?'

'There are two of them now.'

Dad's tired now, perhaps by the effort of casting his mind back so many years, perhaps by the excitement of recalling all those things from the war, the archaic weapons, the out-of-date slang. Perhaps from the sheer confusion of wondering where he is and what it is all about. When Mum suggests a fiesta, we don't argue with either the idea or the word.

We're just getting out of the car when a blue shape

emerges from the Villa Francesca and heads across the square.

'Hey, I've been waiting for you. I've got a message!'

Ferguson strolls over, a teasing smile playing on his lips.

'Guess who you missed while you were out?' he says.

'I've no idea,' I say. 'Not the rep?'

'No, she only comes Saturdays and Wednesdays. It wasn't the rep.'

He's beginning to annoy me.

'Well, who was it?' says Mum. 'No one else knows we're here.'

'No?' says Ferguson, raising an eyebrow at her.

'Why don't you just tell us,' I say. 'Save a lot of time.'

'It was a priest,' he says, pausing to let this sink in. 'He left an address for you. I've got it somewhere.' He begins patting the pockets of his leisure suit, of which there seem to be far more than anyone could possibly need. 'Now where is it?'

I can see Mum growing impatient.

'Ah yes, here it is.' He hands me a piece of a cigarette packet on which is written an address. 'He said to go at three o'clock tomorrow.'

'Right. Thank you very much. It's very nice of you to have taken the trouble.'

'No trouble.' Ferguson stands there smiling, not wanting to be dismissed. 'Relative?'

'Sorry?' I say.

'Relative? The person you're going to see.'

'No,' I say.

'Oh,' he says. 'I just wondered, that's all.'

'It's private,' says Mum, grabbing Dad's hand and dragging him towards the bungalow, wanting to brush Ferguson off and tugging at Dad in annoyance when he turns to smile at Ferguson. 'If you don't mind.'

'Oh, very sorry, I'm sure. Just trying to be friendly.'

119

Mum turns to face him now. 'We like to keep ourselves to ourselves,' she says, and turns towards the bungalow again.

I watch as Ferguson strolls back across the square. He stops outside the Villa Francesca, where Grey is waiting for him and they stand and chat, looking up from time to time in our direction. When they see me looking at them, I turn the other way and gaze across the wasteland and watch two rats which are worrying at a bright green plastic carrier bag and I wonder what can be inside that is so attractive.

In the evening Laura makes *penne all arrabbiata*, red and fiery, one of her specialities, and we eat it with thick, crusty wedges of local bread.

'Talk about hot!' says Mum, wincing over the first mouthful. 'This'll work you, Jim. If it doesn't, nothing will.'

This is our fourth day and Dad still hasn't had a bowel movement. In fact he hasn't had one for nearly a week now, something which is not unexceptional for him, but which we're all finding a bit of a strain in our different ways, Dad because he spends hours sitting on the loo, as Mum insists he does it here and doesn't wait until we're out somewhere, and because he's almost too full to eat anything; Mum because she feels it is her responsibility to intervene in some way and make him go to the loo; and Laura and I because we have to put up with Mum talking about it at increasing length with each passing day.

Dad eats all his pasta, but nothing happens. Without the excitement of Dad going to the loo, the evening stretches before us like a long walk on a hot day. So Laura produces a game she has brought along for just such an evening. It's called Scruples and the idea is that the players are put into situations where they have to make difficult moral choices. Things go quite well until it's Dad's turn.

Laura hands him his card and reads it over his shoulder for him. 'Are you listening, Dad?' she asks, since he's staring at the floor and may be on another planet or in a different time zone from the rest of us.

'Yis.'

'You're in a hotel with a woman who's not your wife,' Laura reads.

Dad's head jerks up. For a moment I wonder how eyes that are so empty can convey so much fear and confusion.

'I am?' he says.

'Yes, you're in a hotel . . . '

Dad's head turns left and then right. He leans back and looks at the ceiling.

'Hotel . . . ?' he says. 'Here . . . ?'

'No, this isn't a hotel,' Laura says.

He smiles and mumbles something we can't make out.

'Imagine this is a hotel,' says Laura. She points at Mum. 'And this isn't your wife. This is a woman you're having a dirty weekend with.'

Dad turns to look at Mum, and lowers his glasses, staring over them at her. He turns back to Laura. 'I am . . . ?'

'Yes, you're having a dirty weekend with this woman.'

'Not Mum?'

'No, not Mum.'

He turns, lowers the glasses again and stares at Mum for a full minute.

'Lil?'

'Yes Jim, it's me. It's all right.'

'Dad, concentrate,' says Laura, thrusting her face at his. 'It's a game. You're in a hotel with a woman who isn't your wife.'

Dad looks at Mum again, then at me, appealing for help. His lower lip starts to tremble.

'Want Mum,' he says.

'It's OK, Dad, Mum's here. Forget all that stuff Laura was saying. It was just a game.

'Let's forget the game,' I say to Laura. 'He's getting upset.'

She starts putting it away, collecting the cards with angry efficiency. Dad won't let go of the card she gave him, but continues to stare at it as though it holds some clue to the mystery of what's going on here.

'This is a hotel?'

Laura snatches the card, startling Dad with her sudden roughness. She stuffs it into the box and tosses the box on to the sideboard.

'Not the best game for Dad, perhaps,' I say. 'I seem to remember saying as much when you talked about bringing it.'

'Oh well, of course you'd know, wouldn't you,' she hisses.

She turns to Mum. 'Come on, Mum,' she says brusquely. 'If Dad's too tired to play a simple game, I think it's time he went to bed. Let's get him ready.'

Mum sighs as she eases herself out of the chair, whose plastic cushion echoes the sound, gratefully re-inflating itself as she removes her weight. She knows it's the end of her evening too, since Dad won't go to bed without her, and is aggrieved because she isn't tired yet but knows better than to argue with Laura in this mood. As they shuffle Dad off I head for bed too. With luck I may be genuinely asleep before Laura is through with Dad and won't even have to escalate the sniping over the game into a full-blown row to avoid having sex with her again tonight. I'm undressed in a moment, and snuggling down between the sheets, which smell comfortingly of milk.

Five

Tuesday

I suppose I expected the War Museum in Valletta to be like the museums I know in London. They occupy whole blocks or streets. One vast chamber leads into another and then another so you soon become lost. Eventually your interest wanders off somewhere in the vastness of it all. You're overfaced, as Laura always feels by one of Mum's loaded dinner plates, glutted by the richness of it all, unable to savour even a mouthful. Instead this museum is like the island itself, small and overcrowded, occupying what is really only one room with a gallery on each side, in Fort St Elmo, where the Knights of St John built their first defences on the island against the Turks.

'Ooh, lovely,' says Mum, peering through the entrance into the museum, which has a curved ceiling, like a cellar, 'I like anything historical, I do.'

She ambles inside with Laura hanging on her arm. Dad and I pause to look at two milestones by the entrance. One of them has been defaced and an accompanying text explains this was an Allied trick to confuse any invading Germans or Italians, leaving them lost and defeated.

'Not much different from the signposts here today,' I say to Dad. 'Must be a tradition.' He thinks this is desperately funny and the teeth start flapping up and down. I can't help wondering how many other tourists have stood here and made the same joke.

It's hard to get a grip on the chronology of the war from the museum as the exhibits are arranged by type rather than time. In the middle are all the vehicles: a plane, a jeep, a boat, a field gun or two. Along one wall are photographs. One shows a half-sunk British battleship in the harbour, others the extensive bomb damage. A range of glass cases contains various military uniforms, Allied and enemy, and so on. It's a jigsaw whose pieces, while insignificant in themselves, build into a picture of what life was like here during the great siege of 1942–3 when Hitler was throwing everything he had against the tiny island: a kaleidoscope fashioned from a metal shell by a German prisoner-of-war, Craven A and Flag cigarette packets, a khaki bandage in its box, a raffle ticket for the Women's Royal Auxiliary Reserve, an air-raid warden's whistle, spectacles for use when wearing a respirator, although it's not specified whether they are to be worn under or over the gas mask, a pack of playing cards.

We pause to look at the island's George Cross, displayed in a glass case with its accompanying letter from George VI, and Dad says, 'Malta GC.' There's the fuselage of a plane, the wings gone, which looks like a bigger version of the balsa-wood models Dad used to make for me when I was small. It's a Gloucester Gladiator named Faith. This fragile-looking machine, and two others like it called Hope and Charity, were the sum of the island's air power when it defied the might of the Luftwaffe at the start of the siege. There's an Italian speedboat, one of several which were apparently packed with explosives and launched unmanned against the island's coastal defences.

'Typical bloody Eyeties,' says Dad, after studying it over the top of his glasses for several minutes.

Suddenly Mum is back, tugging Laura along.

'Jim, Jim, come quick,' she says. 'It's Ike's jeep.'

We stand and look at General Eisenhower's jeep which, the placard says, was used in the invasion of Sicily, launched from Malta in 1943. Apart from the word 'Huskie' – the codename for the invasion – painted along either side of its bonnet, it's an ordinary jeep and all at once I feel a surge of affection for the little island, imagining the people scurrying around to find anything connected with the war, no matter how trivial, and throwing it all in here together.

It's the trivia Mum likes best and she moves slowly along the display cases, squinting to decipher the labels on the various exhibits. 'Look, Jim,' she says, 'an army knife like yours. Just the same.' Or, 'That takes me back, that ration book.' She lingers for a long time over a handkerchief sent home to his wife by a British soldier, until at last she pulls her own hankie from the pocket of her skirt and dabs her eyes, then catches me looking at her and says, 'Talk about sweat. I could fill a bucket.'

Although the museum is small we're in here for hours, and I wonder if I'll ever get Mum and Dad out and fed and toileted in time to see the old lady this afternoon. But when I say, 'How about lunch?' Mum says, 'I should think so. All this reading about people eating rats has given me an appetite. You can feel your ribs touching your backbone just thinking about how hungry they were, can't you, Laura?'

As we're leaving we meet the Ferguson party, who've just come in.

'It's very interesting,' says Mum, so excited by it all she even feels like forgiving Ferguson for letting her be rude to him the day before. 'I love all this sort of thing. Anything historical.'

'Yes, me too,' says Purple, fishing an instamatic camera out of her bag. 'Specially about the war.'

'My Jim was here,' says Mum. 'He'd tell you what they went through if he could talk. He'd have some stories, but he'll never tell them now.'

Dad smiles idiotically, as if to confirm this.

'Shame,' says Pink, 'isn't it, Carol?'

Purple, who is evidently Carol says, 'Yes, after going through all that too. Was it caused by the war?'

'No, it's Parkinson's,' says Mum, as we move away, 'but he's lucky really, it's not the shaking kind.'

Dad smiles at me and says, 'Lucky.'

We make our way to Republic Square, which seems to be the only place to have lunch in Valletta and sit hiding from the midday sun under a large umbrella. With the plane trees around us and the statue of Victoria, complete with pigeons, it feels like an English market town on a summer's day. As we wait for our omelettes, Laura, who hasn't spoken since the museum, except to say, 'Yes' or 'No' or 'Really?' to Mum's rhetorical ramblings, asks, 'Dad, where did you say you came from to have your appendix out here?'

Dad looks at Mum, as if he would like to know too.

'He come in a plane,' she says.

'Yes,' says Laura, 'but where from?'

'I can't remember. Somewhere in Italy I think. I know he had a rough journey.'

As soon as she says this, Dad's face brightens and he begins talking at his express train speed. It's impossible to understand a word he's saying, but it doesn't matter since I know the story by heart. How he needed an emergency operation and had to be taken to the hospital in Malta fast, how he was given a lift in an American Liberator in which he was the only passenger. How the crew were all drunk, and how they had to go through a storm, with Dad lying on a stretcher watching the lightning dancing on the wing tips. I explain all this to Laura while Dad's talking.

When he's finished she still seems puzzled.

'According to the placard next to Eisenhower's jeep, the Allies invaded Italy *from* Malta. So that was after the siege.'

'What are you getting at, Laura?' says Mum, who's no fool when it comes to reading people's faces.

'Well, Dad's son, Anthony, was born in 1945, right?'

'Yes, that's what the letter said,' says Mum. 'June.'

'OK, well that means Dad was here in 1944, doesn't it?'

'Yes.'

'And according to what we've just seen in the museum, the siege ended in 1943. And anyway, if he came from Italy it must have been after the siege was over because we only invaded it then.'

'Yes, but so what?' says Mum.

'Well, that would mean Dad couldn't have been here during the siege, not unless he was here twice, once during the siege and once when he came back from Italy.'

We all look at Dad. He's looking down at the table, touching the patches where the sun has infiltrated the shade of the plane trees, as if it's something tangible which he just cannot grasp.

'So,' says Laura, 'did he come here twice?'

'Oh no,' says Mum. 'Just the once.'

'And how long was that for?'

Mum looks at Dad. 'How long was it, Jim?' He stares back at her, eager for the answer. She turns to Laura, 'About three weeks.'

'Three weeks!' Omelette explodes out of my mouth, scattering yellow shrapnel on the red and white table-cloth. 'Three weeks! But I thought you were here for months.'

Dad's eyes flick backwards and forwards, as though looking for a way to escape.

'Never said that,' he mumbles.

'But all that stuff about it being your favourite out of all

127

the places you went to in the war.'

'It was,' says Mum. 'He liked it because they spoke English. You could get a proper meal here. With gravy. And they have proper toilets too.'

A smile of satisfaction grows on Laura's face as she watches my dismay. She's just torn to shreds my rosy Boys' Own picture of Dad as war hero bravely dodging bombs with the valiant Maltese people. It's her revenge for my insisting on this holiday in the first place. But for the moment I'm too angry with Dad to be annoyed with her.

'All that stuff about the siege you told me when I was a kid. About the daily raids, about the fires, about there being nothing to eat. I thought you were here. I thought you were being bombed every day.'

Dad starts playing with a chip, picking it up and trying to put it into his wine glass. He mutters something which I take to be 'Never said that' again.

'I thought this was where you went through one of the major experiences of your life, and you weren't even here when the fighting was going on. Just three bloody weeks!'

Laura can't help laughing in triumph. Revealing the brevity of Dad's visit is an unexpected bonus of her questioning.

'Exactly, we went to all this trouble to bring him back to somewhere he didn't stay for much longer than the average holiday. We might as well have taken him to Blackpool or some other place where he'd had a good fortnight.'

'Aren't you forgetting something?' says Mum, laying her knife and fork carefully on her empty plate. 'We didn't just come for a holiday. We come to find Anthony. Dad come to find his son.'

I want to scream, 'He's no need to look for a son, he's got one here! The one spoonfeeding him pieces of omelette. The one wiping the dribble off his chin. The one who'll take him inside this café, past the curious stares of strangers to the lavatory, and lift his shrivelled old penis out of his trousers so he can stand there for half an hour trying to pee!' I want to scream all this but I don't because it's this same son who is, even now, conspiring to foist the responsibility on to strangers and condemn his unsuspecting father to wait out his days in a geriatric nursing home. I take out Dad's tablets, place them one by one in his mouth, cradle his head gently in the palm of one hand, hold a glass of water to his lips with the other and tip it carefully into his mouth, then take him to the lavatory, pay the bill while he's trying to pee, and finally lead him back to the car, where Mum says, 'Talk about rush! We'll never get there in time.'

But we do, despite having to keep stopping and asking for directions to the address on the cigarette packet, where Mrs Haines, Father Joseph's old housekeeper, lives. It's a dingy building next to a yard full of used car tyres. There are four doorbells, the top one marked 'Haines'. As I'm ringing it, a young Maltese boy, about seven or eight, comes out of the front door of the building.

'You want Mrs Haines,' he says, holding the door open for us. 'Best to just go up. Save her coming down. She is a very old lady.'

The stairs are steep and uncarpeted, just some dusty green linoleum. There's a smell of damp which seems out of place on this dry rock of an island. There are five flights. Dad takes them at a run, going so fast my main worry is he'll fall flat on his face. Mum stands at the bottom clutching the banister rail and looks up, as though contemplating the north face of the Eiger.

'Talk about steep!' she says. 'Have we really got to go up there?'

'You could wait at the bottom,' I say, clutching Dad's belt to hold him back a moment.

'It might be best,' says Laura. 'You don't want to risk doing anything to your heart, specially in this heat. I'll stay with you.'

Mum doesn't reply but simply opens her handbag, takes out a plastic carrier bag, bends, spreads it on the second step up and sits down.

The woman who opens the door to us cannot be more than five feet tall. Her back is hunched and her flowered cotton dress hangs loose, as though she has no flesh on her bones. Her face reminds me of crazy paving, it's so lined. Her hair is pure white and so thin the pink scalp shows through. But her eyes are bright and sharp.

'Are you the people Father Martin told me was coming?' she asks. I nod and introduce us.

'Well, you better come in, have a cup of tea.'

We stand awkwardly in the doorway, while she busies herself with kettle and teapot. She turns. 'Sit yourselves down. We don't stand on no ceremony here.'

I lower Dad into one of the two battered armchairs in the room and help myself to an upright bentwood chair.

'You're English?' I say.

'Oh yes, I'm a Londoner, I am. Shepherd's Bush, through and through. I come out here in 1927 when I was in service. I was with a family in the forces. Then I met my Tom, he was a Maltese boy, and got married and here I've stayed ever since.'

She sets the teapot down on a little table next to the other armchair and as she sorts out china, milk and sugar, I glance around the room. It is tiny. A primitive sink and an old, but gleaming electric cooker take up most of one wall. On the floor are ill-matched pieces of linoleum, laid in an intricate pattern like a mosaic, so as to cover the boards beneath completely. On top of them are a couple of rugs, any pile long since trodden flat, making me think of a sandwich you've carried around with you too long so

130

that both slices of bread and the filling are compressed into one mass. Nothing in the room dates from later than the 1950s. There's a glass-fronted cabinet in which are some Mills & Boon romances, all dog-eared, and a collection of small glass animals. On the wall is a curious calendar in the shape of a clock, with three hands which can be moved to indicate the month, day of the week and date. Its face is decorated with pictures of girls in red bathing costumes, some children around a bonfire, a snowman surrounded by more children, and a couple – he in grey flannels, she in a red dress with white polka dots – in a field of bluebells. There are two prints of Tower Bridge, obviously by the same artist, but from different angles, one with the bridge down and a red London double-decker passing across it, the other with the bridge raised with a boat steaming under it. I notice that all around the walls are little shelves, attached by hinges so they can be folded down when not needed, as some of them are, while others are up and bear little glass vases containing dusty plastic flowers. There's a built-in dresser made of cheap veneer, the top section glass-fronted and full of plates and cups and saucers, all with Fifties' designs.

'Have you lived here long?' I ask.

'Tom and I moved in 1930. I was in my early thirties then. It was big enough for us two. We never had no children. I would have loved kids, but I couldn't.'

She passes us tea. I intercept Dad's and put it on one of the little shelves.

'Mind you, you should have seen the state of this place when we first come here. It was that dilapidated.' I try not to let her catch me looking at the ceiling, where there's a large brown watermark and from which the paint is flaking, or at the large crack in the rear wall next to the only window which looks out on to the tyre yard.

'My Tom fixed it up. We've spent a fortune on this

place over the years. Hundreds of pounds. But my Tom made it real nice. He was a carpenter by trade, but he could fix anything. Worked in the docks he did.'

'Is Tom . . . ?'

'Passed on seventeen years ago.' She looks at the shelf nearest her chair, on which is a photo of a young woman in a bathing dress, presumably herself but unrecognisable as such, rowing a boat. Next to it the same young woman, in a floral dress stands beside a dusky-skinned young man, hair greased down, wearing a suit and tie and holding a smouldering cigarette between the first and second fingers of his right hand, looking every inch what Dad would have called a spiv. 'And there isn't a day I don't miss him something terrible.'

'You live alone now?'

'Yes. I do all my own cooking and shopping, and cleaning and washing. I manage all right. I've had a bit of trouble with my hip, though.'

'I'm sorry to hear that.'

'They say it's arthritis. The doctor told me I'm ninety years old and it's no more than I should expect, but I don't see that. There's never been no arthritis in my family. Do you know anything about it?'

'Not really, I'm afraid.'

'Only I've heard that once you've got it, you never get rid of it. I hope that's not true. I wouldn't like to have to put up with this for ever.'

There's a pause while we sip our tea. I help Dad to his, thinking how fortunate Mrs Haines is to be all alone in the world, with no loved ones to put her away somewhere.

Mrs Haines nods in Dad's direction. 'What's wrong with 'im, then?'

'Parkinson's disease. He's had it nearly twenty years.'

'Does he talk?'

'Yes, but it's difficult for him, isn't it, Dad?'

Dad comes out with a long speech that lasts all of two minutes. I nod agreement at him.

'I didn't get none of that,' says Mrs Haines. It's obvious she has all her wits about her and feels something like disapproval for those who age without them.

'It is difficult to understand him when you don't know him,' I say.

'Can't they do nothing for it?' she says. 'Will he have to stay like that?'

'They're doing a lot of research on it. They're coming up with new things all the time.'

'I should hope so,' she says. 'Poor man.'

'Anyway, I understand you were Father Joseph's house-keeper during the war?'

'During, before and after. I worked for him for thirty-five years, till Tom got ill and then I stopped. I had to be with my husband, you see. Father Joseph didn't like me leaving, but he understood. "Mrs Haines," he said, "I don't want you to go, but I understand that you have to." Very understanding man. I been to see him up the hospital but I shan't go again. It upset me seeing him like that.'

I pull out the picture of Maria and Anthony and hand it to her.

'We're trying to find this woman, and her son. He was born in 1945, so he'd be forty-three now. My father knew her during the war. When the boy was born she lived in the town, in Triq San Gwann Battista, number 48. Her name was Maria Spiteri.'

She stares at the photo then puts it down on the shelf next to her, gets up and walks across the room to another shelf, on which is a small plastic box which she opens. A plastic ballerina pops up and begins twirling round while the box plays a tinny version of 'Around the World in Eighty Days'. Mrs Haines hums along to it. She takes a key from the box and walks across the room to another shelf on which there is a larger wooden box. She uses the key to open this and takes out a spectacle case. She walks back to her chair, sits down again and puts on a pair of spectacles with winged frames. I can't help thinking these would be a collector's item at Camden Lock market.

She studies the photo hard. Then she begins tapping it with her index finger. 'I remember, I remember. Maria. Yes, I remember her.'

She lays the photo down. 'She was a one for the boys, she was. It was quite a scandal. Well, you can imagine. I mean, they're very big on religion here. I'm a good Catholic girl myself, mind, but they used to find me a bit too outrageous for them. They didn't like my dresses, said they were too short. Some of them actually complained to Father Joseph about me. I said to him, "Father Joseph, do you think my dresses are too short?" "Mrs Haines," he said, "Mrs Haines. God gave you beautiful legs and I cannot think he meant you to keep them all to yourself." He was like that. Another time – '

'So you remember her?'

'Oh yes. They say she had this boy off a Tommy, and then she lived with a Scottish sailor. And there were several men after that, I believe. She was a one for the men, was Maria.'

I glance at Dad and see his face is now as red as the bathing dress on the calendar girl, but whether from embarrassment or from the excessive heat in the stuffy little flat, I can't tell.

'And do you know where she is now?'

'Oh yes, I know that all right.'

Dad's head jerks up and he stares straight at her with his good eye. Even though I have never wanted to find Maria, or Anthony, I cannot keep my voice from quavering in excitement, our quest having seemed so unpromising at the start.

'You do?'

'Yes, she's in the cemetery here. She's been dead, oh, must be thirty years.' There's a trace of superiority in her voice, the disdain of the long-lived for those who give up the struggle early.

Of course, right from the beginning I've known there was a good possibility that Maria might be dead. After all, nearly half a century has passed since her dalliance with Dad. But still I find myself shocked. Somehow I always expected we'd find her alive.

'She was young,' I say.

'Yes, tragic it was – ' begins Mrs Haines, but then Dad, always a beat or two behind in any conversation, interrupts.

'Cemetery?' he asks. 'What cemetery?'

'The one here. It's as you go towards Valletta. Lovely and peaceful it is. My Tom's in there. Lovely plot we got. Beautiful stone, plenty of room for my name on there. He picked it out himself. He had a good eye for anything like that. He was a lovely man – '

This time I interrupt her before she gets any further down memory lane.

'And her son, Anthony? I don't suppose you remember . . . ?'

'Anthony, was that his name? Bless me, course I do. Couldn't meet a nicer fella. Not that I seen him for a long time, but he thinks I'm marvellous for my age, he does. "Mrs Haines," he always says to me, "Mrs Haines, you are marvellous for your age."'

'Do you have his address?'

'Address? No. It's years since I seen him. But I hear about all the people from the old days from time to time. People come to see me, they're very kind. I did hear tell he was working on one of them new developments on the seafront at St Julian's. Big block of, what-you-call-its, apartments. St Peter's Apartments it's called.'

'That's where he works, St Peter's Apartments?'

'Yes, or if not someone there should know.'

Mrs Haines takes the few steps across the flat to see us to the door. I thank her for her help.

'It's all right. It's nice to see someone from the old country again. I do miss it sometimes, but I 'spect it's all changed since I was there.'

'You don't ever think of going back?'

'No, I've nobody there, except my sister. She's always asking me to go back and live with her. But – ' here she turns and indicates the tiny room and its contents with a majestic sweep of her arm, ' – how could I leave all this?'

Mum can hardly contain her excitement when I tell her the news. I suspect she's secretly pleased to hear of Maria's demise. Mum's view of sexual relationships is decidedly romantic by way of *Rebecca* and the Laurence Olivier film version of *Wuthering Heights* and it's not beyond her to worry about Dad going off, even at this late stage, with the great three-week love of his life. Once we're all back in the car I say, 'Where to? Shall we go and find him now?'

'Yes, Nick, let's not leave it another day. We've only got nine days left. Dad wants maximum time with his son. Don't you Dad?'

'*Toilet.*'

'Oh no, Jim, not now.'

'*Toilet.*'

'Just a wee, I hope?'

'*Number twos.*'

'Oh no. Talk about timing!'

'Do you think he really wants to go?' I ask her.

Her face softens. 'He might well do. It has been a week.'

There's nothing for it but to go home. Constipation is a problem for the male side of our family. It's something I suffered from terribly as a child. Indeed, our bodies are reluctant to give up any of their contents. If Dad or I have a cold, it remains firmly stuck in our sinuses. Our noses do not run. Nor do we weep. We keep our tears to ourselves. Our feelings, too, and the words to liberate them, remain firmly locked inside. We cannot let go. Perhaps, I suddenly think, this is part of why I do not want to make love to Laura. I want to hold on to my sperm. All of this means that if Dad does have a bowel movement it may require a considerable amount of time on the loo first, too long for a public lavatory. A reunion with his missing son will have to wait at least another day. For now, Dad has a more pressing engagement.

Dad spends most of the evening sitting on the loo. At first his face is red and the veins in his neck stand out like branches of ivy on the trunk of an oak tree as he strains to expel a week or more's worth of effluent. But finally he tires and starts to doze, his head leaning to the right, touching the wall of the small loo and tipping his whole body over, so it looks as though he may fall at any moment. We leave the door open so whoever is passing can look in and make sure he's OK.

'All right, Dad?' I shout to him, en route to the bedroom to fetch my book, and he lifts his claw and shouts something back which I take to be, 'All right', but which could just as well be the opposite, rendering the whole business of checking on him an exercise in futility.

Mum is not so polite. Every so often she goes in and we hear her shouting, 'You haven't done nothing? I don't wonder with that head leaning like that. Get it up. GET IT UP! Now come on, you're just not trying.'

Dad's annoyed and defensive now, which renders him capable of speech.

'I am trying!' he barks quite clearly.

'No you're not or you'd have done something.'

It goes on like this for most of the evening. Dad refuses to eat anything, shamed perhaps by Mum's accusation that he must be full to bursting. He even waves away a bowl of ice cream which Laura takes in to him and I realise he must be annoyed.

'Let's leave it for tonight, Mum,' I say. 'Perhaps he'll go in the morning.' She gives him extra senna capsules and we turn in for the night.

In our room Laura tells me that now the bathroom's free, she's going to have a bath. 'Make myself nice and fragrant,' she smiles, giving me a long peck on the lips, accompanied by eye signals so obvious they are almost in the *Carry On* class.

As she collects together bathing foam, soap, perfume and all the other weapons from her armoury of smells, I move to open the glass doors which look out on to a small sitting area outside our room, where if we wanted to, we could sit and watch the rats foraging on the wasteland.

'Don't do that, you'll let a mosquito in,' she says.

'But it's so stuffy in here, it's giving me a headache.'

'Please, Nick. You know how I am about mosquitoes.'

'OK. I'll just sit here with heatstroke.'

She flounces towards the door. 'It's better than being bitten to death. Now, read your book for a minute,' she turns and gives me a Barbara Windsor leer, 'and I'll be back in a little while.'

As soon as she's gone, I go over to the doors and open them. My heart is in my mouth as I do it because they are ill-fitting and the bottoms scrape the tiled floor, making a horrible screeching noise which I hope Laura will not hear. Then I have the bright idea of suggesting it's the cry of a rat being killed by one of the many stray cats which are always contemplating the wasteland. I switch on the overhead light and wait, but not for long. In less than a minute I can hear the familiar whine of a mosquito circling the room, just as nearly half a century ago Stukas circled the island, recceing the target, ready to dive and attack.

I look up and see three, no four, wispy little shapes on the ceiling and another one circling. Another rat dies as I shut the doors. I creep back to the bed and snuggle down in the mould of my body which is still there in the sheets, as though I've never left. I've just opened my book when Laura, clad only in a towel, arrives. She smiles. I smile back and give her my best Sid James eyebrow movements. She purses her lips and tweaks the top of the towel, so that it falls slowly away, as if an invisible hand is unwrapping her, then drops to the floor. Naked except for her sandals, she walks around the room to her side of the bed, her largish breasts perfectly poised, the nipples standing to attention on top of them, her stomach flat, her bottom superbly arched, for Laura has absolutely perfect posture. She kicks off the sandals and sits on the bed.

'Well, look who's still got his clothes on,' she says. 'We'll have to do something about that.'

She begins to undo the buttons of my shirt, and her hand slips inside, brushing gently over my nipples. It moves from one to the other for a moment or two, then creeps down my stomach to my fly, where it encounters a momentary resistance from the zip, which is soon overcome with reinforcements from the other hand, and then slides on to my underpants, cupping the contents in its soft grasp.

'I wonder what we have here,' she says, staring into my face and widening her eyes with fake innocence. 'We might have to have a look at this.'

I lie completely passive, cursing my insubordinate penis for the weightiness I feel increasing there.

I look up at the ceiling, as though in ecstasy, and say to myself, 'Come on, you sleepy buggers, before the ack-ack is up and ready.'

Laura springs my penis free and her head moves down

my stomach in a series of soft kisses towards it. She holds it in her hand and smiles at the tip as if at an old friend. Her mouth opens and she's just about to plunge when instead her head jerks upwards and begins to swivel around, scanning the air.

'There's a mosquito!'

And, sure enough, the whine kicks in.

'Damn!' I say, and it's convincing because part of me actually means it, the part that's pointing straight at the ceiling. But almost immediately my penis begins to subside, the blood returns to my head and I'm sane again.

'Let's just carry on and sort it out later,' I say artfully.

'No! You know I hate mosquitoes. I can't do anything while there's one loose in here.'

'I'll get it,' I say and leap up. I grab Laura's towel and begin flapping at the ceiling, jumping up and down on the bed for extra height.

'Got it!' I say. 'I think.'

We both stay absolutely still, apart from our eyes, which roll back and forth as we survey the ceiling.

I climb down from the bed and immediately the whine begins again.

'It's not dead!'

'Perhaps there was more than one.'

'Oh no, how could there be, with the doors shut?'

'Well, we are next to a rubbish dump, there must be thousands out there. And they can get through gaps around doors, they don't need a written invitation.'

Laura jumps off the bed and strides over to the wardrobe. She pulls out a pair of tights and slips them on, then a T-shirt, which she tucks into the tights. She goes to a drawer and pulls out her plug-in mosquito repellent and sticks it into the wall. She takes out a spray and starts spraying the ceiling. She pulls out a tube of cream and rubs it all over her face and arms.

'That doesn't look very sexy,' I say.

'It's not meant to be. Sex is off the menu for tonight. There's no way I'm doing anything that means taking my clothes off and being bitten to death.'

She gets into bed and pulls the sheet right up over her head and from underneath it pins the top down by placing the pillow on top of it. I lie on my back and listen to the whine of a mosquito as it zooms around the room. Suddenly it stops, like the engine of a doodlebug cutting out, and I know that, while sex may not be on the menu tonight, I, most definitely, am.

Six

Wednesday

This morning Laura has a large red swelling on the end of her nose. Somehow it makes all the itching on my arms and legs worthwhile, although when I walk past the bathroom and catch sight of her close to tears as she stares at the spot in the mirror, I feel a pang of guilt. Why do I treat her so badly? I'm lucky to have her, I know I am. She's kind, intelligent, attractive, amusing . . . I could happily spend the rest of my life with her. But not with a couple of kids too. Laura is thirty-six years old and her biological clock is sounding its alarm. Every day she manages to find another article in the newspaper about the current epidemic of infertility, with heartrending case histories of women who left it too late to start a family and are now condemned to a future of childlessness.

'Why don't you want kids?' Laura is always asking me.

'I don't know,' I answer, the way a child might. 'I just don't.'

Ironically, I'm quite good with kids, even if I do say so myself. When Pauline's were small I was always in demand as a bedtime-story reader and babysitter. When they were bigger I used to take them to the park and kick a football around with them, and the funny thing is I always had a good time. I really enjoyed myself, showing them how to bring a ball under control with one touch, how to hit a screamer into the net with the outside of the boot, how to sell a dummy to an unwary defender. It was fun – but only because at the end of the afternoon, when we came back, hot and sweaty, I could hand them over to Pauline to take upstairs for a bath while I jumped in the car and headed home up the A10, the evening stretching before me, unencumbered.

Sometimes, when Laura goes on about me not wanting children, I wonder if it's because of having a father who, after the first few happy years, often seemed like his heart wasn't really in it. Now of course, I tell myself it was the slow, stealthy march of his as yet undiagnosed illness that made him less connected to me or the world around him. The change was so gradual I can't recall when it began. I just remember there came a time when I had to pester him for a game of chess. He would only agree after a lot of pleading. There was always a point where he made a calculation and decided he could get the game over with in less time than it was taking to fend off my demands. Usually he sat hunched over the board, chain-smoking Players until they burned right down to his nicotine-stained fingertips, when he would throw the stub into the fire. I knew I would never ask him to play again the night he reached out for one of my pawns, picked it up, placed his queen on the newly vacated square and absent-mindedly threw the captured pawn into the fire.

I watched it turn red hot amongst the burning coals, a protest sticking in my throat as it crumbled into grey dust. Dad studied the board, oblivious to my distress and the pawn's demise.

'Check,' he said.

This morning the first move Dad makes is to the loo. He's moving so fast Mum can hardly keep up with him. In the

143

small toilet it's difficult for her to get in with him and turn him around, so I take over. I pull his pyjama trousers down, take his hands and let him drop backwards on to the seat.

'OK, Dad, bombs away.' It's the sort of coarse joke I never make, the sort of thing Pauline would say, but today I can't help myself because I'm embarrassed at the situation of me standing here and my father trying to have a shit in front of me. And, if I'm honest, I want to make him laugh, to get a bit of Pauline's popularity.

He smiles, but he doesn't laugh as I expected. I realise it's actually hurting him, trying to go to the lavatory. He's so imprisoned in his pain, he doesn't need me, so I ruffle his hair, which is the nearest I can get to a hug, say, 'Good luck,' and wander off. From the kitchen next door I can hear him sighing and grunting, like an animal giving birth.

Mum is in the kitchen making breakfast. She's got the frying pan out and some eggs and a packet of bacon we bought yesterday. She takes the top off the bottle of olive oil and her nose wrinkles in disgust as she sniffs it, but in the absence of any high-cholesterol lard it will have to do. She slops some into the pan, turns the cooker on, waits for it to heat up and then breaks an egg into it. She pauses with a second egg to look at me as I walk in.

'Something worked him,' she says, with a nod towards the lavatory. 'I think the extra laxative's done the trick. He'll go now. He needs emptying out. Fancy a nice fried egg, Nicholas?'

There's another pained grunt from the loo and a loud splash.

'Ooh Gawd,' says Mum, giggling. She lifts her voice to the next room. 'You haven't fell in, have you, Jim?' She turns to me again. 'Go and tell him to wait while I have my breakfast. I'll go and see to him then. Only I must eat first or I'll drop. It don't do to go without eating in this heat.'

When Mum's finished breakfast she goes in and 'sees to Dad', the code for wiping his bottom, which she does while Dad stands up so she can get at him. I catch a peep of this as I go past the open doorway. Dad is leaning against the wall, sweat dripping from his face which is still red. He looks as if he's just run a marathon, and I suppose he has, in terms of defecation, a week's worth in one go.

I've just finished dressing when there's a knock on the bedroom door and Mum bursts in, 'Nick, come quick, I can't get it to go!'

I don't know what she's talking about and think it must be something in the kitchen, the hot water to wash up with perhaps, or the electric kettle.

'All right, Mum, no need to panic. What's the problem?'

She grabs my hand and drags me to the loo, where she swings me in front of her and pushes me in.

'That. I can't get it to go.'

In the lavatory pan is the largest turd I have ever seen. It's so big it's rearing up several inches out of the water. It's as thick as a man's arm, and it occurs to me that if it only had a hand attached, it would look like a male version of the Lady of the Lake's arm, rising out of the water. The other end of it curves downwards and out of sight around the U-bend. The colour is black and it looks as solid as wood.

'Something's getting through,' says Mum. 'The paper went, but that thing didn't.'

I press the handle on the cistern, which flushes. The loo begins to fill up with water and there's an agonising moment as I watch the level rise higher and higher until it's right up to the rim. I step backwards expecting it to flood, but at that moment the flushing stops and the water level begins to recede. I wait a minute or so while the cistern refills. I press the handle again. It's just the same as the first time, the thing stands there firm and resolute, refusing to be swept away, defying erosion.

'I tried using the brush,' says Mum, indicating a flimsy nylon brush on a little stand on the floor, 'but it's so hard. It's like iron.'

I take the brush and try pushing the turd. It won't move. I push harder and the brush simply bends. The turd is so solid it doesn't even mark the brush. The erosion factor is nil.

'I'll have to get something harder to try to push it down with,' I say. 'Perhaps if we can just get it round the U-bend it will flush away.'

I rush to the bedroom. Laura has given up on her nose and is getting dressed.

'What's all the fuss about?' she says.

I grab a wire coat hanger and dash out again. 'Dad's blocked the loo.'

Standing outside the loo, Dad hears this and his teeth begin flapping. He says something as I pass, but his hysteria only makes him more difficult to understand. I take the hanger and push one end against the offending object.

Nothing happens. I push harder. The hanger starts to bend.

'It's no good, it's well and truly stuck.'

'No wonder Dad had such a job getting it out if it won't even go through that great big pipe,' says Mum. There's the distant rattle of teeth.

I untwist the hook at the top of the hanger and separate the two ends. I try poking at the turd with the end of the wire, hoping to break it up. It doesn't even flinch. I take the hooked end and straighten the wire leading up to it, pushing it down the side of the loo, so that it disappears out of sight into the waste pipe. I try to hook it around the turd to see if I can grapple it out of position. There's a twang and the hook springs free. Nothing has moved. I try

146

again. And again. I'm still trying, getting more and more frantic, sweat pouring off me, when there's a knock at the front door.

'Who's that?' I say.

Mum peers through the shutters of the French windows. 'It's that girl from the travel company.'

'Damn, what am I going to do now?' I leap up and start bending the hanger in two so that I can hide it somewhere.

'Don't answer the door!' says Mum.

'I've got to, the car's outside, she'll know we're here.' The hanger keeps springing back every time I try to bend it. It's like wrestling with an angry snake. Finally I lose my temper and get so mad it yields. I stuff the bent and twisted metal into the pedal bin in the kitchen and go and open the front door, where I am met by Martina's bright smile.

'I hope I didn't wake you up? You are such a long time opening the door I think you are still in bed.'

'Er no, we were just getting my father up. He needs a lot doing for him.'

'Ah yes, poor man. Anyway, I am sure he is glad we get him away from all those stairs, no?' She smiles and shakes her head in disbelief. 'Villa Francesca!' She goes over to the dining table and sits down at it without waiting to be asked.

'Would you like a cup of tea, dear?' asks Mum. 'I've got a nice fresh one just brewed.'

'I think that would be very nice,' says Martina. 'Thank you.'

She pulls a blue plastic folder from her file and takes out a questionnaire.

'The accommodation is all right, yes?'

I nod and she ticks a box.

'You have all your bed linen, yes?'

It goes on like this, and she ticks a dozen or so boxes. I

147

say yes to everything to get rid of her faster, inwardly cursing Mum for offering her tea.

'Now,' Martina says, taking some brochures out of the folder. 'I have to explain you some excursions. Normally, I would have told you on Saturday, but it was not possible with all the mix-up over the accommodation and you having to move. So you have missed one or two this week, but never mind. There are plenty more. These are to all the interesting places of Malta at very reasonable rates. First there is Valletta and the War Museum . . . '

'We done that,' says Mum.

'Then there is the Blue Grotto, including bus to the location and fare for the boat . . . '

'Boat?' says Mum, 'I'm sorry, you won't get me on no boat. I haven't got a head for water. It draws me.'

'Ah, now this one I think perhaps you like,' Martina says. 'It is a half-day trip to the ancient sites of Tarxien followed by an authentic Hawaiian beach barbecue. It's one of our most popular excursions.'

'I don't think so,' says Mum. 'Dad doesn't like foreign food. His tastes are very loyal to Britain. And to be honest, it would be no use getting him on a bus because he has to have free access to a toilet.'

'Ah yes, I see,' says Martina, and begins putting the brochures back in her folder with a sigh of disappointment which I assume comes from her loss of commission for any trips we might have taken.

She stands up and I make for the door, eager to open it for her and get her out before she decides to make a tour of inspection of the bungalow. She pauses awkwardly.

'Er, excuse me, but since you are the one who has mentioned it,' she says. 'I wonder if I may use your toilet now.'

'No, you can't!' Mum almost screams it.

Martina recoils as if slapped.

'What she means is you can't use it because my father's

148

in there just now. He's likely to be some time.'

At that moment the door opens and Laura helps Dad into the room.

'Good morning, Martina,' she says. 'How are you?'

'Please, I need to use the toilet,' says Martina, now looking slightly pinched. I'm starting to think Pauline would love this holiday.

'Go ahead, it's just through there,' says Laura. 'It's empty.'

Martina moves quickly out of the room.

'Idiot!' I hiss at Laura. 'I told you the loo was blocked.'

'I assumed you'd fixed it,' she hisses back.

We all stand around, holding our breath and not daring to speak, anticipating the embarrassment we will feel when Martina reappears. Seconds tick by, minutes. Whole hours pass, and still no sound. Then we hear the loo flushing.

There's a long pause, during which all we can hear is water running in the pipes. Then the loo flushes again. Another long pause, more water running as the cistern fills up. Another flush. The loo door opens and closes. Martina bursts into the room, cheeks glowing red beneath her tanned complexion.

'I'm so sorry,' she says. 'I don't know what is wrong with me. Please excuse me. Nothing like this ever happens to me before!' Before any of us can move she has reached the front door at a run, opened it and disappeared. We hear her car start up and the squeal of tyres as she accelerates out of the square.

We look at one another without speaking.

I walk to the loo, where the plastic seat cover has been lowered. I lift it and see our old friend completely intact, staring back at me. But somehow something is different. I peer at it more closely and notice, nestling underneath it, almost hidden and completely eclipsed by it, a small brown sister. I realise Martina must have used the loo without looking into it, flushed it, looked down, seen Dad's monster and claimed it for her own.

We get to St Peter's Apartments with scarcely any tension because we're still laughing about Martina and the loo, and about the turd. Mum can't bring herself to say the word. 'I never saw such a big piece of business,' she keeps saying. 'I wouldn't have thought it possible.'

Laura has no such coyness and uses the word profligately, since every time she mentions it it's enough to set Dad off laughing again. Watching Laura with my parents, I realise this is what we have most in common, the ability to hide behind a joke.

We find the apartments easily because there's a huge board bearing the name right beside the coast road. It turns out to be a construction site, over which a huge crane stands like a heron beside a Fenland drain watching for fish.

'He may well still be working here,' I say, trying to sound enthusiastic, although, of course, I'm not. I'm actually hoping the trail might go cold here and that Anthony can be consigned, like his poor mother, to history. 'It's still a long way from being finished.'

'Let's hope they've got the drains in,' says Laura, 'with Dad visiting.'

Dad starts to laugh, but Mum interrupts. 'I don't know how you two can joke at a time like this. I've got a flock of butterflies inside me.'

There's a car park next to the site, full of trucks and tradesmen's vans. I drive across it, trying to avoid potholes even bigger than those on the roads, and park. 'Better wait here,' I say. 'I'll go in and ask.'

There's a portakabin with a sign saying SITE OFFICE. A man in overalls and a hard hat is coming out as I approach.

'What's the matter?' he says. 'Can't you read?' He

150

points to a sign which says HARD HATS MUST BE WORN AT ALL TIMES. I apologise and say I only want to ask a question. 'Do you know a man called . . . ?' I begin. He holds his hand up. 'Wait a minute, mister,' he says, and disappears back into the portakabin. He emerges again almost instantly with a bright yellow hard hat, which he holds out to me.

'Put this on,' he says.

I put it on. I feel like someone in one of those primitive tribes where you have to be in possession of a special object, like a peace pipe or a giant sea shell, before you're allowed to speak.

'Now, what is your question, please?'

'Do you know a man named Anthony Spiteri? I believe he may work here.'

I'm sure there's a flicker of recognition in his eyes, but he shakes his head.

'No, I never heard of him. Sorry, mister.' Then he laughs. 'Why do you want him? He owe you money?'

I explain that my father is an old friend of his mother.

'How come? You're British, no?'

'Yes. But my father was here during the war. He met Anthony's mother then.'

His foot starts doodling in the sand, drawing a circle then rubbing it out. He looks down at it as though it belongs to someone else.

'And you sure you are not after money?'

'No, absolutely not. I think he'll be pleased to see my father.'

The man looks up from his doodling and stares at me, trying to make his mind up. I'm willing him to refuse. I want him to say he doesn't know anything so I can return to the car and truthfully tell Mum I've drawn a blank.

'Sure, I know Anthony,' he says. 'Who doesn't?'

'Is he a construction worker? Does he work here?' I ask, trying to hide my disappointment.

151

His face breaks into a smile. 'That's good. Very good. No, he doesn't work here. I don't think Anthony is the hard-hat type of person.'

'Somebody told me he worked here.'

'Well, they told you wrong. Unless maybe he does something for the sales department some time. They have lots of people give out leaflets, you know. But he don't have no regular job here.'

'Do you know where he lives?'

'No. Somewhere around St Julian's, on the Paceville side. That's all I know. Sorry, mister.'

I thank him and turn and walk away. I can tell Mum that Anthony doesn't work here, that the man in the office doesn't know where he lives. It's all I need.

'Hey, mister . . . '

I turn and see him coming after me. I wait as he approaches. He holds out his hand, 'You forget, the hard hat.'

I take it off and hand it back. He weighs it in his hand a moment, still not sure.

'You know,' he says, 'I think he drinks in the Blue Parrot bar, in St Julian's. Yeah, I think that's where he goes.'

If the name Blue Parrot reinforces the growing feeling I have of finding myself in a Raymond Chandler novel, following a trail long gone cold and always one step behind the man I'm searching for, the reality pulls me sharply back to the present. For while the huge, lurid blue plastic parrot sign outside bears the subtitle 'American Bar', the decor is tacky Mediterranean package tour. There's a long polished metal bar, with high metal bar stools against it, and on the opposite wall some tables set in booths. The rest of the floor is empty, ready for the heaving swell of twenty-year-old British, Dutch and Scandinavian tourists who will fill it by nine o'clock tonight. For now, to keep

152

the till ticking over, they offer hamburgers and fries for lunch and the music has been turned down low so as not to put off people who aren't their normal clientèle. A blonde woman in her late twenties is behind the bar cleaning glasses. I leave the others in a huddle at the door and approach her.

'You want lunch?' the girl says in a London accent. 'I can do you nice fish and chips, or there's barbecued chicken, or hamburger, or pork sausages, or lasagne. All with chips and garnish.'

'Actually, we haven't come to eat.'

'Oh, drink then? Beer? Cocktail? We do fifty-three different cocktails.'

'To be honest, I'm just after a little information. I'm looking for someone.'

She turns and picks a pack of Marlboro off the back of the bar. I see she's wearing tight Levi cut-offs. She has long slim legs and a nice bottom. Her breasts are small and the nipples show through her pink T-shirt when she turns around again.

She takes a cigarette from the pack and lights it with a disposable lighter.

'Yeah?' she says.

'His name's Anthony Spiteri.'

'Oh, right.'

'You know him?'

'Yeah, course. He drinks here. Why do you want him? He owe you money, then?'

'No, nothing like that. Nothing to his detriment, I assure you.'

'That's all right then,' she says, holding the hand with the cigarette up, the elbow resting on her other arm, and flicking off ash which isn't there. 'Only if he did owe you I wouldn't tell you where to find him because you'd be behind me in the queue.'

'He owes you money?'

'Just a hundred quid for his bar bill. It's my own fault, I kept meaning to get it off him. Only, you know Anthony . . . '

'I don't, actually. My father was a friend of his mother's.'

'Oh, I see. Well, I'll give you his address.' She takes a pen, and a card from the back of the bar and scribbles something down.

'It's only a walk from here. You turn right out of here and take the first left. Up there about five minutes you come to a new development? There's three villas side by side, with big walls round them. You want the end one.'

'Thanks.'

'Sure you don't want some lunch first?'

I look towards the others.

'Only it might be best,' says the woman. 'Knowing Anthony, he's probably out now. You're more likely to catch him in a bit later on. He'll go back for his siesta.'

We sit in one of the booths, which isn't easy, since it involves sliding along the seats and there isn't much room between them and the table, all of them fixed to the floor. Laura edges in first and I sit Dad on the seat next to her, facing out into the room, then pick up his feet and swivel him round. I slide into the seat opposite Laura and finally Mum squeezes into the one next to me, complaining all the time.

'Talk about squashed!' she says. 'If I eat anything here I'll never get out.'

'It's a good job you got rid of that turd, Dad,' says Laura. 'You'd never have fitted in otherwise.' The teeth rattle.

The bar-girl introduces herself as Nikki. She's from Pimlico, and she and her boyfriend have been running the bar since last year. It's been a bit of a struggle, she tells us, but it should be OK when it's a bit more established.

We order chicken and chips, which turns out to be

surprisingly good, the chicken white and succulent, the chips crisp and golden.

'Big portions,' says Mum to Nikki. 'Wherever are we going to put it?'

'Dad's got a recently vacated space,' says Laura, and is rewarded by more flapping of the dentures. I feel as if I'm being bludgeoned by fun.

As we eat, I explain about Anthony.

'Don't expect too much,' I warn. 'I've mentioned him to two people and they've both asked me if he owes me money.'

'You mustn't judge him before you meet him,' says Mum. 'You don't know if these people are telling you the truth. Besides, the old girl seemed to like him.'

'Yes, but I don't think she knew him that well.'

Mum is about to argue, but notices an especially large chip on the side of her plate, spears it with her fork and bites the end off it.

'Now, Nicholas, you mustn't be so prejudiced,' she says when she's swallowed it. 'I know it's hard for you to accept you've got a brother after all these years, but that's what you've got to do. Think about how I feel, taking another woman's child into my family.'

'Nick's just trying to say you mustn't build this Anthony up into something special or else you might end up being disappointed,' says Laura.

'Dad won't be disappointed,' says Mum. 'Nobody's perfect, he knows that. But when all's said and done, Anthony's his son and I shall love him for that no matter how much money – '

But she doesn't finish because at that moment there's a scrabbling sound behind her and we realise there's someone in the next booth and that they're getting up. A face appears above the screen behind Mum.

'Well, well, well, fancy meeting you here,' says Ferguson. 'I thought I recognised the voices.'

155

'Oh!' says Mum. 'Nearly gave me a heart attack. Popping up on people like that!'

'What brings you here then?' says Ferguson.

There's an awkward silence. We don't know how much of our conversation could be overheard from next door.

'I could ask you the same question,' says Mum.

'Oh, that's easy, the fish and chips. I get withdrawal symptoms if I don't get a fish dinner down me once a week. Nikki's came very highly recommended by some friends of ours.'

'That's all right then,' says Mum. 'I thought you was following us.'

'Oh no,' says Ferguson, with the smile of someone who has just won a hand at cards. 'We were here before you. We saw you come in.'

Pink appears next to him and begins talking about how hot it is. Mum is suddenly anxious to go and hauls herself from the seat.

'Nice seeing you, I'm sure,' she says, pulling at Dad's shoulder so hard he almost falls off his seat. I slide out and Laura and I extricate him from the booth. I go over to the bar and pay Nikki, giving her a generous tip. I turn to go.

'Here, listen,' she says. 'Watch yourself with Anthony. He's got the gift of the gab, know what I mean?'

I don't and I want to ask, but the Ferguson party are all watching, so I simply nod and follow the others out of the bar.

It's the hottest day so far. Outside, the air itself shimmers in the heat, so I feel I'm seeing everything on an old television set, the reception distorting it all. I notice the asphalt on the road is blistering and bubbling and wonder why they haven't found anything better to cover their roads with in a climate where this must happen all the time. Dad's face is already red and sore, although he's only been exposed to the sun for a matter of minutes. His eczema cream has melted and runs down his cheeks, making him look even hotter than he is. Today he's gone native and made the ultimate concession to the heat, he's wearing shorts. I am fearful for his legs, whose skin is so paper-thin it seems in danger of igniting at any moment. I want to pause so Laura can rub some sun cream on them but Mum is already off, her blue floral dress surging ahead, dragging Laura along, like a whale at full speed, oblivious to one of those little cleaner fish clinging to its side, leaving Dad and me to follow as best we may in her wake. I keep wondering why she is driving us all so hard to find Anthony. She says it's for Dad, but it's difficult to believe he could care less or that he is capable of caring about anything at all any more. So what does she hope to find? A remnant of the old Jim, perhaps? An aide-mémiore to the man she married? Something of his old self to refresh her energies again so she will be able to face all she has to do when he plunges into the darkness of his final decline and disappears for her altogether, as he disappeared for me long, long ago? Whatever she's after, she's going for it so fast I have to call her back as she overshoots the turn-off to the villas.

As Dad and I catch up, I see her remove her straw hat and wipe her forehead with her hankie. I can hear her panting from twenty feet away. Laura rolls her eyes and mouths, 'She'll kill herself at this rate!' to me. We have reason to know, better than Mum herself, that this is more than a faint possibility.

'Mum,' I say, 'slow down. You can't go in until we get there, anyway.'

She turns on me. 'Dad's waited forty odd years for this. He can't wait no longer.' She's so worked up she's itching for an argument to release her tension, like a country overpopulated with men spoiling for a war. As usual, I've no desire to take her on.

'We're just taking it slowly because of the heat,' I say. 'Dad's really feeling it.'

'I don't know why we didn't come in the car,' says Laura.

'Because you went charging off before I had chance to fetch it.' I say. 'If you'd waited a minute I could have gone and got it.'

'Charging?' says Mum. 'Who's saying who's charging? I hope you don't mean me because I've never charged nowhere in my life.'

'Look.' I point behind her. 'There's the villa. It's only another hundred yards.'

It's a nice property, the sort of thing I could shift in my sleep if I had to. Eight-foot-high stone walls and elaborate wrought-iron entrance gates. There's no bell to ring, so I lift the latch on one of the gates and push it open. We all march in and stand at the bottom of a sweeping, gravelled driveway, looking at the house. It's single storey but there any resemblance to our own bungalow ends. The place is massive. It's built in local stone. The roof is flat and the honey-coloured walls, now in shadow because the sun is behind the building, are curtained with purple and crimson swatches of bougainvillaea. The windows of the house have bright blue French shutters, all of which are closed. There's a veranda running around the house, separated from the garden by a low wall. In front of the wall are earthenware pots containing shrubs and all shades of flowers, blue, purple, yellow, red, pink.

'A riot of colour,' Mum says, 'isn't it, Laura? A riot of colour.'

We walk gingerly up the driveway, the crunch of the gravel beneath our feet seeming an intrusion.

At the large oak front door, I pull a bell rope. Somewhere off there's the sound of Westminster chimes.

'Talk about posh!' says Mum, and begins smoothing

down her dress. 'Do I look all right, Laura?'

Laura squeezes her arm. 'You look lovely, Mum.'

There's no answer. I try again. We wait another few minutes. Still no reply.

'Looks like he's out,' I say. 'Let's go.'

'Wait a minute,' Laura says. 'I can hear music.'

We all hold our breaths and sure enough, there's the sound of a woman singing, something that sounds like an Italian folksong, probably Maltese.

'It's coming from round the back.'

We troop round the corner of the house, down the side where a gleaming, white Mercedes stands in a carport, and round to the back.

Most of the garden is taken up by a large swimming pool. The ripples on its surface wink invitingly in the glare of the sun, which is made worse by the paved patio, which bounces the light back at us, doubling its intensity in the process. At the end of the pool nearest the house is a solitary sun parasol providing cover for a sun lounger. Stretched out on this on his back lies a man wearing white cotton trousers and a T-shirt. I walk over to him, the others following slowly. His arms hang limply on either side of the sun lounger, hands touching the ground. His face is covered by an open copy of the *Malta Times*, which flutters gently up and down with the regular, deep breathing of someone who is asleep.

One half of me wants to grasp the edges of the paper and whip it off, the other to leave it and the sleeper beneath undisturbed. In all probability, under this temporary veil of newsprint, is my older brother – or rather my half-brother – but in any case someone who is more my flesh-and-blood than Laura, my partner of ten years. I look at the others. Mum is consulting a pocket mirror and patting her hair, although under her rigorous daily spraying regime it's impossible for the cauliflower to have been the slightest bit disturbed or disarranged. Dad is breathing heavily, snorting through his nostrils, although whether from anxiety, or the effort of the walk, or because his mouth is occupied by a chocolate eclair, it's impossible to tell. As always with Dad these days, emotion, illness and blind indifference are indistinguishable.

Laura raises her eyebrows and whispers, 'Well, what do we do now? Do we wake him up?'

I follow the sound of the music, which is coming from a battered transistor radio standing on the patio beneath the lounger, next to a couple of empty Cisk beer bottles. I bend down, fiddle with the controls for a moment, find the right one and turn it off.

It's as though I've switched the man on the lounger on. Immediately he stirs and then sits up, startled. The *Malta Times* slides down his chest. Although the eyes that look up at us, flicking to each of us in turn and back again, like a cornered animal's, are black, they don't absorb the sunlight like you'd expect, but reflect it back, bright and sparkling. The face is tanned and the skin unlined, so that he doesn't look anywhere near his forty-three years, if indeed he is Anthony. The hair is black, longish and slicked back. There's a thick moustache above the full red lips.

'Oh look,' says Mum, 'he looks just like Omar Sharif, doesn't he? Don't you think he's got a look of Omar Sharif about him, Laura?'

'Mum . . . ' Laura says, squeezing her arm.

The man stands up. I notice his T-shirt has a picture of the singer Madonna on it and the slogan 'LIKE A VIRGIN WORLD TOUR 1984'. He has a slight paunch, not much, but enough to push the lower half of Madonna's face forward, giving her a slightly defiant expression. I'm gratified to see that although he's tall for a Maltese – which I find myself thinking, the way I sometimes do think about irrelevant things at important moments, is probably the result of having Dad's genes – he's still a good inch shorter than me.

'I beg your pardon,' he says, the voice slightly accented, like, say, that of an Italian who has lived in England for a number of years, 'I must have dropped off. Who are you? What do you want?'

'We're sorry to barge in on you,' I say, 'but we're looking for Anthony Spiteri.'

'Who wants him?'

'I can't disclose that, not unless I know it's him I'm talking to.'

'Oh, Nick, don't let's have all this messing around,' Mum cries. 'You're like a cat teasing a mouse.'

She shoulders me out of the way as she rushes forward and I have to wave my arms to keep my balance and avoid toppling into the pool.

'Anthony, Anthony,' she says, 'I never thought we'd find you. Hug your poor old Dad.'

Dragging Dad with her, she practically flings him at the stranger, who is forced to catch him. Mum puts her arms round both of them, pressing the three of them together, her now-sobbing face against the stranger's chest.

'Mum, Mum,' I say, tugging at her dress. 'Let go of the man. We don't even know if it is Anthony yet.'

The man looks at me, the eyes confused, so they remind me of Dad's when he was on his drug holiday.

'What is this? What is this woman talking about?'

'We're looking for Anthony Spiteri, son of a woman called Maria Spiteri. We don't intend anything to his detriment. This is my father. He was here during the war. He had an affair with Maria and she had his child, a boy called Anthony.'

Slowly, slowly, his confusion seems to clear. He gazes at Dad, raising an eyebrow.

'You're saying this is my father? This? But he . . . he's so *old*.'

'He's nearly seventy,' I say.

'Actually, no,' says Anthony. 'There's some mistake

here. I must tell you, no way is he my father.'

'This is Jim Taylor. I'm his son, Nicholas. Are you Anthony Spiteri? Are you Maria's son?'

'Actually, I am, but – ' He stares again at Dad, then abruptly turns around, and strides off through an open sliding patio door into the house. The four of us stand looking at one another.

'I expect it's a bit of a shock,' says Mum, dabbing at her eyes with her handkerchief. 'I must say it is to me, and I knew what was happening.'

From inside there's the sound of furniture being moved, or possibly of drawers being opened. Then a long silence. Finally Anthony re-emerges, clutching a photograph in his hand. He holds it out to me. It's the same woman as in Dad's pictures, only this time, no baby, but beside her, arm entwined with hers, stands Dad, tall, upright and lean, in his corporal's uniform, twenty-four years old, smiling, as he looks out into the future.

Anthony raps the picture with the tips of his fingers. 'This is my father. Look at him. How can it possibly be the same man as this – ' he dismisses Dad with a flick of his fingers. 'My father was so young, so tall. This person, he's old and short.'

Mum moves to his side, with surprising speed and delicacy. She touches his arm lightly. 'That's Dad, in your picture. That's the man I remember. But it was a long time ago, Anthony, more than forty years. Your dad's not a well man. He looks a lot shorter because his back's so bent. And then there's his neck . . . ' Abandoning delicacy she bowls over to Dad, grabs hold of his head, which is wilting even more than usual in the heat, and wrenches it upright. 'See? See how tall he'd be if he'd just hold that neck up. I wouldn't lie to you, Anthony. This is your dad.'

Anthony stares at Dad, then glances at the photograph, then back at Dad, as though he's making some kind of difficult calculation. The photo slips from his fingers and flutters to the ground. He takes a step towards Dad, then another, so they're almost touching. Mum releases her hold on Dad's head and takes a step back from him. Anthony raises a hand and reaches it tentatively towards Dad, snaking it round behind him to rest on the back of his neck. He pulls Dad to him, against his chest. He wraps his other arm around Dad and begins to sob.

'Dad,' he says. 'Dad. I thought I would never see you. What took you so long? What took you until you were old and short?'

There's a snuffling noise and a high-pitched whimper and it sounds so like a child I look around the garden, expecting to see one I hadn't noticed before. But there's no one else here. Then it hits me. It's Dad crying, the first time in my life I've ever known this to happen. Mum's face is buried in her hankie. Even Laura has tears in her eyes. Anthony holds Dad for what seems like hours. No one speaks. The only sounds are Mum's stifled sobs, Dad's snuffling, Anthony sniffing catarrh to the back of his nostrils from time to time and the distant steady thump of pile-driving from the construction site down the road. Finally Anthony loosens his arms, releases his grip on Dad and holds him out at arm's length to get a better look at him. I notice there is a damp patch across Madonna's nose as though she too has been crying. Then Anthony cups Dad's face between his hands, pulls it to him and kisses him with great force upon both cheeks. Tears, sweat and eczema cream flow copiously down Dad's face. When Anthony releases him again, Dad smiles weakly and says something, grinning all the time at this new son of his, but speaking too fast and too low for anything to be understood.

Anthony turns to me. 'Actually, what language is this he's speaking? I thought he was supposed to be English.'

'It's his illness. He has Parkinson's disease. It affects the speech,' I explain.

'You have to get used to it,' says Mum, dabbing at her eyes with her limp hankie. 'Dad's just saying how proud he is to have such a fine son and how glad he is to find you at last,' she interprets freely.

'It is not so hard to find me,' says Anthony. 'I have been here all the time. My mother wrote to him, she didn't get any reply. No letter, no money, nothing.'

Mum explains at great length about the delay in the post getting through. 'We tried so hard to find you Anthony, we really did. But we never had no money to get here, not till now, when our Nicholas paid for it all.'

Anthony stares hard at me.

'So you are his son too?' he says.

'Yes.'

'Then . . . you are my brother?'

'Half-brother,' I correct him.

'I never had a brother before. So, so, so. It's all too much to take in. You are my little brother.'

'Well, younger, anyway. I'm not so sure about little.'

He takes my right hand, folding its whiteness in both his large brown hands and shaking it vigorously. He looks into my eyes and looking back into the dark pools of his, it's impossible to catch any glimmer of what he's thinking.

'Hello, brother,' he says.

'Hello,' I say.

Anthony makes a fist and punches me playfully on the shoulder.

'Little Nick, huh?' Everybody else laughs, the laughter that comes from the release of tension, not because anything funny has been said.

'Yes.'

'My kid brother. Well, well, well.' He looks down at his feet, puts a hand over his eyes to shield them from the sun and pauses for a minute or two. He shakes his head, his long hair flicking back and forth.

'This is some day, actually. I never had a father, or knew any brother even existed. My mother has been dead since I was a small child. And then, all at once, in the space of a siesta, I have a family.'

He looks at Laura. 'And you, are you my sister?'

'No,' I say. 'I do have a sister, Pauline, but she's at home just now. This is Laura, my wife.'

'Well then, she is my sister by marriage. Laura!' He puts his arms round her and hugs her, a little too tightly for my liking. He gives her cheeks the same treatment as Dad's. I expect her to recoil, since she hates the smell of tobacco and Anthony reeks of it, but instead she's smiling at him.

'Actually, Nick, she's very pretty. You're lucky I didn't see her first.' He smiles at Laura. 'If he were not my brother, I would take you away from him.'

'Well, he's only your half-brother,' she says and laughs.

'And little ones, you have little ones? I am an uncle, perhaps?'

Laura fixes her smile. 'No, no children,' she says.

Anthony smiles back. There is something terribly formal about his manner and the way he speaks. His English is too perfect, too precise, as only a foreigner's can be.

'All in good time,' he says. 'All in good time.'

Holding both Laura's hands up, he stands back to admire her again.

'Perfect,' he says. 'A genuine English rose.'

And Laura stands there simpering back at him, like an old lady, loving it all.

'Ooooh, ooooh.'

The low moan is coming from Mum, and we turn to see her leaning back against the veranda wall, one hand to her head. Dad has reached out a hand and is stroking hers.

'Lil, Lil,' he says.

165

'Talk about faint! This heat!'

Anthony is beside her in an instant. He puts his right arm round her shoulder and takes her left hand in his, and leads her gently to a patio chair.

'Here,' he says. 'Take the weight off your feet.'

'Weight?' says Mum. 'What weight?' But she's too weak to argue and lets him lower her on to the chair.

'Oh dear,' she says.

Anthony slides over another parasol in a concrete base and puts the umbrella up so Mum is fully in the shade. He pulls another chair under it and I take Dad over and sit him down on it.

'It's very hot. It is necessary to be careful on such days. Let me get you a drink. What would you like? Some mineral water? Or perhaps a glass of orange squash?'

'No, just water. A drop of water before I faint away.'

He vanishes through the patio doors and returns a moment later with a glass of water, ice cubes clinking in it. Mum takes it and tips her head back, sinking it in one go.

'Talk about relief!' she says.

Anthony disappears inside again and comes back with four opened bottles of beer and four glasses and hands them to Dad, Laura and me, keeping one for himself.

He lifts his glass in a toast. 'Cheers. Actually, I'd like to drink to meeting my Dad again and – ' he gives me a mischievous wink, ' – my little brother.'

We clink glasses and I wonder if I'm alone in thinking they make a hollow sound.

I gesture with my arm to indicate the house and gardens.

'It's a nice property you have here,' I say.

'Yes, it is most pleasant. You must take a look around.' He brushes his hair back with his right hand. 'Although, actually, I may be moving somewhere else, depending on business.'

'What business are you in exactly?'

'Buying and selling.'

'Buying and selling what?'

'This and that. Everything. I buy something, then I sell it for more.'

'Yes, but what sort of thing – '

'Nick . . . ' Laura tugs at my sleeve. She nods towards Mum, who is as white as the plastic chair she's sitting on. I go over to her.

'Are you OK, Mum?'

'I just got a bit of angina,' she says. 'It's all the excitement brought it on. I'll be all right though, I slipped one of my tablets under my tongue.'

I know she only does this when she's worried. Panic engulfs me like a sudden hunger. Perhaps I should have cancelled the holiday when I found out about her condition. Perhaps I should have known it would all be too much for her.

'Listen, Anthony, I'm sorry to spoil the party,' I say, though of course I'm not sorry at all, 'but I think we ought to get Mum home so she can rest. Her heart's not too strong.'

'Yes, yes, of course, Nick. We don't want to take any chances do we? You want me to drive her home?'

'No, it's all right, I'll go and get our car. I'll be back in five minutes.'

It's a long hot walk back to the car, but I'm glad to be out of the relentless heat of the garden and away from all the alternating smiling and sobbing. What is it that I don't like about Anthony? Is it something of myself I'm seeing in him for the first time? That slight jowliness, perhaps, or the hair a little too long and the clothes just a shade too youthful for someone his age? Is this how I look to other people? Or maybe it's the thirty seconds it took him to make Dad cry, something I have never managed in all my years.

I've left the car in the full sun. The plastic steering wheel is too hot to touch and I have to wrap a cloth around it so I can hold it. By the time I get back to the villa, I'm sweaty and irritable. I just want to have a cool shower and for the day to be over. As I walk round to the back, I hear Anthony's voice and then laughter. He says something else. More laughter. I can hear Mum's cackle, almost like Pauline's, and Laura, and there's the clicking of Dad's teeth. The laughing stops as I appear and they all look up at me, so I have the uncomfortable feeling they've been laughing at me, though of course, I know this can't be true.

'Ah, Nick,' says Anthony. 'Another beer, perhaps? You look hot.'

'I am hot. It's boiling out there. No more beer, thanks. I want to get Mum home. She needs a bit of peace and quiet after all this excitement.'

'It's all right, Nick, I feel better now. I'm all right.' Mum gives me a look like a child who doesn't want to go to bed.

'You may think you're OK,' I say, 'but carry on getting yourself over excited and you'll make yourself ill. You don't want another heart attack, do you?'

No answer.

'Well, do you?'

'No, but – '

It's funny how I can never take Mum on about anything except her heart. When it comes to that, she defers to me.

'Right then.' I'm businesslike now. 'I didn't go to the expense and trouble of bringing you here to kill you, so let's get you home and have some rest.'

I hold out my hands to her. She takes them in hers. I take a deep breath and pull her up from the chair. Anthony puts his hand behind her and assists with a push.

'It's OK, I can manage,' I tell him. When she's up he

stands up and hugs her. Then Laura. Then Dad, the longest embrace of all. I start to go. Anthony releases Dad, strides over to me and seizes my hand.

'Nicholas, I hardly know what to say to you. Actually, I haven't had time to consider all this yet. But I would like you to know, I am so happy to meet you.'

'Of course. Goodbye.'

I shepherd Mum around the house and to the front gate, where she pauses and turns to Anthony, who has accompanied us, supporting Dad's arm in the way of people who don't know Dad's illness, holding him back when he could walk faster on his own.

'Bye-bye, Anthony,' says Mum. 'We'll see you tomorrow.'

With a great deal of elaboration, he blows her a kiss.

'Goodbye, Mum,' he says.

In the car I crash the gears so badly there's a sound like animals fighting.

'"Mum?"' I say. 'What's he doing calling you "Mum"? You're not his Mum. You're no relation to him.'

'I know,' she says. 'But Anthony said that since he'd lost his own mum and since I was married to his dad, he couldn't help seeing me as a second mother. I thought it was really nice he could think of me like that. After all, he might have seen me as the woman who took your dad away from his mum.'

'Oh God, give me strength!' I crash the gears again and hit the accelerator. The car roars angrily across a roundabout, provoking a fanfare of horns from other drivers.

'What's that supposed to mean?' snaps Mum.

'Oh nothing. Just that . . . he's a bit . . . over the top, isn't he? A bit too emotional?'

I catch Laura's eye in the rearview mirror, but she doesn't respond to my wink. 'It's not a bad thing to let your emotions out, once in a while,' she says. 'It's better than going around thinking you haven't got any.'

A car pulls out of a side road in front of me. I hit the horn hard and keep my hand on it for a good thirty seconds, all the while watching Mum in the mirror as she holds her hands over her ears to blot out the noise.

Back at the bungalow I help Dad into the house in silence. Mum disappears to the loo.

'What's this about seeing him tomorrow?' I ask Laura.

'He's coming here in the morning. He's going to take us all out for the day, show us some of the sights.'

'Oh, so I've been relieved of my duties as tour guide, have I? He's taking over the holiday is he?'

'No, but he's a native. He'll know about things you couldn't possibly. And he's got a good sense of humour. You haven't exactly been a good laugh on this holiday, you know, Nick.'

'Bloody great. We take them on holiday and he just muscles in and takes over.'

'Oh grow up, Nick, what did you expect? Just hello, goodbye, nice to meet you? He's your father's son. It's natural they should spend time together.'

'Christ, Laura, you don't half piss me off sometimes. I thought at least you'd be on my side.'

Dad clears his throat. 'Thirsty,' he says.

'I'll get you a drink of water, Dad.' Laura goes over to the fridge and takes out a bottle of mineral water. 'And a couple of biscuits so you can take your tablets.'

Mum comes in, adjusting the bottom of her dress.

I avoid her eyes. 'I'm going to have a shower,' I say.

'But what about that thing?' she says.

'What thing?'

Laura nods towards the loo. 'I think she means you have some unfinished business.'

* * *

I look into the loo, just to make sure the turd is still there. It is, practically unscathed after countless flushings, although I'm relieved to see that Martina's item has decamped. I go outside and hop over the wall on to the wasteland, and pick my way carefully through the assorted debris of plastic drinks bottles, rusty tin cans, shredded newspaper and decomposing food, trying all the while to ignore the scrapping sounds which doubtless mean rats. Eventually I find what I'm looking for, a piece of broken plank, about two feet long. I pick it up and head back to the loo, where for the next half an hour I beat the turd with it, plunging the jagged end of the plank again and again against it, gradually breaking it down, working off my anger, trying not to let the image of myself beating Anthony over the head keep popping into my mind, until finally it breaks up and slips silently away around the hidden bend.

When Dad is finally put to rest, Laura comes into our bedroom, where I'm already in bed and makes an offer of truce with a friendly smile. I scowl back. I can't be bought off so easily. Besides, in this situation, a smile is foreplay.

'Oh come on Nick, lighten up.' She begins undressing. 'Don't throw the toys out of the cot.'

'I don't see anything to lighten up about. We can't all be Mr Continental Charm, can we?'

'I liked him. He's very nice. I think you're a little bit jealous.'

'Jealous? Of that short-arse!'

'Oh well, if you're going to be silly about it.' She pulls on a cotton nightdress and slips under the sheet. 'Sod you then.'

She turns her back on me.

'I suppose this means we're not having sex?' I bluff.

'What do you think? That you can be like a bear with a

sore behind with me all day and then expect to make love to me?'

'You could always shut your eyes and pretend I was Anthony.'

'Quite frankly, Nick, my imagination's not that good.'

Seven

Thursday

The most amazing thing about a large, white Mercedes convertible, when you're in one for the first time, has nothing to do with the engine or the sumptuousness of its leather seats or the extravagance of its real wood and stainless steel dashboard, or even the clarity of its state-of-the-art stereo cassette deck. It's the size of the back seat, which is so wide three people – even when one of them's Mum – can sit in it without touching. And two of them, Laura and myself, are not only not touching, but are as far apart as we were in bed last night.

I hate myself for being so impressed by the car as I sit silently slumped against the door, listening to the others spewing out praise.

'Talk about comfy!' says Mum. 'You just sink into these seats, don't you, Laura? To be honest, I didn't like that other car. I didn't say nothing, but it was a very hard ride. It wasn't doing Dad's bottom any good at all.'

'It's just wonderful having the top down,' says Laura. 'Especially in this heat. I love the breeze on my face.'

'It's certainly windy back here,' says Mum.

As if to confirm this, a chocolate eclair wrapper the

slipstream has just ripped from Dad's grasp in the front seat zips past her head.

'Stop throwing things, Jim,' she yells. 'And get that neck off Anthony. Let the boy drive.'

I hunch myself further down in my seat to continue with my own in-car entertainment of counting the ways Anthony gets right up my nose:

1   He has flashy, obvious good looks. During breakfast this morning, which was almost totally taken up with discussion of him, it was agreed by Mum and Laura that he did indeed look like Omar Sharif in his *Dr Zhivago* period, before he got older and a bit too Middle-Eastern for Mum's taste. I find it annoying they're so easily impressed. It's not the sort of look I would go for if I were a woman.

2   He apparently has a lot of money. Flash house. Flash car. When it drove into the square in front of the bungalow this morning even the Ferguson men, Blue and Grey, were drawn to their door to look at it approvingly.

3   The man dresses too young. This morning he turned up in an off-white linen suit and a black polo shirt. Just because he doesn't look his age it's no excuse not to dress it.

4   Although he's not married (waiting for the right woman apparently, according to the potted biography he gave the rest of the family while I was getting the car yesterday), he simply adores kids and wants about twenty of them.

5   He's taking over this holiday without so much as asking. This morning, after my suggestion that we go out in the Seat while he followed in his own car was over-ruled, I spread a carrier bag on the front passenger seat of the Mercedes, taking great satisfaction in Anthony's obvious puzzlement. When he asked me what I was doing, I explained this was how we got Dad into a car.

'Actually, no,' he said, grabbed the bag, scrumpled it

and dropped it on the ground. Then he put one arm behind Dad's back, the other behind his knees, and just lifted him off the ground, cradling him in his arms. Dad, who is as stiff as a corpse whenever I try to lift him, immediately relaxed and went as floppy as a newborn baby. With seemingly effortless ease, Anthony leaned into the car and positioned him perfectly on the passenger seat. Then he turned to me and winked. It's the wink I can't forgive.

6   He calls Mum, 'Mum'.

7   He's short.

8   He has this irritating habit of kissing everyone on both cheeks. I know it's something Continentals go in for, but I've never kissed my Dad in my life as far as I can remember, so how come he turns up and just starts doing it? And it's the way he does it to Laura that really gets me. His lips definitely linger on her skin, whereas I've always thought it was meant to be just a formality, a sort of no-contact sport.

Right now Laura's talking to him. Anthony drapes his left arm along the back of the seat behind Dad, in a pro-prietorial way, so he can turn to answer her.

'Have you ever been to England?' Laura says.

'Why, are you inviting me?' He flicks an eye at the road ahead before turning to her again.

'You haven't answered the question,' I say. 'Have you?'

'No, I am not much of a traveller, actually. I have never been further than Sicily, which, of course, is not very far at all.' There's the blast of a horn and Anthony turns away just in time to take avoiding action from an articulated lorry which is bearing down on us. 'But I have one or two business deals going through at the moment, and if they're successful, then I may take some time off. So, it is possible I will turn up on your doorstep.'

'Feel free,' Laura says, 'we've got a spare bedroom.'

Anthony turns right round to flash his teeth at her, so now he's driving while facing in completely the wrong direction. But some sixth sense seems to inform him of traffic hazards, so he always turns round in time to avert a collision by a hair's breadth. It's in this fashion we arrive in an ugly little town which a sign proclaims to be Mosta.

Rising out of the urban sprawl around it is the reason for coming to Mosta, the church of St Mary, or the *koppla* as Anthony says, waving his right arm out of the car towards it. From behind a façade of massive pillars and twin belfries rises a huge dome, the local limestone weathered to a soft apricot hue. Anthony circles it, all the time gesticulating with his right hand, reeling off facts, telling us we are looking at the fourth largest dome in the world by height, and the third largest by volume, that it took twenty-seven years to build without scaffolding, and that it is bigger than St Paul's Cathedral. He manages all this while negotiating numerous cars and tour buses, often driving with both hands busy in the air describing things, or one of them doing no more than hitting the horn occasionally.

'How do you remember all these facts, Anthony?' says Laura. 'It's like having our own personal tour guide.'

He brushes his hand through his hair. 'Well, tourism is the main industry here. Like most other people, I have worked in the tourist industry a little. But mainly it is because I am Maltese. We have pride in such things. It's important to know about your country.'

'He gets it from Dad,' says Mum. 'Nick used to be the same when he was young. Talk about memory! He could have done himself proud at the university, if he'd only stuck at it. What that little head didn't know wasn't worth knowing.'

She reaches out and pats the head in question and I'm

176

quite touched until she addresses the back of Anthony's again.

'You seem to be like me, Anthony. I love anything historical.'

'*Iva,*' says Anthony, swinging the car on to a small car park in the shadow of the dome. 'Malta is all about history. Always someone invading us or trying to invade us. No one here is untouched by history. Look at me. No Second World War, no Dad on Malta, no me.'

Dad turns to him and they grin at one another as Anthony jerks on the handbrake.

As we walk to the entrance of the dome I notice, in support of what Anthony has said, a British red telephone box, obviously still in use. Beside it, on a low wall, sit some old men chewing the fat. One of them holds in one hand a small wire cage, smaller than a shoebox. Inside is a chaffinch, a portable pet. Unaccountably the bird is singing.

At the entrance to the dome there's a box of clothing with a sign: 'Scarfs and shirts for ladies only. Fold it and return it back.' Another sign says: 'No shorts or mini-skirts.' When I point to it because I'm wearing shorts, Anthony waves a dismissive hand and I notice a tour bus disgorging shorts-clad men by the dozen outside. We have to wait a few minutes because Mass is just ending. On the other side of the massive room a priest is intoning into a microphone. Immediately in front of us sits the congregation, mostly women, the ones near us gossiping to one another and paying no attention to the priest.

Eventually the service ends, the congregation leaves and we walk in. Even though I've just witnessed the Mass, I'm surprised for a moment when Anthony bows and crosses himself, as this huge round shape is so unlike a church. But I like its simplicity after the huge baroque confections of most of the architecture here. There's a spacious, echoey feel to it, the whispers of the tourists and the sound of their feet on the stone floor somehow magnified by the shape. Like most people, I find myself looking upwards, past the paintings of saints which circle the interior and into the dome itself, where an intricate pattern of small squares spirals dizzyingly to the apex, where light enters through the round skylight.

My contemplation of it is suddenly interrupted by Mum's voice, which is somehow shouting and whispering at the same time. 'GET IT UP!' she hisses. 'GET THAT NECK UP!'

I look round to see her trying vainly to lift Dad's neck so that it is not only horizontal, her normal aspiration, but pointing upwards so he can see the dome. Of course, there's no chance of this and in the end she gives up, shaking her head in furious exasperation.

Dad has the look of a told-off child, so I point out the floor to him, easily visible with his neck in its favourite reclining position. Looking at the pattern of intricately inlaid stones, I'm reminded of Mrs Haines's different pieces of linoleum.

Anthony takes Dad by the arm and begins to steer him across the church, pointing out items of interest, talking and gesticulating all the while. Mum and Laura trot along on his other side, hanging on his every word as Dad is hanging on his arm.

I let them go, my normal holiday role usurped. It's obvious to me that Anthony is doing all this, not for the pleasure of informing others, but to show off his own knowledge and cleverness. And then I wonder whether I only know this because I do the same.

I wander about aimlessly and pause to see what a group of tourists are huddled around. A guide is standing next to a large bomb, explaining that it's a replica of one the Luftwaffe dropped one afternoon in 1942, which pierced the dome and crashed to the floor of the church, where some 300 members of the congregation were waiting for Mass to begin. The astonished worshippers watched as the bomb flew across the floor but, mercifully, failed to explode.

'Is very lucky for them,' says the guide and the tourists all nod and agree as they move off.

I stand looking at the replica bomb and wonder about luck. Where do you start measuring it? Wasn't it bad luck the Luftwaffe dropped the bomb on the church in the first place? And more bad luck that it happened at service time? And still more bad luck for any individual who happened to be there? But all of this is forgotten in the one piece of good luck, the one bit of luck that actually matters. After all, the bomb didn't explode! How do you measure the luck in one man's life? Is it Dad's good fortune he wasn't killed in the war, or bad luck because it meant he lived long enough to get Parkinson's disease? And what bit of misfortune gave it to him in the first place? Was it something as arbitrary as being downwind of a certain field when the crops were being sprayed? And within this massive piece of bad luck, are there minor pieces of good luck, like having someone as totally dedicated as Mum to look after him for as long as she has, or the not-quite-so disastrous bad luck of having Parkinson's, but not the shaking kind? Does he count himself lucky to have children who care for him more than a little or, when he learns the awful truth, will he think himself unlucky they don't care a little bit more?

I'm starting to make myself dizzy by chasing all these thoughts round in my head, the way I felt a bit dizzy a few moments ago, after staring up into the dome for so long. Being in a circular building doesn't help. Although I try to banish my thoughts and concentrate on looking at the paintings and statues, I find moving from one object to another involves revolving my head. And then suddenly my eyes come to rest on a familiar red and blue uniform amongst a group of tourists a few feet away.

I walk over to her. She is explaining something to her tour group and has her back to me. I wait until her speech is over before I speak. 'Martina, how nice to see you.'

She turns, about to smile, but when she realises who it is her lips freeze before they can really get going. The effect is a grimace. A deep blush suffuses her cheeks.

'Oh it's you. Mr Taylor. Yes, of course. How nice.'

I suddenly realise she is embarrassed to see me because of the incident with the loo. For a moment I have the urge to explain what really happened, but then realise this would probably only make matters worse. I think about luck again. Is it lucky meeting her here? She probably doesn't think so. Perhaps it's just coincidence, that neutral form of chance which has no spin on it, either good or bad. No, it's lucky, I decide, at least for me since I'm actually pleased to see her.

'Nice church,' I say to fill the silence and help ease her embarrassment.

'You like the *koppla*, Mr Taylor?'

'It's very impressive.'

'It is bigger than St Paul's Cathedral in London, yes?'

'Apparently.'

She looks up at the dome and then smiles back at me.

'I not go to St Paul's, but everybody says is bigger here.'

'Oh, I'm sure they're right.'

She smiles, proud of the *koppla*. Her cheeks have returned to their normal colour, but there's still an awkward silence.

'My family are here somewhere,' I say. I turn and sweep the room, finally spotting them on the far side of the church, where Anthony is evidently explaining a large religious painting to the others.

Martina follows my gaze, her smile breaking out again as she sees them but then slowly vanishing before it reaches full power. She stares hard at Anthony, who suddenly turns round, as though aware of the weight of her eyes upon him.

Martina turns to me. She looks worried.

'Mr Taylor, you know this man who is with your family?'

'Yes, he's, well, a sort of relative.'

'Oh, well, perhaps it better I not say anything then.'

'No Martina, please, what is it?'

She glances again towards the others. Anthony has left them and is hurrying in our direction.

'Mr Taylor, I know this man Anthony Spiteri. He is not someone who you can, how you say – '

'Martina!' Anthony is beside us.

'It is nice to see you, Martina,' he says.

She gives him a smile so perfunctory it almost amounts to an insult. 'Hello, Anthony.'

Anthony smiles at me. 'And what has Martina been telling you? You look to be having a serious conversation here.'

'I was just about to tell him – ', begins Martina, but then she stops. She's looking at Laura, Mum and Dad who are ambling towards us. Her face turns bright red again and she's suddenly flustered. 'It doesn't matter,' she says. 'Say hello to your parents from me. I must rush, my party are waiting.'

She walks briskly towards her group, obviously anxious to avoid the further embarrassment of a meeting with the rest of the family. I realise that by the oddest twist of chance Dad's bowels have stopped the flow of Martina's revelations as effectively as they blocked the loo.

Anthony and I watch her rejoin her group. She begins shepherding them towards the entrance, allowing herself just one anxious backward glance at us.

'I do not know what this woman has been saying to you', says Anthony, turning and staring straight into my

181

eyes, as though trying to read something there. 'Actually, I am sure it will be something bad. You see, she has a grudge against me. It is from the time when I did some work in the tourist industry. This woman took a liking to me and made advances towards me. Unfortunately, I was not able to reciprocate her feelings. In fact, I turned her down.' He watches Laura as she leads Mum and Dad to us. 'Women,' he says. 'They just don't like you to turn them down.'

Outside, Anthony begins to make for the car, but Mum says, 'What about eating? Dad must have something to eat, so he can take his tablets.'

'Perhaps Anthony knows a decent restaurant,' I say.

'Yes,' says Laura, 'somewhere the locals go, not one of the tourist traps we usually end up in.'

Anthony screws his face up. 'Not in Mosta. It is not a good place to eat. I can take you somewhere in St Paul's Bay, a very fine restaurant, offering many local dishes, excellent fish.'

'The thing is,' I say with some satisfaction, 'Dad has to have something now. Nothing fancy, just a snack.'

'OK,' says Anthony, 'There is a good *pastizzeria* here. We can buy something from there.'

'You mean a takeaway?'

'Takeaway, yes.'

'And perhaps', says Laura, 'we can try the place in St Paul's Bay tonight?'

I want to kick her. I'd hoped we'd at least be free of Anthony tonight.

The *pastizzeria* is a tiny shop selling ready-cooked food. We end up sitting on a wall not far from the *koppla*, under the shade of a tree, eating *timpana*, a pie containing macaroni, minced meat, liver, tomatoes and eggs, and *pastizzi*, oval pockets of flaky pastry filled with what seem to be mushy peas. Everyone is quiet, as usual too busy eating to talk. The food is good and for the first time today I find myself not wanting to be somewhere else.

The terrace of the restaurant overlooks St Paul's Bay, the water already changing its bright blue daytime colour for the crimson of the setting sun, which sits, huge and contemplative, on the horizon. The other three sides of the garden are walled, whitewashed, with plants trailing down them. There's a pergola from which vines trail, already laden with small grapes. The ground is paved with ancient flagstones and in the centre there's a small fountain, the babbling of the water a restful backcloth to the low murmurs of diners. We sit at a stone table, the surface covered in blue and yellow ceramic tiles, depicting the sun, the moon and the signs of the zodiac.

Anthony sits at the head of the table with Mum on his left hand and Laura on his right. Dad sits beside Mum, and I am beside my wife, facing him. As soon as we're seated, Laura turns away from me, showing as much of her back to me as you can to a person sitting next to you, and is immediately engrossed in Anthony, a statement that last night's hostilities are still in place. This leaves me with only Dad to talk to or, in effect, no one at all.

As soon as we're seated, a short plump man in black trousers and a white shirt comes into the garden and hurries over to our table, smiling and rubbing his hands. Anthony stands up and the two men hug each other. 'Anthony!' the man, who is evidently the *patron*, says, holding Anthony at arm's length to look at him. 'Ugo!' says Anthony. He introduces the man as the restaurant owner.

'He is an old friend of mine,' says Anthony. He flaps a hand over us.

'These are my friends from Britain.'

'Ah, if they are your friends, then I make sure everything is of the very best for you.'

The whole thing strikes me as incredibly false, like two bad actors playing a scene from an old Hollywood movie, and I'm amazed to see Mum and Laura lapping it up.

Ugo begins listing all the specialities they have tonight, mainly fish, for this is a fish restaurant. There's grouper, bream, grilled swordfish, a special pie of dorado, giant prawns, lobster and several other fish I've never heard of. When the list is finished, Anthony fires several questions at Ugo. Which side of the island do the prawns come from? Was the dorado caught today? What size is the bream? He consults us briefly and then orders.

We begin with *minestra*, a thick soup of at least ten different vegetables, chick peas, lentils and pasta, since soup is one thing Dad can always eat easily. Then we move on to giant prawns, as these are a favourite of Laura's. They arrive smoking from the grill, swimming in strong garlic butter. As Mum is busy listening to Anthony providing a running commentary on the food, I'm left to peel Dad's prawns for him, which keeps me so occupied I catch only the occasional word or two of what Anthony is saying, although enough to guess he is talking about his childhood.

'No money,' I hear. 'Big disgrace to have no father.' 'We were poor, I had to work.' 'No education.'

Although he's probably the villain of this history, if only by default, Dad appears to hear none of it, obsessed as he is by the prawns, constantly picking them up and trying to put them in his mouth before I have peeled them. I have to keep tugging them away from his surprisingly strong grip, while at the same time trying to peel another one-handed.

Anthony is saying something about a bomb, which I presume must be the one in the *koppla,* so I lean forward to listen. But at that moment Dad picks up the finger bowl in front of him and tries to drink from it and I have to leave the conversation to snatch it away. He pulls, trying to keep hold of it, but I peel his hands away, like the skin from one of the prawns, and set it back down on the table. I hand him his glass of white wine and he drinks that instead, without appearing to register it is anything different.

When Dad puts his wine glass down I hand him another peeled prawn, hoping it will keep him busy while I catch up on what's being said at the other end of the table. He takes the prawn carefully and holds it up to inspect it, then reaches down and dips it in his wine glass. I remove the glass from his reach, snatch the prawn angrily from his fingers and thrust it between his lips which are barely open. He looks shocked for a moment, but then proceeds to stuff the rest of the prawn into his mouth. I turn once again to hear what Anthony is talking about and hear Mum say, 'It sounds like you've had a hard life, Anthony. You need a wife to help you. Every man needs a woman behind him. Where would your dad be today without me?'

There's a pause while the main course of various fried fish arrives. We all nod appreciatively as Ugo points out the different varieties, although the names mean nothing to me. There's a huge bowl of salad and a big metal tray of finely cut chips.

I cut up pieces of fish for Dad and check them carefully for bones. He begins eating chips with his fingers, pausing whenever I proffer a fragment of fish on the end of his fork to open his mouth, like a baby being spoonfed, so I can slip it in.

'I hope I shall marry soon. I have some deals, some transactions in progress. Then I will be ready.' He combs his hand through his hair.

Mum pauses before plunging a large piece of fish into her mouth. 'What exactly is it you do?' she asks.

'I am an entrepreneur,' says Anthony, as though it's a job, like being a train driver or a postman.

'What exactly does that involve?' I shout from my end of the table.

Anthony gives me a patronising smile. 'A lot of wheeling and dealing,' he says. 'Believe me, Nick, it is too boring too talk about. It sounds exciting, I know, but it is just like any other job.' He smiles at Laura and Mum and picks up his wine glass. 'And who wants to talk about work when they are having such a wonderful time? You want to talk to me about selling houses, Nick?'

Mum and Laura laugh as he sips his wine. I knock back another glass. I'm starting to feel pretty pissed, but there's not much else to do down here with just Dad for company.

When Ugo arrives with the dessert menu, we all hold up our hands and tell him we're too full of his excellent food to eat any more. He smiles and thanks us as waiters scurry around, clearing the dishes.

'*Ice cream.*'

It's the first time Dad has spoken all evening.

'You like ice cream, Dad?' says Anthony.

'Like it? He's a devil for it,' says Mum. 'He'd eat it all day long if I let him.'

Anthony holds up a finger to Ugo.

'Ugo, my friend, one of your ice-cream specials. And make it very special tonight, would you?'

'And perhaps we could have another bottle of this excellent wine?' I say.

I swear Ugo bows and exits backwards, he's so into the Hollywood thing.

Anthony smiles at Dad, 'I'm telling you, Dad, you haven't eaten ice cream until you have tried Ugo's special.'

Moments later Ugo himself arrives bearing an enormous dessert glass in which I count at least half a dozen different coloured balls of ice cream, pink, white, chocolate, green, yellow and caramel, topped by a mountain

186

of whipped cream and pieces of fruit, two cocktail umbrellas and a small firework which is sizzling away, shedding sparklets on to the tablecloth.

'Oh, a sparkler,' says Mum, putting her hands together in glee like a child at a birthday party.

I reach for the new bottle of wine and pour myself another large glass.

'You like fireworks?' says Anthony. 'Let me tell you, Malta is the place for fireworks. One night, you must allow me to take you to a *festa* and show you fireworks like you have never seen before.'

Dad picks up the long spoon that came with the ice cream and scrapes at the mound of cream. A dollop drops into his lap. I start to get up from my seat, but Anthony is out of his faster. He raises a hand to me, 'No, no, sit still, Nick. I will help Dad. I will give him his ice cream.'

He picks up his chair and brings it to our end of the table, places it next to Dad and sits down. He extracts the now burnt-out sparkler and the cocktail umbrellas and tosses them to one side. Very gently he takes the spoon from Dad and digs it deep into the glass, bringing it out laden with pistachio ice cream, and propels it into Dad's gawping mouth.

'It's good?' he says.

Dad takes a moment or two to digest the ice cream.

'Mmm,' he says. Mum, Laura and Anthony laugh. I watch in disbelief as Anthony feeds him the rest of the ice cream, and Dad takes it. All my efforts during the meal are now forgotten and it's as if he'd take food from any stranger who offered to feed him. Perhaps he doesn't care who looks after him, I think, as long as his needs are met. Perhaps I'm driving myself crazy for nothing.

I have another glass of wine.

When the ice cream is done, Ugo returns and there's more smiling and bowing. He places a silver tray in front of Anthony, bearing a folded card which evidently contains the bill. Mum and Laura get up and go off to the loo. Dad is looking down at his lap, his hands busy fiddling with something there, probably the residue of the ice cream he dropped earlier.

Anthony picks up the wine bottle and pours me another glass. He leans across the table, his face suddenly anxious, less confident. 'Listen, Nick I have a small problem.'

I don't say anything. He smacks his lips together, looks out at the sea and drums his fingers on the back of Dad's chair. He looks back at me.

'It is like this, my credit card, it is out of date. They have not sent me a new one. I have only just realised. It's a problem.'

'You can't pay the bill.'

'Sure, I can pay the bill. Only I don't have a way just now. Once the card comes . . . '

'You want me to pay?'

'Well, if you don't mind.'

'All right.' I pick up the bill. I try not to register my shock. It's a lot more expensive than I'd expected. I hold it up to Anthony. 'This seems pretty steep.'

'No, no. Not at all, let me assure you. This is a very good class of restaurant. And also we had quite a bit of wine.' He indicates my glass, which I empty. I'm not really enjoying the drink, but am planning ahead. If Laura makes a move on me tonight, being unable to perform will save me having to think of some other excuse. I take out my wallet. Luckily I cashed some traveller's cheques today, so I have plenty of cash. I put the notes carelessly on the plate.

Anthony immediately summons a waiter with his finger. The waiter takes the money away.

Anthony smiles. 'Thank you, Nick,' he says.

'Don't mention it.'

'Don't worry, I won't. And, Nick, I'd be grateful if you

don't mention it either. Not to Mum and Dad. It is just that I don't want them . . . '

I hold my hand up in a stop sign. 'It's OK. I understand.'

When the women return, I take Dad off to the loo, which involves a tricky journey through the restaurant and up a flight of stairs.

'How was your ice cream, Dad?' I ask.

'Cold,' he replies.

I've just got Dad to the bottom of the stairs on the way back when I hear raised voices. I see Anthony standing at the restaurant bar. Ugo is on the other side. Anthony has his hand held out on the bar, palm up. There's a pile of bank notes on it. He twitches his fingers, evidently asking for more. Ugo hesitates, then shrugs, in a way that somehow expresses disgust and drops another couple of notes on to Anthony's hand. Anthony snaps his hand shut, stuffs the money into his trouser pocket and walks back out into the garden, whistling, without noticing me and Dad. I wonder if we've been overcharged and this is Anthony's commission for bringing us here and helping to rip us off. I decide not to say anything to Mum or Laura. I want to find out just what Anthony's up to before I do.

Even the smooth suspension of a Mercedes cannot prevent feelings of nausea if you have drunk the best part of two bottles of wine and are travelling on Maltese roads, where the potholes fling you about and the sudden swerves and emergency stops necessary to avoid the lunatic locals churn the contents of your stomach to eruption point. And I'm glad German engineering hasn't progressed as far as a chunder-proof vehicle. I want to be sick, especially with Laura now resting her head amorously and ominously upon my shoulder. Throwing

189

up now would definitely put an end to any possibility of sex with the added bonus of messing up Anthony's upholstery. But I have this problem. I'm never sick. It's just like the constipation and never having a runny nose when I have a cold. I haven't thrown up for years. Even when I had salmonella poisoning, I just *felt* sick. But not a drop passed my lips. And it's the same when I'm pissed. I always hold my beer.

While Laura helps put Dad to bed, I down three bottles of Cisk from the fridge in quick succession. It strikes me as being usefully gassy. Nothing happens. I climb into bed and am just practising a fake snore when Laura walks in and catches me doing it with my eyes open.

'What's that funny noise you're making?' she asks.

'It's my stomach. I feel a bit sick.'

'No it isn't. You were doing it in the back of your nose. Anyway, you're never sick.'

'Tonight could be the night,' I say.

It's no use, she isn't listening. She's already whipped all her clothes off and is spraying Shalimar behind her ears and on her wrists. She crawls across the bed to me. I clutch the single sheet to my chest. She begins stroking me through it, and I decide this is more erotic than having her touch my skin, so I pull the sheet back.

We both look at my penis, which is curled up like a prawn and not of the giant variety we've been eating tonight, either.

'Hey, I hope this isn't brewer's droop,' she says. Playfully, she takes the end of my foreskin between her thumb and forefinger and stretches my penis up. With her other hand she twangs it like the string of a double bass.

Fortunately I find this rather painful and not the least bit erotic.

'Ooh, that's nice, do it again,' I say.

She does. My penis remains a picture of limp indifference. Laura kisses me passionately.

'Steady on with the tongue,' I say. 'It's making me more nauseous.'

She breaks away and begins stroking my body. Nothing happens. She moves her hand down to my balls and caresses them. Normally, when I'm a willing participant, at this point I move her hand somewhere else, usually my penis, as if I can't wait, rather than tell her the testicular touching merely tickles. Tonight I allow her to continue. My penis remains resolute. The tickling stops as she moves her hand on to it and begins stroking it. Perhaps because it's been celibate for so long now, in spite of the prodigious quantity of alcohol I've put away, it begins to stir. In desperation, I lie back, close my eyes, and think of England, in particular the Prime Minister, Mrs Thatcher. I imagine the schoolmistressy face and bossy voice. My penis immediately springs to attention. I'm shocked, but I don't have time now to worry about what this says about my politics. I jump out of bed.

'What's up?' ask Laura. 'Besides that.'

'Feel sick. Need some water.'

I dash from the room. In the kitchen I knock back glass after glass of fizzy mineral water. I can't seem to blank out Mrs Thatcher's face. My penis is still stiff. My stomach feels like it's going to burst. I run back to our room, fingers down my throat, removing them just as I get inside the door to prevent Laura seeing and to release a spectacular projectile vomit which crosses the room and splatters against the opposite wall.

'Oh, Nick,' shouts Laura, 'you disgusting pig!'

'Come on,' I protest, retching. 'Once in ten years.'

Laura gets up, leaves the room and comes back a moment later with a bucket of water and a cloth. She begins scrubbing at the wall, which has bits of vomit stuck all over it. I wonder why there are so many carrots in it, when I haven't eaten any for months. I wonder why there are always carrots in vomit, but decide this is not the time to mention it to Laura.

'There's sick stuck all over the wall,' she says.

'Leave it,' I reply, climbing into bed, safe at last. 'When it dries, it'll just look like it's been artexed.'

Second Week

Eight
Friday

I am lying in bed unable to move. My head aches from the wine last night. Someone has superglued my eyelids shut, but I have no desire to open them to the shock of the bright morning light. I feel too rough to sleep, so I'm thinking about Dad. Since I cannot recover the man he was from my memory by going back from what he is now, I've decided to try to reconstruct him from the other direction, assembling his biography right from the start, using the snippets of family information I've gleaned over the years. This is what I know.

Born 1920 in the Fenland village of Willowbank, in the Isle of Ely, four miles from the city itself. Eldest of three children of Harry Frederick Taylor (listed on the birth certificate as Ag. lab. or agricultural labourer, as are all his male ancestors according to the family tree Pauline researched at her genealogy evening class) and Agnes Ada Taylor, née Dockerill. Residence: Folly Farm, Willowbank. At age three discovered with distressed, de-whiskered cat and a pair of scissors. Having removed cat's whiskers, about to cut open her stomach 'to see where the purr comes from'.

At age 8–10 (approximately) goes fishing every morning before school. Village cats follow him home in numbers much to amusement of villagers.

At age 11 passes entry exam to grammar school, the first child from Willowbank to achieve this. In the absence of any other transport, cycles six miles to school across bleak Fenland in all weathers, the north-easterly wind sometimes so strong the bicycle goes backwards if he stops pedalling. Cycles home every evening.

Age 11–18 plays rugby for school team, comes top of his class in maths, becomes a prefect, which earns him the honour of a pink cap. Gains School Certificate.

Is that it? Is that all I know about his childhood? It's almost as sketchy as the early life of Jesus, who at least had a spectacularly interesting adult life to compensate. Not so Dad:

1938 – begins work as a junior clerk at the sugar-beet factory in Queen Adelaide, two miles from Willowbank.

1939 – at the outbreak of war enlists as a private in the Royal East Anglian Foot Regiment.

1939–45 – serves in Canada, North Africa, Italy, Malta, Burma and India, always in a support capacity and without taking part in any military action. Fathers at least one illegitimate child.

1945 – marries childhood sweetheart Lilian Irene Twite by special licence on VJ Day. Spends wedding night in mother-in-law's home, where happy couple are kept awake by jubilant celebrations in the streets outside.

1946 – returns to sugar-beet factory where he spends the rest of his working life, eventually rising to Deputy Office Manager, the supreme achievement only denied him by his enforced early retirement because of Parkinson's disease.

1949 – daughter Pauline born.

1952 – son Nicholas born.

* * *

And what then? I imagine me as my infant self, coming to consciousness one morning in the council house in Willowbank. I'm just trying to open my eyes on the scene, when suddenly there's an explosion of noise in my head.

'Nick! Nick! Wake up!'

For a moment I don't recognise the voice. It doesn't seem to belong in my childhood world. I feel a hand tugging at my shoulder.

'Nick, for goodness' sake, wake up!'

The urgency in Laura's voice is enough to jerk my mind into the here and now. In a flash it knows exactly where it is and immediately instructs my opening eyelids to close up again. I pretend to snore. If Laura is pinning her hopes on a surprise dawn raid when my testosterone levels are high and my penis already conveniently engorged, she's about to be disappointed.

There's the slap slap of her bare feet on the tiled floor as she moves around the bed. For a moment I feel flattered she's prepared to go to such lengths to have me make love to her, but then I remember her desperation has nothing to do with sex, my end being simply the means to another. Besides, the rough manner in which she is shaking my shoulders hardly resonates tenderness.

'Nick, wake up! It's Dad, we can't get him out of bed.'

I'm awake and out of bed instantly, a little *too* instantly if she ever stops to think about it. I pull on my shorts and a T-shirt, wondering what the damp patch on the wall is. Then I remember last night. I follow Laura into Mum and Dad's room. Dad is lying on his back, rigid as death, his claw pulling the sheet protectively to his chin. Only his eyes move to take note of my entrance. Mum sits at the foot of the bed, head lowered, one hand over her eyes.

'What's the matter?' I ask.

'This man,' says Mum. 'He won't get up.'

Dad's eyes flick from me to Mum, and then back to me

again, full of mute appeal, wondering which side I'm going to be on.

'What's the problem, Dad? Why don't you want to get up?'

'Why should I?' he says, anger rendering his speech clear. 'You've only just put me to bed, now you want to get me up in the middle of the night. I'm not having it.'

It's probably the longest comprehensible speech he's made in ten years and I almost feel like congratulating him, but then Mum sighs.

'Oh dear,' she says. 'Whatever did I do to deserve this? I do my best day in, day out. I don't never think of myself. And he never even so much as says, "I love you". But I've got used to that. I don't expect anything else now. I could put up with all that if only he wouldn't turn awkward.'

'Not awkward,' says Dad. 'Fed up with being pulled about.'

I sit down beside Mum, closer to Dad. I put my hand on his.

'Listen Dad, you're a bit confused.'

'Confused? Who is? Me?' He says it like it's the most extraordinary idea he's ever heard.

'Yes, it's not the middle of the night — '

'I've been telling the man that!'

'All right, all right, Mum. It's not the middle of the night, Dad, it's morning. Wait a minute and I'll show you.'

I go over to the window and open the wooden shutters. Bright sunlight cascades into the room, making Dad blink it's so strong.

'Morning?'

'Yes, morning. It's time to get up. That's all Mum was trying to do, get you up.'

'Talk about ungrateful! I don't know why I bother.'

Dad's claw emerges from under the sheet and begins to crawl along it, towards Mum's hand, the one that isn't over her eyes, which is resting on the bed. The claw reaches it and climbs on top of it. It moves backwards and forwards in a desultory stroking motion. Mum's huge body quivers from the centre upwards. Tiny whimpers escape it, as though somehow there's a small child hidden in there.

'I can't go on much longer,' she says. 'I've looked after him the best I can all these years, but I can't take much more of it.'

Laura goes to her and puts her arm around her. Mum buries her face in Laura's shoulder, sobbing.

'Well, Mum,' I begin, thinking I'll never have a better chance than this to break it to her, 'perhaps the time has come to think about letting someone else take the strain . . . '

Before I can say any more, Dad suddenly lets go of Mum's hand and throws back the sheet. He starts trying to lift his legs out of the bed, without success.

Laura helps Mum to her feet. 'Listen,' she says, 'why don't you go and make yourself a nice big breakfast, cheer yourself up? Nick and I will see to Dad.'

'But – ' I stammer.

'Not now,' Laura mouths silently at me. 'She's too upset.'

Mum shuffles out, sniffing, but brightening already at the prospect of food. Although Mum has been on duty twenty-four hours a day, seven days a week, fifty-two weeks a year for the best part of twenty years, she has continued during that time to put on weight. Food is a great comfort to her and helps her lurch from crisis to crisis. Once, when Dad was in hospital after breaking his pelvis, he was so ill when she visited him one afternoon, that she went home and phoned me up in hysterics. It took an hour of patient talking to quieten her. I called her back half-an-hour later to make sure she was OK.

'It's all right, I'm calmer now,' she said. 'I've put my potatoes on.'

* * *

To the sound of the frying pan sizzling away in the kitchen, Laura and I go through Dad's morning routine. It takes much longer than usual partly because I'm a poor substitute for Mum, and – efficient and well-practised though she is – Laura isn't able to be quite as rough with Dad as Mum is. Mainly, though, it's because Dad is so confused. He won't open his mouth for his teeth, but holds it tightly shut, the opposite order somehow being dispatched by his brain. He nearly falls over when Laura pulls his shorts up. He can't find the sleeves of his T-shirt.

We speculate over what's wrong. Could he have missed some of his medication yesterday? Hardly likely since Laura always makes herself responsible for administering his medicine on holiday, and she is Miss Efficiency itself when it comes to the taking of tablets, with the notable exception, of course, of her own. Perhaps it's all the excitement over meeting Anthony? Or the unaccustomed rich diet? Or all the booze he's been allowed? Or all the activity, after all he doesn't do much more than sit in a chair all day at home? Or is the heat too much for him? We run through every possibility, almost certainly prolonging the process of getting him ready since I have the feeling Dad is loving all the concern and behaving even more like a helpless child. We're no nearer to a solution by the time we have combed his hair, and put his glasses on. It's just in time. I hear the chink of Mum's knife and fork being laid down next door, accompanied by a sigh of satisfaction, swiftly followed by the swish of Mercedes wheels on the gravel in the square outside.

As soon as Anthony, preceded by his smile, walks in, I voice my doubts about the wisdom of taking Dad out today.

'Whatever you say, Nick,' says Anthony, 'although, actually, he looks all right to me.' He puts an arm round Dad.

'Hey, Dad, how are you? You are feeling OK, yes? Are you ready to come out with Anthony? You want me to show you a good time?'

Dad breaks into a broad grin and says, 'You betcha.' I feel a vein in the back of my neck start to thump.

Today, it turns out, we're going shopping. Mum, Laura and Anthony arranged this amongst themselves last night.

'You might have asked me,' I hiss at Laura, 'you know I hate shopping.'

Mum overhears. 'Well, we can't always do just what you want, Nicholas,' she says, playing back an old recording from my childhood. 'We're halfway through our holidays and we haven't bought no souvenirs yet. I can't go back without something for Pauline.'

'Anyway, it won't be all shopping,' says Laura. 'We're going to the beach too. It'll be nice for Dad, he'll be able to relax.'

I assume shopping means Valletta, but we head in the opposite direction – although, of course, this being Malta, that needn't mean anything. Eventually we arrive at a sign saying Ta' Qali Craft Village and Anthony turns into what seems to be a collection of Nissen huts. When I mention this, Anthony says '*Iva*, this used to be a British camp. Perhaps you recognise it, Dad, perhaps this where you stayed in the war, after you had your operation. Maybe if we look we will find where you wrote on the wall, *Jim loves Maria*, huh? Did you write that, Dad? Did you draw a little heart and write *Jim loves Maria*? Did you? Huh? Did you write that, Dad?'

Dad, of course, doesn't reply. Nobody else says anything. Then Anthony turns round and flashes his teeth and Laura and Mum laugh too.

The craft village proves to be the sort of tourist trap

Laura and I always avoid on holiday. Why, for instance, would we come all this way and buy knitwear from people who have never had to wear a sweater in their lives? But Mum, of course, loves it, so Laura pretends enthusiasm, seizing her arm and propelling her from one dubious attraction to another. In one hut we are treated to a display of traditional glass blowing: a man rolling a ball of molten glass on the end of a long metal pole until, magically, it transforms itself into an inelegant pink vase. After the display Mum buys a pair of bright purple antelopes for Pauline, who has her own menagerie of miniature glass animals. Anthony buys Mum the glass vase we saw being made and, for Dad, a glass paper-weight with the Maltese Cross engraved on it. In another hut Mum spends a long time looking at locally made silver jewellery, moving from display to display pointing things out to Laura.

Dad and I shuffle along behind. I take my hat off and fan him, as the heat inside the tin buildings reaches boiling point. Anthony has taken Laura's arm and steers her into a shop which sells Maltese lace. There's a delicacy about the shawls and tablecloths hanging up here that's lacking anywhere else in the place. The shopkeeper picks up a large white shawl and holds it up. The pattern is as fine as a spider's web, the workmanship as intricate. She hands it to Laura, who holds it in her hands, wonderingly, and says, 'I would like this.'

Anthony speaks to the stallholder in Malti and she says something back and then indicates Laura and smiles at Anthony, who shakes his head and points at me. The woman bursts into laughter and so does Anthony.

'Do you know what this is?' he says to Laura. 'Actually, it's a christening shawl, for a baby.'

'I know,' she says. 'That's why I want it.'

The woman takes the shawl from her, folds it with great deliberation and care, and wraps it in a sheet of white tissue paper as tenderly as if she were wrapping a baby itself. Laura reaches in her handbag, but Anthony puts his hand over hers, 'No please,' he says. 'A gift from me. I insist.' He pulls some banknotes from his pocket, which I presume are the ones I saw Ugo giving him last night. There's a discussion in Malti with the shopkeeper, the words traded back and forth across the package, and finally Anthony gives her some money. He takes the parcel and hands it to Laura.

'To my brother's wife,' he says. 'I hope you have a use for it soon.'

By now it's past noon and the heat is overpowering. Dad has turned a worrying beetroot colour, so I decide to take him to the café, where he can rest out of the sun while the others continue shopping.

I sit him down under a raffia shade and fetch us a bottle of Cisk each. I pour Dad's beer into a glass and hold it up to his lips so he can sip it. He lifts the claw to the bottom of the glass and pushes it higher, draining it all in one. I give him my beer as well and he drains that too.

'Ahh!' He wipes his lips with the back of the claw. 'Thirsty work.'

'What, shopping?'

'Yis. Shopping. Holidays.'

'Are you having a good time? Is Malta how you thought it would be?'

He doesn't answer.

'What do you think of Anthony?'

He lowers his glasses, and scans the café area, obviously looking for Anthony.

'I said, what do you think of your new son?'

He talks for five minutes without stopping. Every time I think he's finished and begin to say something, he starts off again, his voice animated, rising and falling with excitement. His eyes fix me with the wild look they have sometimes as he talks, as though to stress the importance of what he's saying.

Eventually his voice trails off. We sit in silence, listening to the cicadas rubbing their legs in the olive trees, no less incomprehensible to me than what he has been saying and I think he knows it. He busies himself by picking imaginary pieces of fluff from his T-shirt, while I watch the other tourists come and go until one of them turns into Anthony. He's come to collect us. Mum and Laura have just about finished their shopping and are going to meet us at the car.

We're driving along when Mum fishes in her bag and pulls out two little wads of tissue paper. She hands one to me. 'Here you are, Nick. This is from Dad. He treats both his sons the same.' She unwraps the other wad and reveals a tiny silver Maltese cross on the end of a silver chain. She unfastens it, leans forward, loops it around Anthony's neck and does the clasp up.

'Mum, what's the meaning of this?' he says. He takes one hand from the steering wheel and lifts up the cross to study it. 'You shouldn't do this. I do not wish you to spend your money on me.'

'It's from Dad,' she says. 'He wanted to buy you something.'

'I did?' says Dad.

'But you shouldn't spend your money.'

'We've got more than enough,' says Mum. 'What else have we got to spend it on? What can we do with money?'

'Ah, you never know,' says Anthony. 'You never know what you can buy.'

We drive along in silence for a minute or two. I slip my wad of tissue into my pocket, unopened.

Dad turns his head and shoots Mum a worried look. 'Wallet?'

* * *

204

After lunch we head for the beach, even though I've expressed doubts about the wisdom of exposing Dad to the sun.

'With his skin we ought to be careful.'

'Listen, Nicholas,' Anthony says. 'I know all about the sun on this island. I will look after him. I will be careful. However, I must say to you it is possible to be too careful so that, before you know it, your whole life is over. Live a little.'

'Anthony's right, we should live a little.' Mum throws her hands up in the air. 'I'm fed up with being careful. Sitting around being careful we won't enjoy what bit of life we have left to us.'

'That's right, Mum,' Anthony turns round to face her. There's the scream of a horn and he turns back just in time to swerve out of the path of a tour coach.

He laughs. 'Who wants to be careful?'

I look across at Laura, whose hair is blowing wildly in the slipstream. As she smiles at the back of Anthony's head, her tongue moves slowly over first her top and then her lower lip, moistening them in the dry heat.

We arrive at a big horseshoe-shaped bay and park on the road above the beach. Apart from the brightly coloured sun loungers and umbrellas, the beach itself reminds me of the East Coast resorts we went to when I was a little boy. There are stone steps leading down from the pavement and, halfway, a concrete building which turns out to be the public loos, exactly like in England. The beach itself is sandy and the sea is hundreds of yards away, like it used to be when I was a child when the tide was out. But of course, this being the Mediterranean, there's no tide, so the sea won't be coming any closer.

I help Dad down the steps, making sure his panama is firmly in place. The steps are steep and it takes a long time. When he gets to the bottom, Dad looks into the distance, in the direction of the sea.

'Hunstanton,' he says.

Anthony organises everything. He shouts at a small boy, who runs off and comes back dragging a pile of plastic sun loungers. The boy, who can't be more than eight or nine years old but has the business-like air of a middle-aged man, lifts them off one by one, arranges them in a line parallel to the edge of the distant sea, and then scampers off. He returns with three large parasols which he proceeds to erect between the loungers, first inserting half a plastic pole into the sand, then banging it in with a large mallet. He sticks the remainder of the pole, the bit with the umbrella attached, into the first section, looks up at the sun, and tilts the top. When he's finished all of the loungers are completely in the shade. Anthony hands him a note (so argued over last night, I think, so casually given away now!) which the boy tucks into a bumbag he wears on a belt round his shorts and walks off.

Anthony immediately undresses, pulling off first his polo shirt, to reveal a tanned chest with a thick matting of black hair. Laura can't seem to keep her eyes off it, probably because my own chest is white with only two single hairs, one on each nipple. He drops his slacks to reveal a pair of skimpy black swimming trunks of the sort Continentals always seem to go in for. I can't help noticing these are so well filled it looks as though he has a small animal down them. And I notice Laura noticing too. Her clothes are off in an instant and I catch Anthony appraising her small but perfect figure, the slim legs, the well-rounded but firm bottom, the solid breasts, all revealed in her high-cut, low-cut bikini. Mum has no swimming costume, probably being well beyond the upper size limit they're manufactured in, but does what she always does at the seaside and tucks her skirt into her knickers, revealing legs the texture of moon surface. I slip off my T-shirt and sandals, but keep my shorts on and plonk myself down on a lounger. I didn't want to come here in the first place.

Laura has the sun cream out and is carefully applying some to Dad's back when Anthony takes the tube from her.

'Please, permit me,' he says.

He squeezes a large globule on to Dad's back and begins rubbing it in with the fingertips of both hands, with great firmness, but with infinite tenderness too. He works his fingers upwards towards the shoulders and then kneads them back down to the waist. He lifts an arm, and slides his other hand down and around it and up again. He works his way around to the front and slides his hands across the chest. At times he presses so firmly that Laura is obliged to support Dad to stop him falling over. Anthony's not simply applying sun cream any more, this has turned into a massage and his face is a mask of concentration. Dad's paper thin skin seems to gradually absorb moisture, to lose its parchment quality and become supple and younger. And as Anthony works his shoulders again, their stiffness yields, they relax and drop. He no longer holds his arms stiffly, they swing loose by his sides. Dad's whole frame seems to unbend before our eyes. When he's finished, Anthony puts his hand behind Dad's neck, pulls his face against his own shoulder and holds him like that for a minute.

'I'm glad you came looking for your son,' he says. 'Even after so long a time.'

Then he slaps him on the back playfully as if to disperse any embarrassment, and releases him. He turns and smiles at Laura, who is staring at him, eyes shining.

'I've never seen anyone apply sun cream like that. It was like a massage.'

'Yes, well, actually, I was trained in massage. You would like . . . ?'

Laura lies on her front on a lounger, her arms dangling

either side. Anthony kneels beside her and begins to apply the cream to her shoulders.

'Wait a minute,' she says, and reaches up to release the clasp of her bikini top and push the straps out of the way. Anthony begins to massage. Laura turns her head away from me.

'Uuuh, that's won-der-ful.' Her voice approaches the orgasmic.

I lie back and close my eyes. I try to filter the sounds through my ears so I cannot hear Laura's sighs or the sound of Anthony's fingers slithering across her oiled skin. I listen instead to the babbling of children; an Italian pop song on a distant radio; the barking of a dog somewhere; and soon the gentle rise and fall of Dad's breath, the slight whistle on the outbreath my mantra, as he falls asleep beside me; and imagine some thirty years swept away and all my life before me, and eventually I too drift off to sleep, a five-year-old child.

When I wake up something feels different, perhaps the angle of the sun, or the number of people on the beach, but whatever it is, I can tell immediately it's some time later.

'Nick, Nick! Wake up! You're going all red.'

I open my eyes. Mum is sitting up on her lounger, looking at me with some concern. I must have been asleep for quite a while because the sun has moved round and evaded my parasol so that I'm completely exposed. My chest and arms feel hot, but still look white so I tell myself I can't be burned. I stand up and it's like treading on burning ash, the sand is so hot. I move like a firewalker around the lounger and adjust the angle of the parasol. I find my T-shirt and put it on. As I struggle to pull it over my sweaty body, it's like rubbing myself with a red-hot file.

Dad is still asleep, thankfully not in the sun. I look at

my watch. We've been here a couple of hours.

'Where are Anthony and Laura?' I ask Mum.

'Oh, they went for a swim,' she says. 'They've been gone ages.'

I decide to go and look for them. I put my sandals on and trudge off towards the sea. It seems even further away now than when we arrived, although I know this can't be true. There's an indefinable late afternoon feel to everything, with one or two families already packing their things away. I reach the shoreline and look out at the water. There are hundreds of bodies in it. Then I see them. Anthony has his back, his bronzed back, to me. He is holding Laura in his arms. She is squealing and he is laughing. He strides into the sea and drops her. There's a big splash and a lot of spluttering. Laura rises out of the water and shouts something at him I can't hear. She splashes water up at him and his head jerks back. He shouts something and she turns and runs further into the sea. He runs after her. He dives and begins swimming, a powerful crawl which I only have to compare to my feeble breaststroke to banish any lingering thought I have of taking my clothes off and joining them. I see the two of them bobbing up and down like a pair of randy porpoises. I strain my eyes to look, but in the end all I can see are their heads, so far out now they're just dots on the horizon, and then I can't see them at all.

'Hello, here we are again.'

I turn. Ferguson is standing beside me, wearing a pair of grey swimming shorts with a blue trim. Blue is beside him wearing blue shorts with a grey trim.

'Not swimming?'

'Er no, just watching my wife, and a, er, friend.'

'Oh, you mean Anthony. Incredible swimmer.'

'You've seen them, then?'

'Oh yes,' Ferguson gives me a cryptic look. 'Your wife introduced us. I had a race with him to that rock out there. Made me look stupid, he's so good. Nice bloke though. Very knowledgeable. We had a nice chat, just the two of us, sitting on that rock. Very interesting.'

'Oowww!'

It's bedtime and I'm lying on my back on the bed. I can't lie on my front because every bit of it, apart from where my shorts were, has been burned lobster-red by the sun. Laura is kneeling beside me, applying aftersun cream to my chest.

'Not so hard!' I say. 'You're doing that on purpose.'

'No, I'm not, I just didn't realise how sore it was.' She bends to kiss my lips.

'No, don't!' I scream. 'My face is sore too. If you have to kiss me, just blow one.'

She makes a little sucking sound into the air and carries on with the cream. When she's finished my chest, arms and stomach, she moves down to my legs. It's at this moment my penis reveals a hitherto unknown masochistic streak and begins to get interested. Laura somehow notices even though she's looking at my ankles.

'I see you're not *so* sore,' she says.

'Don't even think about it. There's no way I'm risking anything touching my skin.'

She indicates the white band where my shorts were. 'This bit isn't affected. That's the only bit that matters. I could go on top.'

'I'd love to, sweetheart, but I just couldn't risk it, you know with the vibrations and possible accidental friction. You might get carried away and forget. You could fall on me. It's just not on. I'm really sorry.'

'It's OK, I understand. It's nice to know you still want me. You haven't been very affectionate this holiday. I was getting worried.'

'Aaargh,' I whimper, to deflect the conversation from this dangerous line. 'Sorry, Laura. Can't really talk. It's burning like crazy. It's all I can think about.'

'Poor you, she says, moving her head down towards my pale erogenous zone. 'Let me see if I can take your mind off it.'

And she does, she really does.

Nine

Saturday

Bang! Bang! Bang!

I am running along the beach, my bare feet slapping the wet sand. Behind me, the slapping of someone else's feet syncopates with mine.

Bang! Bang! Bang!

I look over my shoulder. Anthony is chasing me, wearing only his skimpy black swimming trunks. The bulge in them is even more alarming than yesterday. He pauses, puts his hand down the front of them and, with a stage villain's smile, slowly draws out a pistol. He levels it at me. I stop running and turn to face him. I raise my hands, cowboy style.

'No, Anthony, no, don't shoot!' I say. He squeezes the trigger. I close my eyes.

Bang! Bang! Bang! Bang! Bang! Bang!

I open my eyes, and see the whitewashed walls of our bedroom in the bungalow. It was only a dream, after all.

Bang! Bang! Bang!

I shoot upright. I scream. It's as though someone has dragged a razor-sharp knife down my chest, but it's only the sheet sliding off me as I move. I remember my sunburn and put an exploratory fingertip on my chest. It's like dropping a hot coal on to it.

Laura's side of the bed is empty. I climb out slowly and pull on my dressing gown, making little moaning noises as I ease the sleeves over my sore arms. Somehow the noises seem to help.

The door of Mum and Dad's room is open, so I wander in. Mum and Laura are just finishing getting Dad up.

Bang! Bang! Bang!

'What's all the shooting for?' I ask.

'Germans,' says Dad. 'Let them come. We're ready.'

'Maybe it's somebody killing the rats,' says Laura.

'Rats?' says Mum, almost dropping Dad's upper dentures. 'What's this about rats? Where?'

'Cats, Mum, Laura said cats,' I say. 'She meant the strays on the wasteland.' If Mum finds out we're living next door to rats she won't stay in the bungalow a moment longer. I've no wish to move again, so I lift an eyebrow to Laura who says, 'Yes, I said cats. There are so many strays I thought perhaps they were trying to keep the numbers under control.'

'Would they do that?' says Mum. 'They seem such a nice sort of people.'

Bang! Bang! Bang!

I'm waking up now and suddenly I realise it's not gunfire at all. I look out of the window and sure enough there's a small white explosion that's almost lost in the blue morning sky.

'It's fireworks. Someone's letting off fireworks.'

'Of course,' says Laura. 'It's the *festa*!'

Anthony told us all about it yesterday. Today is the big celebration for the Feast of the Assumption, or Santa Marija as the locals call it. There will be fireworks, feasting, drinking, singing and dancing for the whole weekend. Tonight Anthony is taking us to a small town he knows where Santa Marija is the patron saint. The celebrations will go on till all hours, so he has suggested get plenty of rest today. Since he has business to attend to, he won't be picking us up until early evening.

I open the French doors and walk outside. Tiny white starbursts, almost invisible in the bright light, puncture the sky. I turn back to Laura.

'I don't understand these people, they're crazy. What's the point of letting off fireworks in broad daylight when you can't see them?'

'Maybe they're just jolly,' she says. 'Maybe they're exuberant and like to let go and listen to the bangs. Maybe that's why you can't understand them.'

I can't be bothered to argue and wander back to the bathroom to wash and apply calamine lotion to my burns.

According to Anthony, the *festa* is an occasion for the locals to dress up in all their best finery and Mum and Laura need no other encouragement to take out their holiday best and try on different outfits. Laura has the travel iron and is smoothing the creases from her cream linen suit. Mum spends an hour alternately holding up two purple cotton frocks, both hideous, trying to decide between them. They have already divided the day ahead into a series of long baths, hair washing and styling, nail-painting and make-up sessions. Dad sits in the shade on the patio, glad to be out of the hurly-burly. I decide to go into Valletta to buy the English papers and read them over a cup of coffee at Eddie's in Republic Square.

'You could take Dad with you, he might like that,' suggests Laura, when I tell her my plan.

Dad's head jerks round when he hears this. Our eyes meet and for a moment I wonder whether he can see my guilty thoughts, as I always imagined he could when I was a child, and then I comfort myself with the knowledge that he can probably hardly see me, let alone what I'm thinking.

214

*　*　*

I'm thinking about why I don't want to be alone with him. About the burden of conspiracy I have borne for over a week now, since the eve of our departure for Malta when I went to collect Mum and Dad from their flat. Pauline cornered me in the kitchen, while Mum was seeing to Dad in the lavatory, and dropped her bombshell.

'I had a long talk with Dr Large the other day. You know Mum had one of her turns last week?' she said, her face grim.

'Yes, she told me. But she said Dr Large had had a good look at her and said it was OK for her to go on holiday.'

'Oh yes,' said Pauline, fumbling for a cigarette, lighting it and then opening the window because Mum can't stand the smell of smoke. 'The holiday's no problem, she'll have you and Laura to help her, it'll be easier than being at home on her own. It's when they come back. She's not a well woman.'

'What do you mean?'

'Her angina's a lot worse. Dr Large says she can't go on like this much longer before she has another heart attack. He says she won't last more than a few months if she carries on the way she has been.'

She flapped her hand up and down, trying to waft smoke out of the window. A man passing in the street outside stopped to stare through the glass at her, looking confused, and I suddenly realised he thought she was waving at him. Pauline dropped her hand and we both watched the man as he turned and hurried away.

'The thing is', she said, leaning over, her back to me, and blowing smoke directly out of the window, 'I can't do any more for them. In fact, I won't be able to do as much. I've been offered a full-time job. It's not much, typing for a software firm. But my kids are nearly off my hands now and I want to work. God knows we need the money with the road haulage business the way it is.'

215

From next door came the sound of the toilet flushing.

'I wouldn't be able to take them shopping. I wouldn't be able to do so much washing or come here and clean as often.'

I felt a momentary surge of resentment at Pauline's selfishness which receded almost immediately when I thought of my own, of how little practical help, other than holidays, I'd been over the years, while Pauline had borne the brunt of not only the hard work, but having to support Mum through all her petty annoyances and black depressions too.

'So, what do we do?' I asked.

'Dr Large says Dad is deteriorating so fast that Mum won't be able to look after him much longer anyway. He thinks he should go into a home and the sooner the better.'

'A home?'

'What's the alternative? You tell me. If he doesn't, he'll be the death of Mum, and then he'll have to go in a home anyway. Only he won't have her to go and see him every day, the way she would. That will be a lot worse for him.'

'When you say soon, how soon do you mean?'

'Dr Large has spoken to Mrs Cooper. They have a vacancy coming up at The Willows. One of the old dears has had to go into hospital and won't be coming back, sadly. She's paid up until the end of the month. So that would mean Dad would move in a week after you get back from Malta.'

'But what about Mum? She'll never stand for it. You know that.'

'She'll have to be made to see it's the only way. You'll just have to talk her round to it.'

'Me? Why me?'

'Well, to be honest, I think I've done my fair share. It's the only thing I've ever asked you to do. Besides, you're her favourite, you always have been. She'll listen to you.

I thought you could break it to her on the holiday, give her chance to get used to the idea.'

Of course, I have not found the courage to do this yet. And so I cannot sit across a café table from Dad and make small talk all the while knowing I am a leading light in the conspiracy which will end with him captive and catheterised in The Willows.

'I don't think it would be a good idea to take him with me,' I say to Laura. 'Not after yesterday. I think he'd better have a good rest before tonight.'

Dad's still looking at me as I say this. When I finish speaking, he turns his head back to stare out at the little square.

Bowling along in the Seat with the windows wide open and the breeze on my face, I'm suddenly drunk on the freedom of being alone. No Mum to tiptoe warily around. No Dad with all his minor irritations, the speech, the walking, the eating, the dribbling, the crapping or not crapping. No Laura to resist.

In Eddie's I order a cappuccino and settle down with *The Times*. It's funny how disjointed the news all seems. You dip into a story that's been running for several days, you don't know the beginning and know that you won't be seeing tomorrow's paper with the continuation or the end. I find myself wondering how aliens will view us when they open one of those capsules we fire into space and read just one day's paper. Will they want to know the rest of the story? Or will that one snapshot be enough to tell them all they need to know about the human race? Perhaps because I'm out of touch with the news, I soon tire of the paper and lay it down. I sip my cappuccino and look idly around. And then I see them. On the other side of the square, sitting at a table belonging to the other café: Anthony, Ferguson, his friend, and their two wives.

Anthony has his back to me, but I can see from the way his hands flap up and down, landing on the table or on the arm of one of his interlocutors and then taking off again like the pigeons which plague the square, that he is deep in animated conversation. The Ferguson party are watching him too intently to be aware of my presence, but I decide not to take any chances and lift the paper to cover my face again, peeping around the side, my eyes disguised by my sunglasses, to watch them.

They stay like that for half an hour or so, then Anthony calls for and pays the bill and they all leave together, Anthony still talking animatedly, concentrating now on the two women. I watch them turn out of the square and pass out of sight.

The waiter comes and asks if I want more coffee, but I'm too disturbed by what I've seen to enjoy my repose with the papers any more. What can it mean? Why would Anthony be talking to Ferguson? Was their meeting accidental or could it have been pre-arranged? Ferguson had been talking to him when I saw him at the beach yesterday, so could this meeting have been set up then? But if so, why wouldn't Ferguson have mentioned it when he was telling me about meeting Anthony? Why did Anthony say he had business to attend to if he knew he was meeting Ferguson? If he had business with Ferguson, what could it be? But perhaps he just ran into them here. After all, it is really the only place to sit if you're in Valletta, say sightseeing like the Fergusons maybe, or on business like Anthony. On the drive home, I decide not to mention the incident to Laura or Mum. For some reason I can't quite explain, I don't want them asking Anthony about it.

Back at the bungalow Dad is asleep on the patio, head bent over. Inside the place smells of bath salts, nail varnish, shampoo and perfume. Mum and Laura are newly bathed, their skin soft and glowing, their hair freshly coifed. They walk around in their dressing gowns saying things like, 'Laura, do you think I should wear my white scarf round the neck of my dress?' and 'Mum, how do these earrings look with this necklace?' which seem designed to exclude me.

When they're finally ready, they wake Dad and take him off to shave him and wash him and dress him in a clean white shirt and cream trousers. I have only a quick wash as most of me is too sore to scrub and change into the only remotely smart clothes I have, a white shirt and stone chinos. Then there's time to open a Cisk and sit on the patio with the newspaper again. I'm halfway through my second Cisk when Anthony's Mercedes disturbs the gravel of the square. But to my surprise, instead of pulling up outside the bungalow, it continues on round and stops outside the Villa Francesca. The doors open and Ferguson, his friend and their wives pile out. There's a lot of laughing and waving goodbye to Anthony, but they're too far away for me to catch what anyone is saying. Finally, all the doors of the car are slammed shut, and Anthony cruises slowly round the square and pulls up beside our patio. He gets out of the car, whistling to himself and tossing his car keys up and down in one hand.

'Hello Nick, how are you? Did you have a good day?'

'Fine, thanks. I see you brought the Fergusons home.'

He brushes his hand through his hair.

'What? Oh, yes. I ran into them in Valletta. They had travelled there on the bus because Mr Ferguson does not like driving in Valletta, so, since I was coming here anyway, I offered them a lift home.'

'That was very kind of you.'

'Actually, not at all. As I said, I was coming here anyway.'

'So you brought them back from Valletta just now?'

'Yes, didn't I just tell you that? Why all the questions?'

'Oh, only that I was at Eddie's around lunchtime and I saw them there then with someone who looked like you.'

'Yes?'

'Perhaps it wasn't you?'

He considers this for a moment.

'No. It was me. I bumped into them there, as I've already explained to you. We chatted for a little while. They had some sightseeing to do, I had some business to take care of, so I arranged to meet them later to bring them here when I came. You see? It is all very simple.'

'So I see.'

Although Anthony is wearing his cream suit, a white shirt and a painted tie, an Aubrey Beardsley type picture of a woman with red hair in a long white gown, Laura her eau-de-Nil linen suit, Mum her best purple frock, Dad his lightweight jacket, and me my chinos instead of my shorts, at the *festa* we are starlings beside peacocks. The locals are in their finery. The men wear suits or smart trousers and their best anoraks, walking slightly stiffly and uncomfortably, still acclimatising to their unaccustomed garb. As one old man pushes by me, I catch the scent of mothballs. The women are in shining cotton dresses in bright reds and greens and yellows and blues, scarcely muted by their black lace shawls. They seem to be wearing all the jewellery they possess at once, one layer of necklace over another, with so many rings adorning their fingers that simply lifting them to wave at one another seems to challenge gravity. Even the children are scrubbed and dressed up, the little boys with their hair carefully brushed and plastered down with oil, the girls in party frocks with ribbons in their hair.

And the little village, too, is done up to the nines. Everywhere pennants wave a greeting in the evening breeze. Shopfronts are brash with bunting. Banners crisscross the narrow streets. The twin towers of the baroque church of St Mary are illuminated by floodlights. Naked white light bulbs are strung out between the trees in the square like strands of pearls.

Everything is movement. We're forced to park some distance away from the centre since, even with Anthony's alacrity with the horn, the streets became more and more impassable the nearer we get to the main square and the roads closest to it have been sealed off by the police anyway. As we walk towards the epicentre, we're absorbed into a milling throng of revellers. Whole families stroll along, waving and shouting to friends as they pass, sometimes stopping and disappearing through the doorway of an open house, only to reappear later, flushed with wine and good talk, carrying out with them more friends and relatives, swelling the tide of people to a flood. We find ourselves borne along with it, talking and laughing with these people we've never seen before, who are happy to have us at their *festa,* until finally the current comes up against another from the opposite direction and we arrive in the square, progress halted. Now, unable to press forward en masse, the crowd splits once more into its component families, who form little wayward eddies and whirlpools as they move about, seeking out still more friends.

'Talk about crowds!' says Mum, as we collect ourselves outside a small bar, where old men sit drinking beer, watching the hullabaloo with the air of those who've seen it all before.

'Wait until tomorrow,' says Anthony, 'that is when the party really starts. This is just the aperitif.'

He says something else, but it's lost as a rocket explodes into the soft dusk above us. It's followed by another and another and another. Soon the whole sky is full of arcing lines and falling stars, as though someone is playing snakes and ladders in the air. On a wall nearby a Catherine wheel bursts into life, its tail spinning sparks of colour in all directions. A squeal of teenage girls a few feet away scatters as a firecracker thrown by a youth detonates where they are standing, and then regroups on the same spot, giggling over this ancient and dangerous courtship ritual. It's impossible to hear anything as the sky explodes into a kaleidoscope of colour and noise, the patterns made by the fireworks always different but somehow always the same.

And then, when it seems our ears can take no more and will themselves explode, the sky begins to darken once again as the bursts of colour become more scattered and then sparse. The wall of sound slowly separates out into individual explosions, and in time these become more and more sporadic, until only one or two are heard and serve only to emphasise the growing silence. The sky is pitch black, and when it is split by a single rocket, we watch the light fade from it again, recognising it as a signal that the celebrations have entered a new phase. A hush descends on the square, the hubbub is quelled, shouts from one person to another are no longer simultaneous so that, did we but speak Malti, we would be able to make out every word. And then, nothing, except perhaps the hissing of thousands of anticipatory whispers.

Suddenly there is a long moan from what sounds like miles away, which swells until I realise it's not a human voice but a note played on a horn. Immediately the crowd bursts into clapping and cheering as the brass band comes towards us. The crowd parts and we are forced right back almost against the bar. The band, dressed in comic opera uniforms of blue and red with gold braiding and epaulettes, marches past, although marches is hardly the word. Not one of them seems to be in step with another, their lines are ragged, their ranks swaying from side to side in disorderly fashion, and I realise they are not simply ill-drilled but ill-disciplined by nature, congenitally unsuited to their task. They march exactly as they drive.

Behind the band comes a troop of small boys in blue shorts and white shirts, each row carrying a religious banner between them, their little faces aglow with pride. And, behind them, a priest in cassock and surplice, swinging a censer and leading a group of six men wearing white surplices over their black suits, who bear a litter on poles on their shoulders, three of them to each side. On the litter is a brightly painted, life-size statue of Santa Marija. Both it and the litter look solidly wooden, and the men are sweating freely. The litter has a leg at each corner, like a table, and Anthony tells us these men have carried the statue around the town, setting it down at each street corner so the inhabitants can come to their balconies and windows to look at it, to applaud and throw out confetti and streamers. The band peels off to one side of the square, where it continues to play solemn, almost mournful music. The statue is carried to the steps of the church, where the men stand and hold it while the band ceases playing and the priest delivers a blessing, calling out the words in a voice so flat he might be reading a bus timetable. It's this very flatness which I somehow find moving. All around the square people light candles. Next to me is an old woman, her face lit from below by the tiny flame which she shields from the slight breeze with one hand, the lines in her face so deep in the uplight they might have been scored by a knife. The priest finishes the blessing and to a huge cheer the statue is carried back into the church. The band strikes up again, but this time a jolly, dancing tune. The square clears and a few young men and girls begin dancing.

Anthony appears at my side bearing two glasses of white wine, one of which he hands to me. I see that Mum, Dad and Laura are already supplied. Anthony raises his own glass.

'May Santa Marija bless us all,' he says.

We drink our wine.

Anthony takes Mum's glass from her and hands it, and his own, to me. He takes her by the hand and leads her out into the square, where people are dancing in the pool of light from the bulbs strung between the trees. In the din it's impossible to hear what Mum is saying, but it's obvious she's protesting. Anthony calms her with a smile, and insinuates his right arm about her waist. With his left hand he takes her hand and, as the band suddenly slides into a waltz, he moves her off across the floor, like someone pushing out a boat. At first Mum almost staggers, but Anthony dances on his toes, his feet scarcely seeming to touch the ground, his body swaying as though moved by the lightest of breezes, and the impression of an elephant dancing with a mouse is soon lost as his delicacy and subtlety of movement transmit themselves to Mum. All at once they are dancing between the trees, at one with the music, with one another, with the evening. On and on they go, Anthony whirling Mum around as though she is no more than a young girl, out for her first dance.

When there's a break in the music, Anthony leads Mum back on his fingertips, as though the merest touch of these is all it takes to propel her. She arrives flushed and breathless, but smiling like a sixteen-year-old. Anthony releases her for a moment and brings more wine. We drink it eagerly, our throats dry from the smell of gunpowder. Then once again, Anthony dumps the glasses on me, but this time Dad's too. Taking Dad's claw in one hand and one of Mum's in the other, he leads them back to the dance area. There he places their hands together and positions them for dancing, while the band pauses between numbers to shake spittle from their instruments and discuss the next tune. As the music starts up again, Anthony removes his hands from my parents and, as if touched by magic, they begin to dance. There's a momentary altercation while Mum rearranges their hands, so that her arm is now around Dad's waist and his on her shoulder. With her leading now, they move off, Dad shuffling slowly, Mum already lost in the rhythm of the night, steering him along. Of course, Dad cannot easily go backwards, nor from side to side, so Mum moves always in reverse, backing across the whole of the dance area, occasionally bumping another couple out of the way, like an unruly fairground dodgem, although soon the other dancers learn to watch out for her and take evasive action. When she reaches the wall dividing the centre of the square from the road around it and can go no further, she shuffles Dad around, an inch or two at a time, until their original positions are reversed, and dances him back the way they have come.

Anthony returns to us and we all drink more wine as we watch Mum and Dad dancing, on and on, one dance after another, back and forth across the square.

'Anthony, you're full of surprises,' says Laura, 'Where did you learn to dance like that?'

He sips his wine, letting it linger on his lips before replying. 'From one of the nuns who looked after me after my mother was killed. This sister had been a dancer and she still loved to dance.' He reaches a hand up to comb his hair, but sees me watching and lowers it again. 'She had these old records. Fred Astaire, Bing Crosby. She would put one on the old gramophone in the schoolroom and show me the steps. She had natural grace. If she just walked across a room, it was dancing. She loved to dance.'

'Nick won't ever dance with me. He won't even get up and shake around to pop records.'

'Is this true?' Anthony looks at me as though Laura has just told him I won't fuck her, his dark brows raised in amazement.

'It's just not my cup of tea. I look pretty stupid dancing

225

and I'd rather not make a fool of myself. Besides, I can't at the moment. The sunburn.'

'In that case,' he takes hold of Laura's hand by the fingertips, 'you don't mind?'

I know I must seem selfish and petty, but I can't seem to help myself. 'No, go ahead,' I say, taking another swig of wine. 'Anything to keep her happy.'

Laura either doesn't notice my sarcasm or chooses to ignore it and flounces off with him. I watch Anthony confer his gift upon Laura too, so that her normally jerky little movements are somehow ironed out and made smooth and graceful. With a lighter partner, Anthony is able to move faster than he did with Mum and the two of them glide over the asphalt square, Laura leaning back, eyes closed in some kind of ecstasy, almost swept off her feet. When everyone returns hot and sweaty, we have more white wine to cool down, and Anthony goes off in search of food, since the dancing has given Mum an appetite. He returns with *mqarets,* hot, sweet fritters, stuffed with dates, and *qubbajt,* locally made nougat. Munching on these we make our way back through the crowded streets, stopping sometimes when Anthony meets a group of friends, to listen to some villagers singing songs, or pausing at a bar for more wine, so that it takes another couple of hours for us to reach the car and ages more for Anthony to extract it from the logjam of parked vehicles.

Finally we're on our way.

'What a wonderful evening,' says Mum and hums the tune of 'I Could Have Danced All Night'.

'It was great fun,' Laura says. She leans forward and gives Anthony a peck on the cheek. 'Thank you, Anthony.'

'Wonderful,' says Mum, 'wasn't it, Jim?'

Dad grunts a reply, mouth too occupied, or teeth too glued by nougat, to make himself understood, but it doesn't matter since none of us will ever forget the spectacle of what I, at least, know to be his last waltz.

Later, in bed, I ask Laura, 'What's all this about his mother being killed?'

'Weren't you listening the other night in the restaurant when he was talking about the bomb?'

'I thought he was going on about the bomb in the *koppla*.'

'No, it was the bomb that blew the house up. He was only thirteen at the time. He was playing down the street when it happened. He was the first one there.'

I suddenly realise this is what Mrs Haines meant when she said 'tragic'.

'He was the one who found the body?'

'He was the one who didn't find the body. There wasn't any body to find. She was blown to pieces.'

I think about this for a moment or two.

'Listen, Nick, I know you don't like him, but he's had a very difficult life, and he's done well for himself – '

'Humpf!'

'He's done well just to come through, he's a survivor.'

'If you say so.'

'Oh, Nick, are you annoyed because I danced with him tonight? I'd much rather have danced with you.' She reaches out to touch me, but I intercept her hand. I smile at her.

'Sorry. It's the sunburn. I'd love to, but I'm still too sore. Perhaps it will be better tomorrow.'

'That's a shame, I was feeling quite romantic,' she says.

'Well,' I say, lifting the sheet, 'we could always do what we did last night.'

227

Ten

Sunday

This morning, I'm worried about Dad. He just isn't well.
It seems crazy to say that because of course he isn't
well. How could you possibly call a man who cannot
walk or talk, who dribbles, snorts and snuffles, is blind,
covered in eczema, dandruff-dusted, has one hand frozen
into a claw, cannot pee when he wants to, is constipated
and so confused he doesn't know what day or perhaps
even what decade he is in, well? And yet there is a kind
of level of illness in Dad to which we've all grown accus-
tomed, which changes so imperceptibly from day to day
we hardly notice the huge deterioration each year brings,
except on those days which are markers in the calendar,
like Christmas, or his birthday, when, each year, we look
back and remember the things he could do a year ago that
he can't do now. But today he's quite clearly not so well
as he was nine days ago when we were on the plane.
There's no question now of him laughing at pissing all
over the aircraft toilet. Even the word turd would not
raise a smile. His teeth have fallen silent. At breakfast he
sits toying with his All-Bran, stirring the spoon round
and round the bowl, watching it intently, as though he
wonders what it is. Even though it's early, the fireworks

are already going. Every time there's another detonation, Dad's shoulders wince, as if he expects at any moment to be blown to bits, the way his erstwhile lover was so long ago. After a fusillade of reports, he looks up from his bowl and says, 'Ack-ack.'

I try to talk to him, and explain patiently that it's simply fireworks and not bombs, but he shakes his head and says, 'Fireworks? Where would they get fireworks? Don't they know there's a war on?'

Mum sits with her head down, one hand over her eyes. She hasn't said anything, but she's already put away two cooked breakfasts. From time to time she sniffs, or wipes away a tear.

'Oh dear, that man!' she says at last, when it's finally necessary to take out her hankie and blow her nose.

I sit down at the table and help myself to some corn-flakes. Laura walks over to Mum and puts an arm around her shoulders.

'Don't worry, it's probably just the heat and being in a different place.'

'*Do it now!*' she mimes to me over Mum's head.

A sob escapes Mum, but it's muffled as though it's had to fight its way out. 'No, it's not that. It might have hurried things up, but he's breaking up, I know he is. He's getting worse all the time. He's getting worse *faster* than he used to.'

'I don't know about that,' says Laura, 'but it's definitely progressing.'

'*Come on!*' she mouths at me.

Mum suddenly lets go and tears roll down her cheeks. You can almost hear them drip on to the stone floor in between the sound of her sobs.

'I can't take much more of it. I've stood it for twenty years. I wish he'd just die in his sleep and get it over with. I can't take no more.'

Dad stirs his All-Bran faster.

'I can't stand to watch him go no further down, I really can't. Look at him! Look at that neck!'

She's on her feet so quickly, her chair overturns. She rushes round the table to Dad and grabs his head. 'Get it up, bugger you. GET IT UP!' She releases her hold and his head almost falls to the table. All at once she's slapping him about the temples with both her hands, like a toddler in a tantrum. Dad lifts his claw in an attempt to ward off the blows.

For a moment I'm too shocked to move. Then I get up, go over to her, and grab her wrists, holding them tight, trying to still the movement. I'm amazed by the strength in her arms. It's like wrestling a powerful man. Her face turns bright red. Her lips are almost blue. I think of what Pauline told me. Her heart may be ready to explode. I want to let go in case the struggling brings on a seizure, but I dare not for fear of what she may do to Dad.

'Calm down! Calm down!' I say, at the same time all too aware of the panic in my voice that makes it anything but calming. At last, though, the flailing of the arms subsides and they go limp in my hands, like a rag doll's.

Laura cradles Dad's head in her arms, stroking it and saying, 'It's all right, Dad, it's all right. Mum's just a bit upset. She doesn't mean it.'

'That's all you know,' snaps Mum, shaking off my hands and stepping back to get the rest of us in perspective. 'It's not the first time I've hit him. Sometimes I could kill him, especially when he lets that bloody neck go like that. I know you'll think I'm terrible, but sometimes he gets me that frustrated hitting him's the only thing makes me feel better. I know I shouldn't, I know it's not his fault, but I just can't help myself.'

Laura lets go of Dad, who lifts his claw up to his head and scratches at it weakly in a pathetic parody of someone rubbing a bruise. She hugs Mum and strokes her hair. I'm grateful to Laura for this because, although I want to,

I cannot get up and walk around the table and do this. It's as though, like Dad, my legs won't obey the signal my brain is sending them. I spoon cornflakes into my mouth like there's no tomorrow, one spoonful following another before I've had time to swallow it.

'It's not all been bad,' says Laura. 'You have to cling to the good times, like last night. You were so happy then, dancing together. You can still have moments like that.'

'Moments! Moments! Who wants to live their life for moments? Not that there are many any more. I might as well be looking after a lump of wood, it would have more feeling for me.'

Dad lifts a spoonful of soggy cereal towards his mouth. As he tries to turn the bowl of the spoon inwards to his lips, it tilts and a blob of All-Bran falls into his lap.

Her anger, and the energy it gave her, gone, Mum subsides on to a chair. She puts her head in her hands, shaking it to and fro.

'It's no good, I done my best. I just can't go on no more.'

'*Now!*' mouths Laura.

'I think you're right,' I say. 'You can't go on, Mum. The time's come when it's too much for you. We need to think of something else.'

'Easy to say,' she grunts. 'What else is there?'

'Well, Dr Large thinks Dad needs professional nursing care.'

'How do you know what Dr Large thinks? Have you been talking to him behind my back?'

'No, he spoke to Pauline.'

'Pauline! Oh, so you and her have been discussing me, have you? Talk about deceit!'

'Don't be silly, nobody wanted to deceive you. We just didn't know how to tell you.'

'Didn't know how to tell me, my arse! Am I such a monster that my own children can't be straight with me?' The way she looks at me, I'm half-scared she's going to jump out of the chair and sting my legs with the flat of her hand, the way she used to when I was a kid.

'No.' My own temper is starting to rise. 'We just thought you'd react the way you are now.'

'Don't get cross, Mum,' says Laura, sitting herself down beside Mum and taking her hand between her own and stroking it as if it's a kitten. 'Arguing amongst ourselves won't help. We've got to do what's best for you and Dad.'

Mum pulls her hand away, shaking off Laura's caresses as if she's suddenly seen a tarantula crawling there. 'I'm not arguing with you. You're nothing to do with me. You're not even a relative, so mind your own business.'

Laura pulls a face at me, gets up and walks to the back of the room. She stands, arms folded, looking out of the window at the waste ground.

'So,' says Mum, fixing her stare on me, 'what have you and Pauline worked out between you, then? Perhaps you'd be kind enough to let me know.'

'We haven't worked out anything. It's just that Dr Large thinks Dad's condition has deteriorated – '

'What would Dr Large know about it? Your Dad wasn't at all well the day he come to see him in the hospital. He had bronchitis and the antibiotics were making him sleepy. He weren't himself. Dr Large didn't get a true picture.'

'But Mum, you just said yourself, Dad's got much worse. Anyone can see it.'

We both turn and look at Dad, who has been sitting staring at us throughout all this. His lips part in a small smile of embarrassment.

'So what are you saying then? What's the magic answer?'

'There's a place coming up at The Willows.'

'I knew it!'

'They have nurses there who are used to dealing with people like Dad.'

'He'd be miserable there.'

'He'd have company. It might do him good, seeing a few more people, instead of being stuck in your flat all the time.'

'He'd be stuck in a room all day, on his own. In the flat he's got me.' She pulls herself slowly out of her chair, and walks over to Dad. She puts an arm gently around his neck, a relaxed version of the grip she had on him a few minutes ago. 'I'm all the company you need, aren't I, darling?'

'Yis.'

'Mum, you can't go on for ever.'

'I shall go on as long as I can.'

'But he's not going to get better. He's going to get worse. Don't you want Dad to have the best care? They have lots of staff. They can look after him better.'

'Do you really think that? You must be mad. Didn't you see them young girls running up and down in that place, trying to answer them bells? Didn't you see them poor old people left on their own in their rooms or just dozing about half-dead in that day room – '

'Lounge.'

'Call it what you bloody well like, it's not what I call home. Your Dad will go in that place, or any place like it, over my dead body.'

There's nothing for it. I have to say it. 'That's what's going to happen. You know that, after that last turn you had. Dr Large told Pauline what he told you – if you don't ease up you're going to kill yourself.'

'That's my business. And Dr Large should know better than to discuss it with Pauline. I thought doctors were supposed to be confidential. I'll keep going while I can.'

'There's not just you to consider, Mum. There's Dad too. What's going to happen to him if you drop dead? He'll end up in a home anyway, only without you. Think about him.'

233

She tugs his head closer to her, a bit sharply, so he lets out a little yelp of pain. 'I am thinking about him. He's all I've thought about every moment of every day for the last seventeen years. I've promised him I'll never put him in one of those places. He'd hate it in there. They'd make him wear a catheter. You don't want to wear a catheter in your willy, do you, Jim?'

The teeth flap. 'No thanks.'

'See, I told you. I know what your Dad wants. So you and Pauline and Dr Large can just stop talking about him behind our backs and keep your opinions to yourself. When I want to know what you lot think, I'll ask you. Come on, Jim.'

She puts her hands under his arms and tries to pull him up. Dad presses his hands on the table in an effort to lift himself. I go over to help him up, but Mum shrugs my hands roughly off him. Eventually Dad makes it to his feet and Mum leads him out of the room towards their bedroom.

'Come on, my old darling,' she says. 'Don't you worry. I won't never let you down.'

Mum and Dad don't re-emerge until lunchtime. She makes him cheese sandwiches and herself a huge salad. I open a bottle of wine and join them on the patio. We chat politely, pretending nothing has happened. When I try to raise the subject of the future again, Mum holds up her hand.

'Nicholas, dear, I know you mean well, but you're too young to teach your mother to eat eggs. Now, let's get on with having a nice holiday and forget all about it.'

Throughout the afternoon there's a formal politeness between Mum and Laura, after the harsh words which were said this morning. Dad dozes on the patio, and is still worryingly confused whenever he wakes. Mum is over-solicitous to him, demonstrating how well she can manage, translating his incoherent mutterings into the other half of a conversation she has with herself.

When Anthony arrives, I walk out to the Mercedes and lean over the door.

'I don't think we should take Dad out tonight. He doesn't even know what year it is. I think he's too ill.'

'But of course, Nick, if this is what you think. However, let me talk to him.'

As soon as Anthony speaks to Dad, he opens his eyes and smiles. A fusillade of fireworks goes off and he doesn't flinch. Anthony puts a hand on his shoulder. Dad looks bright-eyed now, and I see he's rallied, the way he sometimes can after a good sleep.

'What's this they're telling me?' says Anthony. 'You're not well?'

'Fighting fit,' says Dad, followed by a long ramble in which the only distinct word is 'appendix'.

'You see, Anthony, this is how he is. He still thinks it's the war.'

Anthony straightens up and looks at me with great patience and sympathy. Behind him Laura steps out on to the patio.

'Nick, Nick.' Anthony says, 'Forgive me for being, how shall I put it, blunt. But actually it is necessary. You are not here for long and for that reason I will say something which perhaps will sound impertinent from someone who scarcely knows you. You are so terribly, terribly British. So conventional. I don't mean just your job or your clothes, but your thoughts. What does it matter if your father imagines himself in another time and place? Perhaps he was happier then. And as long as it makes him happy now, why not let him believe what he likes?'

'Yes, but if he gets confused he may become distressed . . . '

'And on the other hand he may dance a waltz or two. It is surely worth the risk.'

* * *

And so Anthony drives us to the restaurant he took us to before because the village it's situated in also has Santa Marija as its patron and is bigger and has a more spectacular *festa*. 'I have a surprise for you,' he says. 'I think you will like it, Mum.'

Ugo greets us as fawningly as before, no doubt looking forward to more of my money, and shows us out into the garden, where he indicates the table where we sat last time, and where a woman in a white dress is already sitting.

Anthony strides over to her, lifts the fingertips of one of her hands to raise her from her seat and says, 'Here, this is my surprise. This is Angela.'

'Hello, Angela,' says Mum. Dad grins so widely his top dentures almost fall out. Suddenly, I can see what his skull will look like.

Mum turns to Anthony. 'Pretty, isn't she?'

And at first glance she is. Her deep tan contrasts with the white dress, and Laura is already looking ruefully at where her own white skin has been turned a glaring red in the sun. Angela's dress is startlingly short, exposing legs whose length will probably provoke even more envy in Laura than their deep brown colour. Her black hair has blonde highlights, and she wears a pair of black sunglasses pushed casually up over it. In keeping with the *festa,* she has surfeited on jewellery, with rings on all her fingers, a large and showy necklace and big, dangly earrings that remind me of the censer the priest was swinging last night. Her eyes are black and seem to have a superior smile in them, mocking something hidden from us. Her lips are red and full, not unlike Anthony's and I imagine the two of them being able to kiss quite passionately without any other parts of their anatomies touching. But when we've finished the introductions, the shaking hands and smiling, and sit down, I realise Angela is one of those people who is not so pretty as she thinks she is, the kind who take you in in the beginning because of their own blind confidence. For one thing, she may be dressed like a twenty-year-old, but closer inspection proves her to be in her early thirties, at least. And while her lips are large, her mouth is somehow small, it can't seem to open very wide, which gives her smile a somewhat pinched and ungenerous effect, as though she doesn't really mean it.

She pats the seat beside her and says something in Malti to Anthony. He smiles and nods, and then helps Dad and Mum to the seats opposite him and Angela. Laura and I sit at the ends of the table, me between Anthony and Mum, Laura between Angela and Dad.

With Ugo hovering, we're all too busy deciding what to have to become further acquainted with Angela, although by the time we've ordered our food I already feel I know her quite well. I suggest the soup for Dad. It's the only thing he can feed himself, and it will free Mum, who I worry might be tired from being extra attentive to him all day after the scene at breakfast, from peeling prawns, or worse. Anthony agrees and proposes we all have the *minestra* again, since it's a traditional Maltese dish, and this is a special Maltese evening.

'If you don't mind,' says Laura, 'I'll have the melon.'

'Oh, melon, it's so boring,' says Anthony. 'Have the soup, or some prawns in garlic butter.'

'No really, I prefer the melon. I'd like something cool.'

'She's watching her figure, I reckon,' says Mum, beaming confidentially at Angela.

'Ah, really?' says Angela. 'Fortunately that is something I don't have to do. I leave that to the men.'

'I must say, it's something I've never had to worry about,' says Mum. She pats the mound of her stomach. 'Although I may have put on a pound or two, these last few years.'

237

Angela stares at Mum, wondering, for a moment, if this is a joke. Finally, detecting no sign of a smile, she raises an eyebrow, then picks up her blue check napkin, opens it out with a vigorous shake and spreads it on her lap, her attention now diverted to Dad, who is trying to tuck his napkin into his collar, with Laura's help.

Anthony suggests another traditional dish, fish pie, for the main course. As everyone concurs, he turns to Laura and puts a hand on hers.

'But of course, if you wish, Laura, you can have something else. They will do a very nice salad for you here.'

'No, the fish pie will be fine,' says Laura, slapping her menu down on the table. 'And I'd like some chips too. I'm not worried about my figure, Anthony.'

'Good for you, Laura,' says Angela, pronouncing the first syllable of Laura to rhyme with 'cow.' 'After all, you are on holiday. You can go on a diet when you get home.'

A bit of a silence hangs over the table after this, and we're all relieved when the soup arrives and supplies us with the practical components to begin to construct a conversation, such as 'Pass the bread, please' and 'Mmm, delicious.'

Angela watches Dad as he spoons the soup into his mouth, and says, 'Marvellous how he can feed himself. And he don't spill too much either.'

This last is a reference to Dad dribbling soup from the edge of his spoon and on to the blue and white check tablecloth, where he watches as it spreads into a stain with an uncanny resemblance to the map of Europe. He puts his spoon down and begins rubbing at the edge of the stain, as though trying to erase Portugal.

Mum snatches hold of his hand.

'Stop that, Jim, and eat your soup. And get that neck up. You wouldn't spill things if you would just get it up.' She manhandles his neck into a more upright position and holds it there while Dad manages a couple more spoonfuls of soup without spilling enough to make even a map of Gozo, let alone a continent.

She lets his neck go. 'See?'

As though it's made of plasticine, his neck gradually declines to its former position.

I decide that Angela has not known Anthony that long, or at least not romantically, because throughout the meal she seems to be struggling to keep her hands off him, in contrast to Laura and me, who have known one another long enough to be quite happy to sit at opposite ends of the table. When Anthony reaches for the bread, Angela's hand follows his to the basket like a lovesick schoolgirl trailing around after her first boyfriend and contrives to bump into it as it picks up a piece of bread, lingering a little too long for the meeting to be accidental. When Anthony says something amusing, she leans her head towards him and lets it rest on his shoulder for the briefest of moments, like a butterfly on a flower, each touch a little fix to keep her going until all these tedious English people have gone and she can tear his clothes off.

And as the dusk closes in and we're united in the intimacy of the circle thrown out by the candles in their little glass jars on the table, it's as well that there is this constant banter between them – the little kisses and endearments, the soft thud of a shoe slipping to the floor and a foot being rubbed against a trouser leg. It covers the awkward moments in the conversation.

During the fish pie Mum asks Angela what she does for a living.

'I am in property,' she replies. 'I sell apartments. For holidays. You know this island has some wonderful apartments, at prices which English people find astonishingly low. For a very reasonable outlay you can have somewhere to return to year after year, whenever you like, or if that is too expensive, for one or two weeks every year, it is – '

'Angela,' Anthony puts his hand around her neck and pulls her head towards him, ruffling her hair, 'don't go into your hard sell. This is *festa* night and these are my relatives. Besides, Nick here is an estate agent too. He doesn't want to talk about work on his vacation.'

'Ah yes, you sell property, too?' she says.

'Yes, for my sins.'

'Now, now, Nick, it's no use moaning about it,' Mum butts in. 'You had your chance. You went to the university, you should have stuck at it instead of leaving before you'd finished.'

Dad spits out a few words, which I interpret as, 'Stick at it, he never stuck at anything.' But Laura responds to him by saying, 'Is it, Dad? Well, let me feed you with your spoon.'

'Which university?' asks Anthony.

'London,' I reply.

He whistles. 'That is an opportunity I would have liked. To go to university, and to London as well . . . ' He manages somehow to convey a shrug with the movement of an eyebrow, and then returns to his fish pie.

When the pie is done, we order another of Ugo's special ice creams for Dad and the rest of us sit drinking coffee, Anthony and Angela smoking Marlboros, while Laura feeds Dad.

The embarrassed silence is gone now and everyone listens as Angela talks. She is giving her opinions on the various nationalities who visit the island: English, too quiet and boring; Scandinavians, too obsessed with sex so that an attractive girl really has to watch herself amongst them; the Dutch, too drunk; the Germans, too ignorant to apologise for what they did . . . I switch off and turn to look at Dad enjoying his ice cream. Laura is holding out the spoon to him, but she's listening intently to Angela and does it automatically, without looking at him. It doesn't matter, for Dad is no longer interested in his dessert. Instead, he's staring up at the metal poles supporting the vines above our heads, that hunted look in his eyes again. I follow his gaze and see a vine leaf twitching back and forth, before it is flung aside and something scuttles along the pole. A bird, I think. I'm about to point it out to the others, when there's another rustling of the leaves and from behind them appears a pink, twitching nose and a set of whiskers, pausing to sniff the air, before the rest of the creature emerges and scampers the length of the pole. Quickly I glance at the others. If Mum finds out she could be dive-bombed by a rat at any moment, she will go hysterical. Fortunately, they are all still listening to Angela and don't even notice when another rat runs along the pole, its feet pinging on the aluminium. It sounds to me like someone playing the kettledrums.

I look again at Dad, who is shaking now. I hiss at Laura. Mum looks at me.

'What, dear?'

'Nothing, I just thought of something I wanted to tell Laura.' Mum goes back to listening to Angela. Laura is now looking at me.

'Laura,' I say, 'remember the scene in *Hamlet* when he kills Polonius? Remember what he says?' We've seen the play together recently.

'What?'

I repeat it and, before she can say anything, roll my eyes upwards. Laura glances up in time to see a long tail flipping from side to side of the pole as its owner scurries along.

Dad is still looking up. I push my chair back and stand. Mum looks at me again.

'Just going to relieve Laura and give Dad the rest of his ice cream, seeing as she's helped him all through the meal.'

'I can do that.'

'No, it's all right, Mum, you listen to Angela. It's very interesting what she's telling us.'

Laura and I swap places. I put my hand on Dad's.

'It's OK, Dad.'

'Rats,' he says.

'What's that you're saying, Dad?' says Anthony, from across the table.

'Rats,' says Dad, but so indistinctly that I only know it's that because I know it's that.

'He's just saying how nice his ice cream thing is,' says Mum. She pats him on the knee. 'You like your ice cream thing, don't you, lovey?'

Dad doesn't answer, just turns to appeal to me, as the others resume their conversation, Laura now plying Angela with questions to keep them all diverted.

'Dad,' I whisper, 'it's all right. There's nothing there.'

'Rats. Lots of the buggers.'

'No, Dad, really there's nothing there. Eat your ice cream.'

'Nothing there?' His eyes scan my face. I wonder if he can see I'm lying through the pinhole. I remember a time when I always thought he'd know if I told a lie, like God or Jesus.

'No, nothing there. It was just the leaves rustling.'

'But . . . saw them . . . saw rats . . . ' His lower lip begins to tremble and his eyes mist with tears. 'Look so real. Look so real.'

Too late I realise I've made the wrong decision. That Mum getting upset and breaking up the meal wouldn't have mattered. That this is far worse. Dad puts his head in his hands and begins to cry, the tears that drip down on to the ice cream so hot steam seems to rise from it. Angela stops talking. Everyone is looking at Dad.

'Jim, whatever's up?' Mum grabs his hands, trying to unmask him, but they resist, glued in place by his fear.

Suddenly he puts his hands on the table, and presses down on them, trying to push himself up, making a superhuman effort, at least for a man with Parkinson's. Face purple, breath rasping through his old lungs, he actually manages it, lifting himself so that his chair tips backwards and I have to catch him because his thighs are too far under the table to allow him to straighten them and stand up. The knuckles on his good hand are white as it grips the edge of the table. He's making a soft bleating sound.

I pull him back a bit and steady him, so he's standing. He jerks his hands and sends the dessert glass skittering across the table and off the other side, where it shatters on the paving stones with an explosion that eclipses the noise of the fireworks that are starting to go off all around. Waiters come running. Everyone is shouting. I hear Angela's voice saying, 'Does he have some kind of fit?' Dad stares up at the vines above us, from which the rats have long since fled, scared off by the commotion. He opens his mouth and lets out a long banshee wail, as though someone has just died. He balls his good hand into a fist and presses it and the claw up to his temples.

'Oh God,' he screams, 'please, don't make me mad. Let me die, but don't make me mad.'

I pay the bill quickly and we hurry Dad outside, Laura and I taking him between us. Because of the meal we're later than last night and the *festa* is already in full swing, the narrow streets pulsating with people dancing to an amplified band. We're forced into single file, which means I have to walk backwards to lead Dad and use one of my few Malti words, *skuzzi*, every time I bump into someone. It takes several minutes and what seems like a thousand *skuzzis* to reach the car. But when we finally get there, Anthony claps his hand to his forehead in one of those melodramatic gestures Continentals – and Mum, of course – go in for and spits out something in Malti which can only be obscenities. I push through the crowd to him and see the problem. When we arrived, Anthony parked with his rear bumper against a wall. Since then someone else has parked in front of him, with their bumper touching the front bumper of the Mercedes so there is no possibility of moving it, short of an airlift by helicopter, until the other driver returns.

Anthony beats his fist on the other car and lets fly with a few more oaths. I put my hand on his shoulder, my delight at his discomposure for a moment outweighing my concern for Dad.

'Hey, Anthony, don't get so upset. It's just thoughtlessness, it's nothing personal.'

He glares at me. 'I hope you are right.'

By now the fireworks are deafening and we have to shout at one another above the reports. Dad winces at every minor explosion and ducks at all the larger ones, so his upper body is in constant motion, like a boxer sparring. Laura is stroking his arm, trying to calm him. Angela is still tugging Mum towards us, rather bravely I can't help thinking, since Mum's bulk means she is not an easy vessel to steer through the heaving crowd.

'What now?' I ask Anthony. 'We've got to get Dad out of here, and home. I'm worried he's having some sort of breakdown. He could have a stroke.'

'Yes, yes, I understand the urgency of the situation,' says Anthony, 'but the car is out of the question. We will have to find a taxi.'

'All right, can we wait in the car, while you go and get one?'

'Is no use staying here, they will not want to bring a taxi in here now, too many people. I did not expect to leave this early, so I didn't worry about the crowds when I parked here. We will have to go to the end of this street and cross the square to find a taxi. I am afraid it is the only way.'

The first part isn't too difficult. We simply follow the direction of the crowd, and let ourselves slip into it, like logs sliding into a river, so that we're swept along. Anthony leads the way with me and Dad behind him. I grip Dad's hand, trying to hold him back to prevent him stumbling forwards under the pressure of the people behind him. Behind me comes Angela, who seems to be complaining all the time, but about what I can't hear over the noise, and behind her are Mum and Laura. Like a fast-moving flood encountering a boulder in a river bed, the crowd responds to Mum's size when it reaches us and moves on around us.

So, although it's uncomfortable, although Dad is shouting wildly, Angela is complaining and Mum is screaming, it's all right until we reach the point where the road meets one corner of the village square. It's now the real problems begin. We have to make our way diagonally across the square, across the general forward flow of the crowd. Anthony makes a cutting motion with his hand to indicate the direction we're heading in and our little phalanx sets off. We're immediately buffeted from the side as we try to cross the traffic of bodies being pushed into the square, but we manage to hang together, with Anthony stopping frequently to make sure everyone is all right. We're gradually moving across the square and, although we're being swept further up it than we would wish, we're still heading for the other side. And then, all at once, it all goes wrong. To our left a brass band strikes up and the noise bears down on us. There's a sudden surge of people that takes me by surprise, someone bowls straight into my shoulder and I feel myself falling. I let go of Dad's hand for fear of pulling him down with me. I'm on the floor and two or three bodies are tumbling over me, one of them an old lady who cries out as she comes

245

down on top of me. For a moment I think I'm going to be buried alive and I scream out to let people know I'm down here, but it's no use because the band is practically on top of me too and I can't even hear my own cries above the relentless oompah pah pah. And then the pressure eases, as though one of the bodies on top of me has been removed, and then another. Someone is speaking in a loud and authoritative voice, which I can hear as the band has passed by now and is retreating into the distance. A couple of people lift the old woman, who begins dusting her clothes off although she has not been in contact with the ground, only with me. A couple of youths help me to my feet.

'British?'

'Yes.'

'You're all right, mister?'

'I think so.'

'You have to be careful at the *festa*, OK?'

I nod and turn, expecting to see Dad standing there, but he's not. I whirl around, trying to catch sight of his greying hair in the crowds sweeping past. I wonder whether, amongst all these others, I would actually recognise the top of his head, the thinning patch at the crown where the skin is only just starting to show through, in spite of his age, and suddenly remember the time when I seemed to know all of him so well, right down to the individual whorls on his then orange-nicotined fingertips. It's no use, I can't see him anywhere.

By now Mum, Laura and Angela have caught me up. We stand in the shelter of a fountain, which is probably the centre of the square, to avoid being swept away by the crowd again.

'Where's Dad?' asks Mum, her eyes a cocktail of fear and hope.

I shake my head. 'I don't know.'

'Jim!' she screams, 'Jim! Where are you?' She tries to

launch herself into the crowd, but Angela grabs her arm and says, 'No, you must stay here. We don't want you lost too.'

Mum begins to cry, her eyes darting back and forth across the crowd.

'Nick, he's not well, you've got to find him, Nick, please.'

'It's all right, Mum. You three just wait here so I know where you are. Dad will be OK. People can see he's disabled. They're nice people here, he won't come to any harm. Keep her calm, Laura, for God's sake.'

I dive into the crowd and begin pushing my way through knowing I must get to the front to where it slows and finally stops at the foot of the church steps, praying Dad will have been washed up there. Once I'm away from Mum, my own panic takes over again. Anything could have happened to him. He could have been knocked down and trampled, or mugged. He doesn't even need other people to hurt him, he could have died from his own illnesses or fallen over and broken something all on his own. The more these images leap into my mind, the more frantic I become. I pull people out of my way. I collide with two blond men in their twenties, probably Swedes, who are kissing one another and break apart to scowl at me and say, 'Hey, watch it, you . . . ' I nearly go head over heels over a child and cry out when it turns and looks up at me with Ronald Reagan's senile face and then realise it's a rubber mask. I bump into the back of a woman, who turns on me and screams, 'Fuck you, mate, what's your problem?' in a Cockney accent, and kicks my shin with her pointed red shoe. I don't care, I push on through, my panic lending me a special strength and impervious to the damage I'm causing. Finally I break out of the other side of the crowd and it's like bursting through a wall, so I nearly tumble over when, for the first time in what seems like hours, my momentum meets no resistance.

I'm at the other side of the square, where Anthony says the taxis are, and yes, he's right, I can see two cars with cab signs parked there, the drivers leaning against them, smoking. I decide to make my way forward along this road to see if I can't get around the back of the church and work my way to the front of it and stand on the steps and look for Dad. I'm just setting off when I see Anthony, hurrying in the opposite direction, back towards the bottom end of the square.

'Anthony!' I call, but he doesn't hear me. I can't understand why he is running away from the cabs rather than towards them, but then I notice how he keeps looking back over his shoulder. Two men in their twenties, wearing jeans and T-shirts, are running after him, their mouths set in angry determination. The very way their arms slice through the air is full of aggression. Anthony dives behind a small group of revellers and ducks suddenly out of sight. For a moment I can't think where he's gone and then I spot what looks like an alley between two houses. I hesitate for a moment. I look around. There's no sign of Dad and it hits me that I'm never going to find him without Anthony. As the two men enter the alley, I break into a run and follow. When I reach the entrance it's pitch dark, until suddenly a rocket explodes in the sky above us and it's as though someone has turned on the light. One of the men is standing behind Anthony, pinning his arms behind his back, while the other man punches him in the stomach. I don't know what to do. I haven't had a fight in my life. As a kid I always managed to joke my way out of being bullied, but now there's no time to think.

'Hey, stop that!' I shout. The men pause and turn to look at me. Another rocket explodes and we can see each other clearly now. They're young and hard, these two. The face of the one doing the punching bears a long scar on one cheek. It takes him only a few seconds to weigh me up. I can see him thinking, 'Tourist.' He turns back to Anthony and punches him again. I run down the alley and before I know what I'm doing, I grab the man's arm as he pulls it back to hit Anthony again. He shakes me off, like a dog shaking off water after a swim, lets go of Anthony with his other hand and turns and punches me on the nose. There's a terrific crack and fireworks explode inside my head. My eyes are closed and all I can see are showers of sparks. They sting with tears. I open them in time to see his fist coming again. I try to duck and it hits the side of my head, so hard I almost fall over. And then I see Anthony, still held from behind by the other man, use his captor for support, and lift both his legs off the ground, pulling his knees up tight, like a spring coiling and letting his feet explode into my assailant's back. The man is pushed towards me and instinctively I open my arms to catch him, so he falls against my chest, but after the initial shock I think quickly and jerk my knee up hard into his crotch.

'Uuhhh!' He clutches his balls and sinks to his knees. He leans on one hand, opens his mouth and retches, the sound hardly audible against the continuing barrage of fireworks, over my shoes. I pause for a moment, wondering what to do, and then know it has to be something drastic as these guys are not fooling around. I bring my right foot up and kick him in the chin. There's a crack like wood splintering. His head recoils and he flips over on to his back. I look up and the other man has released Anthony, throwing him to the ground. He rushes at me, easily parries my punch with his arm and kicks me hard in the balls. For a moment I think he's killed me. The pain is so terrible I can't even breathe. It's as though he's punched all the air out of me and I'm gasping like a fish out of water.

And then, as he's pulling back his arm to hit me, a hand

appears on his shoulder, he's whirled around and Anthony's fist smashes into his face. By now the other man is on his feet and coming for me. Anthony and I stand side by side, backs to the wall, and trade punches with them. My man is still so badly winded from the kick in the balls that I can tell he hasn't much fight in him. I hit him again, just as Anthony hits the guy facing him.

Anthony turns and smiles at me.

'So Nick, we are brothers in arms now!'

Before I can answer, I catch the glint of something shiny in his attacker's hand. The man holds up a thin knife, clutched in his fist. He turns his hand around and around, almost mesmerising us.

He smiles, and nods at Anthony. He says something in Malti. Anthony says something back and the man twirls the knife a bit closer and speaks again. You don't need to know the language to understand.

Anthony reaches in his pocket, pulls something out and throws it to the ground. The man with the knife bends and picks it up, always keeping his eye on Anthony, the knife always ready. Then he turns and runs away. The other man puts his face close to mine and snarls at me like a dog. I'm so shocked I forget to defend myself and he punches me hard in the stomach, so I'm winded all over again. He spits out an insult in Malti and then turns and chases after his mate.

Anthony and I stand, hands on knees, getting our breath for a moment. He gives me a broad smile.

'Well, Nick, you are full of surprises.'

'Yes, I think tonight I even surprised myself. Are you all right, Anthony? You don't look so good.'

He doesn't. His right eye is already puffing up, and there's a cut in the corner. His upper lip is swollen and blood is dripping from it on to his white suit, which is now covered in dust and blood. His shirt is ripped down to the waist, exposing his hairy chest.

'You don't look so good yourself. Your nose is bleeding pretty bad.'

I can't feel my nose at all, only a numbness where it should be. I reach up slowly to touch it in case it isn't there any more. It is, but my hand comes away warm and sticky with blood.

'Here, Nick, take this.' Anthony rips a piece off his shirt and hands it to me. I ball it up and press it against my nose.

'Thank you, Nick, you probably saved my life. I understand I am not your favourite person, but you risked yourself to help me. I appreciate that.'

'I need you to help find Dad.'

'Why? What has happened? You've lost him somehow?'

'What was it about? Why were they trying to hurt you?'

He shrugs and looks around, avoiding my eye now.

'It is about the car, the Merc. There is a little dispute about its ownership. I owe someone some money. He is not a very nice man. He says I must give him the car.'

'That's outrageous.'

'Well, perhaps it is a little bit his car. Anyway, that's why we were blocked in tonight. They found the car and parked their car against it.'

'So how are we going to get it out?'

'Oh it will be gone by now. That was the key I just gave him. I'm not getting knifed for a car. Well, maybe a Rolls-Royce,' and he laughs.

He straightens himself up, as though reasserting his pride, and carefully buttons his jacket over his bare chest. We walk out of the alley together. As the adrenalin from the fight drains from me, the feeling of panic about Dad returns like a large hole inside me. I tell Anthony what happened.

He makes a calming gesture with his hands. 'Don't worry, Nick. Together we will find him.'

The crowd is thinning out, moving on, Anthony says, to the village football pitch, where half a dozen brass bands are playing. We're able to walk up and down now, scanning the faces of everyone we pass, but without success. Then Anthony grabs my arm, 'Nick! Look, over there.'

He points towards one of the wooden benches on the far side of the square, where a small hunched figure sits, the head unmistakably inclined over to one side, so that the only danger Dad appears to be in is that he might, if he were left long enough to lean far enough, topple over to the ground.

'Thank God!' I start to rush towards him, but am held back by the grip of Anthony's hand on my shoulder. I turn to face him.

'Nick, listen.' His face is right in mine, his eyes black and shining. 'Nick, tonight you have helped me, so I will be honest with you. I must tell you what I see. This is a man there is nothing left of. It is hard for me to think of him as my father, not just because he has not been much of a father to me, but because there is no person there any more. He is a shell, an echo of a man, nothing more. But you, Nick, you are a man. You must stop trying to decide if you are his father or his son. You must live your own life. You cannot let it slip by waiting for him to come back. Whatever he was, it is long gone.'

Suddenly my eyes are stinging from the fireworks and I draw my wrist across them to wipe them dry. Anthony pats my arm. 'OK, let's see to our father.'

I'm fearful of what we will find, but when we reach Dad, I see his eyes are closed and he is dozing, breathing peacefully with his usual snorts and rasps. I ask Anthony to go over to the fountain and fetch the others. Suddenly I think of Mum. An image of her clutching her chest and keeling over springs into my mind. I tell myself Laura will have looked after her, and anyway, there's nothing I can do about it now. I sit down beside Dad and stroke his claw.

'Dad, are you OK?'

His eyes come slowly open and he turns towards me. 'Why all the fireworks? What is this, VE Day?'

In the taxi home, Dad is awake but relaxed. When Mum pats his hand he turns and smiles at her. He calls Laura 'Pauline' but apart from that he seems OK. I spend most of the journey explaining to Mum and Laura about the fight, why my nose is bleeding and how Anthony got to look the way he did as he and Angela put us in the cab.

'You should have got the police on them,' says Mum.

'I don't think Anthony would have wanted that somehow.'

I lie in bed while Laura wipes my face with a cool flannel, washing off the dried blood, and puts Germolene from her extensive holiday medical chest on the graze on my temple where I fell over in the crowd. Afterwards she rubs my back, which is bruised and sore from being shoved against the wall. She reaches down and puts her hand between my legs to stroke my balls.

I shriek at the first touch of her fingertips. 'Not now,' I say. 'I haven't got over being kicked yet. They hurt too much.' And for the first time, in bed, this holiday, I'm telling the truth.

Eleven
Monday

The numbness has gone from my nose, which, as if to make up for last night's absence of feeling, now has a surplus, so touching it feels like stabbing it with a knife. When I wake the pain is the first reminder I have of the things that happened last night. I get out of bed, my whole body stiff and aching. It's difficult to move and it hits me that this is how it must be to be Dad. I find the wallet with all our travel documents and information in it and look for the phone number of the doctor listed there. If Dad is as he was last night, then he'll have to see someone. I start making plans for flying home early.

But during his morning levée, as Mum and Laura dress him, the old bugger is talking and laughing away as if nothing has happened. Although I still detect a preponderance of words to do with the war, Mum, who stopped listening to Dad years ago and prefers to make up her own script for him, sees nothing wrong.

'He's all right,' she says, rubbing Sudocrem into his bottom. 'It was just all the heat and excitement. There were too many people there for your Dad. He doesn't like a lot of people.'

Laura and I exchange a private smile. We both know it's Mum who hates crowds.

Because I'm so tired and achy, I long to spend the day in bed, so I try to persuade Mum it might be best if we all just rested, but she says, 'No, Anthony's coming, it's that thing today.'

She means the *xalata*, the day after the *festa*, when everyone just relaxes and takes it easy to recover from the excesses of the weekend. Last night, before we all got separated, Anthony suggested we should go over to Gozo today. He knows of an isolated and deserted beach there where we can rest, far away from the traffic, the fireworks and the crowds. I point out to Mum that since we're on holiday, we can do this any day, we don't have to go out today, when it might be too much for Dad. I ask Dad if he wants to go.

'It will be a long day,' I tell him. 'It means a boat crossing.'

His lip stiffens before he speaks, slowly and deliberately to make himself clear. 'Take more than U-boats to stop me.'

I don't bother to relay this to Mum, as I have good reason to believe the trip will be off anyway because we have a transport problem. Since the Merc is gone and there's no way we can all fit into the Seat, even without Angela, who is part of the proposed party, it will be impossible for us to get to Gozo. So I let Mum and Laura busy themselves making sandwiches for a picnic and packing swimwear and towels, and sit on the patio with Dad.

'Not much of the holiday left now,' I say to him. 'Only three more days.'

He closes his lips over his dentures, which has the effect of making him look like a sad chimpanzee, although whether he is unhappy or not is anybody's guess.

'Cheer up. There'll be other holidays.' Of course, I don't mean any of this because I know he is no longer well enough to travel and will never do so again, but it's so much easier to lie, especially if it makes him happy. 'You never know, you might come back here another year.'

'Yis,' he says. 'For two weeks every year.'

I just smile and go inside for his tablets. I begin sorting them out on the patio table into breakfast, lunch, tea, until the day is measured out before us, eight assorted pills in each pile.

I give Dad the breakfast ones and there's the usual problem of knowing whether or not he's swallowed the one containing the vital dopamine. I ask him to open his mouth, and perversely his brain orders him to clench his jaws tighter together. Eventually I have to prise them apart with my hands and look for the tell-tale blue blob on his tongue or pocketed inside his cheek. Sure enough, it's still there, so I have to pour more water in to try to wash it down, while at the same time preventing Dad, who begins coughing and spluttering the moment the first drop of water trickles down his throat, from spitting it out.

I'm just drying his mouth when I hear a car engine. A motor horn blasts out the first few notes of 'Dixie'. I look up and see a large American four-wheel drive enter the square. It's bright red with enormous silver fenders and huge wheels, so it looks like a jeep on stilts. It screeches to a halt beside the patio and Angela jumps from the driving seat. She's wearing tight denim shorts, a halter-neck top, and mirrored sunglasses. Anthony climbs down, rather more slowly, from the passenger side, dressed in baggy white trousers and T-shirt. He's wearing dark glasses, but the area around the bottom of his left eye is so swollen it protrudes under the edge of the frame. There are numerous cuts and bruises all over his face. He walks a bit stiffly and seems to have aged ten years overnight. He waves a hand towards the car.

'Today we are travelling American style. Actually, this is Angela's vehicle.'

She smiles proudly. 'Is my pride and joy.'

'Well, it's certainly different from the Merc.'

Anthony waves a hand dismissively. 'We don't talk about that today. Thank you very much for last night, Nick, but now I prefer to forget about it.'

This isn't immediately possible, as Mum steps out of the French windows, takes one look at Anthony and says, 'Talk about bashed up!'

Anthony repeats his interdiction, and I'm just thinking about how many things our newly extended family is not allowed to mention, when Mum turns her attention to the jeep.

'It was specially imported from the United States,' Angela tells her.

'Very nice I'm sure,' says Mum. 'But I don't know if I like the idea of being up so high. I haven't got no head for heights. I liked the Mercedes myself.'

Anthony winces at the mention of the word as though she has touched not just a nerve but all his bruises at once.

'Let's get going,' he says. 'We can make a nice long day of it. We'll have plenty time for standing around talking once we get there.'

Of course, first there's the height problem with the jeep. The step up to the doors is so steep we have to lift Dad's leg up, and place his foot upon it. Then, while Anthony and I push from below, Angela pulls him in from above. It's tricky, mainly because of Dad's nervousness. He keeps turning to me and muttering something that sounds like 'tank'. But we manage it because, although Dad's awkward, he's light. Mum is a different prospect. Anthony and I end up with the great cushions of her buttocks resting on our shoulders, pushing upwards, our already bruised backs bowing under the strain, while Laura helps Angela at the top. For a moment it seems we're stuck, that we won't be able to get her up there, but Mum finally gets frustrated, shakes off the women's hands, grabs the steel hand rails inside the door and hauls herself in, making my heart skip a beat as I worry about hers. Throughout all this Anthony smiles and jokes and is completely enthusiastic, whereas I complain and voice doubts about the feasibility of the expedition. But then disability is still a novelty to Anthony. Let him deal with it on a daily basis, year after year, and he will be as weary of it all as I am. For now, the way he talks, there's never any possibility of the trip not happening and within an hour we're driving off the ferry in Gozo.

It's impossible to believe we've travelled only a few kilometres. Instead of the miniature Malta I was expecting, another flat, hard-baked rock, congested with cars and buildings, we find ourselves on an island of green hills, with attractive little villages clinging to them, empty roads, well signposted for the few cars, and scarcely any sign of habitation at all. We drive through fertile fields in which crops are growing. Everything is tidy, there aren't the rusted-up old cars you see by the roadside on the larger island, no old oil drums, no concrete factories.

It's a novelty to drive along without the constant rage of car horns and I find myself dozing off, still tired from the excitement and exertions of last night, still sore from the blows I took. I only wake when the jeep stops.

Although it's in the middle of open countryside, with cultivated fields all around it, and with no obvious source of a congregation to fill it, the church of Ta'Pinu is vast. As we wander towards it, I wonder if it is worth the difficult descent from the jeep and having to climb in again afterwards. It's an uninspiring modern building, with a huge basilica and a bell tower that must be 150 feet high, both plain and dull. But inside it's refreshingly simple after the extravagances of the baroque buildings on Malta, and its very plainness lends it a feeling of reverence. We wander around for a few minutes and then run out of things to look at or comment upon. Anthony explains the story of how, a hundred years ago, some local people heard the voice of Christ here and how since then, it has been a place of pilgrimage and miracles, with people visiting from all over the world to ask for the inter-cession of Our Lady of Pinu. He directs us to a little room at the rear of the church

It's as if we've somehow wandered into one of those surgical appliance shops. There are crutches, callipers, neck braces and plaster casts for feet, legs and arms all over the place, the votive offerings of those who have been able to dispense with these items thanks to the inter-cession of the Virgin. There are several motorcycle crash helmets and photographs of dreadful car accidents, with letters of thanks from those who have walked away from the flattened vehicles, or if they haven't, have recovered from the horrible injuries they sustained, thanks to Our Lady of Pinu. There are framed photographs and letters, not just from Malta, but from all over the world. One wall is devoted to framed Babygros and christening dresses, the tiny garments successfully outgrown by sick children. There are tiny children's shoes. Beside one of them I read a letter:

John and Julia Agius-Vadala wish to thank greatly the Blessed Virgin Mary for her intervention on behalf of their baby daughter Emma in obtaining the healthy development of her feet.

Over Laura's shoulder, I read another letter from a

couple in Canada who, after appealing to Our Lady, have at last been able to conceive a child.

On the wall of the corridor behind the room hang dozens of small tin plates, each embossed with a part of the body: leg, foot, arm, eyes, ear, heart, depending on the disability of the appellant, placed there in the hope the Virgin will intercede on behalf of the afflicted and make them whole. I note the absence of any penises, with or without catheters. I try to imagine what we could hang there for Dad. It would take a whole sheaf of the things for him: a hand, two legs, two eyes and certainly a brain, if they have one of those. He would need a wall just to himself. But fortunately there is a more direct way of asking for help. Anthony brings us some small brown envelopes and some paper, kept in the church for those seeking Our Lady's aid. He writes something on the paper, folds it, places it in an envelope and posts it into a small wooden box in front of the altar.

'It's a prayer,' he says. 'You can ask Our Lady of Pinu for something.'

We all follow suit. First Angela, who smiles coyly at Anthony while she writes on her paper, shielding it from him with her other hand, like a child playing Battleships; then Mum, who pauses with the end of the pencil in her mouth, and says to Anthony, 'I wasn't never much good at writing letters. I don't know what to put.'

'It doesn't matter, Mum. Just write your prayer down. She will understand your request. She will not mind how you express it.'

She writes it quickly and, holding her breath, pops it into the slot. 'Let's hope it works. I need a miracle, I do.'

Then Laura has her turn, and I don't need her swift, surreptitious glance at me to know that she is asking for a child. On this holiday, though, that would be a real miracle, another immaculate conception.

Mine is quite simple. 'Send Dad back' it says. And even

though I don't really believe in God, not being able to get my head round an all-powerful being who invents Parkinson's disease let alone this mumbo-jumbo side-show, I find myself half-believing it might work, the way every week I think my pools coupon might win me a million.

Lastly comes Dad. I put the pencil in his hand and hold the paper flat, so it won't ruck up when he writes. But he hasn't written anything in years, he can't even sign his name any more, and the pencil seems to move at random over the paper, like the automatic writing performed by mediums. It's only when I take it from him and fold it to put in the envelope, that somehow the erratic lines of scribble seem to arrange themselves into one word, *die*.

Getting Dad back in the jeep is difficult enough to demonstrate how much of a miracle we need, but Anthony accomplishes it as cheerfully as ever. As we drive off Mum says, 'Well, what did everyone wish for?'

Anthony smiles at her as you would at a small child. 'It is not a wish, Mum. It is a prayer.'

'Same thing,' she says. 'It probably won't work.'

Anthony says, 'It won't work if you don't have faith.'

'All right, what did everyone pray for then?'

Anthony says, 'They say also you shouldn't tell your prayer to anyone else.'

'Oh, I can't see that,' says Mum. 'That's just super-stition, that is. I'll tell you mine. I wished Dad would get better. It's all I want. It's all I pray for every day.' And she turns away to look out of the window in case we catch her eyes misting over.

'That's just what I prayed for too,' says Anthony. He turns to Dad and smiles. 'I prayed for a complete recovery for you, Dad.'

'Much obliged,' says Dad.

'What about you, Angela?' asks Mum.

Angela begins giggling and says, with a sidelong glance at Anthony, 'I pray that I have a husband soon.'

'Oh,' says Mum, smiling, 'and would that be anyone we know?' She, too, giggles when there's no reply. 'What about you Nick? What did you pray for? Was it for Dad too?'

I'm damned if I'm going to let myself sound like Anthony. I refuse to cheapen what I feel by gushing about it. If Dad doesn't know, he bloody well should do.

'I prefer not to say. Even if it is only superstition, I wouldn't want to risk undermining it.'

'I agree,' says Laura, jumping in fast, 'I'd rather keep mine between myself and Our Lady too.'

No one thinks to ask Dad what he prayed for. We all think we know.

There's only one possible gift for the man who has everything wrong with him.

The road we're on is rough and uneven, so the jeep bounces us up and down and sways us from side to side. Eventually it descends into a small valley and peters out altogether in a rough track full of potholes and we have to hold on to the door handles to stop ourselves being thrown around.

'Talk about bumpy! It's making me feel sick, especially in this heat, I don't mind telling you. I weren't never no good at travelling in the back of cars. I always sat in the front with Dad.'

Angela looks back over her shoulder.

'You think there's room up here in front for *you*?'

Mum glares at her, but only gets the back of her head. 'What's that supposed to mean?' she says to Laura, who wisely shakes her head.

'Just as well you didn't bring the Merc,' I shout forward to Anthony, 'it wouldn't have done the suspension much good.'

He doesn't reply.

Finally the valley opens out, the track disappears altogether and all that's in front of us is the sea, looking impossibly blue. Angela stops the jeep on the edge of the beach and we all pile out, Mum descending slowly and breathing hard, and I think to myself that she really shouldn't be doing this. Dark patches of sweat emanate from the underarms of her purple frock. She stumbles on to the beach and says, 'Oh, stones.'

'Yes', says Anthony, with a little shrug. 'But it is very secluded. We have the place to ourselves. Is it all right?'

'I suppose it will have to be,' says Mum. 'It's just that Dad prefers a sandy beach. That's why we never went to Felixstowe when Nick and Pauline were little. We preferred Clacton or Hunstanton. Lovely sand they got at Clacton.'

Anthony halts midway in dragging a coolbox from the back of the jeep. 'Look, if you don't like it, we can go somewhere else where they have sand. Just say so and we can all get back in the jeep and drive there now.'

Mum gives the jeep a look as though it were a donkey and Anthony has suggested travelling on it.

'No, this'll do. It'll have to.'

It's funny, but the mood of fun and anticipation we set off with this morning, and the joking after the church, has already changed. In spite of the propitious conditions – the peace and tranquillity of the spot, the lovely day – the afternoon is not a success. I'm reminded of how, when I was a child, Mum could throw a black cloud over anything, the weight of her depression hanging over everyone else like an impending thunderstorm. But it's not just Mum today. Something is wrong with the mix of people too. Mum likes Anthony, but she resents Angela. Mum has always disliked and distrusted strangers and kept herself cocooned in her family. Angela is not only an interloper and diverting Anthony's affections from their rightful place – Dad – but has also been rude to Mum too, with the unheard-of implication that Mum may be over-weight. Similarly Laura finds Anthony amusing and charming but is miffed at having her thunder stolen by Angela, who is now his favoured flirting partner. And for Anthony the constant attention needed by Mum and Dad is beginning to pall. As we lie on blankets under the two umbrellas he brought along, Anthony drinks more and more beer from the coolbox. The more he drinks the less willing he is to run around after Dad. I watch him and think it's funny how we share the same father and how now he is starting to resemble someone in whom I recog-nise something of myself. And me? I' m worried that one or possibly even both of my parents may drop dead at any moment. And if they don't, it's just a matter of time for Mum anyway, unless I can somehow bring her round to the idea of The Willows, which I very much doubt. And on top of all that, I'm just fed up with Anthony again, his easy assurance, the way Mum and Dad and Laura and even Angela, who is not too bright, but eminently full of common sense, can't see through him. Besides, my nose hurts now, the short-lived camaraderie of being brothers-in-arms has vanished like fireworks in the night, and I wonder if it was worth the pain, since Anthony probably had no right to the car and may have fully deserved his beating.

After we've had a drink, we occupy ourselves by unpacking the food we've brought and having lunch, keeping our mouths busy on sandwiches and fruit, cool-ing ourselves with more beer, and wine too. But once our mouths have nothing left to do, they find occupation in needling one another. Anthony, Angela and Laura have stripped down to their bathing suits. I once again main-tain my khaki shorts and white T-shirt.

'Hey Nick, why don't you keep cool?' says Anthony.

'You look as if you're going to sell a house.' He stage whispers to Angela, 'Nick doesn't like you to know he hasn't any hairs on his chest.'

I turn away and bury myself in my book.

'You're not going to lie there reading all afternoon, are you?' says Mum.

'It's what I usually do on holiday.'

'Yes, but I thought today we were going to have a nice day together. A nice family day,' she says. She looks over at Angela. 'Not that we are all family, of course.'

Angela turns her back on Mum and begins to rub sun cream into Anthony's back, and then down the backs of his legs, being deliberately suggestive, and occasionally glancing back at Mum to judge the effect.

Mum shifts her bottom, her weight producing a grinding noise from the stones.

'Pebbles! Not what I call a beach.'

Angela rounds on her. 'What does it matter to you? What would you do with sand, huh? Are you going to build sandcastles?'

Mum smiles. 'I might, if I'd remembered my bucket and spade.'

Angela stands up. 'I'm going for a swim. Are you coming, Anthony?'

Anthony crunches his empty beer can in his fist and throws it to one side. 'I'm just comfortable now.'

'Comfortable! On pebbles.'

'I don't want to hear any more about pebbles! Anthony, come and swim with me.'

Anthony gets up. 'What about you, Dad? Want a little paddle? Actually, maybe you could swim.'

'He might do,' says Mum. 'He used to be a good swimmer. Would you, Jim? Would you like a little swim?'

'This is ridiculous,' says Angela. 'How is that man going to swim? He's totally disabled.'

'It's possible he could float,' says Anthony, sizing Dad

265

up. 'How about it Dad? Would you like to go in the sea?'

'Yis,' says Dad. 'If we watch out for the mines.'

Laura and I help get Dad changed. His stick of a body glares whiter than ever in the sun. We plaster him with factor 24 sun cream, covering every bit of his skin. Laura, Anthony and Angela lead him down to the shore. I sit back and watch.

'I don't like that girl,' Mum hisses to me. 'He could do a lot better than her if you ask me.'

I watch them at the edge of the sea, Anthony on one side of Dad, Laura on the other. At the edge of the water they try to pull him in but he keeps lifting one foot in the air as though he's trying to climb a step. Angela runs into the sea, lifting her long brown legs high and plunging them hard into the water, sending spray everywhere. Finally she dives in and begins swimming, a languid breaststroke. Her arms move three or four times and then suddenly she screams and there's a commotion in the water and she shoots upright and stands up. She starts wading to the shore, this time not playfully, but in panic and fast. She reaches the others and points to her shoulder. They examine it and Anthony rubs it with his fingers. They all begin staring down into the shallows and I see they're looking at something. I go down and join them. Anthony points out the transparent blob suffused with purple veins.

'Ah, jellyfish.' I say.

'Medusa. Very nasty sting. Angela has a little one on her shoulder.' He points to a weal of red dots there. 'No swimming today.'

We trail back to the umbrellas. Laura produces some anti-histamine cream, which she applies to Angela's shoulder.

'Thank you,' says Angela frostily.

'Are you all right?' I ask.

'It make me feel sick, I don't know if it is the shock or the poison.'

'I felt sick on that ride down here,' says Mum. 'Still do.'

Angela snaps at her. 'Look, this is a bit more serious than being car sick. It can kill someone if they have an allergic reaction. Car sickness, as everyone knows, goes when you are no longer in the car.'

'That might be true of a car, but we was in a jeep.'

The afternoon drags on, with Anthony trying to keep the peace between Angela and Mum. I try to read my book again, but am vetoed by Mum, who says, 'Not that book again, please! He's always got his head stuck in some book.'

'That so,' says Anthony. 'You read in bed, huh, Nick?' He laughs. 'Maybe that's why you haven't any little ones.'

'Well, correct me if I'm wrong, but you don't seem to have any either.'

'No, but when I marry, I won't mess around, I will have children.'

'So when are you going to marry Angela?' asks Laura. 'I hope you're not stringing her along.'

Angela who is lying face down on her beach towel, jerks her head up, 'No one strings me along. I am not a person for that. I have plenty men want to marry me.'

'Oh yes, I can believe that,' says Laura. 'But if you take my advice, you won't wait too long for the wrong one.'

'Thank you very much, I'm sure. I will make sure that I don't leave it until it's too late to get married. Or have children.' And she puts her head down again.

Anthony has brought an air bed, which he pumps up and lays out for Dad, and Dad lies on this and dozes off. I watch him and wonder where he is, what year or what place. I wonder what he makes of the conversation drifting around his head, if he follows any of it at all. His face is red and blotched from the heat, his moustache matted with sun cream. I squint and try to find in his face something of the man he was, but no matter how hard I try all I can see is now.

At last it's time for us to pack up and head back to the ferry.

'About time too,' says Mum. 'My flesh is like a golf ball from sitting on those pebbles. Just look at the tops of my legs, Laura. The texture of golf balls.'

'It's cellulite,' says Angela.

'Don't talk daft,' says Mum. 'What would a person like me be doing with cellulite?'

On the way up from the beach, Angela puts her foot down and drives at a ferocious pace, so that we're thrown all over the place in the back of the jeep. Every time Mum cries out, I can see Angela's smile widen a centimetre more in her rearview mirror. When we're at last on the proper road Mum says, 'Talk about driving! Still, I don't suppose they have to pass a test here.'

At home Angela refuses Mum's very half-hearted invitation to come in for a cup of tea. 'I have to have an early night, I'm working tomorrow.'

After helping Mum and Dad out, Anthony sees us all to the door.

'See you tomorrow,' he says.

'Yes,' says Mum. 'We're looking forward to it. It will be nice to be just family again.'

As the jeep roars angrily away, I open the fridge, take out a bottle of white wine and pour myself a large glass. I take a good-sized swig. It's refreshing after all the warm stuff we've had at the beach and which has given me a headache.

'There's no way I'm going out with them tomorrow,' I say. 'I've had enough. There's only three days of our holiday left, I want to relax, not be dragged around by him.'

I fold my arms, expecting a fight over this. Dad looks down at the floor, obviously thinking the same. But to my surprise, Mum doesn't explode.

'It's only Anthony, not her. You heard her, she's working.'

'I don't care. It's him I've had enough of. I'm not going out with him.'

Mum smiles. 'That's all right, Nick love. You don't have to. In fact, why don't you and Laura go off on your own? After all you've done a lot bringing us out here. And you'll have a lot more to do to get us home. Me and Dad will go out with Anthony on our own. You and Laura do your own thing. What do you think Laura?'

'Yes, it would be nice to have some time together, wouldn't it, Nick?' she replies as she starts unbuttoning Dad's shirt.

What can I say? Somehow I've engineered for myself the last thing I wanted, a day alone with Laura. I've shot myself with my own firework.

'OK, if that's what you all want,' I say petulantly. 'I'm too tired and sore from last night to argue. I need to sleep now. Please don't wake me up when you come in, Laura.'

'I won't, Nick love. I'll see you in the morning.' And she smiles to herself in the way of a woman who knows she has only to wait to achieve what she wants.

Twelve
Tuesday

Malta is a place for sieges. In the great siege of 1565 the Knights of St John endured for almost five months against the Turks of Suleiman the Magnificent. More than two centuries later it took the Maltese themselves, with help from the British, from September 1798 until September 1800 to recapture Valletta from Napoleon's French garrison. And in the second great siege, the one Dad just missed, which lasted from 1940 to 1943, the British successfully fought off first the Italians and then their German allies.

Right now Laura is laying siege to me, but with infinitely more subtlety than the Stukas which forty-five years ago were dropping their bombs not so far from where we are sitting at a table covered with a red-check cloth at Eddie's Café Regina in Republic Square.

We both have a yearning for English food, the way you seem to when the end of a holiday draws near and you begin to reconnect to your real life. So we have an English breakfast Mum would be proud of: fried eggs, bacon, mushrooms, tomatoes, toast, and even Heinz tomato ketchup. We devour it greedily. I look up and catch Laura in one of those unguarded moments, those times when someone doesn't know you're watching them and you love them most because this is how they really are. She dips a piece of toast into her egg, and lifts it, dribbling orange yolk, to her mouth, and I see her as she must have been at four or five years old, half a lifetime before I knew her, her enjoyment genuine and undisguised. She feels my eyes upon her and looks up. Embarrassed, she wipes a blob of yolk from her chin.

'What?' she says.

'I was just thinking . . . ' I want to say how nice she looks, but I'm afraid to, scared of where it might lead.

'Nice without the kids, isn't it?' I say instead.

She spears a mushroom and pops it into her mouth.

'Mmm.'

I'm not sure if it's an answer, or if she's simply enjoying the mushroom. She swallows it, dips another piece of toast in her egg, and pauses with it on her lips. 'No Sudocrem.'

'No tablets.'

'No *toilet*.'

'No dentures.'

'No GET THAT NECK UP, GET IT UP!'

I take a sip of coffee. It's hot and strong.

'Makes you wonder what we did before we had them,' I say.

There's a long silence while Laura concentrates on cutting up a piece of bacon, sawing at it with great intensity. 'Real kids couldn't be any harder, you know.'

I chew this over with a piece of sausage. 'I haven't the patience for kids. It makes me feel bad that I get so frustrated with Dad. I wish I could be nicer to him.'

'But kids would be different. They'd be rewarding for one thing. And they get more self-sufficient and easier to look after every day, not more helpless and difficult like your Dad.'

'Maybe. But if they get too much for you, you can't just stick them in a home.'

'Do you think Mum will agree to that? Perhaps when she's back home and finds what a struggle it is?'

'No, she'll kill herself first.'

I close my eyes for a moment and I see Dad sitting in a vinyl chair in the day room at The Willows, dozing off, or gazing at nothing with his sightless eyes, the highlight of his day when someone places a cat upon his lap – except, of course, that he will probably think this is one of his small, furry animals and recoil in terror. Or more likely, he's lying in bed alone in his room, an afternoon soap playing unwatched on his television, his day measured out in bags of urine decanted from his bladder by a catheter. And all day he has nothing to do but wonder why I, who once loved him more than all the world, have allowed his world to shrink to this.

In this vision Mum is never there. It's the version of his future where she has kept going until her clogged coronary arteries could take the strain no longer, rather than visit this upon him.

And that is how I know it will be. The worst of both worlds. Mum working herself to death to keep Dad at home and him ending up in The Willows anyway. This is the symbiosis of caring, the carer and cared for equally dependent on one another, the one for tablet-giving and bottom-wiping, the other because existence is so filled with these and all the other thankless tasks, it seems that this is all existence is, until finally, they function as one unit. Mum and Dad are as fused as his false teeth after a glut of Cadbury's chocolate eclairs.

I don't want my mother to work herself to death. I don't want my father shuffled off to die alone in some home. But there is nothing I can do to prevent these things happening.

'Nick . . . ' Laura has allowed me space for my thoughts.

Now she gives me a sympathetic smile.

'Yes?'

'Children wear nappies.'

I force a smile back, even as I'm thinking of the blue-pad geriatric nappy which may be waiting for us all. 'Now you're talking!'

I signal to the waiter who is collecting cups from the next table. He nods and finishes what he's doing before he comes over.

'More coffee, sir?'

'Yes please, unless . . . ' It suddenly occurs to me we haven't even seen St John's Cathedral and we're sitting right next to it. 'Unless you'd like to take a look at St John's,' I say to Laura.

'No thanks. I'd rather sit here. I'm not one for anything historical.'

The waiter waltzes off.

'Poor old Mum.'

'She has a lot to put up with.'

It's still quite early and the square is quiet, the only sounds the hooves of a horse pulling a sightseeing carriage and the cooing of the pigeons. Suddenly Laura reaches across and puts her hand on top of mine. I look up and meet her smile.

'You've changed on this holiday, you know. You're not the same old Nick any more. You've had to cope with an awful lot. It's not easy to suddenly have a brother.'

'I expect it's a bit flat sitting here with me after being with Anthony every day.'

'What on earth are you talking about?'

I take a sip of coffee and watch a woman at the next table shooing a pigeon away as it tries to land beside her toast. 'Well, I thought you liked him. He's always in command. He's got so much bloody energy. He's kind and patient with Dad. He shows him affection. He likes kids.'

'That all?'

273

'He's got a hairy chest.'

She laughs. 'Come here, idiot.'

She pulls my head across the table, in a manner suggesting she's been watching Mum dealing with Dad's neck a bit too much and kisses me on the lips.

'Why would you think I like Anthony? What would I see in him?'

'He's less conventional than me?'

'Oh come on, Nick, why do you give yourself such a hard time? You're worth ten of Anthony.'

'Dad doesn't seem to think so. Even Mum seems to find him more fun than me.'

'You really don't understand anything, do you? Listen, they just got what they came here to find, that's all. Your Mum couldn't stand having this bit of Dad's past that wasn't anything to do with her. Now she's met Anthony and made it hers. And she senses Dad's getting towards the end. She wants everything tied up. No unfinished business.'

'And Dad? Did he find the son he was looking for? The one he's wanted all these years? He seems to think he has.'

'Nick, the man doesn't know what decade he's in. You know how he is with Pauline. He'll go for anyone who hugs him and makes a fuss of him. If he does understand that Anthony's his son, that's all he sees in him.'

The waiter returns with the coffee pot. I shake my head. My mind is racing too fast for my body to stay still. I pay the bill and we get up and take a walk up to the city ramparts, where we stand and look out over the Grand Harbour. It was from here, during the great siege, that the Knights of St John fired the heads of captured Turks from their cannons at the invaders' ships below. If I had been here in 1565, I would be looking out at the decapitated bodies of captured knights, lashed to crosses by the Turks and floated across the Harbour.

I notice my arm is round Laura now and wonder how

that happened. She strokes my back with her hand almost without thinking.

I look out at the sailing boats dotting the harbour and a huge cruise ship pulling into dock. I'm thinking about what Laura said. Have I found what I was looking for on this holiday? Have a couple of weeks being with Dad brought me any closer to remembering what he once was to me? Has the sight of him with Anthony helped, even though it's provoked my jealousy? Or has the whole thing just confirmed what I've thought these last few years, that the past is irretrievable, as gone for ever as a dead mistress and a bombed-out building? Maybe it's like Dad not being able to recognise the hospital. Maybe if you can't find it inside yourself, it's no use looking for it in the ruins that remain.

'Fancy thinking I fancied Anthony!'

'Well, you seemed to be enjoying that massage at the beach.'

'I was. If you must know, I shut my eyes and pretended it was you, and I got really horny and lay there imagining I was screwing you all afternoon.'

Her bare leg brushes against mine, so lightly, only the hairs on them touch. She stands on her toes and kisses me on the lips, tongue probing for mine. She presses her hips against me. I realise I'd have been no good in a siege. I've held out for less than two weeks, and now I'm so tired of the whole business I'm on the brink of surrender. If I don't, eventually Laura and I will be forced into open battle, and I realise that if I get the better of her in that and it's accepted that we will never have children, it will be a Pyrrhic victory – like when the Turks captured Fort St Elmo, below where we stand now, at the crippling cost of 8,000 men – and Laura will go.

And besides, after what she's just said, my rebellious old campaigner is stirring, getting ready for action, and to hell with what I want.

* * *

I decide all the Maltese must be in a permanent state of sexual arousal as I'm now driving like one of them, my right foot alternating between aceelerator and brake in a mad rhythm all its own, my hands jerking the gear lever, swivelling the steering wheel and pounding the horn seemingly simultaneously, my brain only just managing to keep up with what's happening, never more than a second away from disaster, as though it's a computer game where I know I'm going to reach my maximum level any moment now and be shot down. Laura compounds it all by massaging my penis through my trousers until I don't know whether I'm going to crash or come or do both at once.

At the bungalow we're hardly through the door before we're pulling one another's clothes off. As I reach my arms round her and fumble with the clasp of her bra, Laura reaches up and kisses me. For a moment we're still, only our tongues moving, darting in and out of one another's mouths like small fishes, touching thrillingly as they pass. We bundle one another towards the bedroom, almost naked, feet scrambling off the recalcitrant legs of shorts that cling to them and try to hold them back. We're on the bed, and I put my hand between Laura's legs, grasping the soft fur, feeling the welcoming wetness. I roll her over on to her back and kneel between her legs. I look down at her and smile as I grasp the heavy stick of my penis, ready to guide it into her without any preliminaries. But she doesn't smile back. Instead she pushes my shoulders away with her hands, her arms extended straight.

'Nick, wait, there's something I have to tell you. A confession. You can't just do it. It's not safe.'

'I know.'

'No, you don't understand, I've stopped taking the pill.'

'I know. I found the packet the day we moved out of the

276

Villa Francesca. I have a confession too. I've been avoiding making love to you all holiday because of it.'

She pushes me off her and sits up. 'What packet? What are you talking about?'

'It was in with your underwear. You'd taken Monday, Tuesday and Wednesday, but you'd left Thursday, Friday and Saturday.'

'It must have been an old one that was in my knicker drawer at home. I didn't stop taking it a couple of weeks ago. It was three months.'

'Three months! But how . . . ? You could be pregnant already.'

She shakes her head. 'No, no way. Don't you realise Nick how long it is since we've made love? That was one reason I stopped taking the pill. There didn't seem much point in year-round contraception for such a rare event.'

I try to think back, to picture the last time we fucked, and I can't. It's all lost in a kind of general picture of me on top of Laura, in our usual, favoured position. I have no idea what the weather outside was like, or how long her hair was that day, or what was on the TV set playing pointlessly in the background.

'Anyway, what did you mean about avoiding making love?'

'What I said. I wasn't getting tricked into making any babies. So I took evasive action.'

'What?'

For a moment my pleasure in my own ingenuity takes over. 'Well, cutting my knee on purpose; making myself sick; pretending my sunburn was still sore when it wasn't; getting you so drunk you wouldn't realise nothing had happened – '

'I wondered about that. You needn't have worried. It was the wrong time of the month then.'

'– letting those mosquitoes into the room. But the best

277

one was when I faked an orgasm. If I say so myself, that was a touch of genius.'

Unable to stop myself, I explain about the milk and the turkey baster. She listens in silence, until I finish. Then she slaps my face hard. It hurts, especially with my bruises from the fight.

'You bastard! You sneaky, evil, lying bastard!'

'Oh yeah? Well, what about you, if you want to talk about sneaky? You were quite happy to trick me into making you pregnant, weren't you?'

'No, of course I wasn't, you fool.' She rolls off the bed, and, after pausing, her back to me in exaggerated modesty, to put on her dressing gown, marches over to the chest of drawers. She opens a drawer, takes something out and throws it on the bed. A packet of condoms.

'I brought these with me. When it came to the point I was going to tell you. Having a baby isn't something you can trick someone into, it's too important. It's not something you do because you happen to be feeling a bit randy and can't be bothered not to, either.' She glares at my surprisingly still-erect penis. I pull the sheet over myself. 'A baby has to be wanted, by both of you. Or else there's no point, there's just no point.'

She chokes on the last word, puts her hand over her mouth like someone trying to stop themselves vomiting, and rushes from the room.

I'm sitting alone on the patio with my book, a glass of Marsovin and a bowl of olives, when the jeep rolls into the square. Laura is in the bath, going through the cleansing ritual she always indulges in after a serious row. Anthony helps Mum and Dad out of the car efficiently, waving away my offer of assistance, as though he's in a hurry and doesn't really want to get drawn into conversation. After depositing Dad on the patio, he declines my offer of a drink with a diffident smile and turns back to the jeep.

'No thanks, Nick, not today. I have to go. Business to see to. You know how it is. Places to go, people to see.' He laughs, perhaps a little uneasily, but I'm too preoccupied with my own problems to take much notice. 'I'll take a rain cheque on it. Actually, you can buy me a big drink tomorrow. We'll be seeing plenty more of each other yet.'

He kisses Mum and Dad, winks at Mum and climbs into the jeep. He drives back around the square with only the most perfunctory touch of the horn, the first few unfulfilled notes of 'Dixie', by way of farewell. I help Dad to sit down. Mum sinks into a chair, letting out a deep sigh, as though air is escaping from her at the impact.

'Good day?' I ask.

'Oh yes, very nice.'

'Did you go to St John's?'

'No, not exactly.'

'Well, where did you get to?'

She reaches forward and takes an olive from the bowl on the table. 'Oh, all over the place. Here and there.'

She looks up at me, challengingly. She's at her most girlish again, the naughty teenager enjoying keeping her father guessing.

'You're not going to tell me?'

She reaches for another olive. Her hand hovers over the bowl for a moment or two, and then picks up three, clutching them together in its podgy fingers.

'You'll find out soon enough. It's a surprise.'

I realise she must have been out buying us presents to thank us for the holiday and don't push it.

'What about you and Laura? Did you have a nice day?'

I get up and duck inside the door so she can't see my face. 'Yes lovely, thanks.'

I bring out the wine bottle from the fridge and a couple of glasses.

'Drink Dad? I think the sun's well over the yardarm by now.'

'Bugger that,' he says. 'Pour.'

I look at the innocent joy of his smile and think, he doesn't know. He just doesn't know.

Thirteen

Wednesday

I'm trying to eat breakfast, but it's not easy with Mum pacing the floor the way she is. It's not just a matter of the impatience she's radiating, but also the practical difficulty of so large a woman walking to and fro in such a comparatively small area. The living room-cum-dining room of the bungalow is not big and is, as we were all pleased to see when we transferred here from the Villa Francesca, very well equipped with furniture, including not only a cane sofa and matching armchairs and a glass-topped cane coffee table, but also a matching pouffe, a dining table, four chairs and a kind of sideboard, all in the same cane material. The furniture is so arranged that there is not a straight route through it from one side of the room to the other. Consequently Mum, who is walking between the French windows that open out on to the patio and the opposite wall, has to weave from right to left and from left to right, negotiating first the pouffe, then the coffee table, practically circumnavigate an armchair and finally squeeze between the sofa and the back of the dining chair in which I'm sitting.

Her progress is accompanied by podgy flesh colliding with cane, which sounds like ripe fruit falling from a tree, and frequent grunts of 'Talk about crowded! It's like sardines caught in a trap,' and my breakfast is interrupted by regular blows to my back as she comes and goes.

I assume she's upset because she's been thinking about our conversation from a couple of days ago and wonder whether now might be a good moment to bring it up again, when she says, 'Anthony's late.' She peers anxiously out at the square as though trying to discern his presence there, although it's actually so empty that he would immediately stand out on his own even without the bright red jeep. And it's true, he is late. It's nearly half-past ten and he's always been here by ten at the latest, every day. Then I realise Mum's been pacing about and looking out of the window for more than an hour, long before Anthony was late, and it suddenly hits me that something is going on here that I don't know about.

'Sit down, Mum, he'll be here soon,' I say. 'What's the hurry? What are you getting worked up about?'

'Who's getting worked up?' she says and, to disprove the accusation, plonks herself down on the nearest armchair, with all the subtlety of a child playing musical chairs. 'It's just he said he'd be here at ten.'

'Well, it doesn't matter,' says Laura, 'we're only going to the beach, after all.'

'Hmm,' says Mum, and picks up a three-day-old *Guardian* and pretends to read it. Dad looks up from the spoonful of cereal Laura is trying to get down him and says something to Mum which I don't catch, although he's speaking loudly enough to spray soggy pellets of All-Bran all over the table.

'Oh, do be quiet, man,' Mum snaps. 'There's nothing to worry about, I keep telling you. It's perfectly safe.'

At this moment all our heads turn towards the open doorway. A car is approaching. It comes roaring around the square at speed, scattering gravel everywhere as it skids to a halt beside our patio. I expect to see the jeep, but instead there's only a modest little Seat, like the one we have. All four doors open and out step Ferguson, his mate Grey, and Purple and Pink. I notice straight away how flushed and angry all their faces look in contrast to the quiet pastels of their leisure suits.

Ferguson marches across the patio and bangs several times on the glass of the French windows. This is quite unnecessary as they are open and we're all looking at him anyway, but it's obvious from the grim set of his mouth, the lips pinched in so you can hardly see them, that he's getting some kind of satisfaction from this, as though he's making do with hitting the door instead of a person.

'Yes?' I say, as calmly as if he had the demeanour of someone wanting to borrow a cup of sugar.

'Where is he? Where the fuck is he?'

'Talk about language!'

'You haven't heard anything yet, missus. Wait till I get hold of him!'

'Who are you talking about?' I ask.

'Who do you think?' says Grey, who has stepped into the room behind Ferguson. 'That bloody wop, Anthony, that's who.'

I look at Laura and raise an eyebrow. Am I missing something here? She shrugs back.

'I don't understand,' I say. 'What's he got to do with you?'

'Two thousand quid mate, that's what. Two bloody grand he's done us out of.' Ferguson's voice is hoarse, as though this isn't the first bit of shouting he's done this morning. It rasps the nerves like a rusty saw.

'Oh no!'

It's Mum. She has her head in her hands. 'Oh no!'

Dad begins talking, mumbling very fast, looking first at Mum, then at Ferguson, then at me, as though pleading with us to understand what he's saying. None of us does.

I swivel in my seat so I'm facing Ferguson directly.

'Would someone mind explaining just what you're talking about?'

Suddenly all the anger seems to go out of him. He grasps the arm of the cane sofa and lowers himself on to it, the nylon of his leisure suit rustling, his face crushed into a pattern of worry lines, so he sounds and looks like a crumpled paper bag, a pathetic old man.

'This Anthony, he said he was a relative of yours . . . '

'That's true. He is, sort of.'

'Well, he sold us a holiday flat. We paid him – a thousand each, me and my friend here – to have it for a week each a year.'

'You mean a timeshare?'

'Yes. He took us to see it and it was lovely. Two bedrooms, balcony with barbecue – '

'Jacuzzi!' says Pink.

'Satellite TV!' says Purple.

'So?' I say. 'That doesn't sound like a bad deal to me, only a thousand for a week a year. It compares pretty favourably with some of the timeshares I've seen advertised in the papers at home.'

'Yes, that's what we thought,' says Ferguson, 'but we went to see the flat again today and there's this Maltese couple living in it. Moved in this morning.'

'With a baby.' says Purple.

'Lovely baby,' says Pink. 'Little girl.'

'They have lovely babies. Such beautiful brown eyes,' says Laura.

'For Christ's sake, shut up about the baby,' says Ferguson. 'The point is, they showed us their papers. They own the bloody flat. They've just bought it, to live in all year round. It's a residential block. There isn't any timeshare there at all.'

'I don't get it. If there's no timeshare, how could you have bought it?'

'We didn't. Your friend Anthony has bloody conned us

out of our money. Two grand in traveller's cheques we paid him, and all we've got in return is a worthless bit of paper.' He pulls his hand out of his pocket and waves a scrap of typewritten paper at me.

For a moment there's silence, and then I hear a low moaning sound, like wind howling around a winter chimney. Mum is rocking back and forth in her armchair, her handkerchief to her lips, trying to suppress the noise coming from her mouth, which is counterpointed by the steady rhythmic creaking of the cane.

'Mum, you didn't give him money too?'

A great creaking sob.

'Tell me you didn't, Mum!'

'Don't get on to me, Nick,' she says, sniffing and wiping her nose. 'He must have took us to the same place. You'd have done the same. Beautiful it was, lovely tiles on the floor, they'd be no trouble to keep clean, a nice rose-coloured bathroom . . . '

'Lovely shade, that bathroom,' says Pink.

'How much did you give him, Mum?'

'We thought it would be nice to come back every year. And maybe if Dad couldn't manage it, you and Laura could come on your own, and Pauline could come as well. She hasn't met her brother yet.'

'Lucky her!' says Grey.

'How much?'

'What I had in my handbag, and the money out of Dad's wallet.'

'Seven thousand pounds! You gave him seven thousand pounds for a non-existent timeshare.'

'It was for two weeks, Nick.'

She begins to cry again. Dad reaches out and manages to pat her on the shoulder with the claw. The Purple woman stares at the claw as though she can't believe it's human.

'I can't believe he would do that,' says Mum. 'Not take

everything we have in the world. I'm sure there must be some mistake. He'll turn up in a minute, you see if he don't. He won't let us down.'

Ferguson looks away from her, and stares at the wall above her head as though he's just discovered something interesting there. The other members of his party shuffle around in embarrassment. I find myself trying to decide if the sounds I can hear come from their nylon suits or from the rats foraging on the wasteland behind them.

I walk over to Mum and put my arm around her shoulders. 'You know that's not true, Mum. You were worried when he was late this morning. I think deep down you knew, didn't you?'

'Yes,' she says. It comes out almost as 'Yis'.

'So, if you had your doubts, why did you let him have all your money?'

'I don't know. It was such a lovely place. And he said he'd get commission and Dad's never had a chance to give him nothing.'

'Seven grand's a bit steep for a present!'

'I know, I know. But don't get on to me, I was trying to do right.'

The only sound in the room is her sniffing.

'This isn't getting us anywhere,' says Ferguson at last, standing up purposefully. 'The point is, what are we going to do about it? How are we going to get our money back? I say we go to the police.'

'Oh no,' says Mum. 'We don't want our name in anything.'

'It could be tricky to prove,' I say to Ferguson. 'Mum and Dad gave him cash and you gave him traveller's cheques, which amounts to the same thing.'

'It don't amount to seven thousand,' says Mum.

'No, I don't mean it's the same amount, I mean both are impossible to prove. You can be sure Anthony will have covered himself so there's no evidence against him.'

'Well, what do you suggest?' Ferguson shifts from one foot to the other, arms folded.

'Listen, let me see if I can find him. Perhaps I can get him to pay the money back without us having to drag the law into it. After all, that could take months. If I can make him co-operate, you'll get the money back straight away.'

Ferguson looks at his party. 'That's all very well,' says Grey. 'But he's not likely to hang about after pulling a stunt like this, is he? What makes you think you can find him?'

'I don't know that I can. Just give me the rest of today, that's all I ask, just the rest of today.'

They mutter amongst themselves for a couple of minutes.

'All right,' says Ferguson, finally. 'But just today. If we haven't got our money back by the end of it, I'm calling in the cops.'

As I approach Anthony's villa, it's almost noon and the air trembles in the heat. The gate is unlocked and I make my way up the gravelled drive, wincing at the warning crunch the gravel makes with each footstep. I decide ringing the doorbell won't get me anywhere if Anthony is in and sneak past the empty carport to the back. The sun lounger is by the pool, just as it was the first time I came here, only this time there's no figure reclining on it. I make my way to the patio doors and peer inside at an empty kitchen. I notice a crack at the edge of the door, get my fingernails round it and pull. It slides open with a metallic screech. I wait, holding my breath, but there's not a sound.

Inside, the villa is newly and smartly furnished. The kitchen units are real wood. Nice rugs on the floor. Tasteful paintings of views of the island on the walls. But it all looks a bit impersonal. There are no toothbrushes or towels in the main bathroom, no records or books in the living room. It's as if no one lives here – the sort of property that's hard to sell, because it doesn't suggest a lifestyle to potential buyers. Only in the master bedroom are there any signs of recent habitation. The bed is made up, the top sheet flung carelessly to one side. On the floor are a couple of crushed Cisk cans and an ashtray full of cigarette ends. A chest has all its drawers open, as though a burglar has been through them, but they are all empty. The doors of the fitted wardrobe are also open, and it too is empty apart from four or five pairs of men's shoes, all quite new and shiny. I assume Anthony must have forgotten them in his haste to leave. There's a small en-suite off the master bedroom. The door of its wall cabinet is open and the probable contents, a squashed tube of toothpaste, a couple of disposable razors and a tub of talcum powder, are strewn across the floor. The top has come off the talc, leaving a fine white dust over everything, so that I walk out leaving a trail of white footprints behind me. I spend some time hunting around, looking in cupboards, even poking my fingers down the sides of the cushions of the chairs and sofa in the sitting room, searching for any clue to where Anthony might have gone. But there's nothing. No conveniently forgotten scrap of paper with a forwarding address, no airline ticket receipt.

I start the drive back with a heavy heart. How am I going to tell Mum and Dad about this? That Dad's long-lost son has vanished once again, this time leaving them poorer by their life savings? But he has. I have no way of knowing where he's gone, no trace of him. And then, as I turn on to the coast road and go a couple of hundred yards, a sudden flash of blue makes me pull up sharp. Immediately I'm almost blown out of my seat by the blast of a horn behind me and I cower guiltily as a truck pulls out round me, the driver gesticulating wildly. I have no time for him. I'm in a hurry.

Nikki greets me like an old friend when I walk into the Blue Parrot, although she's only met me once before.

'Won't be a minute,' she says, as she arranges a couple of hamburgers on plates and puts chips down next to them, then sprinkles a bit of lettuce and chopped tomato on each plate. She opens the bar door and brings them out to a couple of English girls sitting in one of the booths. Then she steps back behind the bar, closes the door and lights a Marlboro.

'Drink?'

I order a Cisk and buy her a vodka and orange.

'So, did you find Anthony?'

'Found him and lost him again. That's why I'm here.'

'You didn't give him no money did you?' She looks at me in disbelief.

I explain he's borrowed some from my parents. I make out it's a trivial amount, a couple of hundred pounds. Nikki whistles. It's evidently a lot to her. 'I did warn you.'

I explain he's cleared out of the villa. 'Do you know his girlfriend, someone called Angela?' I describe her. 'She works for a property company.'

At first Nikki shakes her head, but then she takes another pull on her cigarette, which somehow seems to help her memory.

'Oh yeah, I got her. Hang on a minute.'

She goes to the back of the bar and picks up a large china ashtray and plonks it down on the bar. It's full of business cards which seem to be advertising nightclubs and taxi firms. She rifles through them.

'I'm sure it's in here somewhere. Yes, here it is! She was in here drinking one night and I was telling her I was looking for a new flat and she gave me her card. This is where she works. It's only a couple of miles down the coast road. I can tell you how to get there easy.'

* * *

Angela's office is in a row of flashy-looking shops. A florist's, an undertaker's, a travel company and this end one, with the sign 'Golden Bay Property Company'. The office has three large wooden desks, each one bearing an electric typewriter. Everything looks new and there's the distinctive smell of new plastic. The bright pink and green carpet appears never to have been walked on, but it must have been, for how else would Angela have reached her desk? Because there she is, the only person in the room, staring so intently at the paper in her typewriter she doesn't look up when I walk in. I go over to her and she continues typing.

'Yes?' she says.

'Angela.'

She looks up, sharply. She's wearing sunglasses so I can't tell exactly what effect my appearance has on her.

'I'm looking for Anthony.'

'Anthony! Don't speak of that *bastard* to me. He has stolen my car and caused me all kind of trouble. And he owes me money too.'

'Join the club.'

I explain what has happened, how he has duped Mum and Dad and Ferguson and his friend into buying a time-share that doesn't exist. As she listens she punctuates my speech with what are obviously expletives in Malti. When I've finished, she slaps the desk with her hand.

'I know it, I know he is up to something. Oh, why am I such a fool? This flat he has showed your parents and their friends, it is a property we have to sell. Is not time-share. Anthony ask me to borrow the keys. He says he has this friend who is looking for a flat, and would like an idea of what he can get for his money, and like a fool I believe him. That was Saturday. He doesn't bring me back the keys. He doesn't bring me back my car. Today the people who have bought the flat move in. I have no keys to give them. I have to get a locksmith to open up the flat

290

and let them in and change the locks. They are not too happy about that, let me tell you. Then they telephone me and say a group of English people have been to their new flat claiming it is a timeshare property. There is a big argument before the English people depart. And I am the one who has to sort all this mess out. All because of that *bastard* Anthony!'

'I've just been to his villa. He's cleared out.'

She puts her head in her hands. 'It's not his villa. The owners are German. They only use it certain weeks of the year. We manage it for them. I let Anthony stay there because he has nowhere to live. He ask me not to tell you this because he wants to make good impression.'

'I suppose it's stupid to ask if you know where he is?'

She looks at me in surprise.

'Oh no, I know where he is. I just cannot leave this office to go there. If I could, I would go and strangle him with my bare hands. He makes such a fool of me.' There's a tremor in her voice as she says this last sentence, and I see a little pool of water building up on the bottom rim of each lens of her sunglasses, a couple of trapped tears.

'Where is he?'

'Well, I don't know about now, but fifteen minutes ago he was at the port in Valletta. He is taking the boat to Sicily. I go down there and tell him what I think of him, but I must wait here for an important negotiation. Is more than my job is worth to leave. My boss is not too pleased with me after this morning.'

'How do you know he's there?'

'He telephone me and tell me that he is taking the boat and is leaving my jeep at the port, with the keys under the seat. Under the seat! Have you any idea how much that car costs? And I am supposed to be grateful to him that he phones and tells me where it is. When all the time I know he only does it because he does not want me to report the car stolen and have the police involved. But that is

291

Anthony all over. Sometimes I think he doesn't know right from wrong.'

'Listen, do you know when the boat goes?'

'I would think less than one hour.'

Pausing only to get directions to the port, I'm out of the door and into the Seat. Once again I find myself driving like a madman, playing my crazy dance with horn, gears, brakes and accelerator. Only the fact that it's the beginning of siesta time and the roads are quieter than normal stops me killing myself, or someone else.

When I reach Valletta, I follow a sign saying 'Port' and two minutes later find myself passing the same sign again. I try again and again I pass the same sign. I find myself wishing I had Pauline's Derek with me. His truck driver's instinct would find the right route in an instant. The third time round I ignore what appears to be the correct road and head where my brain tells me the sea must be. A moment later I see the funnels of large ships and beyond them the sea, but it's a long way below me and I can't see any road leading down to it.

I pull up and jump out of the Seat. I run in the direction of the sea and come to a steep flight of ancient stone steps. I race down them, almost tripping and falling headlong in my haste. At the bottom is a road, which curves down to the sea. As I tear down it, I can see the harbour below me. My road runs into the road which runs alongside the harbour. But any route to the water is blocked off by a high wire-mesh fence which separates the dock from the road. I don't know which way to go and there's no one around to ask, but far off in the distance to my right I can see a ship, so I decide to head for it. I jog along beside the fence until I'm level with the ship, a large, rusting cargo boat. The name on the stern is *Tripoli*. I carry on jogging. Sweat drips from my face. My shirt sticks to my back. I come to another boat, which looks like it might be a car ferry. It's called *Garibaldi*. Close by there's a small, concrete building. A sign above it says 'Terminus'.

Inside are signs for Customs and Passport Control. There's a large, crowded waiting room mainly filled with Arabs, who look like seamen. I push my way through them, scanning every face, but there's no sign of Anthony.

I go outside again, then realise I haven't checked the men's lavatory. I go back in and push my way through to it. There's no one standing at the brown-stained urinals. There are three cubicles. One of them is locked. I stand and wait, moving from foot to foot, reminding myself of the woman in the white high heels who waited outside the loo on the plane when Dad was in it. Precious minutes tick by. Finally the toilet flushes, the door opens and out steps an Arab sailor.

Outside once more, I run along the harbour road, constantly wiping my hand across my forehead as I go to keep the sweat out of my eyes. I'm in the full glare of the sun, my heart is thumping, and I can hardly get my breath any more. And then I see it, parked right in front of me. The red jeep. I open the driver's door, put my hand under the seat and feel the cold touch of the keys. I fish them out and pocket them.

I walk on a hundred yards or so, trying to get my breath back, and then, let into the wall on the opposite side of the road from the harbour, I see a small bar.

There are a couple of battered little wooden tables with faded blue Formica tops, and a few chairs outside. Sitting round one table are three or four sailors drinking beer. At the other, his back to me, smoking a cigarette and staring out to sea, sits Anthony.

When I sit down opposite him, the cigarette almost falls from his fingers. For a moment, his open mouth gulps air, like a fish that's just been landed. And then, with a speed I almost admire, his face recomposes itself.

293

'Ah, Nick,' he says. 'How nice to see you.'

'You can leave the bullshit, Anthony. It won't work any more. In fact, it never did work with me. I'm just here for my parents' money.'

He looks at me as though I've disappointed him. 'Please, Nick,' he says, 'we can at least be civilised with one another. I don't think I have ever been rude to you. Actually, why don't we have a drink? There's plenty of time before my boat leaves.'

He gets up and walks into the humble bar. I can see him through the open door and I don't take my eyes off him for a second in case he makes a run for it. He doesn't even act as if he wants to and strolls out a minute later with two bottles of beer and glasses.

He pours the beers with great deliberation, careful not to spill a drop and places one on the table in front of me. He raises his glass, 'Cheers Nick. Here's to brotherhood.'

'I want the money, you bastard. Are you going to give it to me or am I going to have to take it?'

He takes a sip of beer before replying. Amber drops of it glisten on his moustache. 'What is your rush? Why are you so annoyed? You are angry with me for stealing from your parents.'

'One of them's your parent too. How could you? How could you stoop so low, to steal from your own father, especially when he's old and sick and confused?'

He strokes his chin for a moment or two while he considers this, as though he's trying to decide what to do. Finally, he opens his linen jacket, which I now see has faint pink spots all over the lapels, where his blood was spattered on it on Sunday evening and has been inadequately sponged out, and pulls out a wallet. I can see it is thick with money and for a moment I think he's going to give it back, but instead he takes out an old black-and-white photograph, creased and faded with age, and flings it onto the table.

I pick it up. It's another photograph of Maria, again holding a baby, but this time with a small boy of six or seven years old standing beside her.

I gaze at it for a minute. 'I don't understand.'

'Actually, it's a picture of me. It was taken in 1952. The year you were born, if I'm not mistaken, Nick.'

'Your mother had another baby after you?'

'No, Nick. *I* am the baby.'

I take a gulp of beer. My head is swimming from the heat and the running.

'But this is a picture of a small baby. It can't be more than a few weeks old.'

'That is correct. I was six weeks old.'

I shake my head. 'I don't get it.'

'Well, let me explain. The little boy standing there by his mother is a little blue-eyed boy, as you would see if only this were a coloured photograph. His name is Anthony Spiteri. He was born in 1945 and he was the son of your father and my mother. In 1952 the little baby was born. My mother named me Andrew.'

'You're telling me you're *not* Anthony? But, if that's true, why did you say you were? Why does everyone else seem to think you are? And where's the real Anthony?'

'These are difficult questions to answer. Actually, I have had a difficult life. That is not an excuse for the things I do, but it is an explanation. It was not easy growing up in Malta in the Fifties. The island was very poor. There was extensive bomb damage everywhere. There were food shortages. If most people were poor, we were amongst the poorest. There was my mother with two children. Anthony was seven years older than me. He stood out like a . . . like a . . . sore thumb, is that the expression? For a start there was the blond hair, although that had already started to darken by the time he died. Oh yes, Nick, I am afraid I have to tell you, he is dead. And of course, he had those pale blue eyes, so like your own and, permit me, Dad's. Neither characteristic is common in Malta. His skin was pale too, and he was tall, whereas the Maltese tend to be short and swarthy. So naturally people noticed him, but of course, they all knew the story. How my mother had got herself pregnant by an English soldier while she was working at the hospital. Work and my mother were not normally words which went together. After earning only a baby from this brief acquaintance with employment, Maria was never foolish enough to risk it again. Instead she relied on an ever-changing cast of lovers and boyfriends, one of whom was my father. His name was Archie Hamilton and he was a Scottish sailor who came to Malta on a British destroyer towards the end of the war, which is when he formed a – how do you say? – liaison with my mother. From what your mother has told me, I assume it was Archie who helped my mother write her letters to your father. He stayed on after hostilities ceased.'

I'm desperate to interrupt but Anthony holds up his hand. 'Actually, let me finish, Nick. It is most important that you understand.

'I was born in 1952, but it would be wrong to conclude from this that Archie was a constant figure in Maria's life. He was not, much less in mine. Certainly they lived together in the closing stages of the war and for some months afterwards, but the combination of her fierce Latin temperament and his fiery Scots nature made them ill-suited to close quarters.

'They did, however, maintain some sort of relationship. As my mother's lovers and protectors came and went, Archie remained in the background, always ready to help out with a bit of money or food or ration coupons, always equally ready to indulge in a spot of physical passion as part of the deal. But for my mother, I think, it was more than a business arrangement, not because she was averse to the idea of that – indeed, I am sure at times she bordered on the "professional" and exchanged her favours for money, in such an immediate and undisguised way that there is no other conclusion one can draw – but because she had a great lust and, yes, affection for my father. I remember him as a tall man surmounted by a shock of red hair, with cold green eyes, that twinkled when he was in a good mood and turned dead when he was not, which was when I would run and hide, especially if he was drunk. My mother was an exceptionally beautiful woman, although most of what I remember of her comes from photographs. Her looks were dark and gypsyish. She would have made a good Carmen, she was that type. She had a large bosom, it felt warm and soft, like a new pillow, when she cradled me on her lap and I buried my head there. And another thing about Maria. Although she was so hot tempered and often hit her lovers and was even known to draw a knife when pushed to the extreme, she was never rough with us. She thought it was an act of cowardice for an adult to strike a small child.'

He pauses and takes a sip of beer, gazing out to sea. He looks suddenly weary as though the effort of recollection is sapping his strength. He puts the glass down and looks at me again.

'My mother, I have been told, was so volatile, so bursting with the energy of life, both good and bad, it was impossible to imagine her simply growing old and fading away, the way your father is doing, Nick. She was always a person who was going to explode and that is exactly what she did. It happened in 1958, when I was six and Anthony, my half-brother, thirteen. I wasn't there at the time. Maria did not keep too close an eye on me and I had wandered down the street to play with a friend and so I owe my survival to her neglect. When I left our house Anthony was digging in the garden, if you could call the scrap of barren ground beside our house that. I would like to tell you that our half-brother was eagerly helping his mother by planting vegetables to supplement the family food table but alas, this is not the case. Anthony was already an accomplished thief and was digging a hole in order to bury a Japanese transistor radio, which he had stolen from the jeep of some American servicemen. Naturally, as a small child I had no knowledge of the intimate details of this crime, or why he felt it necessary to hide his booty instead of disposing of it quickly, but I trust his judgement in these matters. As I have said, he was already a promising thief, for one so young. Anyway, Maria, who was desperately honest and believed everything should be earned, albeit horizontally, went into the garden to see what he was doing, no doubt suspecting the worst. It was just as she arrived by his side, according to a neighbour, an old busybody, who was watching from an upper window, that Anthony's shovel struck something hard with the ring of metal upon metal. Maria's last words to him were something like, "Stop this, stop this at once, you'll get us all locked up," but Anthony, already a wilful and disobedient child, took no notice and, perhaps hoping to find buried treasure, maybe left by the Knights of St John or Turkish pirates, thrust his shovel into the ground again and the clash of metal was followed a fraction of a second later by the roar of earth and air being torn apart as the buried German bomb exploded. The noise was so great the whole town stopped what it was doing and looked up. Even a couple of hundred yards away I felt earth showering down upon me, although I did not recognise it as part of my own garden. My eardrums almost burst from the pressure. I ran back home to discover the house a ruin, with scarcely one stone standing upon another and the garden now a crater. There was no trace of my mother or Anthony. Quite what they buried in the cemetery I don't know. Of course, kind people told me at the time it was my mother and my brother, but later I learned it was a few bits of clothing which fluttered to earth over the next few days and some soil from the crater, a representative interment, if you will.'

He leans back and smiles at me. He lifts his glass to his lips and takes a another swallow of beer.

It's a moment or two before I can speak. My mind is racing with what I've just been told and I'm struggling to make sense of it all.

'All right,' I ask finally, 'if all this is true, how come you're called Anthony?'

'You must understand I had a difficult upbringing. At first with the Sisters, who were not very kind, then at various orphanages. I ran away at thirteen and lived by my wits. Sometimes I was forced to do things which were not strictly legal – '

'Oh yes!'

'– in order to survive. Eventually I got into some quite serious trouble. It was much easier to use my family documentation and for Andrew to cease to exist. And so Anthony was reborn.'

Things begin to slip into place. Why Anthony looks no older than me. Because he isn't. Why he embraced Dad and Mum so quickly and eagerly when we first encountered him. Because he saw potential victims to gull.

'And now you're fleeing the country with my parents' and the Fergusons' money?'

'Ah, Nick, if only it were so simple. I am taking the money, yes, because it will make my life a little easier, but actually that is not the reason I am going. You see, those men, the ones who came after the Mercedes, I am afraid they want more than the car from me. They say I owe them considerably more than your parents were generous enough to give me. They are not nice people, these men. If I stay here, I fear Anthony may die all over again, and this time perhaps more permanently than before. So you see, I have to go.'

A ship's foghorn sounds a low moan behind me. Anthony drains the rest of his beer and stands up. He picks up a battered blue holdall from the ground beside him. He puts on his panama and lifts it again by way of salute to me.

'Goodbye, Nick,' he smiles. 'I enjoyed being your big brother for a while.'

He turns and starts to walk away towards the *Garibaldi*. For a split second I'm still too stunned by all he has told me to move. Then I'm up and after him. I grab his shoulder and wheel him round. As he turns, his free hand comes and he punches me right on my nose, which is still so sore from the other night that it feels as if it's going to explode with the impact. For a moment I can't see anything as my eyes fill with water. I almost keel over.

He's walking away again, striding briskly now, as other people run for the ferry. I watch him for a moment or two, and then his arrogance in assuming I'll just give up enrages me. Having gone a lifetime without a fight, I'm now having my second one in less than three days. I run after him and throw myself on his back, my arms around his neck, my legs round his waist, hurling him to the ground. His face hits the hard cobbles of the road. He struggles up and tries to pull away. I grab the collar of his jacket and it peels off him. There's a thump as his wallet hits the ground. He reaches for it and, without stopping to think, I stamp hard on his hand. There's a horrible crunching sound. He pulls the hand back. I pick up the bulging wallet. He sits on the floor, rubbing his injured hand with the other. I open the wallet, find Mum's thick wad of fifty-pound notes and take it out. I'm about to close the wallet when I see the words 'Thomas Cook'. It's Ferguson's traveller's cheques. I take those out too. I leaf through some Maltese lire, take out a hundred pounds' worth and leave the rest. Anthony is getting up. I fling the wallet down for him.

I can see he's thinking about fighting me for the money, but he is still nursing his wounded right hand with his left and he knows there's no way he can beat me. Behind him, the ship's horn sounds again. Without a word, Anthony picks up the wallet, his hat and bag, and runs off. The last I see of him is as he disappears through a gate in the metal fence just as it's being closed.

In the Seat, I feel liquid trickling from my nose. I put my hand up to catch it and look, expecting blood, but instead it's something I've never seen before, my own snot. All the way home, my nose runs profusely and, having no handkerchief as I've never previously needed one, I wipe it on my T-shirt sleeve, the way I remember seeing little children do.

I stop off at Angela's office and give her the keys to the jeep.

'Is there any message from him?' she asks.

'What do you think?' is all I can say.

Nikki isn't at the Blue Parrot so I leave the hundred pounds' worth of lire I took from Anthony with her boyfriend, who's working the bar.

The Ferguson party are waiting at the bungalow and when I produce the money and the traveller's cheques I'm treated like the conquering hero. Ferguson trots off to the Villa Francesca and comes back with a bottle of whisky and a portable cassette player and we end up having a bit of a party, which goes on all afternoon and late into the evening. When the Fergusons pop back to their villa to fetch food, I explain about Anthony to Laura, Mum and Dad.

'Talk about lies! I knew there was something wrong about him all along,' Mum says. 'I didn't say nothing, but

301

I knew.' I'm tempted to ask her why she gave him seven grand in that case, but decide it's best not to excite her any more.

When I get to the part about the bomb, and the death of the real Anthony, Mum goes quiet. She gets up and goes into the kitchen and begins making herself a sandwich. 'That poor little boy,' she sniffs. 'He was your Dad's son. He was your brother. For a child to die like that.'

Dad holds his glass of whisky in his good hand and pushes the bottom up with the claw to tip the last dregs down him.

'Do you understand, Dad? Do you know what I'm saying about Anthony?'

He stares out at the wasteland, where I can make out the dark shapes of the rats, coming out to scavenge in the twilight, and the larger shapes of the cats coming for the rats, and says nothing.

When the Fergusons return we eat the sandwiches, crisps and fruit they bring back and wash it down with more alcohol. In the way of older people who do not drink often, the Fergusons and Mum and Dad become what Mum calls 'merry'. Ferguson puts on a Sinatra tape and the six of them attempt to dance, shuffling around the room ricocheting in slow motion from one piece of cane furniture to another. When they finally stop, flushed and puffing, they all stand looking at Dad.

'He's a credit to you,' says Pink. 'So nicely turned out.'

'I do my best,' says Mum.

'A lot of people wouldn't,' says Purple. 'People don't put themselves out these days. Some of them would just put him in a home.'

'Well, I'm not one of them,' says Mum, deliberately not looking at me. 'He won't go into no home as long as I'm alive.'

They have another drink, the subject changes and they're soon all laughing again.

I would like to join in, but somehow this doesn't seem like a celebration at all. It feels like a wake.

When the party finally breaks up, and the last nylon rustle fades into the night as Blue and Grey and Purple and Pink head back to the Villa Francesca, and Mum, tearful with wine, has been consoled about the real Anthony all over again, Laura helps her put Dad to bed while I lie alone in our room. It could be the alcohol, but every time I close my eyes I have the feeling I'm falling. Not just tripping over, but free-falling through space. There's a horrible emptiness around me as I flail my arms about, reaching out for help, and I realise there is no one to catch me. Dad hasn't been there for years and soon, whatever I do, Mum will be gone too. The safety net of my family is disintegrating. Only today I've lost a brother. And now I too am crashing towards the inevitable end. For a moment I'm frightened to open my eyes in case I find that while they've been closed my whole life has flashed by and I'm lying in my own excrement in a room in somewhere like The Willows with a catheter up my prick. All at once I know what I want. The arms of a family safe around me again.

I hear the door open and close, and for a moment I'm reassured, but then I realise it could be a nurse, come to change my catheter bag, perhaps. The sound of someone moving around the room. A wardrobe door being opened and closed.

Lips brush my nose with a careful kiss, and it hurts and I realise it is still sore and wounded and I am grateful because it means I still have half my life left and time to put things right.

'My husband, the hero.'

I open my eyes and see Laura lying naked beside me, resting on her elbow so she can look down into my eyes.

'That's not what you called me yesterday.'

'I know, but I thought about it, and I decided you're not an evil bastard.'

'Good.'

'Just a stupid one.'

'Can we make love, then?' I ask.

'Of course.' She gets up and walks over to the chest of drawers.

'Laura.'

'Yes?'

'Leave them.'

She turns round to look at me. 'Nick, this is the most fertile time of the month. It's not safe.'

'I'm not interested in being safe any more. I think Anthony's right – '

'Anthony!'

'Yes, you can be too safe and get stuck in the wrong life. Look at him, when his life didn't suit, he just went out and got another one.'

'Nick, what are you talking about?'

'My nose started running today.'

'That's probably because it's been bashed twice in a few days.'

'Laura, get into bed.'

'Nick, we should talk about this some more. Shouldn't we?'

'I've had enough talking to last me a lifetime.'

She closes the drawer, pads softly over to the bed, lifts the sheet and climbs in beside me.

Fourteen
Thursday

It's comforting, but not comfortable, to be back in the Seat again. It's good to be just our old foursome without Anthony and Angela. But we miss the smooth suspension of the Mercedes on the pockmarked roads, the smell of its leather and mostly its roominess. In the Seat Mum looks like one of those figures in a child's toy car, out of scale, as big as the vehicle itself.

But today is our last day and she is anxious to avoid anything contentious. She doesn't want any raw emotions loose in this confined space for fear they will re-open a discussion about the future. She's also embarrassed about the debacle over Anthony and the money and is perhaps worried it may lead us to question her judgement and competence in other things, and so seeks to make reparation for it. When I reminisce about the Mercedes she says, 'Don't worry, Nick, you done your best. You can't help the car.'

Earlier, before we left, there was what should have been a touching scene, but of course couldn't be, when she and Dad thanked us for the holiday.

'We've had a lovely time,' she said and I almost thought she believed it, although the holiday doesn't

seem to have done either of them much good. In spite of
the prodigious amounts of food she's put away here,
Mum seems somehow diminished, not so much in size as
in presence. And Dad, who stood by while she made her
little speech with a smile upon his lips which, because of
the immobility of his features, turned into a mini-
grimace, has faded even further away. His eyes have
paled and are even more lost in his redder-than-ever,
eczema-ridden face. Even his eyebrows have dandruff
now. And he's developed a new habit of leaning back, so
if he lifts a foot to mount a step he could easily topple
backwards. His head leans so far over to the right his neck
looks as if it must be made of rubber, like a cartoon
character's, to stretch so far. I notice Mum has given up
telling him to keep it up.

In the middle of the thanksgiving, Dad said '*Toilet!*'
and was despatched to the loo, leaving Mum to finish
expressing their gratitude alone, although she had no
more words, but buried her face in my chest for a few
minutes. I felt a damp patch forming on my T-shirt and
remembered the way she had moistened Madonna's nose
on Anthony's shirt what now seems a lifetime ago. Just as
Mum was not forthcoming with more words, Dad was
unable to produce anything in the lavatory, although he is
due to because it is now more than a week since the Great
Turd and Mum had plied him with senna pods the night
before, fearful of a mid-air disaster and Dad wanting to do
number twos on tomorrow's flight home.

Now, as I drive along, it's all I can do to keep my mind
on the hazards of the traffic, so occupied is it with
thoughts of the flight home and what will follow. Today's
outing, and even the whole holiday, seems a pathetic
little sop to offer as a hostage against the future.

We arrive once again at the horseshoe-shaped bay, and
leave Dad in the car while Laura and I help Mum down

the steps first. Heights are one of her many phobias and she feels her way gingerly from one step to another, never transferring her considerable weight to the leading foot until she is sure it is firmly established on solid concrete. It takes us an age to manoeuvre her down the first flight of steps, along the little landing where the public lavatories are, and then down the second flight.

'Made it!' I say, when she finally reaches the sand.

'Yes,' she says, turning and gazing up at the steps, which look like a wall from down here, 'but how are we going to get back up again?' It was something she didn't think about when Anthony was here.

'We'll worry about that when the time comes,' says Laura and Mum agrees, although I know this has never been her way, her motto being, 'Why worry about something tomorrow, when you can fret over it today?'

I climb back up the steps to fetch Dad. The sun is right overhead now and ricochets off the white concrete, making the steps hard to look at. Although Dad is normally good on stairs, he's better going up than down. Now his new habit of leaning backwards means he keeps stretching his front leg out, feeling for the next step down, but holding his foot higher than the step he's already on and too scared to lower it until I shout at him. I've never seen him so nervous. I have to shout him down every step. By the time we reach the bottom my arm is slippery with sweat where he's been gripping it so tightly. At last he steps on to the sand. 'Terra firma,' he says.

'They didn't ought to have so many steps,' says Mum, who has been stewing in the heat while she watched his descent. 'They should have worked it out better. Still, you're here now, aren't you, darling?' She gives him a little squeeze. 'All right? You're on the sand now, Jim, don't look so worried.'

Dad looks at her blankly.

'*Toilet!*'

'Oh no, Jim, why didn't you say on the way down? The toilets are up there.'

'I did ask him if he wanted to go when we passed them,' I say.

'Didn't want to then,' mutters Dad.

'Well, you'll have to put your trunks on and have a wee in the sea,' says Mum, 'that's all there is to it.'

'*Number twos!*'

'Oh no, you can't. Not now, Jim. You're just saying it to be awkward. You've sat on that toilet all morning and made us late. You can't want to go now.'

'*Yis.*'

There's nothing for it but for me to take him since Mum can't go into the men's toilets and couldn't be expected to climb the steps anyway. It's a task I've somehow managed to escape in all the years we've been taking them places, thanks to Dad's constipation, unisex disabled loos and sheer good fortune.

'Here,' Mum says, passing me her imitation leather shopping bag, 'take this. The Sudocrem is in there. He'll need some on his bottom after he's been.'

Although Dad is safer going up the stairs, he's not as fast as he usually is. He's hot and exhausted and must be in pain from wanting to go to the loo, but more than these things, he's altogether less able than he was a couple of weeks ago. We make slow progress back up to the landing.

The men's loo smells strongly of shit and urine and it's unusually dirty for a Maltese public convenience. Outside I can hear children shouting, in here only the irritant buzz of flies.

There are two cubicles. I push open the door of the first and immediately close it again. The toilet has no lid. There are faeces all over the bowl, including the rim, and the walls and floor, where a pile of brown shit seems alive with a covering of big black flies.

The other loo has no seat either, and the bowl is faeces stained, but at least the rim is reasonably clean. I walk Dad in backwards, edging him a step at the time. When his calves are pressed against the toilet bowl, I take down his shorts and underpants and, holding him by the hands, lower him carefully, the way a mountaineer might lower his fellow over a precipice, taking more and more of his weight as he goes so that he will not drop too suddenly, which could cause him to skid off the rim and fall on the floor. When he's in place, I retreat, pulling the door to behind me. The stink in the place is appalling, and I can hardly breathe. I feel myself starting to gag, so I step outside, where even the ferocity of the sun on the concrete is a welcome relief. After five minutes or so, I'm beginning to wonder which is worse, the full glare of the sun or the stench inside the loo, but my mind is made up for me when a couple of Maltese youths go inside. I have to follow them to make sure they don't push the door of Dad's cubicle open on him. It's OK, though, because they just use the urinals. As they pee, one of them turns his head and looks at me watching them and says something in Malti to his friend. It's only as they leave, hurrying past me at the entrance, that I realise they think I'm some kind of pervert. I stand outside the entrance for twenty minutes, always going back in when someone enters. One middle-aged Maltese man goes in and pushes open the door of the filthy loo and immediately closes it again. He's about to open the other one when I hold up my hand in a stop sign.

'My father,' I say.

The man looks at me desperately. He's clutching his stomach. He pushes the door and it catches on Dad's legs.

'Aaargh!' Dad screams, although the door has scarcely touched him. The bottom of one of his white, bony legs is revealed to the other man.

'*Skuzzi!*' he mutters and disappears into the dirty loo.

I hurry outside again and feel sorry for the man when he emerges a few minutes later, too ashamed of what his urgency has driven him to to look at me.

After twenty minutes I hear the croak of Dad's voice, 'Nick!'

I push open the door and sidle round the edge of it.

'Finished?'

'Yis.'

I take his hands and pull him up. In the loo are a couple of black turds, but this time on a more human scale. I look round for toilet paper and see there isn't any in the holder on the wall. I'm forced to brave the other cubicle, where again the holder is empty. I'm starting to panic, when I see a thin roll on the window ledge. I grab it and rush back to Dad. I edge along beside him.

A sudden image of him cleaning my bottom when I was a child leaps into my mind. 'Bend over,' I tell him. He bends slightly forward and rests his good hand against the wall. I take a ball of paper and place it between the papery flesh of his old haunches. When I wipe it, I realise his anus is blocked with a thick, sticky mess. I drop the paper in the loo and pull more off the roll. I rub away again, and dispose of the paper, but there still seems to be as much shit as when I started. No matter how hard I wipe, I don't seem able to touch it. I fold several sheets of paper into a wad and try to dig the shit out of him. As I pull it away there always seems to be more left. I make another wad of paper, I dig again. My fingers go through the paper and there's shit all over them, caking the nails. All at once my chest feels empty with panic. Sweat pours down my face and drips on to the concrete floor.

I've been doing this for what seems like half an hour when suddenly the door almost explodes in on Dad's head as someone bangs on it angrily and shouts something in Malti. I shout back, 'Engaged, for fuck's sake,' and carry on with my excavation. The roll of paper grows

310

thinner and thinner, until eventually it runs out altogether. But it's OK, by that time his rectum is clean. Dad breathes heavily as he leans against the wall, not complaining, not saying a word, and I can hear Mum's voice in my head. 'He had lovely habits, your Dad. He was always such a clean man.'

Now all I have to do is remove the sticky mess from my hands and the cheeks of Dad's behind but I'm out of paper. I don't know what to do. I can wash my hands outside, but I can't pull his clothes back on while he's like this. He's covered in the stuff. Only my right hand is dirty and I manage to unzip Mum's shopping bag with my left. I rummage around inside. Several packets of crisps. A bag of chocolate eclairs. A Thermos flask of tea. A tub of Sudocrem. But no loo paper or tissues. Then my hand finds something cool and plastic and I take out a little packet bearing the logo of the airline we flew here with. Mum's carefully hoarded moist wipe! A gift from heaven. I wipe down Dad's buttocks and manage to clean up my hand. I dip it in Sudocrem and apply it liberally to the raw wound of his pressure sore. I pull up his pants and shorts. When he's dressed, I take his hand off the wall and give him a minute to straighten up. I pull him from side to side until he can take a couple of steps so he's out of the way of the door, open it and take him out of the cubicle. I leave him standing there a moment while I wash my hands. I lead him outside. He stands blinking in the bright sunlight, gulping in deep breaths of fresh air.

After a minute or so, I try to start him up again. I stand in front of him marching, lifting up my knees and swinging my arms. He doesn't move.

'Come on, Dad. What is it?' I'm beginning to lose patience, and I hate myself for it.

Slowly he raises his good hand, lifts up his spectacles and stares at me. He lowers the glasses and stretches out his hand towards me, the fingers trembling so much that

311

if you didn't know, if you hadn't been told a thousand times, you might think he had the shaking kind. They touch my hair and rest there for a second or two. I don't know what's happening. His fingers move slowly, stroking my hair from front to back, ruffling it under their stiff caress. He repeats the gesture two or three times.

He says something, but it comes out all throaty and I don't understand it. He clears his throat and tries again.

I can make out 'Nick', but nothing else. He says a whole paragraph and pauses, lips in a grimace-smile, and then he says some more. His eyes mist over and then, extra-ordinarily, he sniffs, as though his nose is beginning to run. He raises the claw to it and when he lowers it again I'm not sure if the moisture on it is mucus from his nostrils or just the usual dribble from his mouth. I put my arm around him and without thinking, kiss him lightly on the cheek. His skin is sharp and scratchy to my lips from the permanent residue of stubble because he's so hard to shave. I take my arm from around him, grasp his claw and lead him by it slowly down the steps.

The beach is even more crowded than last time. Plump Maltese matrons sit in voluminous bathing suits. Old men thin as sticks lie talking together. Pale English youths in baggy shorts fight and throw sand at one another. Groups of brown girls in minuscule bikinis parade up and down, noses in the air as if unaware of the admiration they excite in the old men, who cease talking to watch as they pass.

Mum has her skirt tucked into her knickers. 'Let them look, there isn't nobody knows me here,' she says defiantly.

We sit and eat our lunch, the bread tasting fresh the way it can only in the open air. Between mouthfuls, Mum comments on the other bathers: 'Look at her. I wouldn't show my legs if they were as big as that.' 'Them trunks don't leave much to the imagination.' 'What a lovely little boy. A real little imp. Got imp written all over him.'

I lie back and try to blot her out so I can read my book. Laura digs out my bathing shorts and insists I put them on. My body seems as white as the concrete steps.

The afternoon draws on. I shut my eyes again and hear the distant sound of a car passing on the road, children laughing, a teenage girl squealing, a mother calling to her child, the buzz of a helicopter high overhead, the distant tolling of a church bell. Someone tugs at my hand.

'Come for a swim,' Laura says.

I follow her down the beach, that long walk to the edge of the water again, but this time with no Anthony to envy. Hand in hand we enter the sea. The water is warm, like a bath you've been soaking in too long. It laps gently against my chest as my feet lift off the ground and I begin to swim, finding it hard at first, but then my muscles relax and I scarcely have to move my arms and feet at all to glide through the salty water. Laura is at my side, diving and surfacing, graceful as a dolphin. We swim side by side and I think about the secret swimmer I launched inside her last night, making that first journey, through those untroubled waters, to this troubled life. I stretch out my hand and touch her shoulder. We face one another, tread water and kiss.

When we get back Mum says, 'That was nice, seeing you two enjoy yourselves for once. Was it nice in the water?'

'Lovely,' I say. 'Fancy a paddle, Dad? We might even see if you can float.'

'Yes, take him in with you,' says Mum. 'Don't worry about me, I'll be all right on my own. It'll be nice to get away from him for once.'

We undress Dad and pull on his shorts. Laura takes out the sun block and we spread it all over his translucent flesh.

'Your Dad used to be a very good swimmer,' says Mum, sinking back on her sun lounger as though, thanks to his past experience, he's suddenly going to dive in and swim a mile.

I take his hand, and Laura the claw, and we lead him down the beach. Dad is doing his leaning back, lifting his feet up high, reminding me of Goofy in the Mickey Mouse cartoons. He's talking all the time, obviously excited, but of course we cannot understand a word. As we pass, small boys pause in their sandcastle building, buckets of sand suspended in mid-air, to watch, teenagers cease their endless flirting, the matrons their continuous gossip. Dad looks like a great white stick insect, his long legs pale as bones, his body emaciated. It's easy to read on the faces of other people what they are thinking: 'They are surely not taking that poor old man into the sea.'

Eventually we reach the shoreline and Dad stands still as the first wavelet washes over his stiff old feet. He lets out a little trill of pleasure and takes another couple of steps forward. We help him further into the sea, the beach sloping so gently it takes a long time to gain any depth. At last the water is lapping around his waist and he puts his hands in and splashes them up and down, baptising his chest with the water, lifting a handful and letting it trickle out.

We stand either side of him and hold his elbows. With infinite care we tip him backwards. I expect him to stiffen and resist us, he's always so fearful of everything, even a doorstep, but he leans back and lets himself go. His body is as rigid as a plank and his legs tip upwards. He's on his back. His head, as always, leans to the right and his right shoulder is lower than the left, below the surface of the water so he tips that way. I'm afraid he will sink, but after a moment's anxiety I realise he isn't going to, especially with Laura holding him under one shoulder and me under the other. He splashes his feet up and down and tries to do the same with his hands, but his body is so bent in the middle he can't really float with his hands out of the water. Undeterred he keeps trying anyhow, laughing his head off all the time.

He shouts something, which I can't catch. I smile the usual smile, pretending I understand. He shouts it again. He seems desperate for us to hear.

'What's he saying?' I ask Laura.

'I think it's "Don't let me go!"' she says.

'It's all right, Dad,' I tell him. 'I've got you.'

I turn to Laura. 'Can we get a picture of this? Can you go back and get the camera?'

'Will you be all right holding Dad on your own?'

'Yes, it's no problem, the water's taking his weight.'

She sets off back to the edge of the water, where she turns and waves and then begins running up the beach.

Dad suddenly grips my hand hard with his good hand, the nails digging into my flesh.

'Nick. *Don't let me go! Don't let me go!*'

'It's OK, I've got you Dad. Trust me. I won't let you go.'

'No! No!' he screams.

'It's all right, Dad,' I say firmly. 'I won't let you go.'

He bares his teeth in a smile of frustration.

He lifts his head out of the water in an effort to emphasise what he's saying, making his whole body rock.

'No, Nick, I'm not saying that. I'm saying, *Let me go! Let me go!*'

I look into his dead, watery eyes and perhaps by some trick of the bright light, I could almost swear they are smiling at me.

In a whisper, he says it again, 'Let me go.'

I remember the scratchy feel of his stiff fingers in my scalp this morning and understand at last what it meant. I see him lying on an iron bedstead, dentures smiling at me from a glass on the nightstand. I feel the long slow rape of a catheter tube as it snakes its way up through my penis.

He takes his hand from mine, our fingers slowly separating. I move my other hand from beneath his back where it was supporting him. His middle sags precariously, but he continues to float.

I take a couple of steps back. There's no one near us in the sea, no one looking. Dad lifts his hand and waves, causing his body to lurch dangerously, but his arm returns to the water and he's floating all right again, the sea perfectly calm. He seems to be moving further and further away from me, bobbing up and down with the slight swell of the water, listing dangerously to starboard, reminding me suddenly of the photograph in the War Museum of the stricken British battleship, but somehow floating on. I turn and walk away, the salt stinging my eyes, so they begin to water. I walk out of the sea. No one pays me any attention. I walk up the beach. There seem to be miles of golden sand ahead of me. Past the women who stop gossiping momentarily to stare at me, knowing there's something different about me from the last time they saw me but unable to put a finger on what; past the young children who don't even look up from their sandcastle; past the heedless, frolicking teenagers. In the distance I can make out the concrete steps up to the lavatories and the road, and to the right of them our sun umbrellas, and the large blob beneath them which must be Mum, and a small speck running towards me, which I know to be Laura, with the camera in her hand.

THE END

Kicking Around

Terry Taylor

A gloriously funny novel about growing up.

'In the first five minutes I was butted, kneed, rabbit punched, bear-hugged, kicked, bitten and bollocked. Much worse was happening to anyone actually in the vicinity of the ball . . .'

As with most boys his age, girls weren't high on ten-year-old Tim Armstrong's list of life's priorities. Of course there was his mum, usually to be found in the kitchen behind clouds of cabbagy steam, and there was undoubtedly something comfortably alluring about Miss Cocker, the generously proportioned needlework and handicraft teacher, but on the whole girls, like grown-ups, remained a mystery.

No, Tim's passion was playing games. First it was football, encouraged by the Lancastrian *basso profundo* bellowing of Mr Adam, then on to grammar school and 'ruggah', presided over by the gargantuan Father O'Connell whose unrestrained enthusiasm for the sport was matched only by his girth.

But for all his success on the field, Tim's score rate off it was abysmal. Determined to put this to rights, his hormones were ironically to lead him from youth club to cricket pitch, lured by a vision in pink cheese-cloth with a laugh like a klaxon: Sharon Battersby, the siren of Extra Cover.

Spanning that golden decade when hemlines shortened, morals loosened and England won the World Cup, *Kicking Around* captures the pleasures and pitfalls of growing up with insight, affection and enormous good humour. As you follow this most engaging of heroes on the treacherous path to adulthood, you won't be able to help but cheer him on from the sidelines . . .

0 552 99809 5

BLACK SWAN

The Dress Circle

Laurie Graham

Bobs and Ba live in happy prosperity. They have
children, grandchildren and a chain of car repair
yards. But on a Caribbean holiday, to celebrate
Bobs' fiftieth birthday, it becomes clear that he is a
man with things on his mind.

Has he found a younger woman? Has he bought
another useless race horse? And what's the terrible
secret in the cupboard behind his pool table?

As the gossip starts at the golf club and the kids
stop calling, Ba's life is turned upside down. What
do you do when you find yourself married to a
stranger? It takes events beyond their control to
show Bobs and Ba just what their marriage is made
of. That's the thing about courage. Sometimes it
shows up in the funniest places.

0 552 99760 9

BLACK SWAN

Blast From The Past

Ben Elton

'ELTON AT HIS MOST OUTRAGEOUSLY
ENTERTAINING'
Cosmopolitan

It's 2.15 a.m., you're in bed alone and the phone wakes
you.

Your eyes are wide and your body tense before it has
completed so much as a single ring. And as you wake,
in the tiny moment between sleep and consciousness,
you know already that something is wrong.

Only someone bad would ring at such an hour. Or
someone good with bad news, which would probably
be worse.

You lie in the darkness and wait for the answer
machine to kick in. Your own voice sounds strange as
it tells you that nobody is there but that a message can
be left.

You feel your heart beat. You listen. And then you
hear the one voice in the world you least expect . . .
your very own Blast from the Past.

'ONLY BEN ELTON COULD COMBINE
UNCOMFORTABLE QUESTIONS ABOUT GENDER
POLITICS WITH A GRIPPING, PAGE-TURNING
NARRATIVE AND JOKES THAT MAKE YOU LAUGH
OUT LOUD'
Tony Parsons

0 552 99833 8

BLACK SWAN

A SELECTED LIST OF FINE WRITING
AVAILABLE FROM BLACK SWAN

THE PRICES SHOWN BELOW WERE CORRECT AT THE TIME OF GOING TO PRESS. HOWEVER TRANSWORLD PUBLISHERS RESERVE THE RIGHT TO SHOW NEW RETAIL PRICES ON COVERS WHICH MAY DIFFER FROM THOSE PREVIOUSLY ADVERTISED IN THE TEXT OR ELSEWHERE.

99830 3	SINGLE WHITE E-MAIL	Jessica Adams	£6.99
99820 6	FLANDERS	Patricia Anthony	£6.99
99821 4	HOMING INSTINCT	Diana Appleyard	£6.99
99686 6	BEACH MUSIC	Pat Conroy	£7.99
99715 3	BEACHCOMBING FOR A SHIPWRECKED GOD	Joe Coomer	£6.99
99833 8	BLAST FROM THE PAST	Ben Elton	£6.99
99679 3	SAP RISING	A.A. Gill	£6.99
99760 9	THE DRESS CIRCLE	Laurie Graham	£6.99
99699 8	WINTER BIRDS	Jim Grimsley	£6.99
99609 2	FORREST GUMP	Winston Groom	£6.99
99774 9	THE CUCKOO'S PARTING CRY	Anthea Halliwell	£5.99
99668 8	MYSTERIOUS SKIN	Scott Heim	£6.99
99796 X	A WIDOW FOR ONE YEAR	John Irving	£7.99
99748 X	THE BEAR WENT OVER THE MOUNTAIN		
		William Kotzwinkle	£6.99
99807 9	MONTENEGRO	Starling Lawrence	£6.99
99552 5	TALES OF THE CITY	Armistead Maupin	£6.99
99762 5	THE LACK BROTHERS	Malcolm McKay	£6.99
99785 4	GOODNIGHT, NEBRASKA	Tom McNeal	£6.99
99718 8	IN A LAND OF PLENTY	Tim Pears	£6.99
99783 8	DAY OF ATONEMENT	Jay Rayner	£6.99
99696 3	THE VISITATION	Sue Reidy	£5.99
99747 1	M FOR MOTHER	Marjorie Riddell	£6.99
99777 4	THE SPARROW	Mary Doria Russell	£6.99
99813 3	MOUNT MISERY	Samuel Shem	£7.99
99809 5	KICKING AROUND	Terry Taylor	£6.99
99788 9	OTHER PEOPLE'S CHILDREN	Joanna Trollope	£6.99

All Transworld titles are available by post from:

Book Services By Post, P.O. Box 29, Douglas, Isle of Man IM99 1BQ

Credit cards accepted. Please telephone 01624 675137,
fax 01624 670923 or Internet http://www.bookpost.co.uk.
or e-mail: bookshop@enterprise.net for details

Free postage and packing in the UK. Overseas customers: allow
£1 per book (paperbacks) and £3 per book (hardbacks).